LONGFELLOW:

Henry Wadsworth Longfellow (1807–1882) was the
most popular and admired American poet of the nine-
teenth century. Born in Portland, Maine, and educated
at Bowdoin College, Longfellow resolved at an early age
to become a writer; but until midlife his principal career
was the teaching rather than the writing of literature, first
at his alma mater (1829–35) and then at Harvard (1836–
54). His teaching career was punctuated by two extended
study-tours of Europe, during which Longfellow made
himself fluent in all the major Romance and Germanic
languages. Thanks to a fortunate marriage and the grow-
ing popularity of his work, from his mid-thirties onwards
Longfellow, ensconced in a comfortable Cambridge man-
sion, was able to devote an increasingly large fraction of
his energies to the long narrative historical and mythic
poems that made him a household word, especially *Evan-
geline* (1847), *The Song of Hiawatha* (1855), *The Courtship
of Miles Standish* (1858), and *Tales of a Wayside Inn* (1863,
1872, 1873). Versatile as well as prolific, Longfellow also
won fame as a writer of short ballads and lyrics, and
experimented in the essay, the short story, the novel, and
the verse drama. Taken as a whole, Longfellow's writings
show a breadth of literary learning, an understanding of
western languages and cultures, unmatched by any
American writer of his time.

Lawrence Buell has written two critical-historical books
on nineteenth-century New England writing, *Literary
Transcendentalism* and *New England Literary Culture*, as
well as numerous articles and reviews. He has also edited
a collection of the poetry of Walt Whitman and co-
edited an anthology of the works of Elizabeth Barstow
Stoddard. He is currently Professor and Chairman of the
English Department of Oberlin College.

SELECTED POEMS

Henry Wadsworth Longfellow

Edited with an Introduction by
Lawrence Buell

PENGUIN BOOKS

PENGUIN BOOKS
Published by the Penguin Group
Penguin Group (USA) Inc., 375 Hudson Street, New York, New York 10014, U.S.A.
Penguin Group (Canada), 90 Eglinton Avenue East, Suite 700, Toronto,
Ontario, Canada M4P 2Y3 (a division of Pearson Penguin Canada Inc.)
Penguin Books Ltd, 80 Strand, London WC2R 0RL, England
Penguin Ireland, 25 St Stephen's Green, Dublin 2, Ireland (a division of Penguin Books Ltd)
Penguin Group (Australia), 250 Camberwell Road, Camberwell,
Victoria 3124, Australia (a division of Pearson Australia Group Pty Ltd)
Penguin Books India Pvt Ltd, 11 Community Centre, Panchsheel Park,
New Delhi – 110 017, India
Penguin Group (NZ), 67 Apollo Drive, Rosedale, North Shore 0632, New Zealand
(a division of Pearson New Zealand Ltd)
Penguin Books (South Africa) (Pty) Ltd, 24 Sturdee Avenue, Rosebank,
Johannesburg 2196, South Africa

Penguin Books Ltd, Registered Offices: 80 Strand, London WC2R 0RL, England

This collection first published in Penguin Books 1988
Published simultaneously in Canada

30 29 28

Copyright © Viking Penguin Inc., 1988
All rights reserved

LIBRARY OF CONGRESS CATALOGING IN PUBLICATION DATA
Longfellow, Henry Wadsworth, 1807–1882
Selected poems.
(Penguin classics)
Includes index.
I. Buell, Lawrence.   II. Title.   III. Series.
PS2252.B84 1988   811'.3   87-15994
ISBN 978-0-14-039064-3

Printed in the United States of America.
Set in Bembo

CONTENTS

CONTENTS

INTRODUCTION

HENRY WADSWORTH LONGFELLOW (1807–82) was the first American poet to achieve commercial success and international renown. By the time of his death he was the most popular poet in the English-speaking world. In our century, however, Longfellow's reputation has plunged as a result of the kind of overreaction that often follows an excess of fame. Taught to memorize Longfellow as schoolchildren, our grandparents considered him an American institution. Today, he is apt to be dismissed unread as a symbol of the superficial imitation of fashionable European models that the truly important nineteenth-century American poets— Walt Whitman and Emily Dickinson—had to resist in order to create a distinctive national poetry. Rarely has so respected a writer been so discredited by posterity.

Yet rarely can we find such a clear-cut case of increased critical sophistication giving rise to critical overkill. Longfellow's present image as a shallow minor poet is a by-product of the rise, since 1920, of the intensive academic study of American literature. The scholarship produced by this movement has defined the so-called American Renaissance of the mid-nineteenth century in terms of the work of a select handful of Longfellow's contemporaries—Ralph Waldo Emerson, Henry David Thoreau, Edgar Allan Poe, Nathaniel Hawthorne, Herman Melville, Whitman, and Dickinson. Modern critics have scrutinized their writing with unprecedented keenness and intensity. Several biases, however, have kept them from giving Longfellow a fair hearing.

One is a preference for intricate, difficult, quirkily individual styles over the lucid and the popular. Second and related is a preference for the self-divided, alienated, or pessimistic sensibility as against a socially well-adjusted, optimistic temperament. Third is a literary nationalist tendency to isolate what seems the authentically American traits of a work as the main ground of discussion and praise. In short, Longfellow has fared badly within a critical framework that is scholarly (the fondness for intricacy), modernist (the equation of alienated pessimism with the authentic), and American-centered.

Yet not only are these premises open to question; even if one accepts them, they do not fit Longfellow so well as is commonly thought. Those who come to him with open minds find his work considerably more interesting than they had been led to expect.

For one thing, they will find that the myth of a serene, uncomplicated Longfellow is a gross oversimplification. It is true that Longfellow strove to present an unruffled, humane, urbane face to the world. The motto on his personal bookplate was *non clamor, sed armor:* not clamor, but love. Throughout his life, he attached an extremely high value to politeness, common courtesy, dignity, and good citizenship, as well as to domestic comforts of a level of elegance that Ralph Waldo Emerson, on his visits to Cambridge from small-town Concord, found disorientingly palatial. These tastes reflected Longfellow's fortunate second marriage to the daughter of one of Boston's wealthiest manufacturers and his privileged background as the son of a prominent Maine lawyer and Federalist politician.

Beneath the genteel placidity, however, lay an often restless, melancholy spirit. When Longfellow wrote a grief-stricken acquaintance that "there are natures whose native strength and elasticity enable them to endure the worst, and yet live," he was stating from experience a principle to which he clung in his own way as tenaciously as Hemingway did to his code of masculine taciturnity or Emerson to his self-imposed emotional detachment from all but his immediate family and sometimes even them. "With me," Longfellow once noted, "all deep impressions are silent ones. I like to live on, and enjoy them, without telling those around me that I do enjoy them." Remarks like these suggest that the image of Longfellow as a comfortable, reassuring white-bearded purveyor of the accepted verities—the basis of both his late-Victorian fame and his mid-twentieth-century obloquy—has mistaken the surface for the totality of his mind.

At the surface level, the modulated blandness of Longfellow's verse easily anesthetizes us against looking for deeper effects. The sonorous meter, the proliferation of descriptive imagery, the gently didactic tone seemingly bespeak an uncomplicated muse. Take, for example, the old chestnut "The Day Is Done," an especially good case in point since Longfellow's subject (anticipating Frost's in "Stopping by Woods," "Come In," and other lyrics) is the desire not to probe too deeply into the dark side of existence. In an easy but provocative role reversal, the poem's exhausted speaker makes as if to waive his usual responsibility as the reader's guide, asking the reader to read to him: "Not from the grand old masters," who would be too taxing for the speaker's frayed nerves, but from "some humbler poet" who will lull him to sleep.

> . . . lend to the rhyme of the poet
> The beauty of thy voice.

> And the night shall be filled with music,
> And the cares, that infest the day,

> Shall fold their tents, like the Arabs,
> And as silently steal away.

At the surface level, this passage sums up the way Longfellow's poetry has normally been appraised by modern critics: as a poetry interested in form rather than substance, as a poetry too timid to plumb the depths of human experience, as a conventional sort of poetry rather than serious original work.

Yet "The Day Is Done" could clearly not have been written by an author whose mental horizon was as limited as Longfellow's poetry is said to be. Rather, the poem reflects a consciousness quite aware of the differences between levels of poetic effort and of the competing appeal of each. For the moment, the speaker chooses the reassuringly superficial over the disturbingly profound, but he does not pledge always to choose the same way; and—more important—even in the process of so choosing he makes clear that the soothing song implies a more complicated inner reality ("a feeling of sadness . . . That my soul cannot resist"). Read attentively, the poem expresses Longfellow's version of Frost's dictum that a poem provides "a momentary stay against confusion," a confusion which Longfellow's soothing rhythms partly offset but which is stated so explicitly as to make the triumph of blandness ring somewhat hollow toward the close. If we overlook this struggle between melancholy undertone and surface regulation, we impoverish the poem.

"The Day Is Done" is typical in this respect. Longfellow continually writes about disappointed hopes, the need to accommodate oneself to diminished expectations, and the pressures of coping with the fear that the reality of social or personal chaos is more than we can bear. A patriotic ditty like "Paul Revere's Ride" is less characteristic of Longfellow's voice than poems like "The Slave Singing at Midnight" or "The Arsenal," where the sense of social injustice is so strong that divine intervention seems the only possible remedy. Bizarre though it may seem, Charles Baudelaire's interest in Longfellow (from whom he borrowed a few images for *Flowers of Evil*) was not haphazard. It was entirely fitting that Longfellow aspired for his projected masterpiece, the trilogy *Christus* (1872), to provide "some equivalent expression for the trouble and wrath of life, for its sorrow and its mystery."

Not that Longfellow mainly was, or aimed to be, a "tragic" poet. He preferred to concentrate on how to offset, contain, outlive, or otherwise cope productively with life's trouble and wrath. As in "The Day Is Done," two important coping strategies for Longfellow at the stylistic level were narrative and meter. Because of these, the despair behind the speaker's request doesn't get fully vented. The melodious verse and the story the speaker invents about how he'll spend his evening equip the poem with orderly, ritualized patterns that ward off his fears. So too in *Evangeline,* a poem based on the communal and personal tragedy of the uprooting of a Nova Scotian settlement of Acadian French by the British military during the French and Indian War. The event is horrifying, but the horror is stylized even at the moment of forced embarkation by Longfellow's choice of classical hexameter verse ("There disorder prevailed, and the tumult and stir of embarking" *sounds* harmonious though the scene is not) and stylized again by a modified Romeo-and-Juliet plot of star-crossed lovers separated lifelong to be reunited only for a brief moment before death. The starkness of the tragedy of two agonized, unfulfilled lives is partially offset by the sublimation of their suffering into patterned, parallel action and by the neatness of their reunion at Gabriel's deathbed, a scene both bleakly pathetic and aesthetically satisfying as the realization of the long-deferred hopes of lovers and readers.

The containment of melancholy within formal limits conceded themselves to be limited—this approach to poetry was by no means unique to Longfellow. It was a characteristically Victorian approach, favored especially by Tennyson and Arnold among the major poets, as well as a characteristically New England approach from William Cullen Bryant (who influenced Longfellow more than any other American poet) through Robert Frost to the more recent work of Elizabeth Bishop and Robert Francis. When Longfellow penned "The Day Is Done" in the early 1840s he was working within a mode that had been pioneered in America a generation before in such poems as "Thanatopsis" by Bryant, who in turn had followed in the footsteps of Wordsworth—the "stoic" Wordsworth of "Ode to Duty," "Peele Castle," and "Mutability" rather than the visionary Wordsworth of "Tintern Abbey" and the Spots of Time passages in *The Prelude*. If Longfellow's achievements have been minimized in our century, that is partly because students of American literature have been less interested in the conservative aesthetics of restraint than in the comparatively radical-experimental aesthetics of visionary romanticism. According to the present orthodox version of American poetic history, the latter constitutes the American poetic mainstream, with Whitman (fueled by the Puritan-Transcendental tradition on the one hand and the currents of international visionary romanticism on the other) as the key father-figure. One reason for reading Longfellow more attentively would be to test the limits of this powerful but reductive critical myth.

But it is high time to look more closely at the course of Longfellow's career and at the contents of this anthology.

Longfellow was remembered by his son as a "very methodical and careful" man, cautious and unventuresome. "He always thought it wisest not to do a thing." Unable to forget his father's prohibitions against Civil War enlistment and a later projected excursion to Brazil, Ernest Longfellow may have been right from his own angle of vision; but his judgment is as misleading as helpful. Prudent his father surely was: his biography is not particularly exciting, much less scandalous. But during his life he took at least one very major risk.

He dared to aspire to become a writer by vocation as opposed to hobby at a time when no one in America had ever made a living by poetry before. Although his father could and did subsidize him considerably during the early years, Longfellow's resolution still required much courage. As the loyal scion of two leading New England families he was expected as a matter of course to enter one of the three traditional professions (law, medicine, ministry), and he himself desired a respectable lifestyle, not a starveling bohemian existence. The former was certainly the sequel the Longfellow family planned to Henry's proper Portland boyhood and his undergraduate career at Bowdoin, where his father, a trustee of the college, enrolled him in the class of 1825, a group of young gentlemen that included Nathaniel Hawthorne and future President Franklin Pierce. But with graduation in view, and having managed to place some of his poems and stories in well-regarded magazines, Henry balked. He could not, he wrote his father, argue well enough to be a successful lawyer; he was not good enough to be a minister; and as to medicine, "I utterly and absolutely detest it." He pleaded instead to be allowed to take a postgraduate year at Harvard to study literature—and write.

This vocational crisis was luckily resolved by the munificence of another Bowdoin trustee, who had been so impressed with the young Longfellow's translation of one of Horace's odes that he proposed that the professorship of foreign languages he was donating to Bowdoin be offered to Longfellow. The college did so on condition that Longfellow equip himself for the post by study in Europe at his own expense. Accordingly, with his father's help Longfellow spent the next three years (1826–29), in France, Spain, Italy, and Germany for what today seems the modest sum of $2,604.24. The outlay proved a good investment. An amazingly quick learner, Longfellow returned fluent in all four languages; and he was also to become at least a competent reader of Swedish, Finnish, Danish, Norwegian, Dutch, and Portuguese.

Thus began a professional career spanning several decades, first at Bowdoin (1829–35), then at Harvard (1836–54) after another European sojourn. In the long run, Longfellow felt that teaching interfered with his creative writing. He soon became frustrated with routine language pedagogy, and eventually he came to look at all teaching as a burden rather than as a pleasure. But until mid-life, teaching meant much more to him than simply a respectble base of operations from which to finance a career as a creative writer. Until the mid-1830s, his creative energies were largely consumed by study and teaching. His first six books were language texts. Throughout his academic career his students seem to have regarded him with respect and affection as a devoted, caring teacher—a reputation Longfellow could not have sustained without genuine commitment to his job.

Longfellow's academic career, furthermore, stimulated his work as a writer almost as much as it interfered with it. His ambitious program of self-study, encompassing all the European literatures, provided a foundation of art as well as for teaching. Longfellow's muse thereby became more cosmopolitan than that of any American writer of the century. For the first of his two novels, *Hyperion* (1839), he drew on German sources; for his epic of American Indian culture, *The Song of Hiawatha* (1855), Finnish; for his *Tales of a Wayside Inn* (1863), Chaucer; for his theological-historical trilogy, *Christus: A Mystery* (1872), Dante; for the meter of his two most enduring long poems, *Evangeline* (1847) and *The Courtship of Miles Standish* (1858), Homer and Virgil. A good deal of the rest of his poetic output consisted of translations from many languages (*The Divine Comedy* being his most ambitious project) or transpositions of European originals, such as "The Wreck of the Hesperus" (1840), a ballad modeled on "Sir Patrick Spens."

For all this Longfellow has been castigated for dilettantism and derivativeness: for wide but shallow learning and for undue dependence on imported literary models. These judgments are too hasty. Although Longfellow's knowledge *was* superficial by modern scholarly criteria, it measured up extremely well by those of his day, when even Harvard fell far short of German standards of rigor; and his bibliographical reach was impressive for a creative writer in any era. As to the idea that Longfellow was somehow not a truly American author, that is a reductive myth.

It is true that Longfellow preferred similarly cosmopolitan writers like Washington Irving to homespun geniuses like Whitman. It is true too that Longfellow argued staunchly against the idea that American literature must differ radically from the British. ("As our character and modes of thought do not differ essentially from those of England, our literature cannot.") But to hold that he was uninterested in giving distinctive expression to American subjects is wrongheaded, as the contents of this collection prove. And to argue that distinctive expression must mean resistance to European influence is naive, although unfortunately still quite common, as a legacy of the mid-twentieth century movement to establish American letters as an autonomous field with its own inner cohesion. Even today, few professional students of nineteenth-century American literature are competent and committed to study it in its global context. Therefore we habitually underrate the importance of European influences to so-called native talents of the period like Emerson, Hawthorne, Melville, and Whitman. Here Longfellow can serve us as a corrective, pointing up a major dimension of the period's literary culture that has been suppressed. We would do well to approach him not with chip on shoulder, suspecting him of un-American conduct, but as Henry James did, with fascination at "the secret of his harmony," at the way his "European culture and his native kept house together."

An early symptom of this harmony was Longfellow's response to Irving's *The Sketch Book* (1819–20), a collection of European travel essays and American regional tales ("Rip Van Winkle" and "The Legend of Sleepy Hollow") that impressed not only Longfellow but many readers both at home and in Britain, where for the first time reviewers began to confess that something of literary interest might at last be happening in America. "Every reader has his first book," as Longfellow put it. "I mean to say, one book among all others which in early youth fascinates his imagination, and at once excites and satisfies the desires of his mind. To me, this first book was *The Sketch Book* of Washington Irving." What is especially interesting about Longfellow's response is that Irving inspired him to undertake two imitative projects almost simultaneously: a collection of European travel sketches, based on the experiences of 1829; and a New England sketch book, snippets of remembered and imagined scenes of local culture. The first project became Longfellow's first creative book, *Outre-Mer* (1835); the second became a series of "Schoolmaster" papers for the *New England Magazine* and resurfaced a decade later in the form of Longfellow's second novel, *Kavanagh* (1849), a scantly plotted series of glimpses of village life in Maine. The European and Yankee sketchbook ideas did not so much compete with each other as peacefully coexist in Longfellow's imagination.

Another notable feature of these projects was their future testimony to Longfellow's slow development as a poet. After a burst of undergraduate versifying, Longfellow's muse became channeled into academic and literary prose. Not until his thirties did he return to poetry as his preferred genre; and his penchant thereafter for narrative, even in short poems, was in keeping with this gradual and experimental emergence of his choice of poetry over prose.

Longfellow would also have been aware that a narrative line was more likely to make verse readable and popular. Although he would not have chosen narrative poetry simply for this reason, it is quite clear that popularity mattered to him, not just for economic reasons but because of a commitment to the principle that a literary figure ought not remain self-isolated but assume some sort of public role. Here Longfellow's attitude was more unpretentious and candid than that of his greater contemporaries, who also liked to believe in the social significance of art while defending the artist's right to retreat from the public arena. Emerson, for example, defined his "American Scholar" as the brains of the body social but argued that his duties were all in "self-trust." This highly privatistic way of seeing the scholar's role might be contrasted to the declaration of a Longfellow character in *Hyperion* that "the mind of the scholar, if you would have it large and liberal, should come in contact with other minds," and not just through books. "If he would describe the world, he should live in the world." In the same spirit, Longfellow never felt any of the Transcendentalist

INTRODUCTION

squeamishness at the descent to the marketplace. After finishing "The Wreck of the Hesperus," he proudly wrote: "I have a great notion of working upon *people's feelings*. I am going to have this printed on a sheet, and sold like *Varses*, with a coarse picture on it. I desire a new sensation, and a new set of critics." This gusto at the prospect of sending his poetry further down the social ladder oddly foreshadows Whitman. It is ironic that the self-proclaimed bard of the American masses was much less successful in reaching them than the supposedly elitist Cambridge professor, who proved readier to speak to the American people in language they could understand.

Longfellow's exuberance in the passage just quoted reflected his success with magazine lyrics and his first collected volume, *Voices of the Night* (1839), soon to be followed by the equally successful *Ballads and Other Poems* (1841), which included "Hesperus," "The Skeleton in Armor," and "The Village Blacksmith." Always slow to take affront, even at insulting behavior, by 1846 Longfellow could look tranquilly at some abusive reviews that greeted his new collection, *The Belfry of Bruges and Other Poems,* which contained "The Arsenal at Springfield" and "The Day Is Done." "For all this, I care not a fig. I do not think they will succeed in their attempts to suppress me or the book." They didn't. And Longfellow's next book, *Evangeline* (1847), was his greatest success yet (six printings in nine weeks), thanks in good part to the promotional efforts of his editor, James G. Fields, for whom the acquisition of Longfellow was the first major step in the advance of his firm to first place among American literary publishers by the late 1850s. Longfellow helped to make Ticknor and Fields; and Ticknor and Fields helped ensure the preeminence of Longfellow and other comtemporary New England "fireside" poets (Bryant, James Russell Lowell, John Greenleaf Whittier, Oliver Wendell

Holmes) as the dominant school of American poetry for the rest of the century.

Evangeline, America's first best-seller in verse since Michael Wigglesworth's *The Day of Doom* (1662), consolidated Longfellow's poetic fame, made it possible for him to contemplate retirement from teaching without loss of income, and helped set the pattern of his poetry for the next two decades. Whereas previously he had concentrated on shorter lyrics, the bulk of Longfellow's poetic output after publishing *Evangeline* consisted of sustained works, including *The Golden Legend* (1851), a verse drama about a medieval knight whose disease can be cured only if a maiden is willing to sacrifice her life for him; *Hiawatha* (1855); *Miles Standish* (1858); *Tales of a Wayside Inn* (1863), an imitation of the Canterbury Tales in an American setting and similarly cosmopolitan in range of style and theme; and three verse dramas that were collected together with *The Golden Legend* to form the *Christus* trilogy (1872): the two *New England Tragedies* (1868) of Quaker persecution and Salem witchcraft, which comprised Part III, and *The Divine Tragedy* (1871), a retold life of Christ with which the trilogy began. Longfellow thus established himself as a bard of many aspects of American culture, both past and present, as well as of themes from a broad repertoire of European tradition.

Longfellow's life was not a simple success story, however. To establish himself as a professional man of letters was a toilsome and chancy process, despite the financial backing of first his father and then his father-in-law, industrialist Nathan Appleton, who purchased as a wedding present the Cambridge mansion in which the young professor had lived as a boarder. After his literary debut, Longfellow—like most of his major contemporaries—took some time to find his literary voice. And after he had found it, he had trouble giving it anything like his undivided attention. Indeed despite his confidence in the support of his public, Longfellow was always acutely conscious, like Emerson, of falling far short of his self-created ideals. An early mark of this is his impressive Dantesque sonnet, "Mezzo Cammin," where the speaker, as at the opening of *The Divine Comedy*, takes stock of himself and finds that

> Half of my life is gone, and I have let
> The years slip from me and have not fulfilled
> The aspiration of my youth, to build
> Some tower of song with lofty parapet.

One of the central characters in *Kavanagh* is, significantly, a schoolmaster who dreams of writing a romance but is always distracted, usually by others who take advantage of his good nature. Longfellow did better than that because, after all, he did finish *his* romance. Still, the portrait is a wry bit of self-criticism. Teaching drained him. Social life absorbed him—after several years in Cambridge he confessed that he had almost never studied at night while living there. Wishing like his fictional counterpart to deal graciously even to the impertinent, he found his life "riddled and consumed," as he once grumbled with uncharacteristic testiness, "by a useless and foolish correspondence, till in my despair I curse Cadmus for inventing letters."

The most notable consequence to Longfellow's literary career was the fate of the work that was to have been his magnum opus: *Christus* (1872). The basic idea for this trilogy came to him more than thirty years before its publication, one evening in November of 1841, when it occurred to him "to undertake a long and elaborate poem by the holy name of CHRIST; the theme of which would be the various aspects of Christendom in the Apostolic, Middle, and Modern Ages." He seems to have had in mind a counterpart to *The Divine Comedy*, a three-part religio-historical epic. But although, as Longfellow's first editor says, the subject "seems never to have been long absent from his mind" during his most productive years, he made no real progress for many years after that first sketch. In 1849 he rededicated himself to the task after rolling "another stone [a collection of short pieces] over the hill-top" and managed to produce *The Golden Legend*. Then work stalled again until the late 1850s, when he drafted the first of *The New England Tragedies*, but while working more attentively on the "Puritan Idyll," he actually finished *The Courtship of Miles Standish*. A decade more was to elapse before the *Tragedies* were finally composed and published, and several more before Part I was written and the trilogy as a whole stitched together. At its issue, Longfellow was unusually apprehensive, unusually uncertain how this work of so many years' contemplation would be received. And with reason—although *The Golden Legend* had won favor years before, the other two works and the trilogy as a whole were unenthusiastically received by their first reviewers, and very few readers since then have spoken well of *Christus* or, for that matter, spoken much of it at all.

So far as *The New England Tragedies* are concerned, this readerly resistance is obtuse, as I shall try to show below. But certainly the biblical pastiche of *The Divine Tragedy* does not represent Longfellow at his best, and the epic as a whole tends to fall into the sum of its parts. It is deeply ironic that the intended masterpiece of America's then most popular poet went completely unrecognized as such. Yet there is also a certain poetic justice to that outcome, for the chief if not the only cause of its failure was that Longfellow had for too long directed too much of his energy into the easier projects that established his popularity.

Longfellow's personal setbacks were not limited to such

rarefied experiences as the failure to realize his ideal self-image. On a more earthy and immediate level, he was shattered by his first wife's death after miscarriage during his second European trip (1835); he endured years of frustration (1836–42) before his second wife-to-be consented to return his quixotic passion with anything more than friendship; and after nearly twenty years of happily married life thereafter, he was devastated again by her death in a freak accident in their home, when her gown caught fire. These experiences gave him a deep first-hand understanding of love's frustrations and sorrows. Such experiences underlie much of his work, including some jejune stuff like the posturings of the lovesick protagonist in *Hyperion*, but also his best, like the affectionately comic imbroglio in *Miles Standish*, the somber tenderness of *Evangeline*, and the more keenly tragic pathos of "The Cross of Snow" (1879), Longfellow's sonnet written in memory of his second wife's death. It was fitting that he should have come by the story of the Acadians through the agency of his friend and classmate Hawthorne. Fitting that Hawthorne took note of it in the first place, because his work is full of tales of passion repressed or displaced by forces beyond a person's control; but fitting too that Longfellow should have appropriated the legend for a poem of his own.

The biographical incidents noted above do not total up to anything like a sad or maladjusted life. Overall, Longfellow led a securely bourgeois existence. The point is simply that the melancholy undertone of most of his writing is not to be understood as mere mid-Victorian convention, though it is partly that, but as an authentic reflection of Longfellow's sense of self, his relationships, and the state of his time. Let us look a bit further at the latter. Twentieth-century literary histories, accustomed to look at Longfellow's Cambridge culture from the standpoint of Transcendentalist Concord, too easily pigeonhole him as a creature of the New England Brahmin establishment. And it is true that he took pleasure and pride in being a member of the Boston-Cambridge intellectual and cultural elite, by family, marriage, and personal effort. Yet within and apart from his role as gracious clubman and host, Longfellow maintained in one compartment of his mind the unflappable detachment from official values that socially secure people often attain more readily than ostensible rebels uneasy about their public positions. Thus, as an undergraduate, Longfellow unselfconsciously joined a tiny knot of Unitarian liberals in an institutional climate straightlacedly evangelical to the point of open hostility toward his beliefs. In conservatively Whiggish Cambridge, Longfellow was not kept by the hysterical reaction of his theological colleagues from speaking well of Emerson's Divinity School Address, and he became a quietly committed anti-slavery man before Emerson or Thoreau, even publishing an early series of *Poems on Slavery* (1842) without regard for the animosity he knew it would provoke. Longfellow's closest personal friend was probably Charles Sumner, the abolitionist senator whose confrontational tactics rendered him obnoxious to many Yankees as well as southerners.

To picture Longfellow as a conscientious but quietly independent-minded citizen helps prepare us to fathom an important feature of his poetry that is easily overlooked. It does not merely express his intended readers' common vision of reality but also presses the limits of that understanding and attempts to educate it, on the levels of both style and theme. With respect to meter, for instance, although it is tempting to draw a sharp distinction between Longfellow as a traditionalist and Whitman as a pioneer of free verse, it would be truer to see both as participating in a widely shared post-romantic metrical experimentalism (also seen in Emerson, Dickinson, Poe, Tennyson, and the Brownings) that even in the more conservative practitioners often raised reviewer's eyebrows. To write long narrative English poems using classical hexameter or, as in *Hiawatha,* trochaic tetrameter, was unusual albeit not unprecedented. Longfellow's deployment of those forms was not particularly supple, but the individualism of his choice is noteworthy.

Another example of Longfellow's independence was the low-key but determined campaign for the arts that he directed toward a strongly philistine American public. As William Charvat, one of Longfellow's astutest critics, has noted:

> Longfellow was one of the greatest of all promoters of the arts. Ninety per cent of all the poems he ever wrote contained some favorable reference to poetry, poets, artists, art, scholars, or literature. Bards are sublime, grand, immortal; singers are sweet; songs are beautiful; art is wondrous; books are household treasures. Hans Sachs is remembered after kaisers are forgotten. Michael Angelo is impudent to cardinals. John Alden, the scholar, wins out over Miles Standish, the man of action.[1]

In the late twentieth century the body of educated Americans who take the arts seriously is large enough to make it hard to appreciate how different the cultural situation was a little more than a century ago, when even American intellectuals were half-convinced by the old argument that able-bodied men, if not women, ought to give their primary allegiance to the emerging nation's proper business of nation-building. Hawthorne's work is shot through with shamefaced apol-

[1]William Charvat, "Longfellow," *The Profession of Authorship in America, 1800–1870,* ed. Matthew J. Bruccoli (Columbus: Ohio State Univ. Press, 1968), p. 136.

ogies, partly but only partly tongue-in-cheek, for the effeteness of romancing; Emerson recommends books as a resource for the scholar, but only for his "idle times." Longfellow was afflicted by no such timidity. For one thing, his own sense of literary vocation was more clear-cut than theirs: "I most eagerly aspire after future eminence in literature," he wrote his father from college; "my whole soul burns most ardently for it, and every earthly thought centers in it." For this reason, and perhaps also because of the quick success of his writing, Longfellow felt much more confident about proclaiming the value of art as such, well aware though he was (as is clear from his 1832 essay, "The Defense of Poetry") that his audience did not share the same credo.

But Longfellow's promotion of the arts might also be seen more as a sign of interest-group politics than of intellectual autonomy. For a better example of his willingness to go against the grain, let us return to his would-be masterwork, *Christus*. Above and beyond the problems of unevenness and disunity mentioned earlier, nineteenth-century readers, in a verdict that our more saturnine century has been oddly slow to challenge, were dismayed by the directional movement of the trilogy. According to Longfellow's design, the three parts represent three religio-historical eras and the three Christian virtues: I. The era of Jesus - Faith; II. The medieval era - Hope; III. The "modern" era - Charity. In Longfellow's realization of this design, however, Part III seemed a cruel undoing of parts I–II. Part III consisted of two bleak Puritan dramas: "John Endicott," centering on the oligarchy's persecution of Quakers, and "Giles Corey of the Salem Farms," a recreation of the witchcraft delusion that focuses on the corruption of ordinary people. In Longfellow's two-part exposure of the sins of New England's ancestors, magistrates and citizenry are thus equally implicated.

The New England Tragedies were in some ways familiar reruns of plot motifs that had been popular in New England writing since the 1820s. Indeed, Longfellow's subjects were the two most frequently fictionalized Puritan episodes. The conventional approach to those subjects, however, called for the writer either to present the Puritan era as safely bracketed (a moral stage of history beyond which America had fortunately evolved), or to find some silver lining of staunchness, piety or whatnot in the black cloud of Puritanism. Even Hawthorne engaged in such temporizing. Not Longfellow, whose trilogy allowed the Puritan dispensation to stand for the entire modern era and gave no shred of comfort that the virtue of Charity was being fulfilled in our times. Longfellow's cantankerousness would have seemed all the greater for the fact that the work was issued in the aftermath of the Civil War, when rituals of reconciliation and national optimism were the order of the day. Which may have been precisely why Longfellow was tempted to write as he did, although he never said so.

Longfellow's career, then, shows that although he was not an original genius so much as a versatile adapter of preexisting models he was no conformist, either formally or intellectually. His popularity was based not so much on reinforcing what the public already knew very well as in telling it unfamiliar stories, or variations of familiar ones, in verse forms that were modestly innovative and with deepenings and turns of interpretation that generally stopped short of being subversive, but sometimes directly challenged smug consensus.

This edition contains a generous sampling of Longfellow's work, printed here in the order in which it was originally published. In culling items from his first five collections of lyrics (1839–46), I have been very selective. Although they won Longfellow a wide national audience, they were justly eclipsed by the works that followed. Longfellow is all too often judged by old chestnuts from this era, like "A Psalm of Life"—a much anthologized but hollow declamation piece, printed here for the record, that has haunted Longfellow's reputation like Whitman's "I hear America singing" and "O Captain, my captain!" With a few exceptions like "The Arsenal at Springfield" and its lesser-known companion piece "The Occultation of Orion," Longfellow's self-criticism in "Mezzo Cammin" (1842) was well-founded, and it is appropriate that this latter poem stands at the threshold of the more ambitious work of the 1840s and after. In the shorter lyric as well, Longfellow produced his most haunting, densely packed achievements after mid-life: "The Fire of Drift-Wood," "The Jewish Cemetery at Newport" (despite its mistaken prediction at the close), the sonnet "Nature," and the elegies to his wife and to Hawthorne. Though most of Longfellow's lyrics have deservedly been forgotten, his best stands up well by comparison to the best mid-century Anglo-American work in the same vein.

Longfellow's immensely popular recreations of colonial episodes, *Evangeline* and *The Courtship of Miles Standish*, still retain their appeal despite the simplistic characterizations of the former and the situation-comedy sentimentalism of the latter. They illustrate Longfellow's versatility of tone—the one elegaic, the other pastoral, as well as his adeptness at dramatizing the ironies of the oddly split image of colonial life from posterity's standpoint: heavily idealized on the one hand, an affair of Edenic Acadias or pristine innocent Pilgrim bands; grim, threatening, and unstable on the other, an affair of Indian-fighting and of encroachments on bucolic happiness by conquistadors or Puritan oligarchs. In *Miles Standish* this relationship is explored with special discernment, through the device of having the outraged Standish, convinced that his friend John Alden has played him false when making his proxy proposal to Priscilla Mullins, take out his aggression against the Indians. When Standish returns to Plymouth with a sachem's head, he is ready to forgive all.

In *Evangeline,* the opposition between violence and tranquility is external and melodramatized by comparison: the virtuous Acadians vs. the bullying British. This theme, however, takes on additional resonance when read in the light of the poem's own times, the 1840s, America's decade of greatest mobility and expansionism, in which New Englanders played a leading part. *Evangeline,* like *Walden* and *Uncle Tom's Cabin,* gives oblique expression to the New England diaspora south and westward, a movement that as Longfellow perceived had from the stay-at-home's point of view the consequence of violently breaking up families and communities, thus producing a generation of displaced persons with intense nostalgia for the kind of small, interdependent, pre-industrial village life portrayed at the poem's start. The poem, then, is by no means exclusively about an isolated case of disruption taking place in a sealed chamber of the past. The poem's relentless movement from idyllic pleasure to brooding pathos makes it a stronger although less charming achievement than *Miles Standish,* in which the tone is lighter and a great deal of the plot is handled through dialogue, where Longfellow's formal meter and diction tend to come across as wordy and wooden as contrasted with the stately, sonorous narrative words.

Longfellow was unfortunately much less successful in what ironically became his most famous long narrative poem, *The Song of Hiawatha.* Here, as in *Evangeline,* Longfellow sings of the flourishing and the imminent end of love and of an appealingly innocent but fated culture. As in all his major work, Longfellow treats the events of his narrative from a moral perspective that displays compassion rather than righteous crusading, mercy rather than judgmentalism, peaceable mediation rather than militancy. But these humane values, that enable Longfellow to invest his sympathetic figures in *Evangeline* and *Miles Standish* with moral authority, in *Hiawatha* seem too much like the mark of the tenderfoot. Hiawatha, the noblest of all conceivable primitives, and his companions are too obviously a cardboard concoction of Longfellow's reading in Scandinavian epic and in what contemporary American scholars have called the discourse of savagism: that is, nineteenth century liberal complacent-sympathetic construction of Indian culture as noble, exotic, and doomed. Written in twenty-two self-contained short-units, *Hiawatha* is easily excerptable, and two sections will suffice to give the flavor of this white elephant in the Longfellow canon. They show the poem to be mellifluous, prettily and sometimes even beautifully imagistic, but shallow: a pleasant literary-anthropological tour de force but nothing more.

Hiawatha has become increasingly used against Longfellow as the almost simultaneous first edition of *Leaves of Grass* increasingly has become regarded as the great American poem. On the surface, the contrast seems devastating to Longfellow: seeking to range beyond genteel subjects, Longfellow created an insipid, ethnocentric armchair fantasy, while Whitman dug into the nitty-gritty of American experience. A fairer reading of Longfellow's work, however, would be this: *Hiawatha* was a one-time experiment for him, not to be taken as the quintessence of his muse but as one among other occasional attempts to extend his treatment of American life beyond the regional and cultural boundaries he knew best. Just as Whitman's headier catalogues wear thin once he ranges more than a few score miles from Manhattan, so with Longfellow. Although his experiment failed by any exacting standard, at least it was vigorous enough to establish itself, along with James Fenimore Cooper's novels, ahead of the thousand of other contemporary literary evocations of Indian life.

Miles Standish and Longfellow's other ensuing works printed here are much stronger by comparison. Among works of the 1860s and after, the most ambitious and important are *Christus,* discussed above, and *Tales of a Wayside Inn.* The latter, the first and best of whose three installments was published in the middle of the Civil War, is the work that most fully demonstates Longfellow's literary reach and versatility. In the Chaucerian tradition, *Tales of a Wayside Inn* is a loosely knit collection of short and very diverse narratives purportedly told by a small company (the landlord, a musician, a theologian, a poet, a student, a Sicilian, a Spanish Jew) during three evenings at a Sudbury, Massachusetts, inn that is still famous as the site of that imaginary occasion. The present volume includes the first tales of three of these figures. Their personalities and interaction are not sketched with anything like Chaucer's shrewdness and vivacity, but their twice-told tales ventriloquize and elaborate upon an impressive array of tones and themes in the repertoire of western literature. The first of these, the landlord's "Paul Revere's Ride" (which launches the session) is a rousing vernacular hero story. By contrast, the theologian's "Torquemada" is a horrifying gothic tale of the perversity and anguish of a medieval Spanish nobleman who turns his innocent daughters over to the Inquisition. Those who know Longfellow only by his modern reputation will be astonished at its affinities to Hawthorne and Poe. On the other hand, "The Birds of Killingworth," which the poet tells, is by contrast a cheerful comic fable of error followed by regeneration in a Connecticut town whose overpragmatic farmers find they have made a dreadful mistake in ignoring the schoolmaster's pleas not to massacre the birds that are plaguing their land.

Although the individual narratives stand on their own, it is not amiss to read each as commenting on its predecessors. In this way, as in *Evangeline*, Longfellow obliquely but probingly conducts a series of reflections on the spirit of the times. The latter two pieces probe beneath the landlord's naive patriotism to deplore violence as a means of social problem-solving, to expose the pathology of authoritarianism and bigotry, and, finally, to celebrate the triumph of the humane sensibility over programmatic rigor. Indeed it is noteworthy that the folk hero whom Longfellow allows the landlord to celebrate in the first place is conspicuous for what he sees, feels, and says, not for any military action.

Longfellow continued to compose poetry until shortly before his death, and although the work of his final decade represents, overall, a decline in quality, the best of it deserves to be known. One substantial poem of intermediate length is printed here. *Morituri Salutamus* (1875), delivered by Longfellow as a commencement poem on behalf of his fiftieth year class reunion at Bowdoin College, was undertaken hesitantly but turned out to be one of the finest poems ever delivered at an academic celebration. The title, meaning "We who are about to die salute you"—the Roman gladiator's traditional greeting to the emperor—suggests the combination of gusto and resignation with which the poem meditates philosophically on the outcome of youth and the opportunities of old age.

The last decade has seen a dramatic revival of interest in popular mid-nineteenth-century American literature. Works like Frederick Douglass's *Narrative* of his years as a slave and Harriet Beecher Stowe's *Uncle Tom's Cabin*, to mention only two examples, are now widely reprinted, assigned in college literature courses, and studied by scholars with increasing attention. In the process, the sharp-seeming distinction between "serious" literature (supposedly produced by a tiny handful of authors like Emerson and Melville) and "popular" literature (all the rest, not worth close study) has eroded, and rightly so. We now recognize that the period's "serious" authors were by no means above the marketplace, and that "popular" writing was often undertaken with a deep sense of mission and continues in many cases to make good reading and to afford significant cultural commentary. So far, however, this revival of attention has understandably been directed at the discovery or rediscovery of black and women writers, whose voices history had most fully silenced. Now that they are starting to receive their due, it is time to extend the same scrutiny to the largest single group of neglected popular American writers: white men. Among this group, Longfellow stands at the head of the line. No one can fully comprehend the literary culture of nineteenth-century America without coming to terms with his work, and those who come to it for the first time are likely to be surprised at how absorbing the best of it is.

—Lawrence Buell

SUGGESTIONS FOR FURTHER READING

Arms, George. *The Fields Were Green*. Stanford: Stanford Univ. Press, 1948. A collection and thoughtful critical discussion of Longfellow and other New England "schoolroom" or "fireside" poets.

Arvin, Newton. *Longfellow: His Life and Work*. Boston: Little, Brown, 1962. The best one-volume overview of Longfellow's literary career and major works.

Buell, Lawrence, *New England Literary Culture: From Revolution Through Renaissance*. Cambridge: Cambridge Univ. Press, 1986. Extensive discussion of *The New England Tragedies* and selected other Longfellow poems in chapters 5 and 11.

Charvat, William, "Longfellow" and "Longfellow's Income from His Writings, 1842–1852." In *The Profession of Authorship in America, 1800–1870*. Ed. Matthew J. Bruccoli. Columbus: Ohio State Univ. Press, 1968. Excellent discussion of Longfellow as literary professional at a time when American literary professonalism was just beginning.

Duffey, Bernard. *Poetry in America*. Durham: Duke Univ. Press, 1978. Provides, in section one, a discerning analytical overview of nineteenth-century New England poetics. Valuable, like Arms, for the detail with which it shows Longfellow in relation to his closest poetic peers.

Ferguson, Robert. "Longfellow's Political Fears: Civic Authority and the Role of the Artist in *Hiawatha* and

Miles Standish." *American Literature,* 50 (1978), 187–215.

Hilen, Andrew. *Longfellow and Scandinavia.* New Haven: Yale Univ. Press, 1947. The best case study of Longfellow's knowledge of foreign literatures and the literary uses to which he put it.

Longfellow, Henry Wadsworth. *The Letters of Henry Wadsworth Longfellow.* 6 vols. Ed. Andrew Hilen. Cambridge, Mass.: Harvard Univ. Press, 1967–82. An excellent scholarly edition, with extensive biographical summaries.

Longfellow, Samuel. *Life of Henry Wadsworth Longfellow.* 2 vols. Boston: Ticknor, 1886. The standard nineteenth-century biographical memoir compiled by Longfellow's brother, with generous excerpts from the poet's letters and diary.

Longfellow, Samuel. *Final Memorials of Henry Wadsworth Longfellow.* Boston: Ticknor, 1887. A supplement to the two-volume *Life.*

Mathews, J. Chesley. *Longfellow Reconsidered: A Symposium.* Hartford: Transcendental Books, 1973. A miscellaneous collection of recent scholarly opinion and analysis.

Papers Presented at the Longfellow Commemorative Conference, April 1–3, 1982. Washington, D.C.: GPO, 1982. A useful miscellaneous collection of criticism.

Seelye, John, "Attic Shape: Dusting Off *Evangeline.*" *Virginia Quarterly Review,* 60 (1984), 21–44. A witty, thoughtful reading of the poem as a response to its times, with particular emphasis on its depiction of the west.

Thompson, Lawrance. *Young Longfellow,* 1807–1843. New York: Macmillan, 1838. The most detailed account of Longfellow's intellectually formative years. Intelligent and probing, albeit judgmental.

Wagenknecht, Edward. *Longfellow: A Full-Length Portrait.*

New York: Longmans, Green, 1955. A thoughtful topically arranged study of important aspects of Longfellow's life and career.

Ward, Robert S. "Longfellow's Roots on Yankee Soil." *New England Quarterly*, 41 (1968), 180–192. Eloquently makes the case for seeing Longfellow as a New England writer.

A NOTE ON THE TEXT

The edition used as the basis of this volume is *The Complete Writings of Henry Wadsworth Longfellow* (Boston: Houghton, Mifflin, & Co., 1904). Texts of poems printed here have been checked for accuracy against the first editions.

LONGER WORKS

LONGER WORKS

EVANGELINE*

A TALE OF ACADIE

THIS is the forest primeval. The murmuring pines and
    the hemlocks,
Bearded with moss, and in garments green, indistinct
    in the twilight,
Stand like Druids of eld, with voices sad and prophetic,
Stand like harpers hoar, with beards that rest on their
    bosoms.
Loud from its rocky caverns, the deep-voiced neighboring
    ocean
Speaks, and in accents disconsolate answers the wail of
    the forest.

This is the forest primeval; but where are the hearts
    that beneath it
Leaped like the roe, when he hears in the woodland
    the voice of the huntsman?
Where is the thatch-roofed village, the home of Acadian
    farmers,—
Men whose lives glided on like rivers that water the
    woodlands,
Darkened by shadows of earth, but reflecting an image
    of heaven?
Waste are those pleasant farms, and the farmers forever
    departed!
Scattered like dust and leaves, when the mighty blasts
    of October
Seize them, and whirl them aloft, and sprinkle them
    far o'er the ocean.

Naught but tradition remains of the beautiful village of Grand-Pré.

Ye who believe in affection that hopes, and endures, and is patient,
Ye who believe in the beauty and strength of woman's devotion,
List to the mournful tradition, still sung by the pines of the forest;
List to a Tale of Love in Acadie, home of the happy.

PART THE FIRST

I

IN the Acadian land, on the shores of the Basin of Minas,
Distant, secluded, still the little village of Grand-Pré
Lay in the fruitful valley. Vast meadows stretched to the eastward,
Giving the village its name, and pasture to flocks without number.
Dikes, that the hands of farmers had raised with labor incessant,
Shut out the turbulent tides; but at stated seasons the flood-gates
Opened, and welcomed the sea to wander at will o'er the meadows.
West and south there were fields of flax, and orchards and cornfields
Spreading afar and unfenced o'er the plain; and away to the northward
Blomidon rose, and the forests old, and aloft on the mountains
Sea-fogs pitched their tents, and mists from the mighty Atlantic

Looked on the happy valley, but ne'er from their station
    descended.
There, in the midst of its farms, reposed the Acadian
    village.
Strongly built were the houses, with frames of oak and
    of hemlock,
Such as the peasants of Normandy built in the reign
    of the Henries.
Thatched were the roofs, with dormer-windows; and
    gables projecting
Over the basement below protected and shaded the
    doorway.
There in the tranquil evenings of summer, when brightly
    the sunset
Lighted the village street, and gilded the vanes on the
    chimneys,
Matrons and maidens sat in snow-white caps and in
    kirtles
Scarlet and blue and green, with distaffs spinning the
    golden
Flax for the gossiping looms, whose noisy shuttles within
    doors
Mingled their sounds with the whir of the wheels and
    the songs of the maidens.
Solemnly down the street came the parish priest, and
    the children
Paused in their play to kiss the hand he extended to
    bless them.
Reverend walked he among them; and up rose matrons
    and maidens,
Hailing his slow approach with words of affectionate
    welcome.
Then came the laborers home from the field, and serenely
    the sun sank
Down to his rest, and twilight prevailed. Anon from
    the belfry

Softly the Angelus sounded, and over the roofs of the
   village
Columns of pale blue smoke, like clouds of incense
   ascending,
Rose from a hundred hearths, the home of peace and
   contentment
Thus dwelt together in love these simple Acadian farmers,—
Dwelt in the love of God and of man. Alike were
   they free from
Fear, that reigns with the tyrant, and envy, the vice
   of republics.
Neither locks had they to their doors, nor bars to their
   windows;
But their dwellings were open as day and the hearts
   of the owners;
There the richest was poor, and the poorest lived in
   abundance.

   Somewhat apart from the village, and nearer the Basin
      of Minas,
Benedict Bellefontaine, the wealthiest farmer of Grand-
   Pré,
Dwelt on his goodly acres; and with him, directing
   his household,
Gentle Evangeline lived, his child, and the pride of the
   village.
Stalworth and stately in form was the man of seventy
   winters;
Hearty and hale was he, an oak that is covered with
   snow-flakes;
White as the snow were his locks, and his cheeks as
   brown as the oak-leaves.
Fair was she to behold, that maiden of seventeen summers.
Black were her eyes as the berry that grows on the
   thorn by the wayside,
Black, yet how softly they gleamed beneath the brown
   shade of her tresses!

Sweet was her breath as the breath of kine that feed
    in the meadows.
When in the harvest heat she bore to the reapers at
    noontide
Flagons of home-brewed ale, ah! fair in sooth was the
    maiden.
Fairer was she when, on Sunday morn, while the bell
    from its turret
Sprinkled with holy sounds the air, as the priest with
    his hyssop
Sprinkles the congregation, and scatters blessings upon
    them,
Down the long street she passed, with her chaplet of
    beads and her missal,
Wearing her Norman cap, and her kirtle of blue, and
    the ear-rings,
Brought in the olden time from France, and since, as
    an heirloom,
Handed down from mother to child, through long
    generations.
But a celestial brightness—a more ethereal beauty—
Shone on her face and encircled her form, when, after
    confession,
Homeward serenely she walked with God's benediction
    upon her.
When she had passed, it seemed like the ceasing of
    exquisite music.

  Firmly builded with rafters of oak, the house of the
    farmer
Stood on the side of a hill commanding the sea; and
    a shady
Sycamore grew by the door, with a woodbine wreathing
    around it.
Rudely carved was the porch, with seats beneath; and
    a footpath

Led through an orchard wide, and disappeared in the
  meadow.
Under the sycamore-tree were hives overhung by a
  penthouse,
Such as the traveller sees in regions remote by the
  roadside,
Built o'er a box for the poor, or the blessed image
  of Mary.
Farther down, on the slope of the hill, was the well
  with its moss-grown
Bucket, fastened with iron, and near it a trough for
  the horses.
Shielding the house from storms, on the north, were
  the barns and the farmyard.
There stood the broad-wheeled wains and the antique
  ploughs and the harrows;
There were the folds for the sheep; and there, in his
  feathered seraglio,
Strutted the lordly turkey, and crowed the cock, with
  the selfsame
Voice that in ages of old had startled the penitent
  Peter.*
Bursting with hay were the barns, themselves a village.
  In each one
Far o'er the gable projected a roof of thatch; and a
  staircase,
Under the sheltering eaves, led up to the odorous corn-
  loft.
There too the dove-cot stood, with its meek and innocent
  inmates
Murmuring ever of love; while above it the variant
  breezes
Numberless noisy weathercocks rattled and sang of
  mutation.

  Thus, at peace with God and the world, the farmer
  of Grand-Pré

Lived on his sunny farm, and Evangeline governed his
   household.
Many a youth, as he knelt in church and opened his
   missal,
Fixed his eyes upon her as the saint of his deepest
   devotion;
Happy was he who might touch her hand or the hem
   of her garment!
Many a suitor came to her door, by the darkness
   befriended,
And, as he knocked and waited to hear the sound of
   her footsteps,
Knew not which beat the louder, his heart or the
   knocker of iron;
Or at the joyous feast of the Patron Saint of the village,
Bolder grew, and pressed her hand in the dance as he
   whispered
Hurried words of love, that seemed a part of the music.
But, among all who came, young Gabriel only was
   welcome;
Gabriel Lajeunesse, the son of Basil the blacksmith,
Who was a mighty man in the village, and honored
   of all men;
For, since the birth of time, throughout all ages and
   nations,
Has the craft of the smith been held in repute by the
   people.
Basil was Benedict's friend. Their children from earliest
   childhood
Grew up together as brother and sister; and Father
   Felician,
Priest and pedagogue both in the village, had taught
   them their letters
Out of the selfsame book, with the hymns of the
   church and the plain-song.
But when the hymn was sung, and the daily lesson
   completed,

Swiftly they hurried away to the forge of Basil the
    blacksmith.
There at the door they stood, with wondering eyes to
    behold him
Take in his leathern lap the hoof of the horse as a
    plaything,
Nailing the shoe in its place; while near him the tire
    of the cart-wheel
Lay like a fiery snake, coiled round in a circle of
    cinders.
Oft on autumnal eves, when without in the gathering
    darkness
Bursting with light seemed the smithy, through every
    cranny and crevice,
Warm by the forge within they watched the laboring
    bellows,
And as its panting ceased, and the sparks expired in
    the ashes,
Merrily laughed, and said they were nuns going into
    the chapel.
Oft on sledges in winter, as swift as the swoop of
    the eagle,
Down the hillside bounding, they glided away o'er the
    meadow.
Oft in the barns they climbed to the populous nests
    on the rafters,
Seeking with eager eyes that wondrous stone, which
    the swallow
Brings from the shore of the sea to restore the sight
    of its fledglings;
Lucky was he who found that stone in the nest of
    the swallow!
Thus passed a few swift years, and they no longer
    were children.
He was a valiant youth, and his face, like the face of
    the morning,

Gladdened the earth with its light, and ripened thought
 into action.
She was a woman now, with the heart and hopes of
 a woman.
"Sunshine of Saint Eulalie" was she called; for that was
 the sunshine
Which, as the farmers believed, would load their orchards
 with apples;
She, too, would bring to her husband's house delight
 and abundance,
Filling it with love and the ruddy faces of children.

II

Now had the season returned, when the nights grow
 colder and longer,
And the retreating sun the sign of the Scorpion enters.
Birds of passage sailed through the leaden air, from
 the ice-bound,
Desolate northern bays to the shores of tropical islands
Harvests were gathered in; and wild with the winds
 of September
Wrestled the trees of the forest, as Jacob of old with
 the angel.*
All the signs foretold a winter long and inclement.
Bees, with prophetic instinct of want, had hoarded their
 honey
Till the hives overflowed; and the Indian hunters asserted
Cold would the winter be, for thick was the fur of
 the foxes.
Such was the advent of autumn. Then followed that
 beautiful season,
Called by the pious Acadian peasants the Summer of
 All-Saints!
Filled was the air with a dreamy and magical light;
 and the landscape
Lay as if new-created in all the freshness of childhood.

Peace seemed to reign upon the earth, and the restless
heart of the ocean
Was for a moment consoled. All sounds were in harmony
blended.
Voices of children at play, the crowing of cocks in
the farmyards,
Whir of wings in the drowsy air, and the cooing of
pigeons,
All were subdued and low as the murmurs of love,
and the great sun
Looked with the eye of love through the golden vapors
around him;
While arrayed in its robes of russet and scarlet and
yellow,
Bright with the sheen of the dew, each glittering tree
of the forest
Flashed like the plane-tree the Persian adorned with
mantles and jewels.

Now recommenced the reign of rest and affection
and stillness.
Day with its burden and heat had departed, and twilight
descending
Brought back the evening star to the sky, and the
herds to the homestead.
Pawing the ground they came, and resting their necks
on each other,
And with their nostrils distended inhaling the freshness
of evening.
Foremost, bearing the bell, Evangeline's beautiful heifer,
Proud of her snow-white hide, and the ribbon that
waved from her collar,
Quietly paced and slow, as if conscious of human
affection.
Then came the shepherd back with his bleating flocks
from the seaside,

Where was their favorite pasture. Behind them followed
    the watch-dog,
Patient, full of importance, and grand in the pride of
    his instinct,
Walking from side to side with a lordly air, and superbly
Waving his bushy tail, and urging forward the stragglers;
Regent of flocks was he when the shepherd slept; their
    protector,
When from the forest at night, through the starry silence
    the wolves howled.
Late, with the rising moon, returned the wains from
    the marshes,
Laden with briny hay, that filled the air with its odor.
Cheerily neighed the steeds, with dew on their manes
    and their fetlocks,
While aloft on their shoulders the wooden and ponderous
    saddles,
Painted with brilliant dyes, and adorned with tassels of
    crimson,
Nodded in bright array, like hollyhocks heavy with
    blossoms.
Patiently stood the cows meanwhile, and yielded their
    udders
Unto the milkmaid's hand; whilst loud and in regular
    cadence
Into the sounding pails the foaming streamlets descended.
Lowing of cattle and peals of laughter were heard in
    the farmyard,
Echoed back by the barns. Anon they sank into stillness;
Heavily closed, with a jarring sound, the valves of the
    barn-doors,
Rattled the wooden bars, and all for a season was silent.

  Indoors, warm by the wide-mouthed fireplace, idly
    the farmer
Sat in his elbow-chair and watched how the flames and
    the smoke-wreaths

Struggled together like foes in a burning city. Behind
     him,
Nodding and mocking along the wall, with gestures
     fantastic,
Darted his own huge shadow, and vanished away into
     darkness.
Faces, clumsily carved in oak, on the back of his arm-
     chair
Laughed in the flickering light; and the pewter plates
     on the dresser
Caught and reflected the flame, as shields of armies the
     sunshine.
Fragments of song the old man sang, and carols of
     Christmas,
Such as at home, in the olden time, his fathers before
     him
Sang in their Norman orchards and bright Burgundian
     vineyards.
Close at her father's side was the gentle Evangeline
     seated,
Spinning flax for the loom, that stood in the corner
     behind her,
Silent awhile were its treadles, at rest was its diligent
     shuttle,
While the monotonous drone of the wheel, like the
     drone of a bagpipe,
Followed the old man's song and united the fragments
     together.
As in a church, when the chant of the choir at intervals
     ceases,
Footfalls are heard in the aisles, or words of the priest
     at the altar,
So, in each pause of the song, with measured motion
     the clock clicked.

  Thus as they sat, there were footsteps heard, and,
     suddenly lifted,

Sounded the wooden latch, and the door swung back
    on its hinges.
Benedict knew by the hob-nailed shoes it was Basil
    the blacksmith,
And by her beating heart Evangeline knew who was
    with him.
"Welcome!" the farmer exclaimed, as their footsteps
    paused on the threshold,
"Welcome, Basil, my friend! Come, take thy place on
    the settle
Close by the chimney-side, which is always empty
    without thee;
Take from the shelf overhead thy pipe and the box
    of tobacco;
Never so much thyself art thou as when through the
    curling
Smoke of the pipe or the forge thy friendly and jovial
    face gleams
Round and red as the harvest moon through the mist
    of the marshes."
Then, with a smile of content, thus answered Basil the
    blacksmith,
Taking with easy air the accustomed seat by the fireside:
"Benedict Bellefontaine, thou hast ever thy jest and thy
    ballad!
Ever in cheerfullest mood art thou, when others are
    filled with
Gloomy forebodings of ill, and see only ruin before
    them.
Happy art thou, as if every day thou hadst picked up
    a horseshoe."
Pausing a moment, to take the pipe that Evangeline
    brought him,
And with a coal from the embers had lighted, he slowly
    continued:
"Four days now are passed since the English ships at
    their anchors

Ride in the Gaspereau's mouth, with their cannon pointed
    against us.
What their design may be is unknown; but all are
    commanded
On the morrow to meet in the church, where his
    Majesty's mandate
Will be proclaimed as law in the land. Alas! in the
    meantime
Many surmises of evil alarm the hearts of the people."
Then made answer the farmer: "Perhaps some friendlier
    purpose
Brings these ships to our shores. Perhaps the harvests
    in England
By untimely rains or untimelier heat have been blighted,
And from our bursting barns they would feed their
    cattle and children."
"Not so thinketh the folk in the village," said, warmly,
    the blacksmith,
Shaking his head, as in doubt; then, heaving a sigh,
    he continued:
"Louisburg is not forgotten, nor Beau Séjour, nor Port
    Royal.
Many already have fled to the forest, and lurk on its
    outskirts,
Waiting with anxious hearts the dubious fate of to-
    morrow.
Arms have been taken from us, and warlike weapons
    of all kinds;
Nothing is left but the blacksmith's sledge and the
    scythe of the mower."
Then with a pleasant smile made answer the jovial
    farmer:
"Safer are we unarmed, in the midst of our flocks and
    our cornfields,
Safer within these peaceful dikes, besieged by the ocean,
Than our fathers in forts, besieged by the enemy's
    cannon.

Fear no evil, my friend, and to-night may no shadow
    of sorrow
Fall on this house and hearth; for this is the night of
    the contract.
Built are the house and the barn. The merry lads of
    the village
Strongly have built them and well; and, breaking the
    glebe round about them,
Filled the barn with hay, and the house with food for
    a twelvemonth.
René Leblanc will be here anon, with his papers and
    inkhorn.
Shall we not then be glad, and rejoice in the joy of
    our children?"
As apart by the window she stood, with her hand in
    her lover's,
Blushing Evangeline heard the words that her father
    had spoken,
And, as they died on his lips, the worthy notary entered.

III

Bent like a laboring oar, that toils in the surf of the
    ocean,
Bent, but not broken, by age was the form of the
    notary public;
Shocks of yellow hair, like the silken floss of the maize,
    hung
Over his shoulders; his forehead was high; and glasses
    with horn bows
Sat astride on his nose, with a look of wisdom supernal.
Father of twenty children was he, and more than a
    hundred
Children's children rode on his knee, and heard his
    great watch tick.
Four long years in the time of the war had he languished
    a captive,

Suffering much in an old French fort as the friend of
      the English.
Now, though warier grown, without all guile or suspicion,
Ripe in wisdom was he, but patient, and simple, and
      childlike.
He was beloved by all, and most of all by the children;
For he told them tales of the Loup-garou in the forest,*
And of the goblin that came in the night to water the
      horses,
And of the white Létiche, the ghost of a child who
      unchristened
Died, and was doomed to haunt unseen the chambers
      of children;
And how on Christmas Eve the oxen talked in the stable,
And how the fever was cured by a spider shut up in
      a nutshell,
And of the marvellous powers of four-leaved clover
      and horseshoes,
With whatsoever else was writ in the lore of the village.
Then up rose from his seat by the fireside Basil the
      blacksmith,
Knocked from his pipe the ashes, and slowly extending
      his right hand,
"Father Leblanc," he exclaimed, "thou hast heard the
      talk in the village,
And, perchance, canst tell us some news of these ships
      and their errand."
Then with modest demeanor made answer the notary
      public,
"Gossip enough have I heard, in sooth, yet am never
      the wiser;
And what their errand may be I know not better than
      others.
Yet am I not of those who imagine some evil intention
Brings them here, for we are at peace; and why then
      molest us?"

"God's name!" shouted the hasty and somewhat irascible
    blacksmith;
"Must we in all things look for the how, and the
    why, and the wherefore?
Daily injustice is done, and might is the right of the
    strongest!"
But without heeding his warmth, continued the notary
    public,
"Man is unjust, but God is just; and finally justice
Triumphs; and well I remember a story, that often
    consoled me,
When as a captive I lay in the old French fort at Port
    Royal."
This was the old man's favorite tale, and he loved to
    repeat it
When his neighbors complained that any injustice was
    done them.
"Once in an ancient city, whose name I no longer
    remember,
Raised aloft on a column, a brazen statue of Justice
Stood in the public square, upholding the scales in its
    left hand,
And in its right a sword, as an emblem that justice
    presided
Over the laws of the land, and the hearts and homes
    of the people.
Even the birds had built their nests in the scales of
    the balance,
Having no fear of the sword that flashed in the sunshine
    above them.
But in the course of time the laws of the land were
    corrupted;
Might took the place of right, and the weak were
    oppressed, and the mighty
Ruled with an iron rod. Then it chanced in a nobleman's
    palace

That a necklace of pearls was lost, and ere long a
    suspicion
Fell on an orphan girl who lived as a maid in the
    household.
She, after form of trial condemned to die on the scaffold,
Patiently met her doom at the foot of the statue of
    Justice.
As to her Father in heaven her innocent spirit ascended,
Lo! o'er the city a tempest rose; and the bolts of the
    thunder
Smote the statue of bronze, and hurled in wrath from
    its left hand
Down on the pavement below the clattering scales of
    the balance,
And in the hollow thereof was found the nest of a
    magpie,
Into whose clay-built walls the necklace of pearls was
    inwoven."
Silenced, but not convinced, when the story was ended,
    the blacksmith
Stood like a man who fain would speak, but findeth
    no language;
All his thoughts were congealed into lines on his face,
    as the vapors
Freeze in fantastic shapes on the window-panes in the
    winter.

    Then Evangeline lighted the brazen lamp on the table,
Filled, till it overflowed, the pewter tankard with home-
    brewed
Nut-brown ale, that was famed for its strength in the
    village of Grand-Pré;
While from his pocket the notary drew his papers and
    inkhorn,
Wrote with a steady hand the date and the age of the
    parties,

Naming the dower of the bride in flocks of sheep and
    in cattle.
Orderly all things proceeded, and duly and well were
    completed,
And the great seal of the law was set like a sun on
    the margin.
Then from his leathern pouch the farmer threw on the table
Three times the old man's fee in solid pieces of silver;
And the notary rising, and blessing the bride and the
    bridegroom,
Lifted aloft the tankard of ale and drank to their welfare.
Wiping the foam from his lip, he solemnly bowed and
    departed,
While in silence the others sat and mused by the fireside,
Till Evangeline brought the draught-board out of its
    corner.
Soon was the game begun. In friendly contention the
    old men
Laughed at each lucky hit, or unsuccessful manœuvre,
Laughed when a man was crowned, or a breach was
    made in the king-row.
Meanwhile apart, in the twilight gloom of a window's
    embrasure,
Sat the lovers, and whispered together, beholding the
    moon rise
Over the pallid sea, and the silvery mists of the meadows.
Silently one by one, in the infinite meadows of heaven,
Blossomed the lovely stars, the forget-me-nots of the
    angels.

    That was the evening passed. Anon the bell from
    the belfry
Rang out the hour of nine, the village curfew, and
    straightaway
Rose the guests and departed; and silence reigned in
    the household.

Many a farewell word and sweet good-night on the
    door-step
Lingered long in Evangeline's heart, and filled it with
    gladness.
Carefully then were covered the embers that glowed
    on the hearth-stone,
And on the oaken stairs resounded the tread of the
    farmer.
Soon with a soundless step the foot of Evangeline
    followed.
Up the staircase moved a luminous space in the darkness,
Lighted less by the lamp than the shining face of the
    maiden.
Silent she passed the hall, and entered the door of her
    chamber.
Simple that chamber was, with its curtains of white,
    and its clothes-press
Ample and high, on whose spacious shelves were carefully
    folded
Linen and woollen stuffs by the hand of Evangeline
    woven.
This was the precious dower she would bring to her
    husband in marriage,
Better than flocks and herds, being proofs of her skill
    as a housewife.
Soon she extinguished her lamp, for the mellow and
    radiant moonlight
Streamed through the windows, and lighted the room,
    till the heart of the maiden
Swelled and obeyed its power, like the tremulous tides
    of the ocean.
Ah! she was fair, exceeding fair to behold, as she stood
    with
Naked snow-white feet on the gleaming floor of her
    chamber!
Little she dreamed that below, among the trees of the
    orchard,

Waited her lover and watched for the gleam of her
     lamp and her shadow.
Yet were her thoughts of him, and at times a feeling
     of sadness
Passed o'er her soul, as the sailing shade of clouds in
     the moonlight
Flitted across the floor and darkened the room for a
     moment.
And, as she gazed from the window, she saw serenely
     the moon pass
Forth from the folds of a cloud, and one star follow
     her footsteps,
As out of Abraham's tent young Ishmael wandered with
     Hagar!*

IV

Pleasantly rose next morn the sun on the village of
     Grand-Pré.
Pleasantly gleamed in the soft, sweet air the Basin of
     Minas,
Where the ships, with their wavering shadows, were
     riding at anchor.
Life had long been astir in the village, and clamorous
     labor
Knocked with its hundred hands at the golden gates
     of the morning.
Now from the country around, from the farms and
     neighboring hamlets,
Came in their holiday dresses the blithe Acadian peasants.
Many a glad good-morrow and jocund laugh from the
     young folk
Made the bright air brighter, as up from the numerous
     meadows,
Where no path could be seen but the track of wheels
     in the greensward,
Group after group appeared, and joined, or passed on
     the highway.

Long ere noon, in the village all sounds of labor were
    silenced.
Thronged were the streets with people; and noisy groups
    at the house-doors
Sat in the cheerful sun, and rejoiced and gossiped
    together.
Every house was an inn, where all were welcomed and
    feasted;
For with this simple people, who lived like brothers
    together,
All things were held in common, and what one had
    was another's.
Yet under Benedict's roof hospitality seemed more abun-
    dant:
For Evangeline stood among the guests of her father;
Bright was her face with smiles, and words of welcome
    and gladness
Fell from her beautiful lips, and blessed the cup as she
    gave it.

   Under the open sky, in the odorous air of the orchard,
Stript of its golden fruit, was spread the feast of
    betrothal.
There in the shade of the porch were the priest and
    the notary seated;
There good Benedict sat, and sturdy Basil the black-
    smith.
Not far withdrawn from these, by the cider-press and
    the beehives,
Michael the fiddler was placed, with the gayest of hearts
    and of waistcoats.
Shadow and light from the leaves alternately played on
    his snow-white
Hair, as it waved in the wind; and the jolly face of
    the fiddler
Glowed like a living coal when the ashes are blown
    from the embers.

Gayly the old man sang to the vibrant sound of his
    fiddle,
Tous les Bourgeois de Chartres, and *Le Carillon de Dun-*
    querque,
And anon with his wooden shoes beat time to the
    music.
Merrily, merrily whirled the wheels of the dizzying
    dances
Under the orchard-trees and down the path to the
    meadows;
Old folk and young together, and children mingled
    among them.
Fairest of all the maids was Evangeline, Benedict's
    daughter!
Noblest of all the youths was Gabriel, son of the
    blacksmith!

  So passed the morning away. And lo! with a summons
    sonorous
Sounded the bell from its tower, and over the meadows
    a drum beat.
Thronged ere long was the church with men. Without,
    in the churchyard,
Waited the women. They stood by the graves, and
    hung on the headstones
Garlands of autumn-leaves and evergreens fresh from
    the forest.
Then came the guard from the ships, and marching
    proudly among them
Entered the sacred portal. With loud and dissonant
    clangor
Echoed the sound of their brazen drums from ceiling
    and casement,—
Echoed a moment only, and slowly the ponderous
    portal
Closed, and in silence the crowd awaited the will of
    the soldiers.

Then uprose their commander, and spake from the steps
    of the altar,
Holding aloft in his hands, with its seals, the royal
    commission.
"You are convened this day," he said, "by his Majesty's
    orders.
Clement and kind has he been; but how you have
    answered his kindness,
Let our own hearts reply! To my natural make and
    my temper
Painful the task is I do, which to you I know must
    be grievous.
Yet must I bow and obey, and deliver the will of our
    monarch;
Namely, that all your lands, and dwellings, and cattle
    of all kinds
Forfeited be to the crown; and that you yourselves
    from this province
Be transported to other lands. God grant you may
    dwell there
Ever as faithful subjects, a happy and peaceable people!
Prisoners now I declare you; for such is his Majesty's
    pleasure!"
As, when the air is serene in sultry solstice of summer,
Suddenly gathers a storm, and the deadly sling of the
    hailstones
Beats down the farmer's corn in the field and shatters
    his windows,
Hiding the sun, and strewing the ground with thatch
    from the house-roofs,
Bellowing fly the herds, and seek to break their enclosures;
So on the hearts of the people descended the words
    of the speaker.
Silent a moment they stood in speechless wonder, and
    then arose
Louder and ever louder a wail of sorrow and anger,

And, by one impulse moved, they madly rushed to
    the doorway.
Vain was the hope of escape; and cries and fierce
    imprecations
Rang through the house of prayer; and high o'er the
    heads of the others
Rose, with his arms uplifted, the figure of Basil the
    blacksmith,
As, on a stormy sea, a spar is tossed by the billows.
Flushed was his face and distorted with passion; and
    wildly he shouted,
"Down with the tyrants of England! We never have
    sworn them allegiance!
Death to these foreign soldiers, who seize on our homes
    and our harvests!"
More he fain would have said, but the merciless hand
    of a soldier
Smote him upon the mouth, and dragged him down
    to the pavement.

  In the midst of the strife and tumult of angry contention,
Lo! the door of the chancel opened, and Father Felician
Entered, with serious mien, and ascended the steps of
    the altar.
Raising his reverend hand, with a gesture he awed into
    silence
All that clamorous throng; and thus he spake to his
    people;
Deep were his tones and solemn; in accents measured
    and mournful
Spake he, as, after the tocsin's alarum, distinctly the
    clock strikes.
"What is this that ye do, my children? what madness
    has seized you?
Forty years of my life have I labored among you, and
    taught you,

Not in word alone, but in deed, to love one another!
Is this the fruit of my toils, of my vigils and prayers
and privations?
Have you so soon forgotten all lessons of love and
forgiveness?
This is the house of the Prince of Peace, and would
you profane it
Thus with violent deeds and hearts overflowing with
hatred?
Lo! where the crucified Christ from his cross is gazing
upon you!
See! in those sorrowful eyes what meekness and holy
compassion!
Hark! how those lips still repeat the prayer, 'O Father,
forgive them!'
Let us repeat that prayer in the hour when the wicked
assail us,
Let us repeat it now, and say, 'O Father, forgive
them!' "
Few were his words of rebuke, but deep in the hearts
of his people
Sank they, and sobs of contrition succeeded the passionate
outbreak,
While they repeated his prayer, and said, "O Father,
forgive them!"

Then came the evening service. The tapers gleamed
from the altar.
Fervent and deep was the voice of the priest, and the
people responded,
Not with their lips alone, but their hearts; and the
Ave Maria
Sang they, and fell on their knees, and their souls,
with devotion translated,
Rose on the ardor of prayer, like Elijah ascending to
heaven.

Meanwhile had spread in the village the tidings of
    ill, and on all sides
Wandered, wailing, from house to house the women
    and children.
Long at her father's door Evangeline stood, with her
    right hand
Shielding her eyes from the level rays of the sun, that,
    descending,
Lighted the village street with mysterious splendor, and
    roofed each
Peasant's cottage with golden thatch, and emblazoned
    its windows.
Long within had been spread the snow-white cloth on
    the table;
There stood the wheaten loaf, and the honey fragrant
    with wild-flowers;
There stood the tankard of ale, and the cheese fresh
    brought from the dairy,
And, at the head of the board, the great armchair of
    the farmer.
Thus did Evangeline wait at her father's door, as the
    sunset
Threw the long shadows of trees o'er the broad ambrosial
    meadows.
Ah! on her spirit within a deeper shadow had fallen,
And from the fields of her soul a fragrance celestial
    ascended,—
Charity, meekness, love, and hope, and forgiveness, and
    patience!
Then, all-forgetful of self, she wandered into the village,
Cheering with looks and words the mournful hearts of
    the women,
As o'er the darkening fields with lingering steps they
    departed,
Urged by their household cares, and the weary feet of
    their children.

Down sank the great red sun, and in golden, glimmering
vapors
Veiled the light of his face, like the Prophet descending
from Sinai.
Sweetly over the village the bell of the Angelus sounded.

Meanwhile, amid the gloom, by the church Evangeline
lingered.
All was silent within; and in vain at the door and the
windows
Stood she, and listened and looked, till, overcome by
emotion,
"Gabriel!" cried she aloud with tremulous voice; but
no answer
Came from the graves of the dead, nor the gloomier
grave of the living.
Slowly at length she returned to the tenantless house
of her father.
Smouldered the fire on the hearth, on the board was
the supper untasted,
Empty and drear was each room, and haunted with
phantoms of terror.
Sadly echoed her step on the stair and the floor of
her chamber.
In the dead of the night she heard the disconsolate rain
fall
Loud on the withered leaves of the sycamore-tree by
the window.
Keenly the lightning flashed; and the voice of the echoing
thunder
Told her that God was in heaven, and governed the
world he created!
Then she rememberd the tale she had heard of the
justice of Heaven;
Soothed was her troubled soul, and she peacefully
slumbered till morning.

V

Four times the sun had risen and set; and now on the
    fifth day
Cheerily called the cock to the sleeping maids of the
    farmhouse.
Soon o'er the yellow fields, in silent and mournful
    procession,
Came from the neighboring hamlets and farms the
    Acadian women,
Driving in ponderous wains their household goods to
    the seashore,
Pausing and looking back to gaze once more on their
    dwellings,
Ere they were shut from sight by the winding road
    and the woodland.
Close at their sides their children ran, and urged on
    the oxen,
While in their little hands they clasped some fragments
    of playthings.

Thus to the Gaspereau's mouth they hurried; and
    there on the sea-beach
Piled in confusion lay the household goods of the
    peasants.
All day long between the shore and the ships did the
    boats ply;
All day long the wains came laboring down from the
    village.
Late in the afternoon, when the sun was near to his
    setting,
Echoed far o'er the fields came the roll of drums from
    the churchyard.
Thither the women and children thronged. On a sudden
    the church-doors
Opened, and forth came the guard, and marching in
    gloomy procession

Followed the long-imprisoned, but patient, Acadian farm-
      ers.
Even as pilgrims, who journey afar from their homes
      and their country,
Sing as they go, and in singing forget they are weary
      and wayworn,
So with songs on their lips the Acadian peasants descended
Down from the church to the shore, amid their wives
      and their daughters.
Foremost the young men came; and, raising together
      their voices,
Sang with tremulous lips a chant of the Catholic Missions:
"Sacred heart of the Savior! O inexhaustible fountain!
Fill our hearts this day with strength and submission
      and patience!"
Then the old men, as they marched, and the women
      that stood by the wayside
Joined in the sacred psalm, and the birds in the sunshine
      above them
Mingled their notes therewith, like voices of spirits
      departed.

  Halfway down to the shore Evangeline waited in
      silence,
Not overcome with grief, but strong in the hour of
      affliction,—
Calmly and sadly she waited, until the procession
      approached her,
And she beheld the face of Gabriel pale with emotion.
Tears then filled her eyes, and eagerly running to meet
      him,
Clasped she his hands, and laid her head on his shoulder,
      and whispered,
"Gabriel! be of good cheer! for if we love one another
Nothing, in truth, can harm us, whatever mischances
      may happen!"

Smiling she spake these words; then suddenly paused, for her father

Saw she slowly advancing. Alas! how changed was his aspect!

Gone was the glow from his cheek, and the fire from his eye, and his footstep

Heavier seemed with the weight of the heavy heart in his bosom.

But with a smile and a sigh, she clasped his neck and embraced him,

Speaking words of endearment where words of comfort availed not.

Thus to the Gaspereau's mouth moved on that mournful procession.

There disorder prevailed, and the tumult and stir of embarking.

Busily plied the freighted boats; and in the confusion

Wives were torn from their husbands, and mothers, too late, saw their children

Left on the land, extending their arms, with wildest entreaties.

So unto separate ships were Basil and Gabriel carried,

While in despair on the shore Evangeline stood with her father.

Half the task was not done when the sun went down, and the twilight

Deepened and darkened around; and in haste the refluent ocean

Fled away from the shore, and left the line of the sand-beach

Covered with waifs of the tide, with kelp and the slippery seaweed.

Farther back in the midst of the household goods and the wagons,

Like to a gypsy camp, or a leaguer after a battle,

All escape cut off by the sea, and the sentinels near
    them,
Lay encamped for the night the houseless Acadian farmers.
Back to its nethermost caves retreated the bellowing
    ocean,
Dragging adown the beach the rattling pebbles, and
    leaving
Inland and far up the shore the stranded boats of the
    sailors.
Then, as the night descended, the herds returned from
    their pastures;
Sweet was the moist still air with the odor of milk
    from their udders;
Lowing they waited, and long, at the well-known bars
    of the farmyard, —
Waited and looked in vain for the voice and the hand
    of the milkmaid.
Silence reigned in the streets; from the church no Angelus
    sounded,
Rose no smoke from the roofs, and gleamed no lights
    from the windows.

  But on the shores meanwhile the evening fires had
    been kindled,
Built of the drift-wood thrown on the sands from
    wrecks in the tempest.
Round them shapes of gloom and sorrowful faces were
    gathered,
Voices of women were heard, and of men, and the
    crying of children.
Onward from fire to fire, as from hearth to hearth in
    his parish,
Wandered the faithful priest, consoling and blessing and
    cheering,
Like unto shipwrecked Paul on Melita's desolate seashore.*
Thus he approached the place where Evangeline sat with
    her father,

EVANGELINE

And in the flickering light beheld the face of the old
man,
Haggard and hollow and wan, and without either thought
or emotion,
E'en as the face of a clock from which the hands have
been taken.
Vainly Evangeline strove with words and caresses to
cheer him,
Vainly offered him food; yet he moved not, he looked
not, he spake not,
But, with a vacant stare, ever gazed at the flickering
firelight.
"*Benedicite!*" murmured the priest, in tones of com-
passion.*
More he fain would have said, but his heart was full,
and his accents
Faltered and paused on his lips, as the feet of a child
on the threshold,
Hushed by the scene he beholds, and the awful presence
of sorrow.
Silently, therefore, he laid his hand on the head of the
maiden,
Raising his tearful eyes to the silent stars that above
them
Moved on their way, unperturbed by the wrongs and
sorrows of mortals.
Then sat he down at her side, and they wept together
in silence.

Suddenly rose from the south a light, as in autumn
the blood-red
Moon climbs the crystal walls of heaven, and o'er the
horizon
Titan-like stretches its hundred hands upon the mountain
and meadow,
Seizing the rocks and the rivers, and piling huge shadows
together.

Broader and ever broader it gleamed on the roofs of
the village,
Gleamed on the sky and sea, and the ships that lay
in the roadstead.
Columns of shining smoke uprose, and flashes of flame
were
Thrust through their folds and withdrawn, like the
quivering hands of a martyr.
Then as the wind seized the gleeds and the burning
thatch, and, uplifting,
Whirled them aloft through the air, at once from a
hundred house-tops
Started the sheeted smoke with flashes of flame inter-
mingled.

These things beheld in dismay the crowd on the
shore and on shipboard.
Speechless at first they stood, then cried aloud in their
anguish,
"We shall behold no more our homes in the village
of Grand-Pré!"
Loud on a sudden the cocks began to crow in the
farmyards,
Thinking the day had dawned; and anon the lowing
of cattle
Came on the evening breeze, by the barking of dogs
interrupted.
Then rose a sound of dread, such as startles the sleeping
encampments
Far in the Western prairies of forests that skirt the
Nebraska,
When the wild horses affrighted sweep by with the
speed of the whirlwind,
Or the loud bellowing herds of buffaloes rush to the
river.
Such was the sound that arose on the night, as the
herds and the horses

Broke through their folds and fences, and madly rushed
    o'er the meadows.

  Overwhelmed with the sight, yet speechless, the priest
    and the maiden
Gazed on the scene of terror that reddened and widened
    before them;
And as they turned at length to speak to their silent
    companion,
Lo! from his seat he had fallen, and stretched abroad
    on the seashore
Motionless lay his form, from which the soul had
    departed.
Slowly the priest uplifted the lifeless head, and the
    maiden
Knelt at her father's side, and wailed aloud in her
    terror.
Then in a swoon she sank, and lay with her head on
    his bosom.
Through the long night she lay in deep, oblivious
    slumber;
And when she awoke from the trance, she beheld a
    multitude near her.
Faces of friends she beheld, that were mournfully gazing
    upon her,
Pallid, with tearful eyes, and looks of saddest compassion.
Still the blaze of the burning village illumined the
    landscape,
Reddened the sky overhead, and gleamed on the faces
    around her,
And like the day of doom it seemed to her wavering
    senses.
Then a familiar voice she heard, as it said to the people,
"Let us bury him here by the sea. When a happier
    season
Brings us again to our home from the unknown land
    of our exile,

Then shall his sacred dust be piously laid in the
churchyard."
Such were the words of the priest. And there in haste
by the seaside,
Having the glare of the burning village for funeral
torches,
But without bell or book, they buried the farmer of
Grand-Pré.
And as the voice of the priest repeated the service of
sorrow,
Lo! with a mournful sound, like the voice of a vast
congregation,
Solemnly answered the sea, and mingled its roar with
the dirges.
'Twas the returning tide, that afar from the waste of
the ocean,
With the first dawn of the day, came heaving and
hurrying landward.
Then recommenced once more the stir and noise of
embarking;
And with the ebb of the tide the ships sailed out of
the harbor,
Leaving behind them the dead on the shore, and the
village in ruins.

PART THE SECOND

I

MANY a weary year had passed since the burning of
Grand-Pré,
When on the falling tide the freighted vessels departed,
Bearing a nation, with all its household gods, into exile,
Exile without an end, and without an example in story.
Far asunder, on separate coasts, the Acadians landed;
Scattered were they, like flakes of snow, when the wind
from the northeast

Strikes aslant through the fogs that darken the Banks
of Newfoundland.
Friendless, homeless, hopeless, they wandered from city
to city,
From the cold lakes of the North to sultry Southern
savannas,—
From the bleak shores of the sea to the land where
the Father of Waters
Seizes the hills in his hands, and drags them down to
the ocean,
Deep in their sands to bury the scattered bones of the
mammoth.
Friends they sought and homes; and many, despairing,
heart-broken,
Asked of the earth but a grave, and no longer a friend
nor a fireside.
Written their history stands on tablets of stone in the
churchyards.
Long among them was seen a maiden who waited and
wandered,
Lowly and meek in spirit, and patiently suffering all
things.
Fair was she and young: but alas! before her extended,
Dreary and vast and silent, the desert of life, with its
pathway
Marked by the graves of those who had sorrowed and
suffered before her,
Passions long extinguished, and hopes long dead and
abandoned,
As the emigrant's way o'er the Western desert is marked
by
Camp-fires long consumed, and bones that bleach in
the sunshine.
Something there was in her life incomplete, imperfect,
unfinished;
As if a morning of June, with all its music and sunshine,
Suddenly paused in the sky, and, fading, slowly descended

Into the east again, from whence it late had arisen.
Sometimes she lingered in towns, till, urged by the
      fever within her,
Urged by a restless longing, the hunger and thirst of
      the spirit,
She would commence again her endless search and
      endeavor;
Sometimes in churchyards strayed, and gazed on the
      crosses and tombstones,
Sat by some nameless grave, and thought that perhaps
      in its bosom
He was already at rest, and she longed to slumber
      beside him.
Sometimes a rumor, a hearsay, an inarticulate whisper,
Came with its airy hand to point and beckon her
      forward.
Sometimes she spake with those who had seen her
      beloved and known him,
But it was long ago, in some far-off place or forgotten.
"Gabriel Lajeunesse!" they said; "oh, yes! we have seen
      him.
He was with Basil the blacksmith, and both have gone
      to the prairies;
Coureurs-des-Bois are they, and famous hunters and
      trappers."
"Gabriel Lajeunesse!" said others; "oh yes! we have seen
      him.
He is a Voyageur in the lowlands of Louisiana."
Then would they say, "Dear child! why dream and
      wait for him longer?
Are there not other youths as fair as Gabriel? others
Who have hearts as tender and true; and spirits as
      loyal?
Here is Baptiste Leblanc, the notary's son, who has
      loved thee
Many a tedious year; come, give him thy hand and
      be happy!

Thou art too fair to be left to braid St. Catherine's
    tresses."*
Then would Evangeline answer, serenely but sadly, "I
    cannot!
Whither my heart has gone, there follows my hand,
    and not elsewhere.
For when the heart goes before, like a lamp, and
    illumines the pathway,
Many things are made clear, that else lie hidden in
    darkness."
Thereupon the priest, her friend and father-confessor,
Said, with a smile, "O daughter! thy God thus speaketh
    within thee!
Talk not of wasted affection, affection never was wasted;
If it enrich not the heart of another, its waters, returning
Back to their springs, like the rain, shall fill them full
    of refreshment;
That which the fountain sends forth returns again to
    the fountain,
Patience; acccomplish thy labor; accomplish thy work
    of affection!
Sorrow and silence are strong, and patient endurance
    is godlike.
Therefore accomplish thy labor of love, till the heart
    is made godlike,
Purified, strengthened, perfected, and rendered more
    worthy of heaven!"
Cheered by the good man's words, Evangeline labored
    and waited.
Still in her heart she heard the funeral dirge of the
    ocean,
But with its sound there was mingled a voice that
    whispered, "Despair not!"
Thus did that poor soul wander in want and cheerless
    discomfort,
Bleeding, barefooted, over the shards and thorns of
    existence.

Let me essay, O Muse! to follow the wanderer's
    footsteps;—
Not through each devious path, each changeful year of
    existence,
But as a traveller follows a streamlet's course through
    the valley:
Far from its margin at times, and seeing the gleam of
    its water
Here and there, in some open space, and at intervals
    only;
Then drawing nearer its banks, through sylvan glooms
    that conceal it,
Though he behold it not, he can hear its continuous
    murmur;
Happy, at length, if he find the spot where it reaches
    an outlet.

II

  It was the month of May. Far down the Beautiful
    River,
Past the Ohio shore and past the mouth of the Wabash,
Into the golden stream of the broad and swift Mississippi,
Floated a cumbrous boat, that was rowed by Acadian
    boatmen.
It was a band of exiles: a raft, as it were, from the
    shipwrecked
Nation, scattered along the coast, now floating together,
Bound by the bonds of a common belief and a common
    misfortune;
Men and women and children, who, guided by hope
    or by hearsay,
Sought for their kith and their kin among the few-
    acred farmers
On the Acadian coast, and the prairies of fair Opelousas.
With them Evangeline went, and her guide, the Father
    Felician.

Onward o'er sunken sands, through a wilderness sombre
    with forests,
Day after day they glided down the turbulent river;
Night after night, by their blazing fires, encamped on
    its borders.
Now through rushing chutes, among green islands,
    where plumelike
Cotton-trees nodded their shadowy crests, they swept
    with the current,
Then emerged into broad lagoons, where silvery sandbars
Lay in the stream, and along the wimpling waves of
    their margin,
Shining with snow-white plumes, large flocks of pelicans
    waded.
Level the lanscape grew, and along the shores of the
    river,
Shaded by china-trees, in the midst of luxuriant gardens,
Stood the houses of planters, with negro-cabins and
    dove-cots.
They were approaching the region where reigns perpetual
    summer,
Where through the Golden Coast, and groves of orange
    and citron,
Sweeps with majestic curve the river away to the
    eastward.
They, too, swerved from their course; and, entering
    the Bayou of Plaquemine,
Soon were lost in a maze of sluggish and devious
    waters,
Which, like a network of steel, extended in every
    direction.
Over their heads the towering and tenebrous boughs
    of the cypress
Met in a dusky arch, and trailing mosses in mid-air
Waved like banners that hang on the walls of ancient
    cathedrals.

Deathlike the silence seemed, and unbroken, save by
     the herons
Home to their roosts in the cedar-trees returning at
     sunset,
Or by the owl, as he greeted the moon with demoniac
     laughter.
Lovely the moonlight was as it glanced and gleamed
     on the water,
Gleamed on the columns of cypress and cedar sustaining
     the arches,
Down through whose broken vaults it fell as through
     chinks in a ruin.
Dreamlike, and indistinct, and strange were all things
     around them;
And o'er their spirits there came a feeling of wonder
     and sadness,—
Strange forebodings of ill, unseen and that cannot be
     compassed.
As, at the tramp of a horse's hoof on the turf of the
     prairies,
Far in advance are closed the leaves of the shrinking
     mimosa,
So, at the hoof-beats of fate, with sad forebodings of
     evil,
Shrinks and closes the heart, ere the stroke of doom
     had attained it.
But Evangeline's heart was sustained by a vision, that
     faintly
Floated before her eyes, and beckoned her on through
     the moonlight.
It was the thought of her brain that assumed the shape
     of a phantom.
Through those shadowy aisles had Gabriel wandered
     before her,
And every stroke of the oar now brought him nearer
     and nearer.

Then in his place, at the prow of the boat, rose
      one of the oarsmen,
And, as a signal sound, if others like them peradventure
Sailed on those gloomy and midnight streams, blew a
      blast on his bugle.
Wild through the dark colonnades and corridors leafy
      the blast rang,
Breaking the seal of silence, and giving tongues to the
      forest.
Soundless above them the banners of moss just stirred
      to the music.
Multitudinous echoes awoke and died in the distance,
Over the watery floor, and beneath the reverberant
      branches;
But not a voice replied; no answer came from the
      darkness;
And, when the echoes had ceased, like a sense of pain
      was the silence.
Then Evangeline slept; but the boatmen rowed through
      the midnight,
Silent at times, then singing familiar Canadian boatsongs,
Such as they sang of old on their own Acadian rivers,
While through the night were heard the mysterious
      sounds of the desert,
Far off,—indistinct,—as of wave or wind in the forest,
Mixed with the whoop of the crane and the roar of
      the grim alligator.

Thus ere another noon they emerged from the shades;
      and before them
Lay, in the golden sun, the lakes of the Atchafalaya.
Water-lilies in myriads rocked on the slight undulations
Made by the passing oars, and, resplendent in beauty,
      the lotus
Lifted her golden crown above the heads of the boatmen.

Faint was the air with the odorous breath of magnolia
    blossoms,
And with the heat of noon; and numberless sylvan
    islands,
Fragrant and thickly embowered with blossoming hedges
    of roses,
Near to whose shores they glided along, invited to
    slumber.
Soon by the fairest of these their weary oars were
    suspended.
Under the boughs of Wachita willows, that grew by
    the margin,
Safely their boat was moored; and scattered about on
    the greensward,
Tired with their midnight toil, the weary travellers
    slumbered.
Over them vast and high extended the cope of a cedar.
Swinging from its great arms, the trumpet-flower and
    the grapevine
Hung their ladder of ropes aloft like the ladder of
    Jacob,*
On whose pendulous stairs the angels ascending, de-
    scending,
Were the swift humming-birds, that flitted from blossom
    to blossom.
Such was the vision Evangeline saw as she slumbered
    beneath it.
Filled was her heart with love, and the dawn of an
    opening heaven
Lighted her soul in sleep with the glory of regions
    celestial.

  Nearer, and ever nearer, among the numberless islands,
Darted a light, swift boat, that sped away o'er the
    water,

Urged on its course by the sinewy arms of hunters
    and trappers.

Northward its prow was turned, to the land of the
    bison and beaver.

At the helm sat a youth, with countenance thoughtful
    and careworn.

Dark and neglected locks overshadowed his brow, and
    a sadness

Somewhat beyond his years on his face was legibly
    written.

Gabriel was it, who, weary with waiting, unhappy and
    restless,

Sought in the Western wilds oblivion of self and of
    sorrow.

Swiftly they glided along, close under the lee of the
    island,

But by the opposite bank, and behind a screen of
    palmettos,

So they saw not the boat, where it lay concealed in
    the willows;

All undisturbed by the dash of their oars, and unseen,
    were the sleepers.

Angel of God was there none to awaken the slumbering
    maiden.

Swiftly they glided away, like the shade of a cloud
    on the prairie.

After the sound of their oars on the tholes had died
    in the distance,

As from a magic trance the sleepers awoke, and the
    maiden

Said with a sigh to the friendly priest, "O Father
    Felician!

Something says in my heart that near me Gabriel wanders.

Is it a foolish dream, an idle and vague superstition?

Or has an angel passed, and revealed the truth to my
    spirit?"

Then, with a blush, she added, "Alas for my credulous
      fancy!

Unto ears like thine such words as these have no
      meaning."

But made answer the reverend man, and he smiled as
      he answered,

"Daughter, thy words are not idle; nor are they to
      me without meaning.

Feeling is deep and still; and the word that floats on
      the surface

Is as the tossing buoy, that betrays where the anchor
      is hidden.

Therefore trust to thy heart, and to what the world
      calls illusions.

Gabriel truly is near thee; for not far away to the
      southward

On the banks of the Têche, are the towns of St. Maur
      and St. Martin.

There the long-wandering bride shall be given again
      to her bridegroom,

There the long-absent pastor regain his flock and his
      sheepfold.

Beautiful is the land, with its prairies and forests of
      fruit-trees;

Under the feet a garden of flowers, and the bluest of
      heavens

Bending above, and resting its dome on the walls of
      the forest.

They who dwell there have named it the Eden of
      Louisiana!"

  With these words of cheer they arose and continued
      their journey.

Softly the evening came. The sun from the western
      horizon

Like a magician extended his golden wand o'er the
    landscape;
Twinkling vapor arose; and sky and water and forest
Seemed all on fire at the touch, and melted and mingled
    together.
Hanging between two skies, a cloud with edges of
    silver,
Floated the boat, with its dripping oars, on the motionless
    water.
Filled was Evangeline's heart with inexpressible sweetness.
Touched by the magic spell, the sacred fountains of
    feeling
Glowed with the light of love, as the skies and waters
    around her.
Then from a neighboring thicket the mocking-bird,
    wildest of singers,
Swinging aloft on a willow spray that hung o'er the
    water,
Shook from his little throat such floods of delirious
    music,
That the whole air and the woods and the waves seemed
    silent to listen.
Plaintive at first were the tones and sad; then soaring
    to madness
Seemed they to follow or guide the revel of frenzied
    Bacchantes.
Single notes were then heard, in sorrowful, low lam-
    entation;
Till, having gathered them all, he flung them abroad
    in derision,
As when, after a storm, a gust of wind through the
    tree-tops
Shakes down the rattling rain in a crystal shower on
    the branches.
With such a prelude as this, and hearts that throbbed
    with emotion,

Slowly they entered the Têche, where it flows through
the green Opelousas,
And, through the amber air, above the crest of the
woodland,
Saw the column of smoke that rose from a neighboring
dwelling;—
Sounds of a horn they heard, and the distant lowing
of cattle.

III

Near to the bank of the river, o'ershadowed by oaks,
from whose branches
Garlands of Spanish moss and of mystic mistletoe flaunted,
Such as the Druids cut down with golden hatchets at
Yule-tide,
Stood, secluded and still, the house of the herdsman.
A garden
Girded it round about with a belt of luxuriant blossoms,
Filling the air with fragrance. The house itself was of
timbers,
Hewn from the cypress-tree, and carefully fitted together.
Large and low was the roof; and on slender columns
supported,
Rose-wreathed, vine-encircled, a broad and spacious
veranda,
Haunt of the humming-bird and the bee, extended
around it.
At each end of the house, amid the flowers of the
garden,
Stationed the dove-cots were, as love's perpetual symbol,
Scenes of endless wooing, and endless contentions of
rivals,
Silence reigned o'er the place. The line of shadow and
sunshine
Ran near the tops of the trees; but the house itself
was in shadow,

And from its chimney-top, ascending and slowly ex-
    panding
Into the evening air, a thin blue column of smoke
    rose.
In the rear of the house, from the garden gate, ran
    a pathway
Through the great groves of oak to the skirts of the
    limitless prairie,
Into whose sea of flowers the sun was slowly descending.
Full in his track of light, like ships with shadowy
    canvas
Hanging loose from their spars in a motionless calm
    in the tropics,
Stood a cluster of trees, with tangled cordage of grape-
    vines.

  Just where the woodlands met the flowery surf of
    the prairie,
Mounted upon his horse, with Spanish saddle and stirrups,
Sat a herdsman, arrayed in gaiters and doublet of deerskin.
Broad and brown was the face that from under the
    Spanish sombrero
Gazed on the peaceful scene, with the lordly look of
    its master.
Round about him were numberless herds of kine, that
    were grazing
Quietly in the meadows, and breathing the vapory
    freshness
That uprose from the river, and spread itself over the
    landscape.
Slowly lifting the horn that hung at his side, and
    expanding
Fully his broad, deep chest, he blew a blast, that
    resounded
Wildly and sweet and far, through the still damp air
    of the evening.

Suddenly out of the grass the long white horns of the
 cattle
Rose like flakes of foam on the adverse currents of
 ocean.
Silent a moment they gazed, then bellowing rushed o'er
 the prairie,
And the whole mass became a cloud, a shade in the
 distance.
Then, as the herdsman turned to the house, through
 the gate of the garden
Saw he the forms of the priest and the maiden advancing
 to meet him.
Suddenly down from his horse he sprang in amazement,
 and forward
Rushed with extended arms and exclamations of wonder;
When they beheld his face, they recognized Basil the
 blacksmith.
Hearty his welcome was, as he led his guests to the
 garden.
There in an arbor of roses with endless question and
 answer
Gave they vent to their hearts, and renewed their friendly
 embraces,
Laughing and weeping by turns, or sitting silent and
 thoughtful.
Thoughtful, for Gabriel came not; and now dark doubts
 and misgivings
Stole o'er the maiden's heart; and Basil, somewhat
 embarrassed,
Broke the silence and said, "If you came by the
 Atchafalaya,
How have you nowhere encounterd my Gabriel's boat
 on the bayous?"
Over Evangeline's face at the words of Basil a shade
 passed.
Tears came into her eyes, and she said, with a tremulous
 accent,

"Gone? is Gabriel gone?" and, concealing her face on
his shoulder,
All her o'erburdened heart gave way, and she wept
and lamented.
Then the good Basil said,—and his voice grew blithe
as he said it,—
"Be of good cheer, my child; it is only to-day he
departed.
Foolish boy! he has left me alone with my herds and
my horses.
Moody and restless grown, and tried and troubled, his
spirit
Could no longer endure the calm of this quiet existence.
Thinking ever of thee, uncertain and sorrowful ever,
Ever silent, or speaking only of thee and his troubles,
He at length had become so tedious to men and to
maidens,
Tedious even to me, that at length I bethought me,
and sent him
Unto the town of Adayes to trade for mules with the
Spaniards.
Thence he will follow the Indian trails to the Ozark
Mountains,
Hunting for furs in the forests, on rivers trapping the
beaver.
Therefore be of good cheer; we will follow the fugitive
lover;
He is not far on his way, and the Fates and the streams
are against him.
Up and away to-morrow, and through the red dew
of the morning
We will follow him fast, and bring him back to his
prison."

Then glad voices were heard, and up from the banks
of the river,

Borne aloft on his comrades' arms, came Michael the
fiddler.
Long under Basil's roof had he lived like a god on
Olympus,
Having no other care than dispensing music to mortals.
Far renowned was he for his silver locks and his fiddle.
"Long live Michael," they cried, "our brave Arcadian
minstrel!"
As they bore him aloft in triumphal procession; and
straightway
Father Felician advanced with Evangeline, greeting the
old man
Kindly and oft, and recalling the past, while Basil,
enraptured,
Hailed with hilarious joy his old companions and gossips,
Laughing loud and long, and embracing mothers and
daughters.
Much they marvelled to see the wealth of the cidevant
blacksmith,
All his domains and his herds, and his patriarchal
demeanor;
Much they marvelled to hear his tales of the soil and
the climate,
And of the prairies, whose numberless herds were his
who would take them;
Each one thought in his heart, that he, too, would go
and do likewise.
Thus they ascended the steps, and crossing the breezy
veranda,
Entered the hall of the house, where already the supper
of Basil
Waited his late return; and they rested and feasted
together.

Over the joyous feast the sudden darkness descended.
All was silent without, and, illuming the landscape with
silver,

Fair rose the dewy moon and the myriad stars; but
    within doors,
Brighter than these, shone the faces of friends in the
    glimmering lamplight.
Then from his station aloft, at the head of the table,
    the herdsman
Poured forth his heart and his wine together in endless
    profusion.
Lighting his pipe, that was filled with sweet Natchitoches
    tobacco,
Thus he spake to his guests, who listened, and smiled
    as they listened:
"Welcome once more, my friends, who long have been
    friendless and homeless,
Welcome once more to a home, that is better perchance
    than the old one!
Here no hungry winter congeals our blood like the
    rivers;
Here no stony ground provokes the wrath of the
    farmer.
Smoothly the ploughshare runs through the soil, as a
    keel through the water.
All the year round the orange-groves are in blossom;
    and grass grows
More in a single night than a whole Canadian summer.
Here, too, numberless herds run wild and unclaimed
    in the prairies;
Here, too, lands may be had for the asking, and forests
    of timber
With a few blows of the axe are hewn and framed
    into houses.
After your houses are built, and your fields are yellow—
    with harvests,
No King George of England shall drive you away from
    your homesteads,
Burning your dwellings and barns, and stealing your
    farms and your cattle."

Speaking these words, he blew a wrathful cloud from
      his nostrils,
While his huge, brown hand came thundering down
      on the table,
So that the guests all started; and Father Felician,
      astounded,
Suddenly paused, with a pinch of snuff halfway to his
      nostrils.
But the brave Basil resumed, and his words were milder
      and gayer:
"Only beware of the fever, my friends, beware of the
      fever!
For it is not like that of our cold Acadian climate,
Cured by wearing a spider hung round one's neck in
      a nutshell!"
Then there were voices heard at the door, and footsteps
      approaching
Sounded upon the stairs and the floor of the breezy
      veranda,
It was the neighboring Creoles and small Acadian
      planters,
Who had been summoned all to the house of Basil
      the herdsman.
Merry the meeting was of ancient comrades and neighbors:
Friend clasped friend in his arms; and they who before
      were as strangers,
Meeting in exile, became straightway as friends to each
      other,
Drawn by the gentle bond of a common country together.
But in the neighboring hall a strain of music, proceeding
From the accordant strings of Michael's melodious
      fiddle,
Broke up all further speech. Away, like children delighted,
All things forgotten beside, they gave themselves to
      the maddening
Whirl of the giddy dance, as it swept and swayed to
      the music,

Dreamlike, with beaming eyes and the rush of fluttering garments.

Meanwhile, apart at the head of the hall, the priest and the herdsman
Sat, conversing together of past and present and future;
While Evangeline stood like one entranced, for within her
Olden memories rose, and loud in the midst of the music
Heard she the sound of the sea, and an irrepressible sadness
Came o'er her heart, and unseen she stole forth into the garden.
Beautiful was the night. Behind the black wall of the forest,
Tipping its summit with silver, arose the moon. On the river
Fell here and there through the branches a tremulous gleam of the moonlight,
Like the sweet thoughts of love on a darkened and devious spirit.
Nearer and round about her, the manifold flowers of the garden
Poured out their souls in odors, that were their prayers and confessions
Unto the night, as it went its way, like a silent Carthusian.*
Fuller of fragrance than they, and as heavy with shadows and night-dews,
Hung the heart of the maiden. The calm and the magical moonlight
Seemed to inundate her soul with indefinable longings,
As, through the garden gate, and beneath the shade of the oak-trees,
Passed she along the path to the edge of the measureless prairie.
Silent it lay, with a silvery haze upon it, and fireflies

Gleamed and floated away in mingled and infinite
    numbers.
Over her head the stars, the thoughts of God in the
    heavens,
Shone on the eyes of man, who had ceased to marvel
    and worship,
Save when a blazing comet was seen on the walls of
    that temple,
As if a hand had appeared and written upon them,
    "Upharsin."*
And the soul of the maiden, between the stars and the
    fireflies,
Wandered alone, and she cried, "O Gabriel! O my
    beloved!
Art thou so near unto me, and yet I cannot behold
    thee?
Art thou so near unto me, and yet thy voice does not
    reach me?
Ah! how often thy feet have trod this path to the
    prairie!
Ah! how often thine eyes have looked on the woodlands
    around me!
Ah! how often beneath this oak, returning from labor,
Thou hast lain down to rest, and to dream of me in
    thy slumbers!
When shall these eyes behold, these arms be folded
    about thee?"
Loud and sudden and near the notes of a whippoorwill
    sounded
Like a flute in the woods; and anon, through the
    neighboring thickets,
Farther and farther away it floated and dropped into
    silence.
"Patience!" whispered the oaks from oracular caverns
    of darkness:
And, from the moonlit meadow, a sigh responded, "To-
    morrow!"

Bright rose the sun next day; and all the flowers of
the garden
Bathed his shining feet with their tears, and anointed
his tresses
With the delicious balm that they bore in their vases
of crystal.
"Farewell!" said the priest, as he stood at the shadowy
threshold;
"See that you bring us the Prodigal Son from his
fasting and famine,
And, too, the Foolish Virgin, who slept when the
bridegroom was coming."
"Farewell!" answered the maiden, and, smiling, with
Basil descended
Down to the river's brink, where the boatmen already
were waiting.
Thus beginning their journey with morning, and sunshine,
and gladness,
Swiftly they followed the flight of him who was speeding
before them,
Blown by the blast of fate like a dead leaf over the
desert.
Not that day, nor the next, nor yet the day that
succeeded,
Found they the trace of his course, in lake or forest
or river,
Nor, after many days, had they found him; but vague
and uncertain
Rumors alone were their guides through a wild and
desolate country;
Till, at the little inn of the Spanish town of Adayes,
Weary and worn, they alighted, and learned from the
garrulous landlord,
That on the day before, with horses and guides and
companions,
Gabriel left the village, and took the road of the
prairies.

IV

Far in the West there lies a desert land, where the
    mountains
Lift, through perpetual snows, their lofty and luminous
    summits.
Down from their jagged, deep ravines, where the gorge,
    like a gateway,
Opens a passage rude to the wheels of the emigrant's
    wagon,
Westward the Oregon flows and the Walleway and
    Owyhee.
Eastward, with devious course, among the Windriver
    Mountains,
Through the Sweet-water Valley precipitate leaps the
    Nebraska;
And to the south, from Fontaine-qui-bout and the Spanish
    sierras,
Fretted with sands and rocks, and swept by the wind
    of the desert,
Numberless torrents, with ceaseless sound, descend to
    the ocean,
Like the great chords of a harp, in loud and solemn
    vibrations.
Spreading between these streams are the wondrous,
    beautiful prairies;
Billowy bays of grass ever rolling in shadow and sunshine,
Bright with luxuriant clusters of roses and purple amor-
    phas.
Over them wandered the buffalo herds, and the elk
    and the roebuck,
Over them wandered the wolves, and herds of riderless
    horses;
Fires that blast and blight, and winds that are weary
    with travel;
Over them wander the scattered tribes of Ishmael's
    children,

Staining the desert with blood; and above their terrible
    war-trails
Circles and sails aloft, on pinions majestic, the vulture,
Like the implacable soul of a chieftain slaughtered in
    battle,
By invisible stairs ascending and scaling the heavens.
Here and there rise smokes from the camps of these
    savage marauders;
Here and there rise groves from the margins of swift-
    running rivers;
And the grim, tactiturn bear, the anchorite monk of
    the desert,
Climbs down their dark ravines to dig for roots by
    the brookside,
And over all is the sky, the clear and crystalline heaven,
Like the protecting hand of God inverted above them.

  Into this wonderful land, at the base of the Ozark
    Mountains,
Gabriel far had entered, with hunters and trappers behind
    him.
Day after day, with their Indian guides, the maiden
    and Basil
Followed his flying steps, and thought each day to
    o'ertake him.
Sometimes they saw, or thought they saw, the smoke
    of his camp-fire
Rise in the morning air from the distant plain; but at
    nightfall,
When they had reached the place, they found only
    embers and ashes.
And, though their hearts were sad at times and their
    bodies were weary,
Hope still guided them on, as the magic Fata Morgana
Showed them her lakes of light, that retreated and
    vanished before them.

Once, as they sat by their evening fire, there silently
    entered
Into their little camp an Indian woman, whose features
Wore deep traces of sorrow, and patience as great as
    her sorrow.
She was a Shawnee woman returning home to her
    people,
From the far-off hunting-grounds of the cruel Camanches,
Where her Canadian husband, a Coureur-des-Bois, had
    been murdered.
Touched were their hearts at her story, and warmest
    and friendliest welcome
Gave they, with words of cheer, and she sat and feasted
    among them
On the buffalo-meat and the venison cooked on the
    embers.
But when their meal was done, and Basil and all his
    companions,
Worn with the long day's march and the chase of the
    deer and the bison,
Stretched themselves on the ground, and slept where
    the quivering firelight
Flashed on their swarthy cheeks, and their forms wrapped
    up in their blankets,
Then at the door of Evangeline's tent she sat and
    repeated
Slowly, with soft, low voice, and the charm of her
    Indian accent,
All the tale of her love, with its pleasures, and pains,
    and reverses.
Much Evangeline wept at the tale, and to know that
    another
Hapless heart like her own had loved and had been
    disappointed.
Moved to the depths of her soul by pity and woman's
    compassion,

Yet in her sorrow pleased that one who had suffered
    was near her,
She in turn related her love and all its disasters.
Mute with wonder the Shawnee sat, and when she had
    ended
Still was mute; but at length, as if a mysterious horror
Passed through her brain, she spake, and repeated the
    tale of the Mowis;
Mowis, the bridegroom of snow, who won and wedded
    a maiden,
But, when the morning came, arose and passed from
    the wigwam,
Fading and melting away and dissolving into the sunshine,
Till she beheld him no more, though she followed far
    into the forest.
Then, in those sweet, low tones, that seemed like a
    weird incantation,
Told she the tale of the fair Lilinau, who was wooed
    by a phantom,
That through the pines o'er her father's lodge, in the
    hush of the twilight,
Breathed like the evening wind, and whispered love to
    the maiden,
Till she followed his green and waving plume through
    the forest,
And nevermore returned, nor was seen again by her
    people.
Silent with wonder and strange surprise, Evangeline
    listened
To the soft flow of her magical words, till the region
    around her
Seemed like enchanted ground, and her swarthy guest
    the enchantress.
Slowly over the tops of the Ozark Mountains the moon
    rose,
Lighting the little tent, and with a mysterious splendor

Touching the sombre leaves, and embracing and filling
    the woodland.
With a delicious sound the brook rushed by, and the
    branches
Swayed and sighed overhead in scarcely audible whispers.
Filled with the thoughts of love was Evangeline's heart,
    but a secret,
Subtile sense crept in of pain and indefinite terror,
As the cold, poisonous snake creeps into the nest of
    the swallow.
It was no earthly fear. A breath from the region of
    spirits
Seemed to float in the air of night; and she felt for
    a moment
That, like the Indian maid, she, too, was pursuing a
    phantom.
With this thought she slept, and the fear and the phantom
    had vanished.

    Early upon the morrow the march was resumed; and
    the Shawnee
Said, as they journeyed along, "On the western slope
    of these mountains
Dwells in his little village the Black Robe chief of the
    Mission.
Much he teaches the people, and tells them of Mary
    and Jesus.
Loud laugh their hearts with joy, and weep with pain,
    as they hear him."
Then, with a sudden and secret emotion, Evangeline
    answered,
"Let us go to the Mission, for there good tidings await
    us!"
Thither they turned their steeds; and behind a spur of
    the mountains,
Just as the sound went down, they heard a murmur
    of voices,

And in a meadow green and broad, by the bank of
a river,
Saw the tents of the Christians, the tents of the Jesuit
Mission.
Under a towering oak, that stood in the midst of the
village,
Knelt the Black Robe chief with his children. A crucifix
fastened
High on the trunk of the tree, and overshadowed by
grapevines,
Looked with its agonized face on the multitude kneeling
beneath it.
This was their rural chapel. Aloft, through the intricate
arches
Of its aërial roof, arose the chant of their vespers,
Mingling its notes with soft susurrus and sighs of the
branches.
Silent, with heads uncovered, the travellers, nearer ap-
proaching,
Knelt on the swarded floor, and joined in the evening
devotions.
But when the service was done, and the benediction
had fallen
Forth from the hands of the priest, like seed from the
hands of the sower,
Slowly the reverend man advanced to the strangers,
and bade them
Welcome; and when they replied, he smiled with benignant
expression,
Hearing the homelike sounds of his mother tongue in
the forest,
And, with words of kindness, conducted them into his
wigwam.
There upon mats and skins they reposed, and on cakes
of the maize-ear
Feasted, and slaked their thirst from the water-gourd
of the teacher.

Soon was their story told; and the priest with solemnity
    answered:
"Not six suns have risen and set since Gabriel, seated
On this mat by my side, where now the maiden reposes,
Told me this same sad tale; then arose and continued
    his journey!"
Soft was the voice of the priest, and he spake with
    an accent of kindness;
But on Evangeline's heart fell his words as in winter
    the snow-flakes
Fall into some lone nest from which the birds have
    departed.
"Far to the north he has gone," continued the priest;
    "but in autumn,
When the chase is done, will return again to the
    Mission."
Then Evangeline said, and her voice was meek and
    submissive,
"Let me remain with thee, for my soul is sad and
    afflicted."
So seemed it wise and well unto all; and betimes on
    the morrow,
Mounting his Mexican steed, with his Indian guides
    and companions,
Homeward Basil returned, and Evangeline stayed at the
    Mission.

Slowly, slowly, slowly the days succeeded each other,—
Days and weeks and months; and the fields of maize
    that were springing
Green from the ground when a stranger she came, now
    waving above her,
Lifted their slender shafts, with leaves interlacing, and
    forming
Cloisters for mendicant crows and granaries pillaged by
    squirrels.

Then in the golden weather the maize was husked, and
    the maidens
Blushed at each blood-red ear, for that betokened a
    lover,
But at the crooked laughed, and called it a thief in
    the cornfield.
Even the blood-red ear to Evangeline brought not her
    lover.
"Patience!" the priest would say; "have faith, and thy
    prayer will be answered!
Look at this vigorous plant that lifts its head from the
    meadow,
See how its leaves are turned to the north, as true as
    the magnet;
This is the compass-flower, that the finger of God has
    planted
Here in the houseless wild, to direct the traveller's
    journey
Over the sea-like, pathless, limitless waste of the desert.
Such in the soul of man is faith. The blossoms of
    passion,
Gay and luxuriant flowers, are brighter and fuller of
    fragrance,
But they beguile us, and lead us astray, and their odor
    is deadly.
Only this humble plant can guide us here, and hereafter
Crown us with asphodel flowers, that are wet with
    the dews of nepenthe."

So came the autumn, and passed, and the winter,—
    yet Gabriel came not;
Blossomed the opening spring, and the notes of the
    robin and bluebird
Sounded sweet upon wold and in wood, yet Gabriel
    came not.
But on the breath of the summer winds a rumor was
    wafted,

Sweeter than song of bird, or hue or odor of blossom.
Far to the north and east, it said, in the Michigan
forests,
Gabriel had his lodge by the banks of the Saginaw
River.
And, with returning guides, that sought the lakes of
St. Lawrence,
Saying a sad farewell, Evangeline went from the Mission.
When over weary ways, by long and perilous marches,
She had attained at length the depths of the Michigan
forests,
Found she the hunter's lodge deserted and fallen to
ruin!

Thus did the long sad years glide on, and in seasons
and places
Divers and distant far was seen the wandering maiden;—
Now in the Tents of Grace of the meek Moravian
Missions,
Now in the noisy camps and the battle-fields of the
army,
Now in secluded hamlets, in towns and populous cities.
Like a phantom she came, and passed away unremem-
bered.
Fair was she and young, when in hope began the long
journey;
Faded was she and old, when in disappointment it
ended.
Each succeeding year stole something away from her
beauty,
Leaving behind it, broader and deeper, the gloom and
the shadow.
Then there appeared and spread faint streaks of gray
o'er her forehead,
Dawn of another life, that broke o'er her earthly horizon,
As in the eastern sky the first faint streaks of the
morning.

V

In that delightful land which is washed by the Delaware's
    waters,
Guarding in sylvan shades the name of Penn the apostle,
Stands on the banks of its beautiful stream the city he
    founded.
There all the air is balm, and the peach is the emblem
    of beauty,
And the streets still reëcho the names of the trees of
    the forest,
As if they fain would appease the Dryads whose haunts
    they molested.
There from the troubled sea had Evangeline landed, an
    exile,
Finding among the children of Penn a home and a
    country.
There old René Leblanc had died; and when he departed,
Saw at his side only one of all his hundred descendants.
Something at least there was in the friendly streets of
    the city,
Something that spake to her heart, and made her no
    longer a stranger;
And her ear was pleased with the Thee and Thou of
    the Quakers,
For it recalled the past, the old Acadian country,
Where all men were equal, and all were brothers and
    sisters.
So, when the fruitless search, the disappointed endeavor,
Ended, to recommence no more upon earth, uncom-
    plaining,
Thither, as leaves to the light, were turned her thoughts
    and her footsteps.
As from the mountain's top the rainy mists of the
    morning
Roll away, and afar we behold the landscape below
    us,

Sun-illumined, with shining rivers and cities and hamlets,
So fell the mists from her mind, and she saw the
world far below her,
Dark no longer, but all illumined with love; and the
pathway
Which she had climbed so far, lying smooth and fair
in the distance.
Gabriel was not forgotten. Within her heart was his
image,
Clothed in the beauty of love and youth, at last she
beheld him,
Only more beautiful made by this death-like silence and
absence.
Into her thoughts of him time entered not, for it was
not.
Over him years had no power; he was not changed,
but transfigured;
He had become to her heaart as one who is dead, and
not absent;
Patience and abnegation of self, and devotion to others,
This was the lesson a life of trial and sorrow had
taught her.
So was her love diffused, but, like to some odorous
spices,
Suffered no waste nor loss, though filling the air with
aroma.
Other hope had she none, nor wish in life, but to
follow
Meekly, with reverent steps, the sacred feet of her
Saviour.
Thus many years she lived as a Sister of Mercy;
frequenting
Lonely and wretched roofs in the crowded lanes of the
city,
Where distress and want concealed themselves from the
sunlight,
Where disease and sorrow in garrets languished neglected.

Night after night, when the world was asleep, as the
    watchman repeated
Loud, through the gusty streets, that all was well in
    the city,
High at some lonely window he saw the light of her
    taper.
Day after day, in the gray of the dawn, as slow through
    the suburbs
Plodded the German farmer, with flowers and fruits
    for the market,
Met he that meek, pale face, returning home from its
    watchings.

    Then it came to pass that a pestilence fell on the
    city,
Presaged by wondrous signs, and mostly by flocks of
    wild pigeons,
Darkening the sun in their flight, with naught in their
    craws but an acorn.
And, as the tides of the sea arise in the month of
    September,
Flooding some silver stream, till it spreads to a lake
    in the meadow,
So death flooded life, and, o'erflowing its natural margin,
Spread to a brackish lake the silver stream of existence.
Wealth had no power to bribe, nor beauty to charm,
    the oppressor;
But all perished alike beneath the scourge of his anger;—
Only, alas! the poor, who had neither friends nor
    attendants,
Crept away to die in the almshouse, home of the
    homeless.
Then in the suburbs it stood, in the midst of meadows
    and woodlands;—
Now the city surrounds it; but still, with its gateway
    and wicket

Meek, in the midst of splendor, its humble walls seem
     to echo
Softly the words of the Lord: "The poor ye always
     have with you."
Thither, by night and by day, came the Sister of Mercy.
     The dying,
Looked up into her face, and thought, indeed, to behold
     there
Gleams of celestial light encircle her forehead with
     splendor,
Such as the artist paints o'er the brows of the saints
     and apostles,
Or such as hangs by night o'er a city seen at a distance.
Unto their eyes it seemed the lamps of the city celestial,
Into whose shining gates ere long their spirits would
     enter.

   Thus, on a Sabbath morn, through the streets, deserted
     and silent,
Wending her quiet way, she entered the door of the
     almshouse.
Sweet on the summer air was the odor of flowers in
     the garden;
And she paused on her way to gather the fairest among
     them,
That the dying once more might rejoice in their fragrance
     and beauty.
Then, as she mounted the stairs to the corridors, cooled
     by the east-wind,
Distant and soft on her ear fell the chimes from the
     belfry of Christ Church,
While, intermingled with these, across the meadows
     were wafted
Sounds of psalms, that were sung by the Swedes in
     their church at Wicaco.
Soft as descending wings fell the calm of the hour on
     her spirit:

Something within her said, "At length thy trials are
    ended;"
And, with light in her looks, she entered the chambers
    of sickness.
Noiselessly moved about the assiduous, careful attendants,
Moistening the feverish lip, and the aching brow, and
    in silence
Closing the sightless eyes of the dead, and concealing
    their faces,
Where on their pallets they lay, like drifts of snow by
    the roadside.
Many a languid head, upraised as Evangeline entered,
Turned on its pillow of pain to gaze while she passed,
    for her presence
Fell on their hearts like a ray of the sun on the walls
    of a prison.
And, as she looked around, she saw how Death, the
    consoler,
Laying his hand upon many a heart, had healed it
    forever.
Many familiar forms had disappeared in the nighttime;
Vacant their places were, or filled already by strangers.

  Suddenly, as if arrested by fear or a feeling of wonder,
Still she stood, with her colorless lips apart, while a
    shudder
Ran through her frame, and, forgotten, the flowerets
    dropped from her fingers,
And from her eyes and cheeks the light and bloom
    of the morning.
Then there escaped from her lips a cry of such terrible
    anguish,
That the dying heard it, and started up from their
    pillows.
On the pallet before her was stretched the form of an
    old man.

Long, and thin, and gray were the locks that shaded
  his temples;
But, as he lay in the morning light, his face for a
  moment
Seemed to assume once more the forms of its earlier
  manhood;
So are wont to be changed the faces of those who
  are dying.
Hot and red on his lips still burned the flush of the
  fever,
As if life, like the Hebrew, with blood had besprinkled
  its portals,
That the Angel of Death might see the sign, and pass
  over.
Motionless, senseless, dying, he lay, and his spirit
  exhausted
Seemed to be sinking down through infinite depths in
  the darkness,
Darkness of slumber and death, forever sinking and
  sinking.
Then through those realms of shade, in multiplied
  reverberations,
Heard he that cry of pain, and through the hush that
  succeeded
Whispered a gentle voice, in accents tender and saintlike,
"Gabriel! O my beloved!" and died away into silence.
Then he beheld, in a dream, once more the home of
  his childhood;
Green Acadian meadows, with sylvan rivers among them,
Village, and mountain, and woodlands; and walking
  under their shadow,
As in the days of her youth, Evangeline rose in his
  vision.
Tears came into his eyes; and as slowly he lifted his
  eyelids,
Vanished the vision away, but Evangeline knelt by his
  bedside.

Vainly he strove to whisper her name, for the accents
     unuttered
Died on his lips, and their motion revealed what his
     tongue would have spoken.
Vainly he strove to rise; and Evangeline, kneeling beside
     him,
Kissed his dying lips, and laid his head on her bosom.
Sweet was the light of his eyes; but it suddenly sank
     into darkness,
As when a lamp is blown out by a gust of wind at
     a casement.

   All was ended now, the hope, and the fear, and the
     sorrow,
All the aching of heart, the restless, unsatisfied longing,
All the dull, deep pain, and constant anguish of patience!
And, as she pressed once more the lifeless head to her
     bosom,
Meekly she bowed her own, and murmured, "Father,
     I thank thee!"

———————

Still stands the forest primeval; but far away from its
     shadow,
Side by side, in their nameless graves, the lovers are
     sleeping.
Under the humble walls of the little Catholic churchyard,
In the heart of the city, they lie, unknown and unnoticed.
Daily the tides of life go ebbing and flowing beside
     them,
Thousands of throbbing hearts, where theirs are at rest
     and forever,
Thousands of aching brains, where theirs no longer are
     busy,
Thousands of toiling hands, where theirs have ceased
     from their labors,

Thousands of weary feet, where theirs have completed
their journey!

  Still stands the forest primeval; but under the shade
of its branches
Dwells another race, with other customs and language.
Only along the shore of the mournful and misty Atlantic
Linger a few Acadian peasants, whose fathers from exile
Wandered back to their native land to die in its bosom,
In the fisherman's cot the wheel and the loom are still
busy;
Maidens still wear their Norman caps and their kirtles
of homespun,
And by the evening fire repeat Evangeline's story,
While from its rocky caverns the deep-voiced, neighboring
ocean
Speaks, and in accents disconsolate answers the wail of
the forest.

FROM THE SONG OF HIAWATHA*

III

HIAWATHA'S CHILDHOOD

Downward through the evening twilight,
In the days that are forgotten,
In the unremembered ages,
From the full moon fell Nokomis,
Fell the beautiful Nokomis,
She a wife, but not a mother.
  She was sporting with her women,
Swinging in a swing of grapevines,
When her rival the rejected,
Full of jealousy and hatred,
Cut the leafy swing asunder,
Cut in twain the twisted grapevines,
And Nokomis fell affrighted
Downward through the evening twilight,
On the Muskoday, the meadow,
On the prairie full of blossoms.
"See! a star falls!" said the people;
"From the sky a star is falling!"
  There among the ferns and mosses,
There among the prairie lilies,
On the Muskoday, the meadow,
In the moonlight and the starlight,
Fair Nokomis bore a daughter.
And she called her name Wenonah,
As the first-born of her daughters.
And the daughter of Nokomis

Grew up like the prairie lilies,
Grew a tall and slender maiden,
With the beauty of the moonlight,
With the beauty of the starlight.

And Nokomis warned her often,
Saying oft, and oft repeating,
"Oh, beware of Mudjekeewis,
Of the West-Wind, Mudjekeewis;
Listen not to what he tells you;
Lie not down upon the meadow,
Stoop not down among the lilies,
Lest the West-Wind come and harm you!"

But she heeded not the warning,
Heeded not those words of wisdom,
And the West-Wind came at evening,
Walking lightly o'er the prairie,
Whispering to the leaves and blossoms,
Bending low the flowers and grasses,
Found the beautiful Wenonah,
Lying there among the lilies,
Wooed her with his words of sweetness,
Wooed her with his soft caresses,
Till she bore a son in sorrow,
Bore a son of love and sorrow.

Thus was born my Hiawatha,
Thus was born the child of wonder;
But the daughter of Nokomis,
Hiawatha's gentle mother,
In her anguish died deserted
By the West-Wind, false and faithless,
By the heartless Mudjekeewis.

For her daughter long and loudly
Wailed and wept the sad Nokomis;
"Oh that I were dead!" she murmured,
"Oh that I were dead, as thou art!
No more work, and no more weeping,
Wahonowin! Wahonowin!"

By the shores of Gitche Gumee,
By the shining Big-Sea-Water,
Stood the wigwam of Nokomis,
Daughter of the Moon, Nokomis.
Dark behind it rose the forest,
Rose the black and gloomy pine-trees,
Rose the firs with cones upon them;
Bright before it beat the water,
Beat the clear and sunny water,
Beat the shining Big-Sea-Water.
There the wrinkled old Nokomis
Nursed the little Hiawatha,
Rocked him in his linden cradle,
Bedded soft with moss and rushes,
Safely bound with reindeer sinews;
Stilled his fretful wail by saying,
"Hush! the Naked Bear will hear thee!"
Lulled him into slumber, singing,
"Ewa-yea! my little owlet!
Who is this, that lights the wigwam?
With his great eyes lights the wigwam?
Ewa-yea! my little owlet!"
Many things Nokomis taught him
Of the stars that shine in heaven;
Showed him Ishkoodah, the comet,
Ishkoodah, with fiery tresses;
Showed the Death-Dance of the spirits,
Warriors with their plumes and war-clubs,
Flaring far away to northward
In the frosty nights of Winter;
Showed the broad white road in heaven,
Pathway of the ghosts, the shadows,
Running straight across the heavens,
Crowded with the ghosts, the shadows.
At the door on summer evenings
Sat the little Hiawatha;
Heard the whispering of the pine-trees,

Heard the lapping of the waters,
Sounds of music, words of wonder;
"Minne-wawa!" said the pine-trees,
"Mudway-aushka!" said the water.
  Saw the firefly, Wah-wah-taysee,
Flitting through the dusk of evening,
With the twinkle of its candle
Lighting up the brakes and bushes,
And he sang the song of children,
Sang the song Nokomis taught him:
"Wah-wah-taysee, little firefly,
Little, flitting, white-fire insect,
Little, dancing, white-fire creature,
Light me with your little candle,
Ere upon my bed I lay me,
Ere in sleep I close my eyelids!"
  Saw the moon rise from the water
Rippling, rounding from the water,
Saw the flecks and shadows on it,
Whispered, "What is that, Nokomis?"
And the good Nokomis answered:
"Once a warrior, very angry,
Seized his grandmother, and threw her
Up into the sky at midnight;
Right against the moon he threw her;
'T is her body that you see there."
  Saw the rainbow in the heaven,
In the eastern sky, the rainbow,
Whispered, "What is that, Nokomis?"
And the good Nokomis answered:
" 'T is the heaven of flowers you see there;
All the wild-flowers of the forest,
All the lilies of the prairie,
When on earth they fade and perish,
Blossom in that heaven above us."
  When he heard the owls at midnight,
Hooting, laughing in the forest,

"What is that?" he cried in terror,
"What is that," he said, "Nokomis?"
And the good Nokomis answered:
"That is but the owl and owlet,
Talking in their native language,
Talking, scolding at each other."
    Then the little Hiawatha
Learned of every bird its language,
Learned their names and all their secrets,
How they built their nests in Summer,
Where they hid themselves in Winter,
Talked with them whene'er he met them,
Called them "Hiawatha's Chickens."

    Of all beasts he learned the language,
Learned their names and all their secrets,
How the beavers built their lodges,
Where the squirrels hid their acorns,
How the reindeer ran so swiftly,
Why the rabbit was so timid,
Talked with them whene'er he met them,
Called them "Hiawatha's Brothers."

    Then Iagoo, the great boaster,
He the marvellous story-teller,
He the traveller and the talker,
He the friend of old Nokomis,
Made a bow for Hiawatha;
From a branch of ash he made it,
From an oak-bough made the arrows,
Tipped with flint, and winged with feathers,
And the cord he made of deer-skin.
    Then he said to Hiawatha:
"Go, my son, into the forest,
Where the red deer herd together,
Kill for us a famous roebuck,
Kill for us a deer with antlers!"
    Forth into the forest straightway
All alone walked Hiawatha

Proudly, with his bow and arrows;
And the birds sang round him, o'er him,
"Do not shoot us, Hiawatha!"
Sang the robin, the Opechee,
Sang the bluebird, the Owaissa,
"Do not shoot us, Hiawatha!"
   Up the oak-tree, close beside him,
Sprang the squirrel, Adjidaumo,
In and out among the branches,
Coughed and chattered from the oak-tree,
Laughed, and said between his laughing,
"Do not shoot me, Hiawatha!"
   And the rabbit from his pathway
Leaped aside, and at a distance
Sat erect upon his haunches,
Half in fear and half in frolic,
Saying to the little hunter,
"Do not shoot me, Hiawatha!"
   But he heeded not, nor heard them,
For his thoughts were with the red deer;
On their tracks his eyes were fastened,
Leading downward to the river,
To the ford across the river,
And as one in slumber walked he.
   Hidden in the alder-bushes,
There he waited till the deer came,
Till he saw two antlers lifted,
Saw two eyes look from the thicket,
Saw two nostrils point to windward,
And a deer came down the pathway,
Flecked with leafy light and shadow.
And his heart within him fluttered,
Trembled like the leaves above him,
Like the birch-leaf palpitated,
As the deer came down the pathway.
   Then, upon one knee uprising,
Hiawatha aimed an arrow;

Scarce a twig moved with his motion,
Scarce a leaf was stirred or rustled,
But the wary roebuck started,
Stamped with all his hoofs together,
Listened with one foot uplifted,
Leaped as if to meet the arrow;
Ah! the singing, fatal arrow,
Like a wasp it buzzed and stung him!

Dead he lay there in the forest,
By the ford across the river;
Beat his timid heart no longer;
But the heart of Hiawatha
Throbbed and shouted and exulted,
As he bore the red deer homeward,
And Iagoo and Nokomis
Hailed his coming with applauses.

From the red deer's hide Nokomis
Made a cloak for Hiawatha,
From the red deer's flesh Nokomis
Made a banquet to his honor.
All the village came and feasted,
All the guests praised Hiawatha,
Called him Strong-Heart, Soan-ge-taha!
Called him Loon-Heart, Mahn-go-taysee!

V

HIAWATHA'S FASTING

You shall hear how Hiawatha
Prayed and fasted in the forest,
Not for greater skill in hunting,
Not for greater craft in fishing,
Not for triumphs in the battle,
And renown among the warriors,
But for profit of the people,

For advantage of the nations.
First he built a lodge for fasting,
Built a wigwam in the forest,
By the shining Big-Sea-Water,
In the blithe and pleasant Spring-time,
In the Moon of Leaves he built it,
And, with dreams and visions many,
Seven whole days and nights he fasted.
On the first day of his fasting
Through the leafy woods he wandered;
Saw the deer start from the thicket,
Saw the rabbit in his burrow,
Heard the pheasant, Bena, drumming,
Heard the squirrel, Adjidaumo,
Rattling in his hoard of acorns,
Saw the pigeon, the Omemee,
Building nests among the pine-trees,
And in flocks the wild-goose, Wawa,
Flying to the fen-lands northward,
Whirring, wailing far above him.
"Master of Life!" he cried, desponding,
"Must our lives depend on these things?"
On the next day of his fasting
By the river's brink he wandered,
Through the Muskoday, the meadow,
Saw the wild rice, Mahnomenee,
Saw the blueberry, Meenahga,
And the strawberry, Odahmin,
And the gooseberry, Shahbomin,
And the grapevine, the Bemahgut,
Trailing o'er the alder-branches,
Filling all the air with fragrance!
"Master of Life!" he cried, desponding,
"Must our lives depend on these things?"
On the third day of his fasting
By the lake he sat and pondered,
By the still, transparent water;

Saw the sturgeon, Nahma, leaping,
Scattering drops like beads of wampum,
Saw the yellow perch, the Sahwa,
Like a sunbeam in the water,
Saw the pike, the Maskenozha,
And the herring, Okahahwis,
And the Shawgashee, the craw-fish!
"Master of Life!" he cried, desponding,
"Must our lives depend on these things?"
   On the fourth day of his fasting
In his lodge he lay exhausted;
From his couch of leaves and branches
Gazing with half-open eyelids,
Full of shadowy dreams and visions,
On the dizzy, swimming landscape,
On the gleaming of the water,
On the splendor of the sunset.
And he saw a youth approaching,
Dressed in garments green and yellow
Coming through the purple twilight,
Through the splendor of the sunset;
Plumes of green bent o'er his forehead,
And his hair was soft and golden.
Standing at the open doorway,
Long he looked at Hiawatha,
Looked with pity and compassion
On his wasted form and features,
And, in accents like the sighing
Of the South-Wind in the tree-tops,
Said he, "O my Hiawatha!
All your prayers are heard in heaven,
For you pray not like the others;
Not for greater skill in hunting,
Not for greater craft in fishing,
Not for triumph in the battle,
Nor renown among the warriors,
But for profit of the people,

For advantage of the nations.
"From the Master of Life descending,
I, the friend of man, Mondamin,
Come to warn you and instruct you,
How by struggle and by labor
You shall gain what you have prayed for.
Rise up from your bed of branches,
Rise, O youth, and wrestle with me!"
   Faint with famine, Hiawatha
Started from his bed of branches,
From the twilight of his wigwam
Forth into the flush of sunset
Came, and wrestled with Mondamin;
At his touch he felt new courage
Throbbing in his brain and bosom,
Felt new life and hope and vigor
Run through every nerve and fibre.
   So they wrestled there together
In the glory of the sunset,
And the more they strove and struggled,
Stronger still grew Hiawatha;
Till the darkness fell around them,
And the heron, the Shuh-shuh-gah,
From her nest among the pine-trees,
Gave a cry of lamentation,
Gave a scream of pain and famine.
   " 'T is enough!" then said Mondamin,
Smiling upon Hiawatha,
"But to-morrow, when the sun sets,
I will come again to try you."
And he vanished, and was seen not;
Whether sinking as the rain sinks,
Whether rising as the mists rise,
Hiawatha saw not, knew not,
Only saw that he had vanished,
Leaving him alone and fainting,

With the misty lake below him,
And the reeling stars above him.

   On the morrow and the next day,
When the sun through heaven descending,
Like a red and burning cinder
From the hearth of the Great Spirit,
Fell into the western waters,
Came Mondamin for the trial,
For the strife with Hiawatha;
Came as silent as the dew comes,
From the empty air appearing,
Into empty air returning,
Taking shape when earth it touches,
But invisible to all men
In its coming and its going.

   Thrice they wrestled there together
In the glory of the sunset,
Till the darkness fell around them,
Till the heron, the Shuh-shuh-gah,
From her nest among the pine-trees,
Uttered her loud cry of famine,
And Mondamin paused to listen.

   Tall and beautiful he stood there,
In his garments green and yellow;
To and fro his plumes above him
Waved and nodded with his breathing,
And the sweat of the encounter
Stood like drops of dew upon him.

   And he cried, "O Hiawatha!
Bravely have you wrestled with me,
Thrice have wrestled stoutly with me,
And the Master of Life, who sees us,
He will give to you the triumph!"

   . Then he smiled, and said: "To-morrow
Is the last day of your conflict,
Is the last day of your fasting.

You will conquer and o'ercome me;
Make a bed for me to lie in,
Where the rain may fall upon me,
Where the sun may come and warm me;
Strip these garments, green and yellow,
Strip this nodding plumage from me,
Lay me in the earth, and make it
Soft and loose and light above me.

"Let no hand disturb my slumber,
Let no weed nor worm molest me,
Let not Kahgahgee, the raven,
Come to haunt me and molest me,
Only come yourself to watch me,
Till I wake, and start, and quicken,
Till I leap into the sunshine."

And thus saying, he departed;
Peacefully slept Hiawatha,
But he heard the Wawonaissa,
Heard the whippoorwill complaining,
Perched upon his lonely wigwam;
Heard the rushing Sebowisha,
Heard the rivulet rippling near him,
Talking to the darksome forest;
Heard the sighing of the branches,
As they lifted and subsided
At the passing of the Night-Wind,
Heard them, as one hears in slumber
Far-off murmurs, dreamy whispers:
Peacefully slept Hiawatha.

On the morrow came Nokomis,
On the seventh day of his fasting,
Came with food for Hiawatha,
Came imploring and bewailing,
Lest his hunger should o'ercome him,
Lest his fasting should be fatal.

But he tasted not, and touched not,
Only said to her, "Nokomis,

Wait until the sun is setting,
Till the darkness falls around us,
Till the heron, the Shuh-shuh-gah,
Crying from the desolate marshes,
Tells us that the day is ended."
  Homeward weeping went Nokomis,
Sorrowing for her Hiawatha,
Fearing lest his strength should fail him,
Lest his fasting should be fatal.
He meanwhile sat weary waiting
For the coming of Mondamin,
Till the shadows, pointing eastward,
Lengthened over field and forest,
Till the sun dropped from the heaven,
Floating on the waters westward,
As a red leaf in the Autumn
Falls and floats upon the water,
Falls and sinks into its bosom.
  And behold! the young Mondamin,
With his soft and shining tresses,
With his garments green and yellow,
With his long and glossy plumage,
Stood and beckoned at the doorway,
And as one in slumber walking,
Pale and haggard, but undaunted,
From the wigwam Hiawatha
Came and wrestled with Mondamin.
  Round about him spun the landscape,
Sky and forest reeled together,
And his strong heart leaped within him,
As the sturgeon leaps and struggles
In a net to break its meshes.
Like a ring of fire around him
Blazed and flared the red horizon,
And a hundred suns seemed looking
At the combat of the wrestlers.
  Suddenly upon the greensward

All alone stood Hiawatha,
Panting with his wild exertion,
Palpitating with the struggle;
And before him breathless, lifeless,
Lay the youth, with hair dishevelled,
Plumage torn, and garments tattered,
Dead he lay there in the sunset.
    And victorious Hiawatha
Made the grave as he commanded,
Stripped the garments from Mondamin,
Stripped his tattered plumage from him,
Laid him in the earth, and made it
Soft and loose and light above him;
And the heron, the Shuh-shuh-gah,
From the melancholy moorlands,
Gave a cry of lamentation,
Gave a cry of pain and anguish!
    Homeward then went Hiawatha
To the lodge of old Nokomis,
And the seven days of his fasting
Were accomplished and completed.
But the place was not forgotten
Where he wrestled with Mondamin;
Nor forgotten nor neglected
Was the grave where lay Mondamin,
Sleeping in the rain and sunshine,
Where his scattered plumes and garments
Faded in the rain and sunshine.
    Day by day did Hiawatha
Go to wait and watch beside it;
Kept the dark mould soft above it,
Kept it clean from weeds and insects,
Drove away, with scoffs and shoutings,
Kahgahgee, the king of ravens.
    Till at length a small green feather
From the earth shot slowly upward,
Then another and another,

And before the Summer ended
Stood the maize in all its beauty,
With its shining robes about it,
And its long, soft, yellow tresses;
And in rapture Hiawatha
Cried aloud, "It is Mondamin!
Yes, the friend of man, Mondamin!"
    Then he called to old Nokomis
And Iagoo, the great boaster,
Showed them where the maize was growing,
Told them of his wondrous vision,
Of his wrestling and his triumph,
Of this new gift to the nations,
Which should be their food forever.
    And still later, when the Autumn
Changed the long, green leaves to yellow,
And the soft and juicy kernels
Grew like wampum hard and yellow,
Then the ripened ears he gathered,
Stripped the withered husks from off them,
As he once had stripped the wrestler,
Gave the first Feast of Mondamin,
And made known unto the people
This new gift of the Great Spirit.

THE COURTSHIP
OF MILES STANDISH*

I

MILES STANDISH

In the Old Colony days, in Plymouth the land of the
Pilgrims,
To and fro in a room of his simple and primitive
dwelling,
Clad in doublet and hose, and boots of Cordovan leather,
Strode, with a martial air, Miles Standish the Puritan
Captain.
Buried in thought he seemed, with his hands behind
him, and pausing
Ever and anon to behold his glittering weapons of
warfare,
Hanging in shining array along the walls of the chamber, —
Cutlass and corselet of steel, and his trusty sword of
Damascus,
Curved at the point and inscribed with its mystical
Arabic sentence,
While underneath, in a corner, were fowling-piece,
musket, and matchlock.
Short of stature he was, but strongly built and athletic,
Broad in the shoulders, deep-chested, with muscles and
sinews of iron;
Brown as a nut was his face, but his russet beard was
already
Flaked with patches of snow, as hedges sometimes in
November.

Near him was seated John Alden, his friend, and household
  companion,
Writing with diligent speed at a table of pine by the
  window;
Fair-haired, azure-eyed, with delicate Saxon complexion,
Having the dew of his youth, and the beauty thereof,
  as the captives
Whom Saint Gregory saw, and exclaimed, "Not Angles,
  but Angels."
Youngest of all was he of the men who came in the
  Mayflower.

  Suddenly breaking the silence, the diligent scribe
    interrupting,
Spake, in the pride of his heart, Miles Standish the
  Captain of Plymouth.
"Look at these arms," he said, "the warlike weapons
  that hang here
Burnished and bright and clean, as if for parade or
  inspection!
This is the sword of Damascus I fought with in Flanders;
  this breastplate,
Well I remember the day! once saved my life in a
  skirmish;
Here in front you can see the very dint of the bullet
Fired point-blank at my heart by a Spanish arcabucero.
Had it not been of sheer steel, the forgotten bones of
  Miles Standish
Would at this moment be mould, in their grave in the
  Flemish morasses."
Thereupon answered John Alden, but looked not up
  from his writing:
"Truly the breath of the Lord hath slackened the speed
  of the bullet;
He in his mercy preserved you, to be our shield and
  our weapon!"

Still the Captain continued, unheeding the words of the
    stripling:
"See, how bright they are burnished, as if in an arsenal
    hanging;
That is because I have done it myself, and not left it
    to others.
Serve yourself, would you be well served, is an excellent
    adage;
So I take care of my arms, as you of your pens and
    your inkhorn.
Then, too, there are my soldiers, my great, invincible
    army,
Twelve men, all equipped, having each his rest and
    his matchlock,
Eighteen shillings a month, together with diet and
    pillage,
And, like Caesar, I know the name of each of my
    soldiers!"
This he said with a smile, that danced in his eyes, as
    the sunbeams
Dance on the waves of the sea, and vanish again in
    a moment.
Alden laughed as he wrote, and still the Captain continued:
"Look! you can see from this window my brazen
    howitzer planted
High on the roof of the church, a preacher who speaks
    to the purpose,
Steady, straightforward, and strong, with irresistible logic,
Orthodox, flashing conviction right into the hearts of
    the heathen.
Now we are ready, I think, for any assault of the
    Indians;
Let them come, if they like, and the sooner they try
    it the better,—
Let them come, if they like, be it sagamore, sachem,
    or pow-wow,

Aspinet, Samoset, Corbitant, Squanto, or Tokamaha-
mon!"

Long at the window he stood, and wistfully gazed
on the landscape,
Washed with a cold gray mist, the vapory breath of
the east-wind,
Forest and meadow and hill, and the steel-blue rim of
the ocean,
Lying silent and sad, in the afternoon shadows and
sunshine.
Over his countenance flitted a shadow like those on
the landscape,
Gloom intermingled with light; and his voice was subdued
with emotion,
Tenderness, pity, regret, as after a pause he proceeded:
"Yonder there, on the hill by the sea, lies buried Rose
Standish;
Beautiful rose of love, that bloomed for me by the
wayside!
She was the first to die of all who came in the
Mayflower!
Green above her is growing the field of wheat we have
sown there,
Better to hide from the Indian scouts the graves of
our people,
Lest they should count them and see how many already
have perished!"
Sadly his face he averted, and strode up and down,
and was thoughtful.

Fixed to the opposite wall was a shelf of books, and
among them
Prominent three, distinguished alike for bulk and for
binding;
Bariffe's Artillery Guide, and the Commentaries of Cæsar

Out of the Latin translated by Arthur Goldinge of
    London,
And, as if guarded by these, between them was standing
    the Bible.
Musing a moment before them, Miles Standish paused,
    as if doubtful
Which of the three he should choose for his consolation
    and comfort,
Whether the wars of the Hebrews, the famous campaigns
    of the Romans,
Or the Artillery practice, designed for belligerent Chris-
    tians.
Finally down from its shelf he dragged the ponderous
    Roman,
Seated himself at the window, and opened the book,
    and in silence
Turned o'er the well-worn leaves, where thumb-marks
    thick on the margin,
Like the trample of feet, proclaimed the battle was
    hottest.
Nothing was heard in the room but the hurrying pen
    of the stripling,
Busily writing epistles important, to go by the Mayflower,
Ready to sail on the morrow, or next day at latest,
    God willing!
Homeward bound with the tidings of all that terrible
    winter,
Letters written by Alden, and full of the name of
    Priscilla!
Full of the name and the fame of the Puritan maiden
    Priscilla!

II

LOVE AND FRIENDSHIP

Nothing was heard in the room but the hurrying pen
    of the stripling,
Or an occasional sigh from the laboring heart of the
    Captain,
Reading the marvellous words and achievements of Julius
    Cæsar.
After a while he exclaimed, as he smote with his hand,
    palm downwards,
Heavily on the page: "A wonderful man was this Cæsar!
You are a writer, and I am a fighter, but here is a
    fellow
Who could both write and fight, and in both was
    equally skilful!"
Straightway answered and spake John Alden, the comely,
    the youthful:
"Yes, he was equally skilled, as you say, with his pen
    and his weapons.
Somewhere have I read, but where I forget, he could
    dictate
Seven letters at once, at the same time writing his
    memoirs."
"Truly," continued the Captain, not heeding or hearing
    the other,
"Truly a wonderful man was Caius Julius Cæsar!
Better be first, he said, in a little Iberian village,
Than be second in Rome, and I think he was right
    when he said it.
Twice was he married before he was twenty, and many
    times after;
Battles five hundred he fought, and a thousand cities
    he conquered;
He, too, fought in Flanders, as he himself has recorded;
Finally he was stabbed by his friend, the orator Brutus!

Now, do you know what he did on a certain occasion
in Flanders,
When the rear-guard of his army retreated, the front
giving way too,
And the immortal Twelfth Legion was crowded so
closely together
There was no room for their swords? Why, he seized
a shield from a soldier,
Put himself straight at the head of his troops, and
commanded the captains,
Calling on each by his name, to order forward the
ensigns;
Then to widen the ranks, and give more room for
their weapons;
So he won the day, the battle of something-or-other.
That's what I always say; if you wish a thing to be
well done,
You must do it yourself, you must not leave it to
others!"

All was silent again; the Captain continued his reading.
Nothing was heard in the room but the hurrying pen
of the stripling
Writing epistles important to go next day by the
Mayflower,
Filled with the name and the fame of the Puritan maiden
Priscilla;
Every sentence began or closed with the name of Priscilla,
Till the treacherous pen, to which he confided the secret,
Strove to betray it by singing and shouting the name
of Priscilla!
Finally closing his book, with a bang of the ponderous
cover,
Sudden and loud as the sound of a soldier grounding
his musket,
Thus to the young man spake Miles Standish the Captain
of Plymouth:

"When you have finished your work, I have something
    important to tell you.
Be not, however, in haste; I can wait; I shall not be
    impatient!"
Straightway Alden replied, as he folded the last of his
    letters,
Pushing his papers aside, and giving respectful attention:
"Speak; for whenever you speak, I am always ready
    to listen,
Always ready to hear whatever pertains to Miles Standish."
Thereupon answered the Captain, embarrassed, and culling
    his phrases:
" 'T is not good for a man to be alone, say the
    Scriptures.
This I have said before, and again and again I repeat
    it:
Every hour in the day, I think it, and feel it, and say
    it.
Since Rose Standish died, my life has been weary and
    dreary;
Sick at heart have I been, beyond the healing of friendship;
Oft in my lonely hours have I thought of the maiden
    Priscilla.
She is alone in the world; her father and mother and
    brother
Died in the winter together; I saw her going and
    coming,
Now to the grave of the dead, and now to the bed
    of the dying,
Patient, courageous, and strong, and said to myself,
    that if ever
There were angels on earth, as there are angels in
    heaven,
Two have I seen and known; and the angel whose
    name is Priscilla
Holds in my desolate life the place which the other
    abandoned.

Long have I cherished the thought, but never have
    dared to reveal it,
Being a coward in this, though valiant enough for the
    most part.
Go to the damsel Priscilla, the loveliest maiden of
    Plymouth,
Say that a blunt old Captain, a man not of words but
    of actions,
Offers his hand and his heart, the hand and heart of
    a soldier.
Not in these words, you know, but this in short is
    my meaning;
I am a maker of war, and not a maker of phrases.
You, who are bred as a scholar, can say it in elegant
    language,
Such as you read in your books of the pleadings and
    wooings of lovers,
Such as you think best adapted to win the heart of
    a maiden."

When he had spoken, John Alden, the fair-haired,
    taciturn stripling,
All aghast at his words, surprised, embarrassed, bewil-
    dered,
Trying to mask his dismay by treating the subject with
    lightness,
Trying to smile, and yet feeling his heart stand still
    in his bosom,
Just as a timepiece stops in a house that is stricken
    by lightning,
Thus made answer and spake, or rather stammered than
    answered:
"Such a message as that, I am sure I should mangle
    and mar it;
If you would have it well done,—I am only repeating
    your maxim,—

You must do it yourself, you must not leave it to
      others!"
But with the air of a man whom nothing can turn
      from his purpose,
Gravely shaking his head, made answer the Captain of
      Plymouth:
"Truly the maxim is good, and I do not mean to
      gainsay it;
But we must use it discreetly, and not waste powder
      for nothing.
Now, as I said before, I was never a maker of phrases.
I can march up to a fortress and summon the place
      to surrender,
But march up to a woman with such a proposal, I
      dare not.
I'm not afraid of bullets, nor shot from the mouth of
      a cannon,
But of a thundering 'No!' point-blank from the mouth
      of a woman,
That I confess I'm afraid of, nor am I ashamed to
      confess it!
So you must grant my request, for you are an elegant
      scholar,
Having the graces of speech, and skill in the turning
      of phrases."
Taking the hand of his friend, who still was reluctant
      and doubtful,
Holding it long in his own, and pressing it kindly,
      he added:
"Though I have spoken thus lightly, yet deep is the
      feeling that prompts me;
Surely you cannot refuse what I ask in the name of
      our friendship!"
Then made answer John Alden: "The name of friendship
      is sacred;
What you demand in that name, I have not the power
      to deny you!"

So the strong will prevailed, subduing and moulding
the gentler,
Friendship prevailed over love, and Alden went on his
errand.

III

THE LOVER'S ERRAND

So the strong will prevailed, and Alden went on his
errand,
Out of the street of the village, and into the paths of
the forest,
Into the tranquil woods, where bluebirds and robins
were building
Towns in the populous trees, with hanging-gardens of
verdure,
Peaceful, aërial cities of joy and affection and freedom.
All around him was calm, but within him commotion
and conflict,
Love contending with friendship, and self with each
generous impulse.
To and fro in his breast his thoughts were heaving
and dashing,
As in a foundering ship, with every roll of the vessel,
Washes the bitter sea, the merciless surge of the ocean!
"Must I relinquish it all," he cried with a wild lamentation,—
"Must I relinquish it all, the joy, the hope, the illusion?
Was it for this I have loved, and waited, and worshipped
in silence?
Was it for this I have followed the flying feet and the
shadow
Over the wintry sea, to the desolate shores of New
England?
Truly the heart is deceitful, and out of its depths of
corruption

Rise, like an exhalation, the misty phantoms of passion;
Angels of light they seem, but are only delusions of
    Satan.
All is clear to me now; I feel it, I see it distinctly!
This is the hand of the Lord; it is laid upon me in
    anger,
For I have followed too much the heart's desires and
    devices,
Worshipping Astaroth blindly, and impious idols of Baal.*
This is the cross I must bear; the sin and the swift
    retribution."

So through the Plymouth woods John Alden went
    on his errand;
Crossing the brook at the ford, where it brawled over
    pebble and shallow,
Gathering still, as he went, the May-flowers blooming
    around him,
Fragrant, filling the air with a strange and wonderful
    sweetness,
Children lost in the woods, and covered with leaves
    in their slumber.
"Puritan flowers," he said, "and the type of Puritan
    maidens,
Modest and simple and sweet, the very type of Priscilla!
So I will take them to her; to Priscilla the May-flower
    of Plymouth,
Modest and simple and sweet, as a parting gift will
    I take them;
Breathing their silent farewells, as they fade and wither
    and perish,
Soon to be thrown away as is the heart of the giver."
So through the Plymouth woods John Alden went on
    his errand;
Came to an open space, and saw the disk of the ocean,
Sailless, sombre and cold with the comfortless breath
    of the east-wind;

Saw the new-built house, and people at work in a meadow;
Heard, as he drew near the door, the musical voice of Priscilla
Singing the hundredth Psalm, the grand old Puritan anthem,
Music that Luther sang to the sacred words of the Psalmist,
Full of the breath of the Lord, consoling and comforting many.
Then, as he opened the door, he beheld the form of the maiden
Seated beside her wheel, and the carded wool like a snow-drift
Piled at her knee, her white hands feeding the ravenous spindle,
While with her foot on the treadle she guided the wheel in its motion.
Open wide on her lap lay the well-worn psalm-book of Ainsworth,
Printed in Amsterdam, the words and the music together,
Rough-hewn, angular notes, like stones in the wall of a churchyard,
Darkened and overhung by the running vine of the verses.
Such was the book from whose pages she sang the old Puritan anthem,
She, the Puritan girl, in the solitude of the forest,
Making the humble house and the modest apparel of homespun
Beautiful with her beauty, and rich with the wealth of her being!
Over him rushed, like a wind that is keen and cold and relentless,
Thoughts of what might have been, and the weight and woe of his errand;
All the dreams that had faded, and all the hopes that had vanished,

All his life henceforth a dreary and tenantless mansion,
Haunted by vain regrets, and pallid, sorrowful faces.
Still he said to himself, and almost fiercely he said it,
"Let not him that putteth his hand to the plough look
      backwards;
Though the ploughshare cut through the flowers of life
      to its fountains,
Though it pass o'er the graves of the dead and the
      hearths of the living,
It is the will of the Lord; and his mercy endureth forever!"

So he entered the house: and the hum of the wheel
      and the singing
Suddenly ceased; for Priscilla, aroused by his step on
      the threshold,
Rose as he entered, and gave him her hand, in signal
      of welcome,
Saying, "I knew it was you, when I heard your step
      in the passage;
For I was thinking of you, as I sat there singing and
      spinning."
Awkward and dumb with delight, that a thought of
      him had been mingled
Thus in the sacred psalm, that came from the heart
      of the maiden,
Silent before her he stood, and gave her the flowers
      for an answer,
Finding no words for his thought. He remembered that
      day in the winter,
After the first great snow, when he broke a path from
      the village,
Reeling and plunging along through the drifts that
      encumbered the doorway,
Stamping the snow from his feet as he entered the
      house, and Priscilla
Laughed at his snowy locks, and gave him a seat by
      the fireside,

Grateful and pleased to know he had thought of her
in the snow-storm.
Had he but spoken then! perhaps not in vain had he
spoken;
Now it was all too late; the golden moment had
vanished!
So he stood there abashed, and gave her the flowers
for an answer.

Then they sat down and talked of the birds and the
beautiful spring-time,
Talked of their friends at home, and the Mayflower
that sailed on the morrow.
"I have been thinking all day," said gently the Puritan
maiden,
"Dreaming all night, and thinking all day, of the hedge-
rows of England,—
They are in blossom now, and the country is all like
a garden;
Thinking of lanes and fields, and the song of the lark
and the linnet,
Seeing the village street, and familiar faces of neighbors
Going about as of old, and stopping to gossip together,
And, at the end of the street, the village church, with
the ivy
Climbing the old gray tower, and the quiet graves in
the churchyard.
Kind are the people I live with, and dear to me my
religion;
Still my heart is so sad, that I wish myself back in
Old England.
You will say it is wrong, but I cannot help it: I almost
Wish myself back in Old England, I feel so lonely and
wretched."

Thereupon answered the youth: "Indeed I do not
condemn you;

Stouter hearts than a woman's have quailed in this
    terrible winter.
Yours is tender and trusting, and needs a stronger to
    lean on;
So I have come to you now, with an offer and proffer
    of marriage
Made by a good man and true, Miles Standish the
    Captain of Plymouth!"

  Thus he delivered his message, the dexterous writer
    of letters,—
Did not embellish the theme, nor array it in beautiful
    phrases,
But came straight to the point, and blurted it out like
    a school-boy;
Even the Captain himself could hardly have said it more
    bluntly.
Mute with amazement and sorrow, Priscilla the Puritan
    maiden
Looked into Alden's face, her eyes dilated with wonder,
Feeling his words like a blow, that stunned her and
    rendered her speechless;
Till at length she exclaimed, interrupting the ominous
    silence:
"If the great Captain of Plymouth is so very eager to
    wed me,
Why does he not come himself, and take the trouble
    to woo me?
If I am not worth the wooing, I surely am not worth
    the winning!"
Then John Alden began explaining and smoothing the
    matter,
Making it worse as he went, by saying the Captain
    was busy,—
Had no time for such things;—such things! the words
    grating harshly

Fell on the ear of Priscilla; and swift as a flash she
    made answer:
"Has he no time for such things, as you call it, before
    he is married,
Would he be likely to find it, or make it, after the
    wedding?
That is the way with you men; you don't understand
    us, you cannot.
When you have made up your minds, after thinking
    of this one and that one,
Choosing, selecting, rejecting, comparing one with an-
    other,
Then you make known your desire, with abrupt and
    sudden avowal,
And are offended and hurt, and indignant, perhaps, that
    a woman
Does not respond at once to a love that she never
    suspected,
Does not attain at a bound the height to which you
    have been climbing.
This is not right nor just: for surely a woman's affection
Is not a thing to be asked for, and had for only the
    asking.
When one is truly in love, one not only says it, but
    shows it.
Had he but waited a while, had he only showed that
    he loved me,
Even this Captain of yours—who knows?—at last might
    have won me,
Old and rough as he is; but now it never can happen."

    Still John Alden went on, unheeding the words of
    Priscilla,
Urging the suit of his friend, explaining, persuading,
    expanding;
Spoke of his courage and skill, and of all his battles
    in Flanders,

How with the people of God he had chosen to suffer
affliction;
How, in return for his zeal, they had made him Captain
of Plymouth;
He was a gentleman born, could trace his pedigree
plainly
Back to Hugh Standish of Duxbury Hall, in Lancashire,
England,
Who was the son of Ralph, and the grandson of Thurston
de Standish;
Heir unto vast estates, of which he was basely defrauded,
Still bore the family arms, and had for his crest a cock
argent
Combed and wattled gules, and all the rest of the
blazon.
He was a man of honor, of noble and generous nature;
Though he was rough, he was kindly; she knew how
during the winter
He had attended the sick, with a hand as gentle as
woman's;
Somewhat hasty and hot, he could not deny it, and
headstrong,
Stern as a soldier might be, but hearty, and placable
always,
Not to be laughed at and scorned, because he was little
of stature;
For he was great of heart, magnanimous, courtly,
courageous;
Any woman in Plymouth, nay, any woman in England,
Might be happy and proud to be called the wife of
Miles Standish!

But as he warmed and glowed, in his simple and
eloquent language,
Quite forgetful of self, and full of the praise of his
rival,

Archly the maiden smiled, and, with eyes overrunning
    with laughter,
Said, in a tremulous voice, "Why don't you speak for
    yourself, John?"

IV

JOHN ALDEN

Into the open air John Alden, perplexed and bewildered,
Rushed like a man insane, and wandered alone by the
    seaside;
Paced up and down the sands, and bared his head to
    the east-wind,
Cooling his heated brow, and the fire and fever within
    him.
Slowly as out of the heavens, with apocalyptical splendors,
Sank the City of God, in the vision of John the Apostle,
So, with its cloudy walls of chrysolite, jasper, and
    sapphire,
Sank the broad red sun, and over its turrets uplifted
Glimmered the golden reed of the angel who measured
    the city.

"Welcome, O wind of the East!" he exclaimed in
    his wild exultation,
"Welcome, O wind of the East, from the caves of the
    misty Atlantic!
Blowing o'er fields of dulse, and measureless meadows
    of sea-grass,
Blowing o'er rocky wastes, and the grottos and gardens
    of ocean!
Lay thy cold, moist hand on my burning forehead,
    and wrap me
Close in thy garments of mist, to allay the fever within
    me!"

Like an awakened conscience, the sea was moaning
and tossing,
Beating remorseful and loud the mutable sands of the
seashore.
Fierce in his soul was the struggle and tumult of passions
contending;
Love triumphant and crowned, and friendship wounded
and bleeding,
Passionate cries of desire, and importunate pleadings of
duty!
"Is it my fault," he said, "that the maiden has chosen
between us?
Is it my fault that he failed,—my fault that I am the
victor?"
Then within him there thundered a voice, like the voice
of the Prophet:
"It hath displeased the Lord!"—and he thought of David's
transgression,*
Bathsheba's beautiful face, and his friend in the front
of the battle!
Shame and confusion of guilt, and abasement and self-
condemnation,
Overwhelmed him at once; and he cried in the deepest
contrition:
"It hath displeased the Lord! It is the temptation of
Satan!"

Then, uplifting his head, he looked at the sea, and
beheld there
Dimly the shadowy form of the Mayflower riding at
anchor,
Rocked on the rising tide, and ready to sail on the
morrow;
Heard the voices of men through the mist, the rattle
of cordage
Thrown on the deck, the shouts of the mate, and the
sailors' "Ay, ay, Sir!"

Clear and distinct, but not loud, in the dripping air
    of the twilight.
Still for a moment he stood, and listened, and stared
    at the vessel,
Then went hurriedly on, as one who, seeing a phantom,
Stops, then quickens his pace, and follows the beckoning
    shadow.
"Yes, it is plain to me now," he murmured; "the hand
    of the Lord is
Leading me out of the land of darkness, the bondage
    of error,
Through the sea, that shall lift the walls of its waters
    around me,
Hiding me, cutting me off, from the cruel thoughts
    that pursue me.
Back will I go o'er the ocean, this dreary land will
    abandon,
Her whom I may not love, and him whom my heart
    has offended.
Better to be in my grave in the green old churchyard
    in England,
Close by my mother's side, and among the dust of
    my kindred;
Better be dead and forgotten, than living in shame and
    dishonor;
Sacred and safe and unseen, in the dark of the narrow
    chamber
With me my secret shall lie, like a buried jewel that
    glimmers
Bright on the hand that is dust, in the chambers of
    silence and darkness,—
Yes, as the marriage-ring of the great espousal hereafter!"

  Thus as he spake, he turned, in the strength of his
    strong resolution,
Leaving behind him the shore, and hurried along in
    the twilight,

Through the congenial gloom of the forest silent and
    sombre,
Till he beheld the lights in the seven houses of Plymouth,
Shining like seven stars in the dusk and mist of the
    evening.
Soon he entered his door, and found the redoubtable
    Captain
Sitting alone, and absorbed in the martial pages of
    Cæsar,
Fighting some great campaign in Hainault or Brabant
    or Flanders.
"Long have you been on your errand," he said with
    a cheery demeanor,
Even as one who is waiting an answer, and fears not
    the issue.
"Not far off is the house, although the woods are
    between us;
But you have lingered so long, that while you were
    going and coming
I have fought ten battles and sacked and demolished
    a city.
Come, sit down, and in order relate to me all that
    has happened."

Then John Alden spake, and related the wondrous
    adventure,
From begining to end, minutely, just as it happened;
How he had seen Priscilla, and how he had sped in
    his courtship,
Only smoothing a little, and softening down her refusal.
But when he came at length to the words Priscilla had
    spoken,
Words so tender and cruel: "Why don't you speak for
    yourself, John?"
Up leaped the Captain of Plymouth, and stamped on
    the floor, till his armor

Clanged on the wall, where it hung, with a sound of
    sinister omen.
All his pent-up wrath burst forth in a sudden explosion,
E'en as a hand-grenade, that scatters destruction around
    it.
Wildly he shouted, and loud: "John Alden! you have
    betrayed me!
Me, Miles Standish, your friend! have supplanted, de-
    frauded, betrayed me!
One of my ancestors ran his sword through the heart
    of Wat Tyler;*
Who shall prevent me from running my own through
    the heart of a traitor?
Yours is the greater treason, for yours is a treason to
    friendship!
You, who lived under my roof, whom I cherished and
    loved as a brother;
You, who have fed at my board, and drunk at my
    cup, to whose keeping
I have intrusted my honor, my thoughts the most sacred
    and secret,—
You too, Brutus! ah, woe to the name of friendship
    hereafter!
Brutus was Cæsar's friend, and you were mine, but
    henceforward
Let there be nothing between us save war, and implacable
    hatred!"

  So spake the Captain of Plymouth, and strode about
    in the chamber,
Chafing and choking with rage; like cords were the
    veins on his temples.
But in the midst of his anger a man appeared at the
    doorway,
Bringing in uttermost haste a message of urgent im-
    portance,

Rumors of danger and war and hostile incursions of
  Indians!
Straightway the Captain paused, and, without further
  question or parley,
Took from the nail on the wall his sword with its
  scabbard of iron,
Buckled the belt round his waist, and, frowning fiercely,
  departed.
Alden was left alone. He heard the clank of the scabbard
Growing fainter and fainter, and dying away in the
  distance.
Then he arose from his seat, and looked forth into
  the darkness,
Felt the cool air blow on his cheek, that was hot with
  the insult,
Lifted his eyes to the heavens, and, folding his hands
  as in childhood,
Prayed in the silence of night to the Father who seeth
  in secret.

  Meanwhile the choleric Captain strode wrathful away
  to the council,
Found it already assembled, impatiently waiting his
  coming;
Men in the middle of life, austere and grave in deportment,
Only one of them old, the hill that was nearest to
  heaven,
Covered with snow, but erect, the excellent Elder of
  Plymouth.
God had sifted three kingdoms to find the wheat for
  this planting,
Then had sifted the wheat, as the living seed of a
  nation;
So say the chronicles old, and such is the faith of the
  people!
Near them was standing an Indian, in attitude stern
  and defiant;

Naked down to the waist, and grim and ferocious in
    aspect;
While on the table before them was lying unopened
    a Bible,
Ponderous, bound in leather, brass-studded, printed in
    Holland,
And beside it outstretched the skin of a rattlesnake
    glittered,
Filled, like a quiver, with arrows; a signal and challenge
    of warfare,
Brought by the Indian, and speaking with arrowy tongues
    of defiance.
This Miles Standish beheld, as he entered, and heard
    them debating
What were an answer befitting the hostile message and
    menace,
Talking of this and of that, contriving, suggesting,
    objecting;
One voice only for peace, and that the voice of the
    Elder,
Judging it wise and well that some at least were converted,
Rather than any were slain, for this was but Christian
    behavior!
Then out spake Miles Standish, the stalwart Captain
    of Plymouth,
Muttering deep in his throat, for his voice was husky
    with anger,
"What! do you mean to make war with milk and the
    water of roses?
Is it to shoot red squirrels you have your howitzer
    planted
There on the roof of the church, or is it to shoot red
    devils?
Truly the only tongue that is understood by a savage
Must be the tongue of fire that speaks from the mouth
    of the cannon!"

Thereupon answered and said the excellent Elder of
    Plymouth,
Somewhat amazed and alarmed at this irreverent language:
"Not so thought St. Paul, nor yet the other Apostles;
Not from the cannon's mouth were the tongues of fire
    they spake with!"
But unheeded fell this mild rebuke on the Captain,
Who had advanced to the table, and thus continued
    discoursing:
"Leave this matter to me, for to me by right it
    pertaineth.
War is a terrible trade; but in the cause that is righteous,
Sweet is the smell of powder; and thus I answer the
    challenge!"

Then from the rattlesnake's skin, with a sudden,
    contemptuous gesture,
Jerking the Indian arrows, he filled it with powder and
    bullets
Full to the very jaws, and handed it back to the savage,
Saying, in thundering tones: "Here, take it! this is your
    answer!"
Silently out of the room then glided the glistening
    savage,
Bearing the serpent's skin, and seeming himself like a
    serpent,
Winding his sinuous way in the dark to the depths of
    the forest.

V

THE SAILING OF THE MAYFLOWER

Just in the gray of the dawn, as the mists uprose from
    the meadows,

There was a stir and a sound in the slumbering village
of Plymouth;
Clanging and clicking of arms, and the order imperative,
"Forward!"
Given in tone suppressed, a tramp of feet, and then
silence.
Figures ten, in the mist, marched slowly out of the
village.
Standish the stalwart it was, with eight of his valorous
army,
Led by their Indian guide, by Hobomok, friend of the
white men,*
Northward marching to quell the sudden revolt of the
savage.
Giants they seemed in the mist, or the mighty men
of King David;
Giants in heart they were, who believed in God and
the Bible,—
Ay, who believed in the smiting of Midianites and
Philistines.*
Over them gleamed far off the crimson banners of
morning;
Under them loud on the sands, the serried billows,
advancing,
Fired along the line, and in regular order retreated.

Many a mile had they marched, when at length the
village of Plymouth
Woke from its sleep, and arose, intent on its manifold
labors.
Sweet was the air and soft; and slowly the smoke from
the chimneys
Rose over roofs of thatch, and pointed steadily east-
ward;
Men came forth from the doors, and paused and talked
of the weather,

Said that the wind had changed, and was blowing fair
    for the Mayflower;
Talked of their Captain's departure, and all the dangers
    that menaced,
He being gone, the town, and what should be done
    in his absence.
Merrily sang the birds, and the tender voices of women
Consecrated with hymns the common cares of the
    household.
Out of the sea rose the sun, and the billows rejoiced
    at his coming;
Beautiful were his feet on the purple tops of the
    mountains;
Beautiful on the sails of the Mayflower riding at anchor,
Battered and blackened and worn by all the storms of
    the winter.
Loosely against her masts was hanging and flapping her
    canvas,
Rent by so many gales, and patched by the hands of
    the sailors.
Suddenly from her side, as the sun rose over the ocean,
Darted a puff of smoke, and floated seaward; anon
    rang
Loud over field and forest the cannon's roar, and the
    echoes
Heard and repeated the sound, the signal-gun of departure!
Ah! but with louder echoes replied the hearts of the
    people!
Meekly, in voices subdued, the chapter was read from
    the Bible,
Meekly the prayer was begun, but ended in fervent
    entreaty!
Then from their houses in haste came forth the Pilgrims
    of Plymouth,
Men and women and children, all hurrying down to
    the seashore,

Eager, with tearful eyes, to say farewell to the May-
flower,
Homeward bound o'er the sea, and leaving them here
in the desert.

Foremost among them was Alden. All night he had
lain without slumber,
Turning and tossing about in the heat and unrest of
his fever.
He had beheld Miles Standish, who came back late
from the council,
Stalking into the room, and heard him mutter and
murmur,
Sometimes it seemed a prayer, and sometimes it sounded
like swearing.
Once he had come to the bed, and stood there a
moment in silence;
Then he had turned away, and said: "I will not awake
him;
Let him sleep on, it is best; for what is the use of
more talking!"
Then he extinguished the light, and threw himself down
on his pallet,
Dressed as he was, and ready to start at the break of
the morning,—
Covered himself with the cloak he had worn in his
campaigns in Flanders,—
Slept as a soldier sleeps in his bivouac, ready for
action.
But with the dawn he arose; in the twilight Alden
beheld him
Put on his corselet of steel, and all the rest of his
armor,
Buckle about his waist his trusty blade of Damascus,
Take from the corner his musket, and so stride out
of the chamber.

Often the heart of the youth had burned and yearned
    to embrace him,
Often his lips had essayed to speak, imploring for
    pardon;
All the old friendship came back, with its tender and
    grateful emotions;
But his pride overmastered the nobler nature within
    him,—
Pride, and the sense of his wrong, and the burning
    fire of the insult.
So he beheld his friend departing in anger, but spake
    not,
Saw him go forth to danger, perhaps to death, and
    he spake not!
Then he arose from his bed, and heard what the people
    were saying,
Joined in the talk at the door, with Stephen and Richard
    and Gilbert,
Joined in the morning prayer, and in the reading of
    Scripture,
And, with the others, in haste went hurrying down
    to the seashore,
Down to the Plymouth Rock, that had been to their
    feet as a doorstep
Into a world unknown,—the corner-stone of a nation!

There with his boat was the Master, already a little
    impatient
Lest he should lose the tide, or the wind might shift
    to the eastward,
Square-built, hearty, and strong, with an odor of ocean
    about him,
Speaking with this one and that, and cramming letters
    and parcels
Into his pockets capacious, and messages mingled together
Into his narrow brain, till at last he was wholly bewildered.

Nearer the boat stood Alden, with one foot placed on
    the gunwale,
One still firm on the rock, and talking at times with
    the sailors,
Seated erect on the thwarts, all ready and eager for
    starting.
He too was eager to go, and thus put an end to his
    anguish,
Thinking to fly from despair, that swifter than keel is
    or canvas,
Thinking to drown in the sea the ghost that would
    rise and pursue him.
But as he gazed on the crowd, he beheld the form
    of Priscilla
Standing dejected among them, unconscious of all that
    was passing.
Fixed were her eyes upon his, as if she divined his
    intention,
Fixed with a look so sad, so reproachful, imploring,
    and patient,
That with a sudden revulsion his heart recoiled from
    its purpose,
As from the verge of a crag, where one step more
    is destruction.
Strange is the heart of man, with its quick, mysterious
    instincts!
Strange is the life of man, and fatal or fated are mo-
    ments,
Whereupon turn, as on hinges, the gates of the wall
    adamantine!
"Here I remain!" he exclaimed, as he looked at the
    heavens above him,
Thanking the Lord whose breath had scattered the mist
    and the madness,
Wherein, blind and lost, to death he was staggering
    headlong.

"Yonder snow-white cloud, that floats in the ether above
    me,
Seems like a hand that is pointing and beckoning over
    the ocean.
There is another hand, that is not so spectral and ghost-
    like,
Holding me, drawing me back, and clasping mine for
    protection.
Float, O hand of cloud, and vanish away in the ether!
Roll thyself up like a fist, to threaten and daunt me;
    I heed not
Either your warning or menace, or any omen of evil!
There is no land so sacred, no air so pure and so
    wholesome,
As is the air she breathes, and the soil that is pressed
    by her footsteps.
Here for her sake will I stay, and like an invisible
    presence
Hover around her forever, protecting, supporting her
    weakness;
Yes! as my foot was the first that stepped on this rock
    at the landing,
So, with the blessing of God, shall it be the last at
    the leaving!"

  Meanwhile the Master alert, but with dignified air
    and important,
Scanning with watchful eye the tide and the wind and
    the weather,
Walked about on the sands, and the people crowded
    around him
Saying a few last words, and enforcing his careful
    remembrance.
Then, taking each by the hand, as if he were grasping
    a tiller,

Into the boat he sprang, and in haste shoved off to
        his vessel,
Glad in his heart to get rid of all this worry and
        flurry,
Glad to be gone from a land of sand and sickness and
        sorrow,
Short allowance of victual, and plenty of nothing but
        Gospel!
Lost in the sound of the oars was the last farewell of
        the Pilgrims.
O strong hearts and true! not one went back in the
        Mayflower!
No, not one looked back, who had set his hand to
        this ploughing!

Soon were heard on board the shouts and songs of
        the sailors
Heaving the windlass round, hoisting the ponderous
        anchor.
Then the yards were braced, and all sails set to the
        west-wind,
Blowing steady and strong; and the Mayflower sailed
        from the harbor,
Rounded the point of the Gurnet, and leaving far to
        the southward
Island and cape of sand, and the Field of the First
        Encounter,
Took the wind on her quarter, and stood for the open
        Atlantic,
Borne on the send of the sea, and the swelling hearts
        of the Pilgrims.

Long in silence they watched the receding sail of the
        vessel,
Much endeared to them all, as something living and
        human;

Then, as if filled with the spirit, and wrapt in a vision
    prophetic,
Baring his hoary head, the excellent Elder of Plymouth
Said, "Let us pray!" and they prayed, and thanked the
    Lord and took courage.
Mournfully sobbed the waves at the base of the rock,
    and above them
Bowed and whispered the wheat on the hill of death,
    and their kindred
Seemed to awake in their graves, and to join in the
    prayer that they uttered.
Sun-illumined and white, on the eastern verge of the
    ocean
Gleamed the departing sail, like a marble slab in a
    graveyard;
Buried beneath it lay forever all hope of escaping.
Lo! as they turned to depart, they saw the form of
    an Indian,
Watching them from the hill; but while they spake
    with each other,
Pointing with outstretched hands, and saying, "Look!"
    he had vanished.
So they returned to their homes; but Alden lingered
    a little,
Musing alone on the shore, and watching the wash of
    the billows
Round the base of the rock, and the sparkle and flash
    of the sunshine,
Like the spirit of God, moving visibly over the waters.

VI

PRISCILLA

Thus for a while he stood, and mused by the shore
    of the ocean,

Thinking of many things, and most of all of Priscilla;
And as if thought had the power to draw to itself,
    like the loadstone,
Whatsoever it touches, by subtile laws of its nature,
Lo! as he turned to depart, Priscilla was standing beside
    him.

"Are you so much offended, you will not speak to
    me?" said she.
"Am I so much to blame, that yesterday, when you
    were pleading
Warmly the cause of another, my heart, impulsive and
    wayward,
Pleaded your own, and spake out, forgetful perhaps of
    decorum?
Certainly you can forgive me for speaking so frankly,
    for saying
What I ought not to have said, yet now I can never
    unsay it;
For there are moments in life, when the heart is so
    full of emotion,
That if by chance it be shaken, or into its depths like
    a pebble
Drops some careless word, it overflows, and its secret,
Spilt on the ground like water, can never be gathered
    together.
Yesterday I was shocked, when I heard you speak of
    Miles Standish,
Praising his virtues, transforming his very defects into
    virtues,
Praising his courage and strength, and even his fighting
    in Flanders,
As if by fighting alone you could win the heart of
    a woman,
Quite overlooking yourself and the rest, in exalting
    your hero.
Therefore I spake as I did, by an irresistible impulse.

You will forgive me, I hope, for the sake of the
    friendship between us,
Which is too true and too sacred to be so easily broken!"
Thereupon answered John Alden, the scholar, the friend
    of Miles Standish
"I was not angry with you, with myself alone I was
    angry,
Seeing how badly I managed the matter I had in my
    keeping."
"No!" interrupted the maiden, with answer prompt and
    decisive;
"No; you were angry with me, for speaking so frankly
    and freely.
It was wrong, I acknowledge; for it is the fate of a
    woman
Long to be patient and silent, to wait like a ghost that
    is speechless,
Till some questioning voice dissolves the spell of its
    silence.
Hence in the inner life of so many suffering women
Sunless and silent and deep, like subterranean rivers
Running through caverns of darkness, unheard, unseen,
    and unfruitful,
Chafing their channels of stone, with endless and profitless
    murmurs."
Thereupon answered John Alden, the young man, the
    lover of women:
"Heaven forbid it, Priscilla; and truly they seem to me
    always
More like the beautiful rivers that watered the Garden
    of Eden,
More like the river Euphrates, through deserts of Havilah
    flowing,
Filling the land with delight, and memories sweet of
    the garden!"
"Ah, by these words, I can see," again interrupted the
    maiden,

"How very little you prize me, or care for what I am
saying,
When from the depths of my heart, in pain and with
secret misgiving,
Frankly I speak to you, asking for sympathy only and
kindness,
Straightway you take up my words, that are plain and
direct and in earnest,
Turn them away from their meaning, and answer with
flattering phrases.
This is not right, is not just, is not true to the best
that is in you;
For I know and esteem you, and feel that your nature
is noble,
Lifting mine up to a higher, a more ethereal level.
Therefore I value your friendship, and feel it perhaps
the more keenly
If you say aught that implies I am only as one among
many,
If you make use of those common and complimentary
phrases
Most men think so fine, in dealing and speaking with
women,
But which women reject as insipid, if not as insulting."

Mute and amazed was Alden; and listened and looked
at Priscilla,
Thinking he never had seen her more fair, more divine
in her beauty.
He who but yesterday pleaded so glibly the cause of
another,
Stood there embarrassed and silent, and seeking in vain
for an answer.
So the maiden went on, and little divined or imagined
What was at work in his heart, that made him so
awkward and speechless.

"Let us then, be what we are, and speak what we
    think, and in all things
Keep ourselves loyal to truth, and the sacred professions
    of friendship.
It is no secret I tell you, nor am I ashamed to declare
    it:
I have liked to be with you, to see you, to speak
    with you always.
So I was hurt at your words, and a little affronted
    to hear you
Urge me to marry your friend, though he were the
    Captain Miles Standish.
For I must tell you the truth: much more to me is
    your friendship
Than all the love he could give, were he twice the
    hero you think him."
Then she extended her hand, and Alden, who eagerly
    grasped it,
Felt all the wounds in his heart, that were aching and
    bleeding so sorely,
Healed by the touch of that hand, and he said, with
    a voice full of feeling:
"Yes, we must ever be friends; and of all who offer
    you friendship
Let me be ever the first, the truest, the nearest and
    dearest!"

  Casting a farewell look at the glimmering sail of the
    Mayflower,
Distant, but still in sight, and sinking below the horizon,
Homeward together they walked, with a strange, indefinite
    feeling,
That all the rest had departed and left them alone in
    the desert.
But, as they went through the fields in the blessing
    and smile of the sunshine,
Lighter grew their hearts, and Priscilla said very archly:

"Now that our terrible Captain has gone in pursuit of
the Indians,
Where he is happier far than he would be commanding
a household,
You may speak boldly, and tell me of all that happened
between you,
When you returned last night, and said how ungrateful
you found me."
Thereupon answered John Alden, and told her the whole
of the story,—
Told her his own despair, and the direful wrath of
Miles Standish.
Whereat the maiden smiled, and said between laughing
and earnest,
"He is a little chimney, and heated hot in a moment!"
But as he gently rebuked her, and told her how he
had suffered,—
How he had even determined to sail that day in the
Mayflower,
And had remained for her sake, on hearing the dangers
that threatened,—
All her manner was changed, and she said with a
faltering accent,
"Truly I thank you for this: how good you have been
to me always!"

Thus, as a pilgrim devout, who toward Jerusalem
journeys,
Taking three steps in advance, and one reluctantly
backward,
Urged by importunate zeal, and withheld by pangs of
contrition;
Slowly but steadily onward, receding yet ever advancing,
Journeyed this Puritan youth to the Holy Land of his
longings,
Urged by the fervor of love, and withheld by remorseful
misgivings.

VII

THE MARCH OF MILES STANDISH

Meanwhile the stalwart Miles Standish was marching
    steadily northward,
Winding through forest and swamp, and along the trend
    of the seashore,
All day long, with hardly a halt, the fire of his anger
Burning and crackling within, and the sulphurous odor
    of powder
Seeming more sweet to his nostrils than all the scents
    of the forest.
Silent and moody he went, and much he revolved his
    discomfort;
He who was used to success, and to easy victories
    always,
Thus to be flouted, rejected, and laughed to scorn by
    a maiden,
Thus to be mocked and betrayed by the friend whom
    most he had trusted!
Ah! 't was too much to be borne, and he fretted and
    chafed in his armor!

"I alone am to blame," he muttered, "for mine was
    the folly.
What has a rough old soldier, grown grim and gray
    in the harness,
Used to the camp and its ways, to do with the wooing
    of maidens?
'T was but a dream,—let it pass,—let it vanish like
    so many others!
What I thought was a flower, is only a weed, and is
    worthless;
Out of my heart will I pluck it, and throw it away,
    and henceforward

Be but a fighter of battles, a lover and wooer of
    dangers!"
Thus he revolved in his mind his sorry defeat and
    discomfort,
While he was marching by day or lying at night in
    the forest,
Looking up at the trees, and the constellations beyond
    them.

   After a three days' march he came to an Indian
    encampment
Pitched on the edge of a meadow, between the sea
    and the forest;
Women at work by the tents, and warriors, horrid
    with war-paint,
Seated about a fire, and smoking and talking together;
Who, when they saw from afar the sudden approach
    of the white men,
Saw the flash of the sun on breastplate and sabre and
    musket,
Straightway leaped to their feet, and two, from among
    them advancing,
Came to parley with Standish, and offer him furs as
    a present;
Friendship was in their looks, but in their hearts there
    was hatred.
Braves of the tribe were these, and brothers, gigantic
    in stature,
Huge as Goliath of Gath, or the terrible Og, king of
    Bashan;*
One was Pecksuot named, and the other was called
    Wattawamat.
Round their necks were suspended their knives in
    scabbards of wampum,
Two-edged, trenchant knives, with points as sharp as
    a needle.

Other arms had they none, for they were cunning and
    crafty.
"Welcome, English!" they said,—these words they had
    learned from the traders
Touching at times on the coast, to barter and chaffer
    for peltries.
Then in their native tongue they began to parley with
    Standish,
Through his guide and interpreter, Hobomok, friend
    of the white man,
Begging for blankets and knives, but mostly for muskets
    and powder,
Kept by the white man, they said, concealed, with the
    plague, in his cellars,
Ready to be let loose, and destroy his brother the red
    man!
But when Standish refused, and said he would give
    them the Bible,
Suddenly changing their tone, they began to boast and
    to bluster.
Then Wattawamat advanced with a stride in front of
    the other,
And, with a lofty demeanor, thus vauntingly spake to
    the Captain:
"Now Wattawamat can see, by the fiery eyes of the
    Captain,
Angry is he in his heart; but the heart of the brave
    Wattawamat
Is not afraid at the sight. He was not born of a woman,
But on a mountain at night, from an oak-tree riven
    by lightning,
Forth he sprang at a bound, with all his weapons about
    him,
Shouting, 'Who is there here to fight with the brave
    Wattawamat?' "
Then he unsheathed his knife, and, whetting the blade
    on his left hand,

Held it aloft and displayed a woman's face on the
    handle;
Saying, with bitter expression and look of sinister
    meaning:
"I have another at home, with the face of a man on
    the handle;
By and by they shall marry; and there will be plenty
    of children!"

  Then stood Pecksuot forth, self-vaunting, insulting
    Miles Standish:
While with his fingers he patted the knife that hung
    at his bosom,
Drawing it half from its sheath, and plunging it back,
    as he muttered,
"By and by it shall see; it shall eat; ah, ha! but shall
    speak not!
This is the mighty Captain the white men have sent
    to destroy us!
He is a little man; let him go and work with the
    women!"

  Meanwhile Standish had noted the faces and figures
    of Indians
Peeping and creeping about from bush to tree in the
    forest,
Feigning to look for game, with arrows set on their
    bow-strings,
Drawing about him still closer and closer the net of
    their ambush.
But undaunted he stood, and dissembled and treated
    them smoothly;
So the old chronicles say, that were writ in the days
    of the fathers.
But when he heard their defiance, the boast, the taunt,
    and the insult,

All the hot blood of his race, of Sir Hugh and of
       Thurston de Standish,
Boiled and beat in his heart, and swelled in the veins
       of his temples.
Headlong he leaped on the boaster, and, snatching his
       knife from its scabbard,
Plunged it into his heart, and, reeling backward, the
       savage
Fell with his face to the sky, and a fiendlike fierceness
       upon it.
Straight there arose from the forest the awful sound
       of the war-whoop,
And, like a flurry of snow on the whistling wind of
       December,
Swift and sudden and keen came a flight of feathery
       arrows.
Then came a cloud of smoke, and out of the cloud
       came the lightning,
Out of the lightning thunder; and death unseen ran
       before it.
Frightened the savages fled for shelter in swamp and
       in thicket,
Hotly pursued and beset; but their sachem, the brave
       Wattawamat,
Fled not; he was dead. Unswerving and swift had a
       bullet
Passed through his brain, and he fell with both hands
       clutching the greensward,
Seeming in death to hold back from his foe the land
       of his fathers.

There on the flowers of the meadow the warriors
       lay, and above them,
Silent, with folded arms, stood Hobomok, friend of
       the white man.
Smiling at length he exclaimed to the stalwart Captain
       of Plymouth:

"Pecksuot bragged very loud, of his courage, his strength,
and his stature,—
Mocked the great Captain, and called him a little man;
but I see now
Big enough have you been to lay him speechless before
you!"

Thus the first battle was fought and won by the
stalwart Miles Standish.
When the tidings thereof were brought to the village
of Plymouth,
And as a trophy of war the head of the brave Wattawamat
Scowled from the roof of the fort, which at once was
a church and a fortress,
All who beheld it rejoiced, and praised the Lord, and
took courage.
Only Priscilla averted her face from this spectre of
terror,
Thanking God in her heart that she had not married
Miles Standish;
Shrinking, fearing almost, lest, coming home from his
battles,
He should lay claim to her hand, as the prize and
reward of his valor.

VIII

THE SPINNING-WHEEL

Month after month passed away, and in autumn the
ships of the merchants
Came with kindred and friends, with cattle and corn
for the Pilgrims.
All in the village was peace; the men were intent on
their labors,

Busy with hewing and building, with garden-plot and
    with merestead,
Busy with breaking the glebe, and mowing the grass
    in the meadows,
Searching the sea for its fish, and hunting the deer in
    the forest.
All in the village was peace; but at times the rumor
    of warfare
Filled the air with alarm, and the apprehension of danger.
Bravely the stalwart Standish was scouring the land
    with his forces,
Waxing valiant in fight and defeating the alien armies,
Till his name had become a sound of fear to the
    nations.
Anger was still in his heart, but at times the remorse
    and contrition
Which in all noble natures succeed the passionate outbreak,
Came like a rising tide, that encounters the rush of
    a river,
Staying its current awhile, but making it bitter and
    brackish.

   Meanwhile Alden at home had built him a new
    habitation,
Solid, substantial, of timber rough-hewn from the firs
    of the forest.
Wooden-barred was the door, and the roof was covered
    with rushes;
Latticed the windows were, and the window-panes were
    of paper,
Oiled to admit the light, while wind and rain were
    excluded.
There too he dug a well, and around it planted an
    orchard:
Still may be seen to this day some trace of the well
    and the orchard.

Close to the house was the stall, where, safe and secure
    from annoyance,
Raghorn, the snow-white bull, that had fallen to Alden's
    allotment
In the division of cattle, might ruminate in the nighttime;
Over the pastures he cropped, made fragrant by sweet
    pennyroyal.

Oft when his labor was finished, with eager feet
    would the dreamer
Follow the pathway that ran through the woods to the
    house of Priscilla,
Led by illusions romantic and subtile deceptions of
    fancy,
Pleasure disguised as duty, and love in the semblance
    of friendship.
Ever of her he thought, when he fashioned the walls
    of his dwelling;
Ever of her he thought, when he delved in the soil
    of his garden;
Ever of her he thought when he read in his Bible on
    Sunday
Praise of the virtuous woman, as she is described in
    the Proverbs,—
How the heart of her husband doth safely trust in her
    always,
How all the days of her life she will do him good,
    and not evil,
How she seeketh the wool and the flax and worketh
    with gladness,
How she layeth her hand to the spindle and holdeth
    the distaff,
How she is not afraid of the snow for herself or her
    household,
Knowing her household are clothed with the scarlet
    cloth of her weaving!

So as she sat at her wheel one afternoon in the
    autumn,
Alden, who opposite sat, and was watching her dexterous
    fingers,
As if the thread she was spinning were that of his life
    and his fortune,
After a pause in their talk, thus spake to the sound
    of the spindle.
"Truly, Priscilla," he said, "when I see you spinning
    and spinning,
Never idle a moment, but thrifty and thoughtful of
    others,
Suddenly you are transformed, are visibly changed in
    a moment;
You are no longer Priscilla, but Bertha the Beautiful
    Spinner."*
Here the light foot on the treadle grew swifter and
    swifter; the spindle
Uttered an angry snarl, and the thread snapped short
    in her fingers;
While the impetuous speaker, not heeding the mischief,
    continued:
"You are the beautiful Bertha, the spinner, the queen
    of Helvetia;
She whose story I read at a stall in the streets of
    Southampton,
Who, as she rode on her palfrey, o'er valley and meadow
    and mountain,
Ever was spinning her thread from a distaff fixed to
    her saddle.
She was so thrifty and good, that her name passed
    into a proverb.
So shall it be with your own, when the spinning-wheel
    shall no longer
Hum in the house of the farmer, and fill its chambers
    with music.

Then shall the mothers, reproving, relate how it was
    in their childhood,
Praising the good old times, and the days of Priscilla
    the spinner!"
Straight uprose from her wheel the beautiful Puritan
    maiden,
Pleased with the praise of her thrift from him whose
    praise was the sweetest,
Drew from the reel on the table a snowy skein of her
    spinning,
Thus making answer, meanwhile, to the flattering phrases
    of Alden:
"Come, you must not be idle; if I am a pattern for
    housewives,
Show yourself equally worthy of being the model of
    husbands.
Hold this skein on your hands, while I wind it, ready
    for knitting;
Then who knows but hereafter, when fashions have
    changed and the manners,
Fathers may talk to their sons of the good old times
    of John Alden!"
Thus, with a jest and a laugh, the skein on his hands
    she adjusted,
He sitting awkwardly there, with his arms extended
    before him,
She standing graceful, erect, and winding the thread
    from his fingers,
Sometimes chiding a little his clumsy manner of holding,
Sometimes touching his hands, as she disentangled expertly
Twist or knot in the yarn, unawares—for how could
    she help it?—
Sending electrical thrills through every nerve in his
    body.

  Lo! in the midst of this scene, a breathless messenger
    entered,

Bringing in hurry and heat the terrible news from the
    village.
Yes; Miles Standish was dead!—an Indian had brought
    them the tidings,—
Slain by a poisoned arrow, shot down in the front of
    the battle,
Into an ambush beguiled, cut off with the whole of
    his forces;
All the town would be burned, and all the people be
    murdered!
Such were the tidings of evil that burst on the hearts
    of the hearers.
Silent and statue-like stood Priscilla, her face looking
    backward
Still at the face of the speaker, her arms uplifted in
    horror;
But John Alden, upstarting, as if the barb of the arrow
Piercing the heart of his friend had struck his own,
    and had sundered
Once and forever the bonds that held him bound as
    a captive,
Wild with excess of sensation, the awful delight of his
    freedom,
Mingled with pain and regret, unconscious of what he
    was doing,
Clasped, almost with a groan, the motionless form of
    Priscilla,
Pressing her close to his heart, as forever his own,
    and exclaiming:
"Those whom the Lord hath united, let no man put
    them asunder!"

Even as rivulets twain, from distant and separate
    sources,
Seeing each other afar, as they leap from the rocks,
    and pursuing

Each one its devious path, but drawing nearer and
    nearer,
Rush together at last, at their trysting-place in the forest;
So these lives that had run thus far in separate channels,
Coming in sight of each other, then swerving and
    flowing asunder,
Parted by barriers strong, but drawing nearer and nearer,
Rushed together at last, and one was lost in the other.

IX

THE WEDDING-DAY

Forth from the curtain of clouds, from the tent of
    purple and scarlet,
Issued the sun, the great High Priest, in his garments
    resplendent,
Holiness unto the Lord, in letters of light, on his
    forehead,
Round the hem of his robe the golden bells and
    pomegranates.
Blessing the world he came, and the bars of vapor
    beneath him
Gleamed like a grate of brass, and the sea at his feet
    was a laver!

  This was the wedding-morn of Priscilla the Puritan
    maiden.
Friends were assembled together; the Elder and Magistrate
    also
Graced the scene with their presence, and stood like
    the Law and the Gospel,
One with the sanction of earth and one with the blessing
    of heaven.
Simple and brief was the wedding, as that of Ruth
    and of Boaz.*

Softly the youth and the maiden repeated the words
    of betrothal,
Taking each other for husband and wife in the Magistrate's
    presence,
After the Puritan way, and the laudable custom of
    Holland.
Fervently then, and devoutly, the excellent Elder of
    Plymouth
Prayed for the hearth and the home, that were founded
    that day in affection,
Speaking of life and of death, and imploring Divine
    benedictions.

  Lo! When the service was ended, a form appeared
    on the threshold,
Clad in armor of steel, a sombre and sorrowful figure!
Why does the bridegroom start and stare at the strange
    apparition?
Why does the bride turn pale, and hide her face on
    his shoulder?
Is it a phantom of air,—a bodiless, spectral illusion?
Is it a ghost from the grave, that has come to forbid
    the betrothal?
Long had it stood there unseen, a guest uninvited,
    unwelcomed;
Over its clouded eyes there had passed at times an
    expression
Softening the gloom and revealing the warm heart hidden
    beneath them,
As when across the sky the driving rack of the raincloud
Grows for a moment thin, and betrays the sun by its
    brightness.
Once it had lifted its hand, and moved its lips, but
    was silent,
As if an iron will had mastered the fleeting intention.
But when were ended the troth and the prayer and
    the last benediction,

Into the room it strode, and the people beheld with
    amazement
Bodily there in his armor Miles Standish, the Captain
    of Plymouth!
Grasping the bridegroom's hand, he said with emotion,
    "Forgive me!
I have been angry and hurt,—too long have I cherished
    the feeling;
I have been cruel and hard, but now, thank God! it
    is ended.
Mine is the same hot blood that leaped in the veins
    of Hugh Standish,
Sensitive, swift to resent, but as swift in atoning for
    error.
Never so much as now was Miles Standish the friend
    of John Alden."
Thereupon answered the bridegroom: "Let all be forgotten
    between us,—
All save the dear, old friendship, and that shall grow
    older and dearer!"
Then the Captain advanced, and, bowing, saluted Priscilla,
Gravely, and after the manner of old-fashioned gentry
    in England,
Something of camp and of court, of town and of
    country, commingled,
Wishing her joy of her wedding, and loudly lauding
    her husband.
Then he said with a smile: "I should have remembered
    the adage,
If you would be well served, you must serve yourself;
    and moreover,
No man can gather cherries in Kent at the season of
    Christmas!"

Great was the people's amazement, and greater yet
    their rejoicing,

Thus to behold once more the sunburnt face of their
    Captain,
Whom they had mourned as dead; and they gathered
    and crowded about him,
Eager to see him and hear him, forgetful of bride and
    of bridegroom,
Questioning, answering, laughing, and each interrupting
    the other,
Till the good Captain declared, being quite overpowered
    and bewildered,
He had rather by far break into an Indian encampment,
Than come again to a wedding to which he had not
    been invited.

  Meanwhile the bridegroom went forth and stood with
    the bride at the doorway,
Breathing the perfumed air of that warm and beautiful
    morning.
Touched with autumnal tints, but lonely and sad in
    the sunshine,
Lay extended before them the land of toil and privation;
There were the graves of the dead, and the barren
    waste of the seashore,
There the familiar fields, the groves of pine, and the
    meadows;
But to their eyes transfigured, it seemed as the Garden
    of Eden,
Filled with the presence of God, whose voice was the
    sound of the ocean.

  Soon was their vision disturbed by the noise and stir
    of departure,
Friends coming forth from the house, and impatient of
    longer delaying,
Each with his plan for the day, and the work that
    was left uncompleted,

Then, from a stall near at hand, amid exclamations of
    wonder,
Alden the thoughtful, the careful, so happy, so proud
    of Priscilla,
Brought out his snow-white bull, obeying the hand of
    its master,
Led by a cord that was tied to an iron ring in its
    nostrils,
Covered with crimson cloth, and a cushion placed for
    a saddle.
She should not walk, he said, through the dust and
    heat of the noonday;
Nay, she should ride like a queen, not plod along like
    a peasant.
Somewhat alarmed at first, but reassured by the others,
Placing her hand on the cushion, her foot in the hand
    of her husband,
Gayly, with joyous laugh, Priscilla mounted her palfrey.
"Nothing is wanting now," he said with a smile, "but
    the distaff;
Then you would be in truth my queen, my beautiful
    Bertha!"

  Onward the bridal procession now moved to their
    new habitation,
Happy husband and wife, and friends conversing together.
Pleasantly murmured the brook, as they crossed the
    ford in the forest,
Pleased with the image that passed, like a dream of
    love through its bosom,
Tremulous, floating in air, o'er the depths of the azure
    abysses.
Down through the golden leaves the sun was pouring
    his splendors,
Gleaming on purple grapes, that, from branches above
    them suspended,

Mingled their odorous breath with the balm of the pine
      and the fir-tree,
Wild and sweet as the clusters that grew in the valley
      of Eshcol.*
Like a picture it seemed of the primitive, pastoral ages,
Fresh with the youth of the world, and recalling Rebecca
      and Isaac,*
Old and yet ever new, and simple and beautiful always,
Love immortal and young in the endless succession of
      lovers.
So through the Plymouth woods passed onward the
      bridal procession.

FROM TALES OF A WAYSIDE INN*

THE LANDLORD'S TALE

PAUL REVERE'S RIDE*

Listen, my children, and you shall hear
Of the midnight ride of Paul Revere,
On the eighteenth of April, in Seventy-five;
Hardly a man is now alive
Who remembers that famous day and year.

He said to his friend, "If the British march
By land or sea from the town to-night,
Hang a lantern aloft in the belfry arch
Of the North Church tower as a signal light,—
One, if by land, and two, if by sea;
And I on the opposite shore will be,
Ready to ride and spread the alarm
Through every Middlesex village and farm,
For the country folk to be up and to arm"
Then he said, "Good-night!" and with muffled oar
Silently rowed to the Charlestown shore,
Just as the moon rose over the bay,
Where swinging wide at her moorings lay
The Somerset, British man-of-war;
A phantom ship, with each mast and spar
Across the moon like a prison bar,
And a huge black hulk, that was magnified
By its own reflection in the tide.

Meanwhile, his friend, through alley and street,
Wanders and watches with eager ears,
Till in the silence around him he hears
The muster of men at the barrack door,
The sound of arms, and the tramp of feet,
And the measured tread of the grenadiers,
Marching down to their boats on the shore.

Then he climbed the tower of the Old North Church,
By the wooden stairs, with stealthy tread,
To the belfry-chamber overhead,
And startled the pigeons from their perch
On the sombre rafters, that round him made
Masses and moving shapes of shade,—
By the trembling ladder, steep and tall,
To the highest window in the wall,
Where he paused to listen and look down
A moment on the roofs of the town,
And the moonlight flowing over all.
Beneath, in the churchyard, lay the dead,
In their night-encampment on the hill,
Wrapped in silence so deep and still
That he could hear, like a sentinel's tread,
The watchful night-wind, as it went
Creeping along from tent to tent,
And seeming to whisper, "All is well!"
A moment only he feels the spell
Of the place and the hour, and the secret dread
Of the lonely belfry and the dead;
For suddenly all his thoughts are bent
On a shadowy something far away,
Where the river widens to meet the bay,—
A line of black that bends and floats
On the rising tide, like a bridge of boats.

Meanwhile, impatient to mount and ride,
Booted and spurred, with a heavy stride

On the opposite shore walked Paul Revere.
Now he patted his horse's side,
Now gazed at the landscape far and near,
Then, impetuous, stamped the earth,
And turned and tightened his saddle-girth;
But mostly he watched with eager search
The belfry-tower of the Old North Church,
As it rose above the graves on the hill,
Lonely and spectral and sombre and still.
And lo! as he looks, on the belfry's height
A glimmer, and then a gleam of light!
He springs to the saddle, the bridle he turns,
But lingers and gazes, till full on his sight
A second lamp in the belfry burns!
A hurry of hoofs in a village street,
A shape in the moonlight, a bulk in the dark,
And beneath, from the pebbles, in passing, a spark
Struck out by a steed flying fearless and fleet:
That was all! And yet, through the gloom and the
      light,
The fate of a nation was riding that night;
And the spark struck out by that steed, in his flight,
Kindled the land into flame with its heat.
He has left the village and mounted the steep,
And beneath him, tranquil and broad and deep,
Is the Mystic, meeting the ocean tides;
And under the alders, that skirt its edge,
Now soft on the sand, now loud on the ledge,
Is heard the tramp of his steed as he rides.

It was twelve by the village clock,
When he crossed the bridge into Medford town.
He heard the crowing of the cock,
And the barking of the farmer's dog,
And felt the damp of the river fog,
That rises after the sun goes down.

It was one by the village clock,
When he galloped into Lexington.
He saw the gilded weathercock
Swim in the moonlight as he passed,
And the meeting-house windows, blank and bare,
Gaze at him with a spectral glare,
As if they already stood aghast
At the bloody work they would look upon.

It was two by the village clock,
When he came to the bridge in Concord town.
He heard the bleating of the flock,
And the twitter of birds among the trees,
And felt the breath of the morning breeze
Blowing over the meadows brown.
And one was safe and asleep in his bed
Who at the bridge would be first to fall,
Who that day would be lying dead,
Pierced by a British musket-ball.

You know the rest. In the books you have read,
How the British Regulars fired and fled,—
How the farmers gave them ball for ball,
From behind each fence and farm-yard wall,
Chasing the red-coats down the lane,
Then crossing the fields to emerge again
Under the trees at the turn of the road,
And only pausing to fire and load.

So through the night rode Paul Revere;
And so through the night went his cry of alarm
To every Middlesex village and farm,—
A cry of defiance and not of fear,
A voice in the darkness, a knock at the door,
And a word that shall echo forevermore!
For, borne on the night-wind of the Past,
Through all our history, to the last,

In the hour of darkness and peril and need,
The people will waken and listen to hear
The hurrying hoof-beats of that steed,
And the midnight message of Paul Revere.

THE THEOLOGIAN'S TALE

TORQUEMADA*

In the heroic days when Ferdinand
And Isabella ruled the Spanish land,
And Torquemada, with his subtle brain,
Ruled them, as Grand Inquisitor of Spain,
In a great castle near Valladolid,
Moated and high and by fair woodlands hid,
There dwelt, as from the chronicles we learn,
An old Hidalgo proud and taciturn,
Whose name has perished, with his towers of stone,
And all his actions save this one alone;
This one, so terrible, perhaps 't were best
If it, too, were forgotten with the rest;
Unless, perchance, our eyes can see therein
The martyrdom triumphant o'er the sin;
A double picture, with its gloom and glow,
The splendor overhead, the death below.

This sombre man counted each day as lost
On which his feet no sacred threshold crossed;
And when he chanced the passing Host to meet,
He knelt and prayed devoutly in the street;
Oft he confessed; and with each mutinous thought,
As with wild beasts at Ephesus, he fought.
In deep contrition scourged himself in Lent,
Walked in processions, with his head down bent,
At plays of Corpus Christi oft was seen,

And on Palm Sunday bore his bough of green.
His sole diversion was to hunt the boar
Through tangled thickets of the forest hoar,
Or with his jingling mules to hurry down
To some grand bull-fight in the neighboring town,
Or in the crowd with lighted taper stand,
When Jews were burned, or banished from the land.
Then stirred within him a tumultuous joy;
The demon whose delight is to destroy
Shook him, and shouted with a trumpet tone,
"Kill! kill! and let the Lord find out his own!"

And now, in that old castle in the wood,
His daughters, in the dawn of womanhood,
Returning from their convent school, had made
Resplendent with their bloom the forest shade,
Reminding him of their dead mother's face,
When first she came into that gloomy place,—
A memory in his heart as dim and sweet
As moonlight in a solitary street,
Where the same rays, that lift the sea, are thrown
Lovely but powerless upon walls of stone.
These two fair daughters of a mother dead
Were all the dream had left him as it fled.
A joy at first, and then a growing care,
As if a voice within him cried, "Beware!"
A vague presentiment of impending doom,
Like ghostly footsteps in a vacant room,
Haunted him day and night; a formless fear
That death to some one of his house was near,
With dark surmises of a hidden crime,
Made life itself a death before its time.
Jealous, suspicious, with no sense of shame,
A spy upon his daughters he became;
With velvet slippers, noiseless on the floors,
He glided softly through half-open doors;
Now in the room, and now upon the stair,

He stood beside them ere they were aware;
He listened in the passage when they talked,
He watched them from the casement when they walked,
He saw the gypsy haunt the river's side,
He saw the monk among the cork-trees glide;
And, tortured by the mystery and the doubt
Of some dark secret, past his finding out,
Baffled he paused; then reassured again
Pursued the flying phantom of his brain.
He watched them even when they knelt in church;
And then, descending lower in his search,
Questioned the servants, and with eager eyes
Listened incredulous to their replies;
The gypsy? none had seen her in the wood!
The monk? a mendicant in search of food!

At length the awful revelation came,
Crushing at once his pride of birth and name;
The hopes his yearning bosom forward cast
And the ancestral glories of the past,
All fell together, crumbling in disgrace,
A turret rent from battlement to base.
His daughters talking in the dead of night
In their own chamber, and without a light,
Listening, as he was wont, he overheard,
And learned the dreadful secret, word by word;
And hurrying from his castle, with a cry
He raised his hands to the unpitying sky,
Repeating one dread word, till bush and tree
Caught it, and shuddering answered, "Heresy!"

Wrapped in his cloak, his hat drawn o'er his face,
Now hurrying forward, now with lingering pace,
He walked all night the alleys of his park,
With one unseen companion in the dark,
The demon who within him lay in wait
And by his presence turned his love to hate,

Forever muttering in an undertone,
"Kill! kill! and let the Lord find out his own!"

Upon the morrow, after early Mass,
While yet the dew was glistening on the grass,
And all the woods were musical with birds,
The old Hidalgo, uttering fearful words,
Walked homeward with the Priest, and in his room
Summoned his trembling daughters to their doom.
When questioned, with brief answers they replied,
Nor when accused evaded or denied;
Expostulations, passionate appeals,
All that the human heart most fears or feels,
In vain the Priest with earnest voice essayed;
In vain the father threatened, wept, and prayed;
Until at last he said, with haughty mien,
"The Holy Office, then, must intervene!"

And now the Grand Inquisitor of Spain,
With all the fifty horsemen of his train,
His awful name resounding, like the blast
Of funeral trumpets, as he onward passed,
Came to Valladolid, and there began
To harry the rich Jews with fire and ban.
To him the Hidalgo went, and at the gate
Demanded audience on affairs of state,
And in a secret chamber stood before
A venerable graybeard of fourscore,
Dressed in the hood and habit of a friar;
Out of his eyes flashed a consuming fire,
And in his hand the mystic horn he held,
Which poison and all noxious charms dispelled.
He heard in silence the Hidalgo's tale,
Then answered in a voice that made him quail:
"Son of the Church! when Abraham of old
To sacrifice his only son was told,
He did not pause to parley nor protest,

But hastened to obey the Lord's behest.
In him it was accounted righteousness;
The Holy Church expects of thee no less!"

A sacred frenzy seized the father's brain,
And Mercy from that hour implored in vain.
Ah! who will e'er believe the words I say?
His daughters he accused, and the same day
They both were cast into the dungeon's gloom,
That dismal antechamber of the tomb,
Arraigned, condemned, and sentenced to the flame,
The secret torture and the public shame.

Then to the Grand Inquisitor once more
The Hidalgo went more eager than before,
And said: "When Abraham offered up his son,
He clave the wood wherewith it might be done.
By his example taught, let me too bring
Wood from the forest for my offering!"
And the deep voice, without a pause, replied:
"Son of the Church! by faith now justified,
Complete thy sacrifice, even as thou wilt;
The Church absolves thy conscience from all guilt!"

Then this most wretched father went his way
Into the woods, that round his castle lay,
Where once his daughters in their childhood played
With their young mother in the sun and shade.
Now all the leaves had fallen; the branches bare
Made a perpetual moaning in the air,
And screaming from their eyries overhead
The ravens sailed athwart the sky of lead.
With his own hands he lopped the boughs and bound
Fagots, that crackled with foreboding sound,
And on his mules, caparisoned and gay
With bells and tassels, sent them on their way.

Then with his mind on one dark purpose bent,
Again to the Inquisitor he went,
And said: "Behold, the fagots I have brought,
And now, lest my atonement be as naught,
Grant me one more request, one last desire,—
With my own hand to light the funeral fire!"
And Torquemada answered from his seat,
"Son of the Church! Thine offering is complete;
Her servants through all ages shall not cease
To magnify thy deed. Depart in peace!"

Upon the market-place, builded of stone
The scaffold rose, whereon Death claimed his own.
At the four corners, in stern attitude,
Four statues of the Hebrew Prophets stood,
Gazing with calm indifference in their eyes
Upon this place of human sacrifice,
Round which was gathering fast the eager crowd,
With clamor of voices dissonant and loud,
And every roof and window was alive
With restless gazers, swarming like a hive.

The church-bells tolled, the chant of monks drew near,
Loud trumpets stammered forth their notes of fear,
A line of torches smoked along the street,
There was a stir, a rush, a tramp of feet,
And, with its banners floating in the air,
Slowly the long procession crossed the square,
And, to the statues of the Prophets bound,
The victims stood, with fagots piled around.
Then all the air a blast of trumpets shook,
And louder sang the monks with bell and book,
And the Hidalgo, lofty, stern, and proud,
Lifted his torch, and, bursting through the crowd,
Lighted in haste the fagots, and then fled,
Lest those imploring eyes should strike him dead!
O pitiless skies! why did your clouds retain

For peasants' fields their floods of hoarded rain?
O pitiless earth! why open no abyss
To bury in its chasm a crime like this?

That night, a mingled column of fire and smoke
From the dark thickets of the forest broke,
And, glaring o'er the landscape leagues away,
Made all the fields and hamlets bright as day.
Wrapped in a sheet of flame the castle blazed,
And as the villagers in terror gazed,
They saw the figure of that cruel knight
Lean from a window in the turret's height,
His ghastly face illumined with the glare,
His hands upraised above his head in prayer,
Till the floor sank beneath him, and he fell
Down the black hollow of that burning well.

Three centuries and more above his bones
Have piled the oblivious years like funeral stones;
His name has perished with him, and no trace
Remains on earth of his afflicted race;
But Torquemada's name, with clouds o'ercast,
Looms in the distant landscape of the Past,
Like a burnt tower upon a blackened heath,
Lit by the fires of burning woods beneath!

THE POET'S TALE

THE BIRDS OF KILLINGWORTH*

It was the season, when through all the land
  The merle and mavis build, and building sing
Those lovely lyrics, written by His hand,
  Whom Saxon Caedmon calls the Blithe-heart King;*
When on the boughs the purple buds expand,

The banners of the vanguard of the Spring,
And rivulets, rejoicing, rush and leap,
And wave their fluttering signals from the steep.

The robin and the bluebird, piping loud,
  Filled all the blossoming orchards with their glee;
The sparrows chirped as if they still were proud
  Their race in Holy Writ should mentioned be;
And hungry crows, assembled in a crowd,
  Clamored their piteous prayer incessantly,
Knowing who hears the ravens cry, and said:
"Give us, O Lord, this day, our daily bread!"

Across the Sound the birds of passage sailed,
  Speaking some unknown language strange and sweet
Of tropic isle remote, and passing hailed
  The village with the cheers of all their fleet;
Or quarrelling together, laughed and railed
  Like foreign sailors, landed in the street
Of seaport town, and with outlandish noise
Of oaths and gibberish frightening girls and boys.

Thus came the jocund Spring in Killingworth,
  In fabulous days, some hundred years ago;
And thrifty farmers, as they tilled the earth,
  Heard with alarm the cawing of the crow,
That mingled with the universal mirth,
  Cassandra-like, prognosticating woe;*
They shook their heads, and doomed with dreadful
        words
To swift destruction the whole race of birds.

And a town-meeting was convened straightway
  To set a price upon the guilty heads
Of these marauders, who, in lieu of pay,
  Levied blackmail upon the garden-beds
And cornfields, and beheld without dismay

The awful scarecrow, with his fluttering shreds;
The skeleton that waited at their feast,
Whereby their sinful pleasure was increased.

Then from his house, a temple painted white,
   With fluted columns, and a roof of red,
The Squire came forth, august and splendid sight!
   Slowly descending, with majestic tread,
Three flights of steps, nor looking left nor right,
   Down the long street he walked, as one who said,
"A town that boasts inhabitants like me
Can have no lack of good society!"

The Parson, too, appeared, a man austere,
   The instinct of whose nature was to kill;
The wrath of God he preached from year to year,
   And read, with fervor, Edwards on the Will;*
His favorite pastime was to slay the deer
   In Summer on some Adirondac hill;
E'en now, while walking down the rural lane,
He lopped the wayside lilies with his cane.

From the Academy, whose belfry crowned
   The hill of Science with its vane of brass,
Came the Preceptor, gazing idly round,
   Now at the clouds, and now at the green grass,
And all absorbed in reveries profound
   Of fair Almira in the upper class,
Who was, as in a sonnet he had said,
As pure as water, and as good as bread.

And next the Deacon issued from his door,
   In his voluminous neck-cloth, white as snow;
A suit of sable bombazine he wore;
   His form was ponderous, and his step was slow;
There never was so wise a man before;
   He seemed the incarnate "Well, I told you so!"

And to perpetuate his great renown
There was a street named after him in town.

These came together in the new town-hall,
  With sundry farmers from the region round.
The Squire presided, dignified and tall,
  His air impressive and his reasoning sound;
Ill fared it with the birds, both great and small;
  Hardly a friend in all that crowd they found,
But enemies enough, who every one
Charged them with all the crimes beneath the sun.

When they had ended, from his place apart
  Rose the Preceptor, to redress the wrong,
And, trembling like a steed before the start,
  Looked round bewildered on the expectant throng;
Then thought of fair Almira, and took heart
  To speak out what was in him, clear and strong,
Alike regardless of their smile or frown,
And quite determined not to be laughed down.

"Plato, anticipating the Reviewers,
  From his Republic banished without pity
The Poets; in this little town of yours,
  You put to death, by means of a Committee,
The ballad-singers and the Troubadours,
  The street-musicians of the heavenly city,
The birds, who make sweet music for us all
In our dark hours, as David did for Saul.*

"The thrush that carols at the dawn of day
  From the green steeples of the piny wood;
The oriole in the elm; the noisy jay,
  Jargoning like a foreigner at his food;
The bluebird balanced on some topmost spray,
  Flooding with melody the neighborhood;

Linnet and meadow-lark, and all the throng
That dwell in nests, and have the gift of song.

"You slay them all! and wherefore? for the gain
   Of a scant handful more or less of wheat,
Or rye, or barley, or some other grain,
   Scratched up at random by industrious feet,
Searching for worm or weevil after rain!
   Or a few cherries, that are not so sweet
As are the songs these uninvited guests
Sing at their feast with comfortable breasts.

"Do you ne'er think what wondrous beings these?
   Do you ne'er think who made them, and who taught
The dialect they speak, where melodies
   Alone are the interpreters of thought?
Whose household words are songs in many keys,
   Sweeter than instrument of man e'er caught!
Whose habitations in the tree-tops even
Are halfway houses on the road to heaven!

"Think, every morning when the sun peeps through
   The dim, leaf-latticed windows of the grove,
How jubilant the happy birds renew
   Their old, melodious madrigals of love!
And when you think of this, remember too
   'T is always morning somewhere, and above
The awakening continents, from shore to shore,
Somewhere the birds are singing evermore.

"Think of your woods and orchards without birds!
   Of empty nests that cling to boughs and beams
As in an idiot's brain remembered words
   Hang empty 'mid the cobwebs of his dreams!
Will bleat of flocks or bellowing of herds
   Make up for the lost music, when your teams

Drag home the stingy harvest, and no more
The feathered gleaners follow to your door?

"What! would you rather see the incessant stir
  Of insects in the windrows of the hay,
And hear the locust and the grasshopper
  Their melancholy hurdy-gurdies play?
Is this more pleasant to you than the whirr
  Of meadow-lark, and her sweet roundelay,
Or twitter of little field-fares, as you take
Your nooning in the shade of bush and brake?

"You call them thieves and pillagers; but know,
  They are the winged wardens of your farms,
Who from the cornfields drive the insidious foe,
  And from your harvests keep a hundred harms;
Even the blackest of them all, the crow,
  Renders good service as your man-at-arms,
Crushing the beetle in his coat of mail,
And crying havoc on the slug and snail.

"How can I teach your children gentleness,
  And mercy to the weak, and reverence
For Life, which, in its weakness or excess,
  Is still a gleam of God's omnipotence,
Or Death, which, seeming darkness, is no less
  The selfsame light, although averted hence,
When by your laws, your actions, and your speech,
You contradict the very things I teach?"

With this he closed; and through the audience went
  A murmur, like the rustle of dead leaves;
The farmers laughed and nodded, and some bent
  Their yellow heads together like their sheaves;
Men have no faith in fine-spun sentiment
  Who put their trust in bullocks and in beeves.

THE BIRDS OF KILLINGWORTH

The birds were doomed; and, as the record shows,
A bounty offered for the heads of crows.

There was another audience out of reach,
  Who had no voice nor vote in making laws,
But in the papers read his little speech,
  And crowned his modest temples with applause;
They made him conscious, each one more than each,
  He still was victor, vanquished in their cause.
Sweetest of all the applause he won from thee,
O fair Almira at the Academy!

And so the dreadful massacre began;
  O'er fields and orchards, and o'er woodland crests,
The ceaseless fusillade of terror ran.
  Dead fell the birds, with blood-stains on their breasts,
Or wounded crept away from sight of man,
  While the young died of famine in their nests;
A slaughter to be told in groans, not words,
The very Saint Bartholomew of Birds!*

The Summer came, and all the birds were dead;
  The days were like hot coals; the very ground
Was burned to ashes; in the orchards fed
  Myriads of caterpillars, and around
The cultivated fields and garden-beds
  Hosts of devouring insects crawled, and found
No foe to check their march, till they had made
The land a desert without leaf or shade.

Devoured by worms, like Herod, was the town,*
  Because, like Herod, it had ruthlessly
Slaughtered the Innocents. From the trees spun down
  The canker-worms upon the passers-by,
Upon each woman's bonnet, shawl, and gown,
  Who shook them off with just a little cry;

They were the terror of each favorite walk,
The endless theme of all the village talk.

The farmers grew impatient, but a few
  Confessed their error, and would not complain,
For after all, the best thing one can do
  When it is raining, is to let it rain.
Then they repealed the law, although they knew
  It would not call the dead to life again;
As school-boys, finding their mistake too late,
Draw a wet sponge across the accusing slate.

That year in Killingworth the Autumn came
  Without the light of his majestic look,
The wonder of the falling tongues of flame,
  The illumined pages of his doomsday book.
A few lost leaves blushed crimson with their shame,
  And drowned themselves despairing in the brook,
While the wild wind went moaning everywhere,
Lamenting the dead children of the air!

But the next Spring a stranger sight was seen,
  A sight that never yet by bard was sung,
As great a wonder as it would have been
  If some dumb animal had found a tongue!
A wagon, overarched with evergreen,
  Upon whose boughs were wicker cages hung,
All full of singing birds, came down the street,
Filling the air with music wild and sweet.

From all the country round these birds were brought,
  By order of the town, with anxious quest,
And, loosened from their wicker prisons, sought
  In woods and fields the places they loved best,
Singing loud canticles, which many thought
  Were satires to the authorities addressed,

While others, listening in green lanes, averred
Such lovely music never had been heard!

But blither still and louder carolled they
  Upon the morrow, for they seemed to know
It was the fair Almira's wedding-day,
  And everywhere, around, above, below,
When the Preceptor bore his bride away,
  Their songs burst forth in joyous overflow,
And a new heaven bent over a new earth
Amid the sunny farms of Killingworth.

THE NEW ENGLAND TRAGEDIES*

I. JOHN ENDICOTT*

DRAMATIS PERSONAE

JOHN ENDICOTT	*Governor.*
JOHN ENDICOTT	*His son.*
RICHARD BELLINGHAM	*Deputy Governor.*
JOHN NORTON	*Minister of the Gospel.*
EDWARD BUTTER	*Treasurer.*
WALTER MERRY	*Tithing-man.*
NICHOLAS UPSALL	*An old citizen.*
SAMUEL COLE	*Landlord of the Three Mariners.*

SIMON KEMPTHORN
RALPH GOLDSMITH } *Sea-Captains.*

WENLOCK CHRISTISON
EDITH, *his daughter* } *Quakers.*
EDWARD WHARTON

Assistants, Halberdiers, Marshal, etc.

The Scene is in Boston in the year 1665.

PROLOGUE

TO-NIGHT we strive to read, as we may best,
This city, like an ancient palimpsest;
And bring to light, upon the blotted page,
The mournful record of an earlier age,
That, pale and half effaced, lies hidden away
Beneath the fresher writing of to-day.

Rise, then, O buried city that hast been;
Rise up, rebuilded in the painted scene,
And let our curious eyes behold once more
The pointed gable and the pent-house door,
The Meeting-house with leaden-latticed panes,
The narrow thoroughfares, the crooked lanes!

Rise, too, ye shapes and shadows of the Past,
Rise from your long-forgotten graves at last;
Let us behold your faces, let us hear
The words ye uttered in those days of fear!
Revisit your familiar haunts again,—
The scenes of triumph, and the scenes of pain,
And leave the footprints of your bleeding feet
Once more upon the pavement of the street!

Nor let the Historian blame the Poet here,
If he perchance misdate the day or year,
And group events together, by his art,
That in the Chronicles lie far apart;
For as the double stars, though sundered far,
Seem to the naked eye a single star,
So facts of history, at a distance seen,
Into one common point of light convene.

"Why touch upon such themes?" perhaps some friend
May ask, incredulous; "and to what good end?
Why drag again into the light of day
The errors of an age long passed away?"
I answer: "For the lesson that they teach:
The tolerance of opinion and of speech.
Hope, Faith, and Charity remain,—these three;
And greatest of them all is Charity."*

Let us remember, if these words be true,
That unto all men Charity is due;
Give what we ask; and pity, while we blame,

Lest we become copartners in the shame,
Lest we condemn, and yet ourselves partake,
And persecute the dead for conscience' sake.

Therefore it is the author seeks and strives
To represent the dead as in their lives,
And lets at times his characters unfold
Their thoughts in their own language, strong and bold;
He only asks of you to do the like;
To hear him first, and, if you will, then strike.

ACT I

SCENE I.—*Sunday afternoon. The interior of the Meeting-
house. On the pulpit, an hour-glass; below, a box for
contributions.* JOHN NORTON *in the pulpit.* GOVERNOR
ENDICOTT *in a canopied seat, attended by four halberdiers.
The congregation singing.*

> The Lord descended from above,
>   And bowed the heaven high;
> And underneath his feet He cast
>   The darkness of the sky.

> On Cherubim and Seraphim
>   Right royally He rode,
> And on the wings of mighty winds
>   Came flying all abroad.

NORTON (*rising and turning the hour-glass on the pulpit*)
I heard a great voice from the temple saying
Unto the Seven Angels, Go your ways;
Pour out the vials of the wrath of God
Upon the earth. And the First Angel went
And poured his vial on the earth; and straight

There fell a noisome and a grievous sore
On them which had the birth-mark of the Beast,
And them which worshipped and adored his image.*
On us hath fallen this grievous pestilence.
There is a sense of terror in the air;
And apparitions of things horrible
Are seen by many. From the sky above us
The stars fall; and beneath us the earth quakes!
The sound of drums at midnight from afar,
The sound of horsemen riding to and fro,
As if the gates of the invisible world
Were opened, and the dead came forth to warn us,—
All these are omens of some dire disaster
Impending over us, and soon to fall.
Moreover, in the language of the Prophet,
Death is again come up into our windows,
To cut off little children from without,
And young men from the streets, And in the midst
Of all these supernatural threats and warnings
Doth Heresy uplift its horrid head;
A vision of Sin more awful and appalling
Than any phantasm, ghost, or apparition,
As arguing and portending some enlargement
Of the mysterious Power of Darkness!

EDITH *barefooted, and clad in sackcloth, with her hair hanging
loose upon her shoulders, walks slowly up the aisle, followed
by* WHARTON *and other Quakers. The congregation starts
up in confusion.*

EDITH (*to* NORTON, *raising her hand*)

Peace!

NORTON

Anathema maranatha! The Lord cometh!

EDITH

Yea, verily He cometh, and shall judge
The shepherds of Israel who do feed themselves,
And leave their flocks to eat what they have trodden
Beneath their feet.

NORTON

Be silent, babbling woman!
Saint Paul commands all women to keep silence
Within the churches.

EDITH

Yet the women prayed
And prophesied at Corinth in his day;
And, among those on whom the fiery tongues
Of Pentecost descended, some were women!

NORTON

The Elders of the Churches, by our law,
Alone have power to open the doors of speech
And silence in the Assembly. I command you!

EDITH

The law of God is greater than your laws!
Ye build your church with blood, your town with
        crime;
The heads thereof give judgment for reward;
The priests thereof teach only for their hire;
Your laws condemn the innocent to death;
And against this I bear my testimony!

NORTON

What testimony?

EDITH

That of the Holy Spirit,
Which, as your Calvin says, surpasseth reason.

NORTON

The laborer is worthy of his hire.

EDITH

Yet our great Master did not teach for hire,
And the Apostles without purse or scrip
Went forth to do his work. Behold this box
Beneath thy pulpit. Is it for the poor?
Thou canst not answer. It is for the Priest;
And against this I bear my testimony.

NORTON

Away with all these Heretics and Quakers!
Quakers, forsooth! Because a quaking fell
On Daniel, at beholding of the Vision,
Must ye needs shake and quake? Because Isaiah
Went stripped and barefoot, must ye wail and howl?
Must ye go stripped and naked? must ye make*
A wailing like the dragons, and a mourning
As of the owls? Ye verify the adage
That Satan is God's ape! Away with them!

> *Tumult. The Quakers are driven out with violence,*
> EDITH *following slowly. The congregation retires in*
> *confusion.*

Thus freely do the Reprobates commit
Such measure of iniquity as fits them
For the intended measure of God's wrath,
And even in violating God's commands
Are they fulfilling the divine decree!
The will of man is but an instrument
Disposed and predetermined to its action
According unto the decree of God,

Being as much subordinate thereto
As is the axe unto the hewer's hand!
> *He descends from the pulpit, and joins* GOVERNOR
> ENDICOTT, *who comes forward to meet him.*

The omens and the wonders of the time,
Famine, and fire, and shipwreck, and disease,
The blast of corn, the death of our young men,
Our sufferings in all precious, pleasant things,
Are manifestations of the wrath divine,
Signs of God's controversy with New England.
These emissaries of the Evil One,
These servants and ambassadors of Satan,
Are but commissioned executioners
Of God's vindictive and deserved displeasure.
We must receive them as the Roman Bishop
Once received Attila, saying, I rejoice
You have come safe, whom I esteem to be
The scourge of God, sent to chastise his people.*
This very heresy, perchance, may serve
The purposes of God to some good end.
With you I leave it; but do not neglect
The holy tactics of the civil sword.

ENDICOTT

And what more can be done?

NORTON

The hand that cut
The Red Cross from the colors of the king*
Can cut the red heart from this heresy.
Fear not. All blasphemies immediate
And heresies turbulent must be suppressed
By civil power.

ENDICOTT

But in what way suppressed?

JOHN ENDICOTT

NORTON

The Book of Deuteronomy declares
That if thy son, thy daughter, or thy wife,
Ay, or the friend which is as thine own soul,
Entice thee secretly, and say to thee,
Let us serve other gods, then shall thine eye
Not pity him, but thou shalt surely kill him,
And thine own hand shall be the first upon him
To slay him.

ENDICOTT

Four already have been slain;
And others banished upon pain of death.
But they come back again to meet their doom,
Bringing the linen for their winding-sheets.
We must not go too far. In truth, I shrink
From shedding of more blood. The people murmur
At our severity.

NORTON

Then let them murmur!
Truth is relentless; justice never wavers;
The greatest firmness is the greatest mercy;
The noble order of the Magistracy
Cometh immediately from God, and yet
This noble order of the Magistracy
Is by these Heretics despised and outraged.

ENDICOTT

To-night they sleep in prison. If they die,
They cannot say that we have caused their death.
We do but guard the passage, with the sword
Pointed towards them; if they dash upon it,
Their blood will be on their own heads, not ours.

NORTON

Enough. I ask no more. My predecessor
Coped only with the milder heresies
Of Antinomians and of Anabaptists.
He was not born to wrestle with these fiends.
Chrysostom in his pulpit; Augustine
In disputation; Timothy in his house!
The lantern of Saint Botolph's ceased to burn*
When from the portals of that church he came
To be a burning and a shining light
Here in the wilderness. And, as he lay
On his death-bed, he saw me in a vision
Ride on a snow-white horse into this town.
His vision was prophetic; thus I came,
A terror to the impenitent, and Death
On the pale horse of the Apocalypse
To all the accursed race of Heretics!

Exeunt.

SCENE II.—*A street. On one side,* NICHOLAS UPSALL'S
house; on the other, WALTER MERRY'S, *with a flock of
pigeons on the roof.* UPSALL *seated in the porch of his
house.*

UPSALL

O day of rest! How beautiful, how fair,
How welcome to the weary and the old!
Day of the Lord! and truce to earthly cares!
Day of the Lord, as all our days should be!
Ah, why will man by his austerities
Shut out the blessed sunshine and the light,
And make of thee a dungeon of despair!

WALTER MERRY (*entering and looking round him*)

All silent as a graveyard! No one stirring;
No footfall in the street, no sound of voices!

By righteous punishment and perseverance,
And perseverance in that punishment,
At last I've brought this contumacious town
To strict observance of the Sabbath day.
Those wanton gospellers, the pigeons yonder,
Are now the only Sabbath-breakers left.
I cannot put them down. As if to taunt me,
They gather every Sabbath afternoon
In noisy congregation on my roof,
Billing and cooing. Whir! take that, ye Quakers.

   Throws a stone at the pigeons. Sees UPSALL.
Ah! Master Nicholas!

UPSALL

   Good afternoon,
Dear neighbor Walter.

MERRY

   Master Nicholas,
You have to-day withdrawn yourself from meeting.

UPSALL

Yea, I have chosen rather to worship God
Sitting in silence here at my own door.

MERRY

Worship the Devil! You this day have broken
Three of our strictest laws. First, by abstaining
From public worship. Secondly, by walking
Profanely on the Sabbath.

UPSALL

   Not one step.
I have been sitting still here, seeing the pigeons
Feed in the street and fly about the roofs.

MERRY

You have been in the street with other intent
Than going to and from the Meeting-house.
And, thirdly, you are harboring Quakers here.
I am amazed!

UPSALL

   Men sometimes, it is said,
Entertain angels unawares.

MERRY

    Nice angels!
Angels in broad-brimmed hats and russet cloaks,
The color of the Devil's nutting-bag! They came
Into the Meeting-house this afternoon
More in the shape of devils than of angels.
The women screamed and fainted; and the boys
Made such an uproar in the gallery
I could not keep them quiet.

UPSALL

     Neighbor Walter,
Your persecution is of no avail.

MERRY

'T is prosecution, as the Governor says,
Not persecution.

UPSALL

   Well, your prosecution;
Your hangings do no good.

MERRY

    The reason is,
We do not hang enough. But, mark my words,

We'll scour them; yea, I warrant ye, we'll scour them!
And now go in and entertain your angels,
And don't be seen here in the street again
Till after sundown!—There they are again!

> *Exit* UPSALL. MERRY *throws another stone at the*
> *pigeons, and then goes into his house.*

SCENE III.—*A room in* UPSALL'S *house. Night.* EDITH,
WHARTON, *and other Quakers seated at a table.* UPSALL
seated near them. Several books on the table.

WHARTON

William and Marmaduke, our martyred brothers,
Sleep in untimely graves, if aught untimely
Can find place in the providence of God,
Where nothing comes too early or too late.
I saw their noble death. They to the scaffold
Walked hand in hand. Two hundred armed men
And many horsemen guarded them, for fear
Of rescue by the crowd, whose hearts were stirred.

EDITH

O holy martyrs!

WHARTON

                    When they tried to speak,
Their voices by the roll of drums were drowned.
When they were dead they still looked fresh and
        fair,
The terror of death was not upon their faces.
Our sister Mary, likewise, the meek woman,
Has passed through martyrdom to her reward;
Exclaiming, as they led her to her death,
"These many days I've been in Paradise."
And, when she died, Priest Wilson threw the hang-
        man

His handkerchief, to cover the pale face
He dared not look upon.

EDITH

                As persecuted,
Yet not forsaken; as unknown, yet known;
As dying, and behold we are alive;
As sorrowful, and yet rejoicing alway;
As having nothing, yet possessing all!

WHARTON

And Leddra, too, is dead. But from his prison,
The day before his death, he sent these words
Unto the little flock of Christ: "Whatever
May come upon the followers of the Light,—
Distress, affliction, famine, nakedness,
Or perils in the city or the sea,
Or persecution, or even death itself,—
I am persuaded that God's armor of Light,
As it is loved and lived in, will preserve you.
Yea, death itself; through which you will find entrance
Into the pleasant pastures of the fold,
Where you shall feed forever as the herds
That roam at large in the low valleys of Achor.
And as the flowing of the ocean fills
Each creek and branch thereof, and then retires,
Leaving behind a sweet and wholesome savor;
So doth the virtue and the life of God
Flow evermore into the hearts of those
Whom He hath made partakers of his nature;
And, when it but withdraws itself a little,
Leaves a sweet savor after it, that many
Can say they are made clean by every word
That He hath spoken to them in their silence."

EDITH (*rising, and breaking into a kind of chant*)

Truly we do but grope here in the dark,
Near the partition-wall of Life and Death,
At every moment dreading or desiring
To lay our hands upon the unseen door!
Let us, then, labor for an inward stillness,—
An inward stillness and an inward healing;
That perfect silence where the lips and heart
Are still, and we no longer entertain
Our own imperfect thoughts and vain opinions,
But God alone speaks in us, and we wait
In singleness of heart, that we may know
His will, and in the silence of our spirits,
That we may do His will, and do that only!

> *A long pause, interrupted by the sound of a drum*
> *approaching; then shouts in the street, and a loud*
> *knocking at the door.*

MARSHAL

Within there! Open the door!

MERRY

Will no one answer?

MARSHAL

In the King's name! Within there!

MERRY

Open the door!

UPSALL (*from the window*)

It is not barred. Come in. Nothing prevents you.
The poor man's door is ever on the latch,
He needs no bolt nor bar to shut out thieves;

He fears no enemies, and has no friends
Importunate enough to need a key.

Enter JOHN ENDICOTT, *the* MARSHAL, MERRY, *and a crowd.*
  Seeing the Quakers silent and unmoved, they pause,
  awestruck. ENDICOTT *opposite* EDITH.

MARSHAL

In the King's name do I arrest you all!
Away with them to prison. Master Upsall,
You are again discovered harboring here
These ranters and disturbers of the peace.
You know the law.

UPSALL

   I know it, and am ready
To suffer yet again its penalties.

EDITH (*to* ENDICOTT)

"Why dost thou persecute me, Saul of Tarsus?"

ACT II

SCENE I.—JOHN ENDICOTT'*s room. Early morning.*

JOHN ENDICOTT

"Why dost thou persecute me, Saul of Tarsus?"
All night these words were ringing in mine ears!*
A sorrowful sweet face; a look that pierced me
With meek reproach; a voice of resignation
That had a life of suffering in its tone;
And that was all! And yet I could not sleep,
Or, when I slept, I dreamed that awful dream!
I stood beneath the elm-tree on the Common
On which the Quakers have been hanged, and heard
A voice, not hers, that cried amid the darkness,

"This is Aceldama, the field of blood!
I will have mercy, and not sacrifice!"
        (*Opens the window, and looks out.*)
The sun is up already; and my heart
Sickens and sinks within me when I think
How many tragedies will be enacted
Before his setting. As the earth rolls round,
It seems to me a huge Ixion's wheel,
Upon whose whirling spokes we are bound fast,
And must go with it! Ah, how bright the sun
Strikes on the sea and on the masts of vessels,
That are uplifted in the morning air,
Like crosses of some peaceable crusade!
It makes me long to sail for lands unknown,
No matter whither! Under me, in shadow,
Gloomy and narrow lies the little town,
Still sleeping, but to wake and toil awhile,
Then sleep again. How dismal looks the prison,
How grim and sombre in the sunless street,—
The prison where she sleeps, or wakes and waits
For what I dare not think of,—death, perhaps!
A word that has been said may be unsaid:
It is but air. But when a deed is done
It cannot be undone, nor can our thoughts
Reach out to all the mischiefs that may follow.
'T is time for morning prayers, I will go down.
My father, though severe, is kind and just;
And when his heart is tender with devotion,—
When from his lips have fallen the words, "Forgive
        us
As we forgive,"—then will I intercede
For these poor people, and perhaps may save them.
                                        Exit.

SCENE II.—*Dock Square. On one side, the tavern of the
Three Mariners. In the background, a quaint building with
gables; and, beyond it, wharves and shipping.* CAPTAIN

KEMPTHORN *and others seated at a table before the door.*
SAMUEL COLE *standing near them.*

KEMPTHORN

Come, drink about! Remember Parson Melham,
And bless the man who first invented flip!
                                        They drink.

COLE

Pray, Master Kempthorn, where were you last night?

KEMPTHORN

On board the Swallow, Simon Kempthorn, master,
Up for Barbadoes, and the Windward Islands.

COLE

The town was in a tumult.

KEMPTHORN

                And for what?

COLE

Your Quakers were arrested.

KEMPTHORN

                How my Quakers?

COLE

Those you brought in your vessel from Barbadoes.
They made an uproar in the Meeting-house
Yesterday, and they're now in prison for it.
I owe you little thanks for bringing them
To the Three Mariners.

KEMPTHORN

          They have not harmed you.
I tell you, Goodman Cole, that Quaker girl
Is precious as a sea-bream's eye. I tell you
It was a lucky day when first she set
Her little foot upon the Swallow's deck,
Bringing good luck, fair winds, and pleasant weather.

COLE

I am a law-abiding citizen;
I have a seat in the new Meeting-house,
A cow-right on the Common; and, besides,
Am corporal in the Great Artillery.
I rid me of the vagabonds at once.

KEMPTHORN

Why should you not have Quakers at your tavern
If you have fiddlers?

COLE

          Never! never! never!
If you want fiddling you must go elsewhere,
To the Green Dragon and the Admiral Vernon,
And other such disreputable places.
But the Three Mariners is an orderly house,
Most orderly, quiet, and respectable.
Lord Leigh said he could be as quiet here
As at the Governor's. And have I not
King Charles's Twelve Good Rules, all framed and
        glazed,
Hanging in my best parlor?

KEMPTHORN

Here's a health
To good King Charles. Will you not drink the King?
Then drink confusion to old Parson Palmer.

COLE

And who is Parson Palmer? I don't know him.

KEMPTHORN

He had his cellar underneath his pulpit,
And so preached o'er his liquor, just as you do.

A drum within.

COLE

Here comes the Marshal.

MERRY (*within*)

Make room for the Marshal.

KEMPTHORN

How pompous and imposing he appears!
His great buff doublet bellying like a mainsail,
And all his streamers fluttering in the wind.
What holds he in his hand?

COLE

A Proclamation.

Enter the MARSHAL, *with a proclamation; and* MERRY, *with
a halberd. They are preceded by a drummer, and followed
by the hangman, with an armful of books, and a crowd
of people, among whom are* UPSALL *and* JOHN ENDICOTT.
A pile is made of the books.

MERRY

Silence, the drum! Good citizens, attend
To the new laws enacted by the Court.

MARSHALL (*reads*)

"Whereas a cursed sect of Heretics
Has lately risen, commonly called Quakers,
Who take upon themselves to be commissioned
Immediately of God, and furthermore
Infallibly assisted by the Spirit
To write and utter blasphemous opinions,
Despising Government and the order of God
In Church and Commonwealth, and speaking evil
Of Dignities, reproaching and reviling
The Magistrates and Ministers, and seeking
To turn the people from their faith, and thus
Gain proselytes to their pernicious ways;—
This Court, considering the premises,
And to prevent like mischief as is wrought
By their means in our land, doth hereby order,
That whatsoever master or commander
Of any ship, bark, pink, or catch shall bring
To any roadstead, harbor, creek, or cove
Within this Jurisdiction any Quakers,
Or other blasphemous Heretics, shall pay
Unto the Treasurer of the Commonwealth
One hundred pounds, and for default thereof
Be put in prison, and continue there
Till the said sum be satisfied and paid."

COLE

Now, Simon Kempthorn, what say you to that?

KEMPTHORN

I pray you, Cole, lend me a hundred pounds!

MARSHAL (*reads*)

"If any one within this Jurisdiction
Shall henceforth entertain, or shall conceal
Quakers, or other blasphemous Heretics,

Knowing them so to be, every such person
Shall forfeit to the country forty shillings
For each hour's entertainment or concealment,
And shall be sent to prison, as aforesaid,
Until the forfeiture be wholly paid."

Murmurs in the crowd.

KEMPTHORN

Now, Goodman Cole, I think your turn has come!

COLE

Knowing them so to be!

KEMPTHORN

At forty shillings
The hour, your fine will be some forty pounds!

COLE

Knowing them so to be! That is the law.

MARSHAL (*reads*)

"And it is further ordered and enacted,
If any Quaker or Quakers shall presume
To come henceforth into this Jurisdiction,
Every male Quaker for the first offence
Shall have one ear cut off; and shall be kept
At labor in the Workhouse, till such time
As he be sent away at his own charge.
And for the repetition of the offence
Shall have his other ear cut off, and then
Be branded in the palm of his right hand.
And every woman Quaker shall be whipt
Severely in three towns; and every Quaker,
Or he or she, that shall for a third time
Herein again offend, shall have their tongues

Bored through with a hot iron, and shall be
Sentenced to Banishment on pain of Death."

Loud murmurs.

(*The voice of* CHRISTISON *in the crowd*)
O patience of the Lord! How long, how long,
Ere thou avenge the blood of Thine Elect?

MERRY

Silence, there, silence! Do not break the peace!

MARSHAL (*reads*)

"Every inhabitant of this Jurisdiction
Who shall defend the horrible opinions
Of Quakers, by denying due respect
To equals and superiors, and withdrawing
From Church Assemblies, and thereby approving
The abusive and destructive practices
Of this accursed sect, in opposition
To all the orthodox received opinions
Of godly men, shall be forthwith committed
Unto close prison for one month; and then
Refusing to retract and to reform
The opinions as aforesaid, he shall be
Sentenced to Banishment on pain of Death.
By the Court. Edward Rawson, Secretary."
Now, hangman, do your duty. Burn those books.

*Loud murmurs in the crowd. The pile of books is
lighted.*

UPSALL

I testify against these cruel laws!
Forerunners are they of some judgment on us;
And, in the love and tenderness I bear
Unto this town and people, I beseech you,
O Magistrates, take heed, lest ye be found
As fighters against God!

JOHN ENDICOTT (*taking* UPSALL'*s hand*)

                         Upsall, I thank you
For speaking words such as some younger man,
I, or another, should have said before you.
Such laws as these are cruel and oppressive;
A blot on this fair town, and a disgrace
To any Christian people.

MERRY (*aside, listening behind them*)

                             Here's sedition!
I never thought that any good would come
Of this young popinjay, with his long hair
And his great boots, fit only for the Russians
Or barbarous Indians, as his father says!

THE VOICE

Woe to the bloody town! and rightfully
Men call it the Lost Town! The blood of Abel
Cries from the ground, and at the final judgment
The Lord will say, "Cain, Cain! where is thy brother?"*

MERRY

Silence there in the crowd!

UPSALL (*aside*)

              'T is Christison!

THE VOICE

O foolish people, ye that think to burn
And to consume the truth of God, I tell you
That every flame is a loud tongue of fire
To publish it abroad to all the world
Louder than tongues of men!

KEMPTHORN (*springing to his feet*)
                    Well said, my hearty.
There's a brave fellow! There's a man of pluck!
A man who's not afraid to say his say,
Though a whole town's against him. Rain, rain, rain,
Bones of Saint Botolph, and put out this fire!
        The drum beats. Exeunt all but MERRY, KEMPTHORN,
            and COLE.

MERRY

And now that matter's ended, Goodman Cole,
Fetch me a mug of ale, your strongest ale.

KEMPTHORN (*sitting down*)

And me another mug of flip; and put
Two gills of brandy in it.

                                    Exit COLE.

MERRY

                    No; no more.
Not a drop more, I say. You've had enough.

KEMPTHORN

And who are you, sir?

MERRY

                    I'm a Tithing-man,*
And Merry is my name.

KEMPTHORN

                    A merry name!
I like it; and I'll drink your merry health
Till all is blue.

MERRY

And then you will be clapped
Into the stocks, with the red letter D
Hung round about your neck for drunkenness.
You're a free-drinker,—yes, and a free-thinker!

KEMPTHORN

And you are Andrew Merry, or Merry Andrew.

MERRY

My name is Walter Merry, and not Andrew.

KEMPTHORN

Andrew or Walter, you're a merry fellow;
I'll swear to that.

MERRY

No swearing, let me tell you.
The other day one Shorthose had his tongue
Put into a cleft stick for profane swearing.

COLE *brings the ale.*

KEMPTHORN

Well, where's my flip? As sure as my name's
Kempthorn—

MERRY

Is your name Kempthorn?

KEMPTHORN

That's the name I go by.

MERRY

What, Captain Simon Kempthorn of the Swallow?

KEMPTHORN

No other.

MERRY (*touching him on the shoulder*)
   Then you're wanted. I arrest you
In the King's name.

KEMPTHORN
   And where's your warrant?

MERRY (*unfolding a paper, and reading*)
          Here.

Listen to me. "Hereby you are required,
In the King'a name, to apprehend the body
Of Simon Kempthorn, mariner, and him
Safely to bring before me, there to answer
All such objections as are laid to him,
Touching the Quakers." Signed, John Endicott.

KEMPTHORN

Has it the Governor's seal?

MERRY
   Ay, here it is.

KEMPTHORN

Death's head and cross-bones. That's a pirate's flag!

MERRY

Beware how you revile the Magistrates;
You may be whipped for that.

KEMPTHORN

Then mum's the word.
Exeunt MERRY *and* KEMPTHORN.

COLE

There's mischief brewing! Sure, there's mischief brewing!
I feel like Master Josselyn when he found
The hornet's nest, and thought it some strange fruit,
Until the seeds came out, and then he dropped it.
Exit.

SCENE III.—*A room in the Governor's house. Enter* GOVERNOR
ENDICOTT *and* MERRY.

ENDICOTT

My son, you say?

MERRY

Your Worship's eldest son.

ENDICOTT

Speaking against the laws?

MERRY

Ay, worshipful sir.

ENDICOTT

And in the public market-place?

MERRY

I saw him
With my own eyes, heard him with my own ears.

ENDICOTT

Impossible!

MERRY

      He stood there in the crowd
With Nicholas Upsall, when the laws were read
To-day against the Quakers, and I heard him
Denounce and vilipend them as unjust,
And cruel, wicked, and abominable.

ENDICOTT

Ungrateful son! O God! thou layest upon me
A burden heavier than I can bear!
Surely the power of Satan must be great
Upon the earth, if even the elect
Are thus deceived and fall away from grace!

MERRY

Worshipful sir! I meant no harm—

ENDICOTT

                    'T is well.
You've done your duty, though you've done it roughly,
and every word you've uttered since you came
Has stabbed me to the heart!

MERRY

                  I do beseech
Your Worship's pardon!

ENDICOTT

        He whom I have nurtured
And brought up in the reverence of the Lord!
The child of all my hopes and my affections!
He upon whom I leaned as a sure staff

For my old age! It is God's chastisement
For leaning upon any arm but His!

MERRY

Your Worship!—

ENDICOTT

And this comes from holding parley
With the delusions and deceits of Satan.
At once, forever, must they be crushed out,
Or all the land will reek with heresy!
Pray, have you any children?

MERRY

No, not any.

ENDICOTT

Thank God for that. He has delivered you
From a great care. Enough; my private griefs
Too long have kept me from the public service.
> Exit MERRY. ENDICOTT *seats himself at the table and arranges his papers.*
The hour has come; and I am eager now
To sit in judgment on these Heretics.

A knock.

Come in. Who is it? (*Not looking up.*)

JOHN ENDICOTT

It is I.

ENDICOTT (*restraining himself*)

Sit down.

JOHN ENDICOTT (*sitting down*)

I come to intercede for these poor people
Who are in prison, and await their trial.

JOHN ENDICOTT

ENDICOTT

It is of them I wish to speak with you.
I have been angry with you, but 't is passed.
For when I hear your footsteps come or go,
See in your features your dead mother's face,
And in your voice detect some tone of hers,
All anger vanishes, and I remember
The days that are no more, and come no more,
When as a child you sat upon my knee,
And prattled of your playthings, and the games
You played among the pear-trees in the orchard!

JOHN ENDICOTT

Oh, let the memory of my noble mother
Plead with you to be mild and merciful!
For mercy more becomes a Magistrate
Than the vindictive wrath which men call justice!

ENDICOTT

The sin of heresy is a deadly sin.
'T is like the falling of the snow, whose crystals
The traveller plays with, thoughtless of his danger,
Until he sees the air so full of light
That it is dark; and blindly staggering onward,
Lost, and bewildered, he sits down to rest;
There falls a pleasant drowsiness upon him,
And what he thinks is sleep, alas! is death.

JOHN ENDICOTT

And yet who is there that has never doubted?
And doubting and believing, has not said,
"Lord, I believe; help thou my unbelief"?

ENDICOTT

In the same way we trifle with our doubts,
Whose shining shapes are like the stars descending;

Until at last, bewildered and dismayed,
Blinded by that which seemed to give us light,
We sink to sleep, and find that it is death,
(*Rising*)
Death to the soul through all eternity!
Alas that I should see you growing up
To man's estate, and in the admonition
And nurture of the Law, to find you now
Pleading for Heretics!

JOHN ENDICOTT (*rising*)

In the sight of God,
Perhaps all men are Heretics. Who dares
To say that he alone has found the truth?
We cannot always feel and think and act
As those who go before us. Had you done so,
You would not now be here.

ENDICOTT

Have you forgotten
The doom of Heretics, and the fate of those
Who aid and comfort them? Have you forgotten
That in the market-place this very day
You trampled on the laws? What right have you,
An inexperienced and untravelled youth,
To sit in judgment here upon the acts
Of older men and wiser than yourself,
Thus stirring up sedition in the streets,
And making me a byword and a jest?

JOHN ENDICOTT

Words of an inexperienced youth like me
Were powerless if the acts of older men
Went not before them. 'T is these laws themselves
Stir up sedition, not my judgment of them.

ENDICOTT

Take heed, lest I be called, as Brutus was,
To be the judge of my own son! Begone!
When you are tired of feeding upon husks,
Return again to duty and submission,
But not till then.

JOHN ENDICOTT

I hear and I obey!

Exit.

ENDICOTT

Oh happy, happy they who have no children!
He's gone! I hear the hall door shut behind him.
It sends a dismal echo through my heart,
As if forever it had closed between us,
And I should look upon his face no more!
Oh, this will drag me down into my grave,—
To that eternal resting-place wherein
Man lieth down, and riseth not again!
Till the heavens be no more he shall not wake,
Nor be roused from his sleep; for Thou dost change
His countenance, and sendest him away!

Exit.

ACT III

Scene I.—*The Court of Assistants.* Endicott, Bellingham,
Atherton, *and other magistrates.* Kempthorn, Merry,
and constables. Afterwards Wharton, Edith, *and* Christison.

ENDICOTT

Call Captain Simon Kempthorn.

MERRY

Simon Kempthorn,
Come to the bar!

KEMPTHORN *comes forward.*

ENDICOTT

You are accused of bringing
Into this Jurisdiction, from Barbadoes,
Some persons of that sort and sect of people
Known by the name of Quakers, and maintaining
Most dangerous and heretical opinions;
Purposely coming here to propagate
Their heresies and errors; bringing with them
And spreading sundry books here, which contain
Their doctrines most corrupt and blasphemous,
And contrary to the truth professed among us.
What say you to this charge?

KEMPTHORN

I do acknowledge,
Among the passengers on board the Swallow
Were certain persons saying Thee and Thou.
They seemed a harmless people, mostways silent,
Particularly when they said their prayers.

ENDICOTT

Harmless and silent as the pestilence!
You'd better have brought the fever or the plague
Among us in your ship! Therefore, this Court,
For preservation of the Peace and Truth,
Hereby commands you speedily to transport,
Or cause to be transported speedily,
The aforesaid persons hence unto Barbadoes,
From whence they came; you paying all the charges
Of their imprisonment.

KEMPTHORN

Worshipful sir,
No ship e'er prospered that has carried Quakers
Against their will! I knew a vessel once—

ENDICOTT

And for the more effectual performance
Hereof you are to give security
In bonds amounting to one hundred pounds.
On your refusal, you will be committed
To prison till you do it.

KEMPTHORN

But you see
I cannot do it. The law, sir, of Barbadoes
Forbids the landing Quakers on the island.

ENDICOTT

Then you will be committed. Who comes next?

MERRY

There is another charge against the Captain.

ENDICOTT

What is it?

MERRY

Profane swearing, please your Worship.
He cursed and swore from Dock Square to the Court-
house.

ENDICOTT

Then let him stand in the pillory for one hour.
                    Exit KEMPTHORN *with constable.*
Who's next?

MERRY

The Quakers.

ENDICOTT

Call them.

MERRY

Edward Wharton,
Come to the bar!

WHARTON

Yea, even to the bench.

ENDICOTT

Take off your hat.

WHARTON

My hat offendeth not.
If it offendeth any, let him take it;
For I shall not resist.

ENDICOTT

Take off his hat.
Let him be fined ten shillings for contempt.

MERRY *takes off* WHARTON's *hat.*

WHARTON

What evil have I done?

ENDICOTT

Your hair's too long;
And in not putting off your hat to us

You've disobeyed and broken that commandment
Which sayeth "Honor thy father and thy mother."

WHARTON

John Endicott, thou are become too proud;
And lovest him who putteth off the hat,
And honoreth thee by bowing of the body,
And sayeth "Worshipful sir!" 'T is time for thee
To give such follies over, for thou mayest
Be drawing very near unto thy grave.

ENDICOTT

Now, sirrah, leave your canting. Take the oath.

WHARTON

Nay, sirrah me no sirrahs!

ENDICOTT

                    Will you swear?

WHARTON

Nay, I will not.

ENDICOTT

                    You made a great disturbance
And uproar yesterday in the Meeting-house,
Having your hat on.

WHARTON

                    I made no disturbance;
For peacefully I stood, like other people.
I spake no words; moved against none my hand;
But by the hair they haled me out, and dashed
Their books into my face.

ENDICOTT

You, Edward Wharton,
On pain of death, depart this Jurisdiction
Within ten days. Such is your sentence. Go.

WHARTON

John Endicott, it had been well for thee
If this day's doings thou hadst left undone.
But, banish me as far as thou hast power,
Beyond the guard and presence of my God
Thou canst not banish me!

ENDICOTT

Depart the Court;
We have no time to listen to your babble.
Who's next?

Exit WHARTON.

MERRY

This woman, for the same offence.

EDITH *comes forward.*

ENDICOTT

What is your name?

EDITH

'T is to the world unknown,
But written in the Book of Life.

ENDICOTT

Take heed
It be not written in the Book of Death!
What is it?

EDITH

Edith Christison.

ENDICOTT (*with eagerness*)
                    The daughter
Of Wenlock Christison?

EDITH

I am his daughter.

ENDICOTT

Your father hath given us trouble many times.
A bold man and a violent, who sets
At naught the authority of our Church and State,
And is in banishment on pain of death.
Where are you living?

EDITH

In the Lord.

ENDICOTT

                              Make answer
Without evasion. Where?

EDITH

                    My outward being
Is in Barbadoes.

ENDICOTT

Then why come you here?

EDITH

I come upon an errand of the Lord.

ENDICOTT

'T is not the business of the Lord you're doing;
It is the Devil's. Will you take the oath?
Give her the Book.

> MERRY *offers the book.*

EDITH

                You offer me this Book
To swear on; and it saith, "Swear not at all,
Neither by heaven, because it is God's Throne,
Nor by the earth, because it is his footstool!"*
I dare not swear.

ENDICOTT

                You dare not? Yet you Quakers
Deny this Book of Holy Writ, the Bible,
To be the Word of God.

EDITH (*reverentially*)

                Christ is the Word,
The everlasting oath of God. I dare not.

ENDICOTT

You own yourself a Quaker,—do you not?

EDITH

I own that in derision and reproach
I am so called.

ENDICOTT

                Then you deny the Scripture
To be the rule of life.

EDITH

Yea, I believe
The Inner Light, and not the Written Word,
To be the rule of life.

ENDICOTT

And you deny
That the Lord's Day is holy.

EDITH

Every day
Is the Lord's Day. It runs through all our lives,
As through the pages of the Holy Bible,
"Thus saith the Lord."

ENDICOTT

You are accused of making
An horrible disturbance, and affrighting
The people in the Meeting-house on Sunday.
What answer make you?

EDITH

I do not deny
That I was present in your Steeple-house
On the First Day; but I made no disturbance.

ENDICOTT

Why came you there?

EDITH

Because the Lord commanded.
His word was in my heart, a burning fire
Shut up within me and consuming me,
And I was very weary with forbearing;
I could not stay.

ENDICOTT

'T was not the Lord that sent you;
As an incarnate devil did you come!

EDITH

On the First Day, when, seated in my chamber,
I heard the bells toll, calling you together,
The sound struck at my life, as once at his,
The holy man, our Founder, when he heard
The far-off bells toll in the Vale of Beavor.*
It sounded like a market bell to call
The folk together, that the Priest might set
His wares to sale. And the Lord said within me,
"Thou must go cry aloud against that Idol,
And all the worshippers thereof." I went
Barefooted, clad in sackcloth, and I stood
And listened at the threshold; and I heard
The praying and the singing and the preaching,
Which were but outward forms, and without power.
Then rose a cry within me, and my heart
Was filled with admonitions and reproofs.
Remembering how the Prophets and Apostles
Denounced the covetous hirelings and diviners,
I entered in, and spake the words the Lord
Commanded me to speak. I could no less.

ENDICOTT

Are you a Prophetess?

EDITH

Is it not written,
"Upon my handmaidens will I pour out
My spirit, and they shall prophesy"?*

ENDICOTT

Enough;
For out of your own mouth are you condemned!
Need we hear further?

THE JUDGES

We are satisfied.

ENDICOTT

It is sufficient. Edith Christison,
The sentence of the Court is, that you be
Scourged in three towns, with forty stripes save one,
Then banished upon pain of death!

EDITH

Your sentence
Is truly no more terrible to me
Than had you blown a feather into the air,
And, as it fell upon me, you had said,
"Take heed it hurt thee not!" God's will be done!

WENLOCK CHRISTISON (*unseen in the crowd*)

Woe to the city of blood! The stone shall cry
Out of the wall; the beam from out the timber
Shall answer it! Woe unto him that buildeth
A town with blood, and stablisheth a city
By his iniquity!

ENDICOTT

Who is it makes
Such outcry here?

CHRISTISON (*coming forward*)

I, Wenlock Christison!

JOHN ENDICOTT

ENDICOTT

Banished on pain of death, why come you here?

CHRISTISON

I come to warn you that you shed no more
The blood of innocent men! It cries aloud
For vengeance to the Lord!

ENDICOTT

               Your life is forfeit
Unto the law; and you shall surely die,
And shall not live.

CHRISTISON

         Like unto Eleazer,*
Maintaining the excellence of ancient years
And the honor of his gray head, I stand before you;
Like him disdaining all hypocrisy,
Lest, through desire to live a little longer,
I get a stain to my old age and name!

ENDICOTT

Being in banishment, on pain of death,
You come now in among us in rebellion.

CHRISTISON

I come not in among you in rebellion,
But in obedience to the Lord of Heaven.
Not in contempt to any Magistrate,
But only in the love I bear your souls,
As ye shall know hereafter, when all men
Give an account of deeds done in the body!
God's righteous judgments ye cannot escape.

JOHN ENDICOTT

ONE OF THE JUDGES

Those who have gone before you said the same,
And yet no judgment of the Lord hath fallen
Upon us.

CHRISTISON

      He but waiteth till the measure
Of your iniquities shall be filled up,
And ye have run your race. Then will his wrath
Descend upon you to the uttermost!
For thy part, Humphrey Atherton, it hangs
Over thy head already. It shall come
Suddenly, as a thief doth in the night,
And in the hour when least thou thinkest of it!

ENDICOTT

We have a law, and by that law you die.

CHRISTISON

I, a free man of England and freeborn,
Appeal unto the laws of mine own nation!

ENDICOTT

There's no appeal to England from this Court!
What! do you think our statutes are but paper?
Are but dead leaves that rustle in the wind?
Or litter to be trampled under foot?
What say ye, Judges of the Court,—what say ye?
Shall this man suffer death? Speak your opinions.

ONE OF THE JUDGES

I am a mortal man, and die I must,
And that erelong; and I must then appear
Before the awful judgment-seat of Christ,
To give account of deeds done in the body.

My greatest glory on that day will be,
That I have given my vote against this man.

CHRISTISON

If, Thomas Danforth, thou hast nothing more
To glory in upon that dreadful day
Than blood of innocent people, then thy glory
Will be turned into shame! The Lord hath said it!

ANOTHER JUDGE

I cannot give consent, while other men
Who have been banished upon pain of death
Are now in their own houses here among us.

ENDICOTT

Ye that will not consent, make record of it.
I thank my God that I am not afraid
To give my judgment. Wenlock Christison,
You must be taken back from hence to prison,
Thence to the place of public execution,
There to be hanged till you be dead—dead—dead!

CHRISTISON

If ye have power to take my life from me,—
Which I do question,—God hath power to raise
The principle of life in other men,
And send them here among you. There shall be
No peace unto the wicked, saith my God.
Listen, ye Magistrates, for the Lord hath said it!
The day ye put his servitors to death,
That day the Day of your own Visitation,
The Day of Wrath, shall pass above your heads,
And ye shall be accursed forevermore!
            (*To* EDITH, *embracing her*)
Cheer up, dear heart! they have not power to
        harm us.

Exeunt CHRISTISON *and* EDITH *guarded. The Scene closes.*

SCENE II.—*A street. Enter* JOHN ENDICOTT *and* UPSALL.

JOHN ENDICOTT

Scourged in three towns! and yet the busy people
Go up and down the streets on their affairs
Of business or of pleasure, as if nothing
Had happened to disturb them or their thoughts!
When bloody tragedies like this are acted,
The pulses of a nation should stand still;
The town should be in mourning, and the people
Speak only in low whispers to each other.

UPSALL

I know this people; and that underneath
A cold outside there burns a secret fire
That will find vent, and will not be put out,
Till every remnant of these barbarous laws
Shall be to ashes burned, and blown away.

JOHN ENDICOTT

Scourged in three towns! It is incredible
Such things can be! I feel the blood within me
Fast mounting in rebellion, since in vain
Have I implored compassion of my father!

UPSALL

You know your father only as a father;
I know him better as a Magistrate.
He is a man both loving and severe;
A tender heart; a will inflexible.
None ever loved him more than I have loved him.
He is an upright man and a just man
In all things save the treatment of the Quakers.

JOHN ENDICOTT

Yet I have found him cruel and unjust
Even as a father. He has driven me forth
Into the street; has shut his door upon me,
With words of bitterness. I am as homeless
As these poor Quakers are.

UPSALL

           Then come with me.
You shall be welcome for your father's sake,
And the old friendship that has been between us.
He will relent erelong. A father's anger
Is like a sword without a handle, piercing
both ways alike, and wounding him that wields it
No less than him that it is pointed at.

                          Exeunt.

SCENE III.—- *The prison. Night.* EDITH *reading the Bible
by a lamp.*

EDITH

"Blessed are ye when men shall persecute you,
And shall revile you, and shall say against you
All manner of evil falsely for my sake!
Rejoice, and be exceeding glad, for great
Is your reward in heaven. For so the prophets,
Which were before you, have been persecuted."

Enter JOHN ENDICOTT.

JOHN ENDICOTT

Edith!

EDITH

Who is it speaketh?

JOHN ENDICOTT

               Saul of Tarsus;
As thou didst call me once.

EDITH (*coming forward*)

               Yea, I remember.
Thou art the Governor's son.

JOHN ENDICOTT

               I am ashamed
Thou shouldst remember me.

EDITH

               Why comest thou
Into this dark guest-chamber in the night?
What seekest thou?

JOHN ENDICOTT

Forgiveness!

EDITH

               I forgive
All who have injured me. What hast thou done?

JOHN ENDICOTT

I have betrayed thee, thinking that in this
I did God service. Now, in deep contrition,
I come to rescue thee.

EDITH

From what?

JOHN ENDICOTT

               From prison.

EDITH

I am safe here within these gloomy walls.

JOHN ENDICOTT

From scourging in the streets, and in three towns!

EDITH

Remembering who was scourged for me, I shrink not
Nor shudder at the forty stripes save one.

JOHN ENDICOTT

Perhaps from death itself!

EDITH

                I fear not death,
Knowing who died for me.

JOHN ENDICOTT (*aside*)

                Surely some divine
Ambassador is speaking through those lips
And looking through those eyes! I cannot answer!

EDITH

If all these prison doors stood opened wide
I would not cross the threshold,—not one step.
There are invisible bars I cannot break;
There are invisible doors that shut me in,
And keep me ever steadfast to my purpose.

JOHN ENDICOTT

Thou hast the patience and the faith of Saints!

EDITH

Thy Priest hath been with me this day to save me,
Not only from the death that comes to all,
But from the second death!

JOHN ENDICOTT

JOHN ENDICOTT

        The Pharisee!
My heart revolts against him and his creed!
Alas! the coat that was without a seam
Is rent asunder by contending sects;
Each bears away a portion of the garment,
Blindly believing that he has the whole!

EDITH

When Death, the Healer, shall have touched our eyes
With moist clay of the grave, then shall we see
The truth as we have never yet beheld it.
But he that overcometh shall not be
Hurt of the second death. Has he forgotten
The many mansions in our father's house?

JOHN ENDICOTT

There is no pity in his iron heart!
The hands that now bear stamped upon their palms
The burning sign of Heresy, hereafter
Shall be uplifted against such accusers,
And then the imprinted letter and its meaning
Will not be Heresy, but Holiness!

EDITH

Remember, thou condemnest thine own father!

JOHN ENDICOTT

I have no father! He has cast me off.
I am as homeless as the wind that moans
And wanders through the streets. Oh, come with me!
Do not delay. Thy God shall be my God,
And where thou goest I will go.*

EDITH

                              I cannot.
Yet will I not deny it, nor conceal it;
From the first moment I beheld thy face
I felt a tenderness in my soul towards thee.
My mind has since been inward to the Lord,
Waiting his word. It has not yet been spoken.

JOHN ENDICOTT

I cannot wait. Trust me. Oh, come with me!

EDITH

In the next room, my father, an old man,
Sitteth imprisoned and condemned to death,
Willing to prove his faith by martyrdom;
And thinkest thou his daughter would do less?

JOHN ENDICOTT

Oh, life is sweet, and death is terrible!

EDITH

I have too long walked hand in hand with death
To shudder at that pale familiar face.
But leave me now. I wish to be alone.

JOHN ENDICOTT

Not yet. Oh, let me stay.

EDITH

                    Urge me no more.

JOHN ENDICOTT

Alas! good-night. I will not say good-by!

EDITH

Put this temptation underneath thy feet.
To him that overcometh shall be given
The white stone with the new name written on it,
That no man knows save him that doth receive it,
And I will give thee a new name, and call thee
Paul of Damascus and not Saul of Tarsus.*

> *Exit* ENDICOTT. EDITH *sits down again to read the Bible.*

ACT IV

SCENE I.—*King Street, in front of the town-house.* KEMPTHORN *in the pillory.* MERRY *and a crowd of lookers-on.*

KEMPTHORN (*sings*)

The world is full of care,
  Much like unto a bubble;
Women and care, and care and women,
  And women and care and trouble.

Good Master Merry, may I say confound?

MERRY

Ay, that you may.

KEMPTHORN

                Well, then, with your permission,
Confound the Pillory!

MERRY

                That's the very thing
The joiner said who made the Shrewsbury stocks.

He said, Confound the stocks, because they put him
Into his own. He was the first man in them.

KEMPTHORN

For swearing, was it?

MERRY

No, it was for charging;
He charged the town too much; and so the town,
To make things square, set him in his own stocks,
And fined him five pound sterling,—just enough
To settle his own bill.

KEMPTHORN

And served him right;
But, Master Merry, is it not eight bells?

MERRY

Not quite.

KEMPTHORN

For, do you see? I'm getting tired
Of being perched aloft herein this cro' nest
Like the first mate of a whaler, or a Middy
Mast-headed, looking out for land! Sail ho!
Here comes a heavy-laden merchantman
With the lee clews eased off, and running free
Before the wind. A solid man of Boston.
A comfortable man, with dividends,
And the first salmon, and the first green peas.
                                        A gentleman passes.
He does not even turn his head to look.
He's gone without a word. Here comes another,
A different kind of craft on a taut bow-line,—
Deacon Giles Firmin the apothecary,

A pious and a ponderous citizen,
Looking as rubicund and round and splendid
As the great bottle in his own shop window!

DEACON FIRMIN passes.

And here's my host of the Three Mariners,
My creditor and trusty taverner,
My corporal in the Great Artillery!
He's not a man to pass me without speaking.

COLE looks away and passes.

Don't yaw so; keep your luff, old hypocrite!
Respectable, ah yes, respectable,
You, with your seat in the new Meeting-house,
Your cow-right on the Common! But who's this?
I did not know the Mary Ann was in!
And yet this is my own friend, Captain Goldsmith,
As sure as I stand in the bilboes here.
Why, Ralph, my boy!

Enter RALPH GOLDSMITH.

GOLDSMITH

Why, Simon, is it you?
Set in the bilboes?

KEMPTHORN

Chock-a-block, you see,
And without chafing-bear.

GOLDSMITH

And what's it for?

KEMPTHORN

Ask that starbowline with the boat-hook there,
That handsome man.

MERRY (bowing)

For swearing.

KEMPTHORN

> In this town
They put sea-captains in the stocks for swearing
And Quakers for not swearing. So look out.

GOLDSMITH

I pray you set him free; he meant no harm;
'T is an old habit he picked up afloat.

MERRY

Well, as your time is out, you may come down.
The law allows you now to go at large
Like Elder Oliver's horse upon that Common.

KEMPTHORN

Now, hearties, bear a hand! Let go and haul.
> KEMPTHORN *is set free, and comes forward, shaking*
> GOLDSMITH's *hand.*

KEMPTHORN

Give me your hand, Ralph. Ah, how good it feels!
The hand of an old friend.

GOLDSMITH

> God bless you, Simon!

KEMPTHORN

Now let us make a straight wake for the tavern
Of the Three Mariners, Samuel Cole commander;
Where we can take our ease, and see the shipping,
And talk about old times.

GOLDSMITH

> First I must pay
My duty to the Governor, and take him
His letters and despatches. Come with me.

KEMPTHORN

I'd rather not. I saw him yesterday.

GOLDSMITH

Then wait for me at the Three Nuns and Comb.

KEMPTHORN

I thank you. That's too near to the town pump.
I will go with you to the Governor's,
And wait outside there, sailing off and on;
If I am wanted, you can hoist a signal.

MERRY

Shall I go with you and point out the way?

GOLDSMITH

Oh no, I thank you. I am not a stranger
Here in your crooked little town.

MERRY

How now, sir?
Do you abuse our town?

Exit.

GOLDSMITH

Oh, no offence.

KEMPTHORN

Ralph, I am under bonds for a hundred pound.

GOLDSMITH

Hard lines. What for?

KEMPTHORN

To take some Quakers back
I brought here from Barbadoes in the Swallow.

JOHN ENDICOTT

And how to do it I don't clearly see,
For one of them is banished, and another
Is sentenced to be hanged! What shall I do?

GOLDSMITH

Just slip your hawser on some cloudy night;
Sheer off, and pay it with the topsail, Simon!

Exeunt.

SCENE II.—*Street in front of the prison. In the background
a gateway and several flights of steps leading up terraces
to the Governor's house. A pump on one side of the
street.* JOHN ENDICOTT, MERRY, UPSALL, *and others. A
drum beats.*

JOHN ENDICOTT

Oh shame, shame, shame!

MERRY

      Yes, it would be a shame
But for the damnable sin of Heresy!

JOHN ENDICOTT

A woman scourged and dragged about our streets!

MERRY

Well, Roxbury and Dorchester must take
Their share of shame. She will be whipped in each!
Three towns, and Forty Stripes save one; that makes
Thirteen in each.

JOHN ENDICOTT

     And are we Jews or Christians?
See where she comes, amid a gaping crowd!
And she a child. Oh, pitiful! pitiful!

223

There's blood upon her clothes, her hands, her feet!
> *Enter* MARSHAL *and a drummer,* EDITH, *stripped to
> the waist, followed by the hangman with a scourge,
> and a noisy crowd.*

EDITH

Here let me rest one moment. I am tired.
Will some one give me water?

MERRY

              At his peril.

UPSALL

Alas! that I should live to see this day!

A WOMAN

Did I forsake my father and my mother
And come here to New England to see this?

EDITH

I am athirst. Will no one give me water?

JOHN ENDICOTT (*making his way through the crowd with water*)

In the Lord's name!

EDITH (*drinking*)

           In his name I receive it!
Sweet as the water of Samaria's well*
This water tastes. I thank thee. Is it thou?
I was afraid thou hadst deserted me.

JOHN ENDICOTT

Never will I desert thee, nor deny thee.
Be comforted.

MERRY

O Master Endicott,
Be careful what you say.

JOHN ENDICOTT

Peace, idle babbler!

MERRY

You'll rue these words!

JOHN ENDICOTT

Art thou not better now?

EDITH

They've struck me as with roses.

JOHN ENDICOTT

Ah, these wounds!
These bloody garments!

EDITH

It is granted me
To seal my testimony with my blood.

JOHN ENDICOTT

O blood-red seal of man's vindictive wrath!
O roses of the garden of the Lord!
I, of the household of Iscariot,*
I have betrayed in thee my Lord and Master!

WENLOCK CHRISTISON *appears above, at the window of
prison, stretching out his hands through the bars.*

CHRISTISON

Be of good courage, O my child! my child!
Blessed art thou when men shall persecute thee!

Fear not their faces, saith the Lord, fear not,
For I am with thee to deliver thee.

A CITIZEN

Who is it crying from the prison yonder?

MERRY

It is old Wenlock Christison.

CHRISTISON

Remember
Him who was scourged, and mocked, and crucified!
I see his messengers attending thee.
Be steadfast, oh, be steadfast to the end!

EDITH (*with exultation*)

I cannot reach thee with these arrms, O father!
But closely in my soul do I embrace thee
And hold thee. In thy dungeon and thy death
I will be with thee, and will comfort thee!

MARSHAL

Come, put an end to this. Let the drum beat.
The drum beats. Exeunt all but JOHN ENDICOTT,
UPSALL, *and* MERRY.

CHRISTISON

Dear child, farewell! Never shall I behold
Thy face again with these bleared eyes of flesh;
And never wast thou fairer, lovelier, dearer
Than now, when scourged and bleeding, and insulted
For the truth's sake. O pitiless, pitiless town!
The wrath of God hangs over thee; and the day
Is near at hand when thou shalt be abandoned
To desolation and the breeding of nettles.

The bittern and the cormorant shall lodge
Upon thine upper lintels, and their voice
Sing in thy windows. Yea, thus saith the Lord!

JOHN ENDICOTT

Awake! awake! ye sleepers, ere too late,
And wipe these bloody statutes from your books!

Exit.

MERRY

Take heed; the walls have ears!

UPSALL

At last, the heart
Of every honest man must speak or break!
Enter GOVERNOR ENDICOTT *with his halberdiers.*

ENDICOTT

What is this stir and tumult in the street?

MERRY

Worshipful sir, the whipping of a girl,
And her old father howling from the prison.

ENDICOTT (*to his halberdiers*)

Go on.

CHRISTISON

Antiochus! Antiochus!
O thou that slayest the Maccabees! The Lord*
Shall smite thee with incurable disease,
And no man shall endure to carry thee!

MERRY

Peace, old blasphemer!

227

CHRISTISON

I both feel and see
The presence and the waft of death go forth
Against thee, and already thou dost look
Like one that's dead!

MERRY (*pointing*)

And there is your own son,
Worshipful sir, abetting the sedition.

ENDICOTT

Arrest him. Do not spare him.

MERRY (*aside*)

His own child!
There is some special providence takes care
That none shall be too happy in this world!
His own first-born.

ENDICOTT

O Absalom, my son!*
*Exeunt; the Governor with his halberdiers ascending
the steps of his house.*

SCENE III.—*The Governor's private room. Papers upon the
table.* ENDICOTT *and* BELLINGHAM.

ENDICOTT

There is a ship from England has come in,
Bringing despatches and much news from home.
His Majesty was at the Abbey crowned;
And when the coronation was complete
There passed a mighty tempest o'er the city,
Portentous with great thunderings and lightnings.

BELLINGHAM

After his father's, if I well remember,
There was an earthquake, that foreboded evil.

ENDICOTT

Ten of the Regicides have been put to death!
The bodies of Cromwell, Ireton, and Bradshaw
Have been dragged from their graves, and publicly
Hanged in their shrouds at Tyburn.

BELLINGHAM

Horrible!

ENDICOTT

Thus the old tyranny revives again!
Its arm is long enough to reach us here,
As you will see. For, more insulting still
Than flaunting in our faces dead men's shrouds,
Here is the King's Mandamus, taking from us,
From this day forth, all power to punish Quakers.

BELLINGHAM

That takes from us all power; we are but puppets,
And can no longer execute our laws.

ENDICOTT

His Majesty begins with pleasant words,
"Trusty and well-beloved, we greet you well;"
Then with a ruthless hand he strips from me
All that which makes me what I am; as if
From some old general in the field, grown gray
In service, scarred with many wounds,
Just at the hour of victory, he should strip
His badge of office and his well-gained honors,
And thrust him back into the ranks again.

Opens the Mandamus, and hands it to BELLINGHAM;
and, while he is reading, ENDICOTT *walks up and
down the room.*

Here, read it for yourself; you see his words
Are pleasant words—considerate—not reproachful—
Nothing could be more gentle—or more royal;
But then the meaning underneath the words,
Mark that. He says all people known as Quakers
Among us, now condemned to suffer death
Or any corporal punishment whatever,
Who are imprisoned, or may be obnoxious
To the like condemnation, shall be sent
Forthwith to England, to be dealt with there
In such wise as shall be agreeable
Unto the English law and their demerits.
Is it not so?

BELLINGHAM (*returning the paper*)
Ay, so the paper says.

ENDICOTT

It means we shall no longer rule the Province;
It means farewell to law and liberty,
Authority, respect for Magistrates,
The peace and welfare of the Commonwealth.
If all the knaves upon this continent
Can make appeal to England, and so thwart
The ends of truth and justice by delay,
Our power is gone forever. We are nothing
But ciphers, valueless save when we follow
Some unit; and our unit is the King!
'T is he that gives us value.

BELLINGHAM
                          I confess
Such seems to be the meaning of this paper,

But being the King's Mandamus, signed and sealed,
We must obey, or we are in rebellion.

ENDICOTT

I tell you, Richard Bellingham,—I tell you,
That this is the beginning of a struggle
Of which no mortal can foresee the end.
I shall not live to fight the battle for you,
I am a man disgraced in every way;
This order takes from me my self-respect
And the respect of others. 'T is my doom,
Yes, my death-warrant, but must be obeyed!
Take it, and see that it is executed
So far as this, that all be set at large;
But see that none of them be sent to England
To bear false witness, and to spread reports
That might be prejudicial to ourselves.

Exit BELLINGHAM.

There's a dull pain keeps knocking at my heart,
Dolefully saying, "Set thy house in order,
For thou shalt surely die, and shalt not live!"
For me the shadow on the dial-plate
Goeth not back, but on into the dark!

Exit.

SCENE IV.—*The street. A crowd, reading a placard on the door of the Meeting-house.* NICHOLAS UPSALL *among them. Enter* JOHN NORTON.

NORTON

What is this gathering here?

UPSALL

   One William Brand,
An old man like ourselves, and weak in body,
Has been so cruelly tortured in his prison,

The people are excited, and they threaten
To tear the prison down.

NORTON

What has been done?

UPSALL

He has been put in irons, with his neck
And heels tied close together, and so left
From five in the morning until nine at night.

NORTON

What more was done?

UPSALL

He has been kept five days
In prison without food, and cruelly beaten,
So that his limbs were cold, his senses stopped.

NORTON

What more?

UPSALL

And is this not enough?

NORTON

Now hear me.
This William Brand of yours has tried to beat
Our Gospel Ordinances black and blue;
And, if he has been beaten in like manner,
It is but justice, and I will appear
In his behalf that did so. I suppose
That he refused to work.

UPSALL

He was too weak.
How could an old man work, when he was starving?

JOHN ENDICOTT

NORTON

And what is this placard?

UPSALL

        The Magistrates,
To appease the people and prevent a tumult,
Have put up these placards throughout the town,
Declaring that the jailer shall be dealt with
Impartially and sternly by the Court.

NORTON (*tearing down the placard*)

Down with this weak and cowardly concession,
This flag of truce with Satan and with Sin!
I fling it in his face! I trample it
Under my feet! It is his cunning craft,
The masterpiece of his diplomacy,
To cry and plead for boundless toleration.
But toleration is the first-born child
Of all abominations and deceits.
There is no room in Christ's triumphant army
For tolerationists. And if an Angel
Preach any other gospel unto you
Than that ye have received, God's malediction
Descend upon him! Let him be accursed!

                                  Exit.

UPSALL

Now, go thy ways, John Norton! go thy ways,
Thou Orthodox Evangelist, as men call thee!
But even now there cometh out of England,
Like an o'ertaking and accusing conscience,
An outraged man, to call thee to account
For the unrighteous murder of his son!   *Exit.*

JOHN ENDICOTT

EDITH

How beautiful are these autumnal woods!
The wilderness doth blossom like the rose,
And change into a garden of the Lord!
How silent everywhere! Alone and lost
Here in the forest, there comes over me
An inward awfulness. I recall the words
Of the Apostle Paul: "In journeyings often,
Often in perils in the wilderness,
In weariness, in painfulness, in watchings,
In hunger and thirst, in cold and nakedness;"*
And I forget my weariness and pain,
My watchings, and my hunger and my thirst.
The Lord hath said that He will seek his flock
In cloudy and dark days, and they shall dwell
Securely in the wilderness, and sleep
Safe in the woods! Whichever way I turn,
I come back with my face towards the town.
Dimly I see it, and the sea beyond it.
O cruel town! I know what waits me there,
And yet I must go back; for ever louder
I hear the inward calling of the Spirit,
And must obey the voice. O woods, that wear
Your golden crown of martyrdom, blood-stained,
From you I learn a lesson of submission,
And am obedient even unto death,
If God so wills it.   *Exit.*

JOHN ENDICOTT (*within*)
Edith! Edith! Edith!

                                              He enters.

It is in vain! I call, she answers not;
I follow, but I find no trace of her!

Blood! blood! The leaves above me and around me
Are red with blood! The pathways of the forest,
The clouds that canopy the setting sun,
And even the little river in the meadows
Are stained with it! Where'er I look, I see it!
Away, thou horrible vision! Leave me! leave me!
Alas! yon winding stream, that gropes its way
Through mist and shadow, doubling on itself,
At length will find, by the unerring law
Of nature, what it seeks. O soul of man,
Groping through mist and shadow, and recoiling
Back on thyself, are, too, thy devious ways
Subject to law? and when thou seemest to wander
The farthest from thy goal, art thou still drawing
Nearer and nearer to it, till at length
Thou findest, like the river, what thou seekest?

Exit.

ACT V

Scene I.—*Daybreak. Street in front of* Upsall's *house. A
light in the window. Enter* John Endicott.

JOHN ENDICOTT

O silent, sombre, and deserted streets,
To me ye're peopled with a sad procession,
And echo only to the voice of sorrow!
O houses full of peacefulness and sleep,
Far better were it to awake no more
Than wake to look upon such scenes again!
There is a light in Master Upsall's window.
The good man is already risen, for sleep

Deserts the couches of the old.

Knocks at UPSALL's *door.*

UPSALL (*at the window*)

Who's there?

JOHN ENDICOTT

Am I so changed you do not know my voice?

UPSALL

I know you. Have you heard what things have happened?

JOHN ENDICOTT

I have heard nothing.

UPSALL

Stay; I will come down.

JOHN ENDICOTT

I am afraid some dreadful news awaits me!
I do not dare to ask, yet am impatient
To know the worst. Oh, I am very weary
With waiting and with watching and pursuing!

Enter UPSALL.

UPSALL

Thank God, you have come back! I've much to tell
      you.
Where have you been?

JOHN ENDICOTT

            You know that I was seized,
Fined, and released again. You know that Edith,

After her scourging in three towns, was banished
Into the wilderness, into the land
That is not sown; and there I followed her,
But found her not. Where is she?

UPSALL

                    She is here.

JOHN ENDICOTT

Oh, do not speak that word, for it means death!

UPSALL

No, it means life. She sleeps in yonder chamber.
Listen to me. When news of Leddra's death
Reached England, Edward Burroughs, having boldly
Got access to the presence of the King,
Told him there was a vein of innocent blood
Opened in his dominions here, which threatened
To overrun them all. The King replied,
"But I will stop that vein!" and he forthwith
Sent his Mandamus to our Magistrates,
That they proceed no further in this business.
So all are pardoned, and all set at large.

JOHN ENDICOTT

Thank God! This is a victory for truth!
Our thoughts are free. They cannot be shut up
In prison walls, nor put to death on scaffolds!

UPSALL

Come in; the morning air blows sharp and cold
Through the damp streets.

JOHN ENDICOTT

                  It is the dawn of day
That chases the old darkness from our sky,

And fills the land with liberty and light.

Exeunt.

SCENE II.—*The parlor of the Three Mariners. Enter* KEMP-
THORN.

KEMPTHORN

A dull life this,—a dull life anyway!
Ready for sea; the cargo all aboard,
Cleared for Barbadoes, and a fair wind blowing
From nor'-nor'-west; and I, an idle lubber,
Laid neck and heels by that confounded bond!
I said to Ralph, says I, "What's to be done?"
Says he: "Just slip your hawser in the night;
Sheer off, and pay it with the topsail, Simon."
But that won't do; because, you see, the owners
Somehow or other are mixed up with it.
Here are King Charles's Twelve Good Rules, that Cole
Thinks as important as the Rule of Three.
                    (*Reads*)
"Make no comparisons; make no long meals."
Those are good rules and golden for a landlord
To hang in his best parlor, framed and glazed!
"Maintain no ill opinions; urge no healths."
I drink the King's, whatever he may say,
And, as to ill opinions, that depends.
Now of Ralph Goldsmith I've a good opinion,
And of the bilboes I've an ill opinion;
And both of these opinions I'll maintain
As long as there's a shot left in the locker.

Enter EDWARD BUTTER *with an ear-trumpet.*

BUTTER

Good morning, Captain Kempthorn.

KEMPTHORN

Sir, to you.
You've the advantage of me. I don't know you.
What may I call your name?

BUTTER

That's not your name?

KEMPTHORN

Yes, that's my name. What's yours?

BUTTER

My name is Butter.
I am the treasurer of the Commonwealth.

KEMPTHORN

Will you be seated?

BUTTER

What say? Who's conceited?

KEMPTHORN

Will you sit down?

BUTTER

Oh, thank you.

KEMPTHORN

Spread yourself
Upon this chair, sweet Butter.

BUTTER (*sitting down*)

A fine morning.

KEMPTHORN

Nothing's the matter with it that I know of.
I have seen better, and I have seen worse.
The wind 's nor'west. That's fair for them that sail.

BUTTER

You need not speak so loud; I understand you.
You sail to-day.

KEMPTHORN

No, I don't sail to-day.
So, be it fair or foul, it matters not.
Say, will you smoke? There's choice tobacco here.

BUTTER

No, thank you. It's against the law to smoke.

KEMPTHORN

Then, will you drink? There's good ale at this inn.

BUTTER

No, thank you. It's against the law to drink.

KEMPTHORN

Well, almost everything's against the law
In this good town. Give a wide berth to one thing,
You're sure to fetch up soon on something else.

BUTTER

And so you sail to-day for dear Old England.
I am not one of those who think a sup
Of this New England air is better worth
Than a whole draught of our Old England's ale.

KEMPTHORN

Nor I. Give me the ale and keep the air.
But, as I said, I do not sail to-day.

BUTTER

Ah yes; you sail to-day.

KEMPTHORN

        I'm under bonds
To take some Quakers back to Barbadoes;
And one of them is banished, and another
Is sentenced to be hanged.

BUTTER

        No, all are pardoned,
All are set free, by order of the Court;
But some of them would fain return to England.
You must not take them. Upon that condition
Your bond is cancelled.

KEMPTHORN

        Ah, the wind has shifted!
I pray you, do you speak officially?

BUTTER

I always speak officially. To prove it,
Here is the bond.

        Rising and giving a paper.

KEMPTHORN

        And here's my hand upon it.
And, look you, when I say I'll do a thing
The thing is done. Am I now free to go?

BUTTER

What say?

KEMPTHORN

    I say, confound the tedious man
With his strange speaking-trumpet! Can I go?

BUTTER

You're free to go, by order of the Court.
Your servant, sir.

                            Exit.

KEMPTHORN (*shouting from the window*)

    Swallow, ahoy! Hallo!
If ever a man was happy to leave Boston,
That man is Simon Kempthorn of the Swallow!

Reenter BUTTER.

BUTTER

Pray, did you call?

KEMPTHORN

    Call? Yes, I hailed the Swallow.

BUTTER

That's not my name. My name is Edward Butter.
You need not speak so loud.

KEMPTHORN (*shaking hands*)

    Good-by! Good-by!

BUTTER

Your servant, sir.

KEMPTHORN

And yours a thousand times!

Exeunt.

SCENE III.—GOVERNOR ENDICOTT's *private room. An open window.* ENDICOTT *seated in an arm-chair.* BELLINGHAM *standing near.*

ENDICOTT

O lost, O loved! wilt thou return no more?
O loved and lost, and loved the more when lost!
How many men are dragged into their graves
By their rebellious children! I now feel
The agony of a father's breaking heart
In David's cry, "O Absalom, my son!"

BELLINGHAM

Can you not turn your thoughts a little while
To public matters? There are papers here
That need attention.

ENDICOTT

Trouble me no more!
My business now is with another world.
Ah, Richard Bellingham! I greatly fear
That in my righteous zeal I have been led
To doing many things which, left undone,
My mind would now be easier. Did I dream it,
Or has some person told me, that John Norton
Is dead?

BELLINGHAM

You have not dreamed it. He is dead,
And gone to his reward. It was no dream.

243

ENDICOTT

Then it was very sudden; for I saw him
Standing where you now stand, not long ago.

BELLINGHAM

By his own fireside, in the afternoon,
A faintness and a giddiness came o'er him;
And, leaning on the chimney-piece, he cried,
"The hand of God is on me!" and fell dead.

ENDICOTT

And did not some one say, or have I dreamed it,
That Humphrey Atherton is dead?

BELLINGHAM

         Alas!
He too is gone, and by a death as sudden.
Returning home one evening, at the place
Where usually the Quakers have been scourged,
His horse took fright, and threw him to the ground,
So that his brains were dashed about the street.

ENDICOTT

I am not superstitious, Bellingham,
And yet I tremble lest it may have been
A judgment on him.

BELLINGHAM

        So the people think.
They say his horse saw standing in the way
The ghost of William Leddra, and was frightened.
And furthermore, brave Richard Davenport,
The captain of the Castle, in the storm
Has been struck dead by lightning.

ENDICOTT

Speak no more
For as I listen to your voice it seems
As if the Seven Thunders uttered their voices,
And the dead bodies lay about the streets
Of the disconsolate city! Bellingham,
I did not put those wretched men to death.
I did but guard the passage with the sword
Pointed towards them, and they rushed upon it!
Yet now I would that I had taken no part
In all that bloody work.

BELLINGHAM

The guilt of it
Be on their heads, not ours.

ENDICOTT

Are all set free?

BELLINGHAM

All are at large.

ENDICOTT

And none have been sent back
To England to malign us with the King?

BELLINGHAM

The ship that brought them sails this very hour,
But carries no one back.

A distant cannon.

ENDICOTT

What is that gun?

BELLINGHAM

Her parting signal. Through the window there,
Look, you can see her sails, above the roofs,
Dropping below the Castle, outward bound.

ENDICOTT

O white, white, white! Would that my soul had wings
As spotless as those shining sails to fly with!
Now lay this cushion straight. I thank you. Hark!
I thought I heard the hall door open and shut!
I thought I heard the footsteps of my boy!

BELLINGHAM

It was the wind. There's no one in the passage.

ENDICOTT

O Absalom, my son! I feel the world
Sinking beneath me, sinking, sinking, sinking!
Death knocks! I go to meet him! Welcome, Death!
        *Rises, and sinks back dead; his head falling aside
        upon his shoulder.*

BELLINGHAM

O ghastly sight! Like one who has been hanged!
Endicott! Endicott! He makes no answer!
        (*Raises* ENDICOTT's *head*)
He breathes no more! How bright this signet-ring
Glitters upon his hand, where he has worn it.
Through such long years of trouble, as if Death
Had given him this memento of affection,
And whispered in his ear, "Remember me!"
How placid and how quiet is his face,
Now that the struggle and the strife are ended!
Only the acrid spirit of the times
Corroded this true steel. Oh, rest in peace,
Courageous heart! Forever rest in peace!

II. GILES COREY OF THE SALEM FARMS*

Dramatis Personae

GILES COREY	Farmer.
JOHN HATHORNE	Magistrate.
COTTON MATHER	Minister of the Gospel.
JONATHAN WALCOT	A youth.
RICHARD GARDNER	Sea-Captain.
JOHN GLOYD	Corey's hired man.
MARTHA	Wife of Giles Corey.
TITUBA	An Indian Woman.
MARY WALCOT	One of the Afflicted.

The Scene is in Salem in the year 1692.

PROLOGUE

Delusions of the days that once have been,
Witchcraft and wonders of the world unseen,
Phantoms of air, and necromantic arts
That crushed the weak and awed the stoutest hearts,—
These are our theme to-night; and vaguely here,
Through the dim mists that crowd the atmosphere,
We draw the outlines of weird figures cast
In shadow on the background of the Past.

Who would believe that in the quiet town
Of Salem, and amid the woods that crown
The neighboring hillsides, and the sunny farms
That fold it safe in their paternal arms,—
Who would believe that in those peaceful streets,
Where the great elms shut out the summer heats,
Where quiet reigns, and breathes through brain and
        breast
The benediction of unbroken rest,—

Who would believe such deeds could find a place
As these whose tragic history we retrace?

'T was but a village then: the goodman ploughed
His ample acres under sun or cloud;
The goodwife at her doorstep sat and spun,
And gossiped with her neighbors in the sun;
The only men of dignity and state
Were then the Minister and the Magistrate,
Who ruled their little realm with iron rod,
Less in the love than in the fear of God;
And who believed devoutly in the Powers
Of Darkness, working in this world of ours,
In spells of Witchcraft, incantations dread,
And shrouded apparitions of the dead.

Upon this simple folk "with fire and flame,"
Saith the old Chronicle, "the Devil came;
Scattering his firebrands and his poisonous darts,
To set on fire of Hell all tongues and hearts!
And 't is no wonder; for, with all his host,
There most he rages where he hateth most,
And is most hated; so on us he brings
All these stupendous and portentous things!"

Something of this our scene to-night will show;
And ye who listen to the Tale of Woe,
Be not too swift in casting the first stone,
Nor think New England bears the guilt alone.
This sudden burst of wickedness and crime
Was but the common madness of the time,
When in all lands, that lie within the sound
Of Sabbath bells, a Witch was burned or drowned.

GILES COREY

ACT I

SCENE I.—*The woods near Salem Village. Enter* TITUBA, *with a basket of herbs.*

TITUBA

Here's monk's-hood, that breeds fever in the blood;
And deadly nightshade, that makes men see ghosts;
And henbane, that will shake them with convulsions;
And meadow-saffron and black hellebore,
That rack the nerves, and puff the skin with dropsy;
And bitter-sweet, and briony, and eye-bright,
That cause eruptions, nosebleed, rheumatisms;
I know them, and the places where they hide
In field and meadow; and I know their secrets,
And gather them because they give me power
Over all men and women. Armed with these,
I, Tituba, an Indian and a slave,
Am stronger than the captain with his sword,
Am richer than the merchant with his money,
Am wiser than the scholar with his books,
Mightier than Ministers and Magistrates,
With all the fear and reverence that attend them!
For I can fill their bones with aches and pains,
Can make them cough with asthma, shake with palsy,
Can make their daughters see and talk with ghosts,
Or fall into delirium and convulsions.
I have the Evil Eye, the Evil Hand;
A touch from me, and they are weak with pain,
A look from me, and they consume and die.
The death of cattle and the blight of corn,
The shipwreck, the tornado, and the fire,—
These are my doings, and they know it not.
Thus I work vengeance on mine enemies,

Who, while they call me slave, are slaves to me!

Exit TITUBA.

Enter MATHER, *booted and spurred, with a riding-whip in his hand.*

MATHER

Methinks that I have come by paths unknown
Into the land and atmosphere of Witches;
For, meditating as I journeyed on,
Lo! I have lost my way! If I remember
Rightly, it is Scribonius the learned
That tells the story of a man who, praying
For one that was possessed by Evil Spirits,
Was struck by Evil Spirits in the face;
I, journeying to circumvent the Witches,
Surely by Witches have been led astray.
I am persuaded there are few affairs
In which the Devil doth not interfere.
We cannot undertake a journey even,
But Satan will be there to meddle with it
By hindering or by furthering. He hath led me
Into this thicket, stuck me in the face
With branches of the trees, and so entangled
The fetlocks of my horse with vines and brambles,
That I must needs dismount, and search on foot
For the lost pathway leading to the village.

(*Reenter* TITUBA)

What shape is this? What monstrous apparition,
Exceeding fierce, that none may pass that way?
Tell me, good woman, if you are a woman—

TITUBA

I am a woman, but I am not good.
I am a Witch!

MATHER

> Then tell me, Witch and woman,
For you must know the pathways through this wood,
Where lieth Salem Village?

TITUBA

> Reverend sir,
The village is near by. I'm going there
With these few herbs. I'll lead you. Follow me.

MATHER

First say, who are you? I am loath to follow
A stranger in this wilderness, for fear
Of being misled, and left in some morass.
Who are you?

TITUBA

> I am Tituba the Witch,
Wife of John Indian.

MATHER

> You are Tituba?
I know you then. You have renounced the Devil,
And have become a penitent confessor.
The Lord be praised! Go on, I'll follow you.
Wait only till I fetch my horse, that stands
Tethered among the trees, not far from here.

TITUBA

Let me get up behind you, reverend sir.

MATHER

The Lord forbid! What would the people think,
If they should see the Reverend Cotton Mather

Ride into Salem with a Witch behind him?
The Lord forbid!

TITUBA

                    I do not need a horse!
I can ride through the air upon a stick,
Above the tree-tops and above the houses,
And no one see me, no one overtake me!

Exeunt.

SCENE II.—*A room at* JUSTICE HATHORNE'S. *A clock in the corner. Enter* HATHORNE *and* MATHER.

HATHORNE

You are welcome, reverend sir, thrice welcome here
Beneath my humble roof.

MATHER

                    I thank your Worship.

HATHORNE

Pray you be seated. You must be fatigued
With your long ride through unfrequented woods.

They sit down.

MATHER

You know the purport of my visit here,—
To be advised by you, and counsel with you,
And with the Reverend Clergy of the village,
Touching these witchcrafts that so much afflict you;
And see with mine own eyes the wonders told
Of spectres and the shadows of the dead,
That come back from their graves to speak with men.

HATHORNE

Some men there are, I have known such, who think
That the two worlds—the seen and the unseen,

The world of matter and the world of spirit—
Are like the hemispheres upon our maps,
And touch each other only at a point.
But these two worlds are not divided thus,
Save for the purposes of common speech.
They form one globe, in which the parted seas
All flow together and are intermingled,
While the great continents remain distinct.

MATHER

I doubt it not. The spiritual world
Lies all about us, and its avenues
Are open to the unseen feet of phantoms
That come and go, and we perceive them not,
Save by their influence, or when at times
A most mysterious Providence permits them
To manifest themselves to mortal eyes.

HATHORNE

You, who are always welcome here among us,
Are doubly welcome now. We need your wisdom,
Your learning in these things, to be our guide.
The Devil hath come down in wrath upon us,
And ravages the land with all his hosts.

MATHER

The Unclean Spirit said, "My name is Legion!"
Multitudes in the Valley of Destruction!
But when our fervent, well-directed prayers,
Which are the great artillery of Heaven,
Are brought into the field, I see them scattered
And driven like Autumn leaves before the wind.

HATHORNE

You, as a Minister of God, can meet them
With spiritual weapons; but, alas!

I, as a Magistrate, must combat them
With weapons from the armory of the flesh.

MATHER

These wonders of the world invisible,—
These spectral shapes that haunt our habitations,—
The multiplied and manifold afflictions
With which the aged and the dying saints
Have their death prefaced and their age imbittered,—
Are but prophetic trumpets that proclaim
The Second Coming of our Lord on earth.
The evening wolves will be much more abroad,
When we are near the evening of the world.

HATHORNE

When you shall see, as I have hourly seen,
The sorceries and the witchcrafts that torment us,
See children tortured by invisible spirits,
And wasted and consumed by powers unseen,
You will confess the half has not been told you.

MATHER

It must be so. The death-pangs of the Devil
Will make him more a Devil than before;
And Nebuchadnezzar's furnace will be heated
Seven times more hot before its putting out.*

HATHORNE

Advise me, reverend sir. I look to you
For counsel and for guidance in this matter.
What further shall we do?

MATHER

     Remember this,
That as a sparrow falls not to the ground

Without the will of God, so not a Devil
Can come down from the air without his leave.
We must inquire.

HATHORNE

Dear sir, we have inquired;
Sifted the matter thoroughly through and through,
And then resifted it.

MATHER

If God permits
These Evil spirits from the unseen regions
To visit us with surprising informations,
We must inquire what cause there is for this,
But not receive the testimony borne
By spectres as conclusive proof of guilt
In the accused.

HATHORNE

Upon such evidence
We do not rest our case. The ways are many
In which the guilty do betray themselves.

MATHER

Be careful. Carry the knife with such exactness,
That on one side no innocent blood be shed
By too excessive zeal, and, on the other
No shelter given to any work of darkness.

HATHORNE

For one, I do not fear excess of zeal.
What do we gain by parleying with the Devil?
You reason, but you hesitate to act!
Ah, reverend sir! believe me, in such cases
The only safety is in acting promptly.

'T is not the part of wisdom to delay
In things where not to do is still to do
A deed more fatal than the deed we shrink from.
You are a man of books and meditation,
But I am one who acts.

MATHER

        God give us widsom
In the directing of this thorny business,
And guide us, lest New England should become
Of an unsavory and sulphurous odor
In the opinion of the world abroad!

The clock strikes.

I never hear the striking of a clock
Without a warning and an admonition
That time is on the wing, and we must quicken
Our tardy pace in journeying Heavenward,
As Israel did in journeying Canaan-ward!

They rise.

HATHORNE

Then let us make all haste; and I will show you
In what disguises and what fearful shapes
The Unclean Spirits haunt this neighborhood,
And you will pardon my excess of zeal.

MATHER

Ah, poor New England! He who hurricanoed
The house of Job is making now on thee
One last assault, more deadly and more snarled
With unintelligible circumstances
Than any thou hast hitherto encountered!

Exeunt.

SCENE III.—*A room in* WALCOT's *house.* MARY WALCOT
seated in an arm-chair. TITUBA *with a mirror.*

MARY

Tell me another story, Tituba.
A drowsiness is stealing over me
Which is not sleep; for, though I close mine eyes,
I am awake, and in another world.
Dim faces of the dead and of the absent
Come floating up before me,—floating, fading,
And disappearing.

TITUBA

Look into this glass.
What see you?

MARY

Nothing but a golden vapor.
Yes, something more. An island, with the sea
Breaking all round it, like a blooming hedge.
What land is this?

TITUBA

It is San Salvador,
Where Tituba was born. What see you now?

MARY

A man all black and fierce.

TITUBA

That is my father:
He was an Obi man, and taught me magic,—
Taught me the use of herbs and images.
What is he doing?

MARY

Holding in his hand
A waxen figure. He is melting it
Slowly before a fire.

TITUBA

And now what see you?

MARY

A woman lying on a bed of leaves,
Wasted and worn away. Ah, she is dying!

TITUBA

That is the way the Obi men destroy*
The people they dislike! That is the way
Some one is wasting and consuming you.

MARY

You terrify me, Tituba! Oh, save me
From those who make me pine and waste away!
Who are they? Tell me.

TITUBA

That I do not know.
But you will see them. They will come to you.

MARY

No, do not let them come! I cannot bear it!
I am too weak to bear it! I am dying.

Falls into a trance.

TITUBA

Hark! there is some one coming.

Enter HATHORNE, MATHER, *and* WALCOT.

WALCOT

There she lies,
Wasted and worn by devilish incantations!
O my poor sister!

MATHER

Is she always thus?

WALCOT

Nay, she is sometimes tortured by convulsions.

MATHER

Poor child! How thin she is! How wan and wasted!

HATHORNE

Observe her. She is troubled in her sleep.

MATHER

Some fearful vision haunts her.

HATHORNE

You now see
With your own eyes, and touch with your own hands,
The mysteries of this Witchcraft.

MATHER

One would need
The hands of Briareus and the eyes of Argus
To see and touch them all.

HATHORNE

You now have entered
The realm of ghosts and phantoms,—the vast realm

Of the unknown and the invisible,
Through whose wide-open gates there blows a wind
From the dark valley of the shadow of Death,
That freezes us with horror.

MARY (*starting*)

　　　　　　Take her hence!
Take her away from me. I see her there!
She's coming to torment me!

WALCOT (*taking her hand*)

　　　　　　O my sister!
What frightens you? She neither hears nor sees me.
She's in a trance.

MARY

Do you not see her there?

TITUBA

My child, who is it?

MARY

　　　　　　Ah, I do not know.
I cannot see her face.

TITUBA

How is she clad?

MARY

She wears a crimson bodice. In her hand
She holds an image, and is pinching it
Between her fingers. Ah, she tortures me!
I see her face now. It is Goodwife Bishop!
Why does she torture me? I never harmed her!

And now she strikes me with an iron rod!
Oh, I am beaten!

MATHER

This is wonderful!
I can see nothing! Is this apparition
Visibly there, and yet we cannot see it?

HATHORNE

It is. The spectre is invisible
Unto our grosser senses, but she sees it.

MARY

Look! look! there is another clad in gray!
She holds a spindle in her hand, and threatens
To stab me with it! It is Goodwife Corey!
Keep her away! Now she is coming at me!
O mercy! mercy!

WALCOT (*thrusting with his sword*)

There is nothing there!

MATHER (*to* HATHORNE)

Do you see anything?

HATHORNE

The laws that govern
The spiritual world prevent our seeing
Things palpable and visible to her.
These spectres are to us as if they were not.
Mark her; she wakes.

> TITUBA *touches her, and she awakes.*

MARY

Who are these gentlemen?

WALCOT

They are our friends. Dear Mary, are you better?

MARY

Weak, very weak.
   (*Taking a spindle from her lap, and holding it up*)
                    How came this spindle here?

TITUBA

You wrenched it from the hand of Goodwife Corey
When she rushed at you.

HATHORNE

                    Mark that, reverend sir!

MATHER

It is most marvellous, most inexplicable!

TITUBA (*picking up a bit of gray cloth from the floor*)

And here, too, is a bit of her gray dress,
That the sword cut away.

MATHER

                    Beholding this,
It were indeed by far more credulous
To be incredulous than to believe.
None but a Sadducee, who doubts of all
Pertaining to the spiritual world,
Could doubt such manifest and damning proofs!

HATHORNE

Are you convinced?

MATHER (*to* MARY)

                    Dear child, be comforted!
Only by prayer and fasting can you drive

These Unclean Spirits from you. An old man
Gives you his blessing. God be with you, Mary!

ACT II

SCENE I.—GILES COREY's *farm. Morning. Enter* COREY,
with a horseshoe and a hammer.

COREY

The Lord hath prospered me. The rising sun
Shines on my Hundred Acres and my woods
As if he loved them! On a morn like this
I can forgive mine enemies, and thank God
For all his goodness unto me and mine.
My orchard groans with russets and pear-mains;
My ripening corn shines golden in the sun;
My barns are crammed with hay, my cattle thrive;
The birds sing blithely on the trees around me!
And blither than the birds my heart within me.
But Satan still goes up and down the earth;
And to protect this house from his assaults,
And keep the powers of darkness from my door,
This horseshoe will I nail upon the threshold.
                              Nails down the horseshoe.
There, ye night-hags and witches that torment
The neighborhood, ye shall not enter here!—
What is the matter in the field?—John Gloyd!
The cattle are all running to the woods!—
John Gloyd! Where is the man?
                    (*Enter* JOHN GLOYD)
                              Look there!
What ails the cattle? Are they all bewitched?
They run like mad.

GLOYD

Look there! They have been overlooked.

COREY

The Evil Eye is on them sure enough.
Call all the men. Be quick. Go after them!

Exit GLOYD *and enter* MARTHA.

MARTHA

What is amiss?

COREY

The cattle are bewitched.
They are broken loose and making for the woods.

MARTHA

Why will you harbor such delusions, Giles?
Bewitched? Well, then it was John Gloyd bewitched
     them;
I saw him even now take down the bars
And turn them loose! They're only frolicsome.

COREY

The rascal!

MARTHA

I was standing in the road,
Talking with Goodwife Proctor, and I saw him.

COREY

With Proctor's wife? And what says Goodwife Proctor?

MARTHA

Sad things indeed; the saddest you can hear
Of Bridget Bishop. She's cried out upon!

COREY

Pour soul! I 've known her forty year or more.
She was the widow Wasselby; and then

She married Oliver, and Bishop next.
She's had three husbands. I remember well
My games of shovel-board at Bishop's tavern
In the old merry days, and she so gay
With her red paragon bodice and her ribbons!
Ah, Bridget Bishop always was a Witch!

MARTHA

They'll little help her now,—her cap and ribbons,
And her red paragon bodice, and her plumes,
With which she flaunted in the Meeting-house!
When next she goes there, it will be for trial.

COREY

When will that be?

MARTHA

This very day at ten.

COREY

Then get you ready. We will go and see it.
Come; you shall ride behind me on the pillion.

MARTHA

Not I. You know I do not like such things.
I wonder you should. I do not believe
In Witches nor in Witchcraft.

COREY

Well, I do.
There's a strange fascination in it all,
That draws me on and on, I know not why.

MARTHA

What do we know of spirits good or ill,
Or of their power to help us or to harm us?

COREY

Surely what's in the Bible must be true.
Did not an Evil Spirit come on Saul?
Did not the Witch of Endor bring the ghost
Of Samuel from his grave? The Bible says so.

MARTHA

That happened very long ago.

COREY

                                   With God
There is no long ago.

MARTHA

                    There is with us.

COREY

And Mary Magdalene had seven devils,
And he who dwelt among the tombs a legion!*

MARTHA

God's power is infinite. I do not doubt it.
If in His Providence he once permitted
Such things to be among the Israelites,
It does not follow He permits them now,
And among us who are not Israelites.
But we will not dispute about it, Giles.
Go to the village, if you think it best,
And leave me here; I'll go about my work.

                              Exit into the house.

COREY

And I will go and saddle the gray mare.
The last word always. That is woman's nature.
If an old man will marry a young wife,

He must make up his mind to many things.
It's putting new cloth into an old garment,
When the strain comes, it is the old gives way.

Goes to the door.

O Martha! I forgot to tell you something.
I've had a letter from a friend of mine,
A certain Richard Gardner of Nantucket,
Master and owner of a whaling-vessel;
He writes that he is coming down to see us.
I hope you'll like him.

MARTHA

I will do my best.

COREY

That's a good woman. Now I will be gone.
I've not seen Gardner for this twenty year;
But there is something of the sea about him,—
Something so open, generous, large, and strong,
It makes me love him better than a brother.

Exit.

MARTHA *comes in the door.*

MARTHA

Oh these old friends and cronies of my husband,
These captains from Nantucket and the Cape,
That come and turn my house into a tavern
With their carousing! Still, there's something frank
In these seafaring men that makes me like them.
Why, here's a horseshoe nailed upon the doorstep!
Giles has done this to keep away the Witches.
I hope this Richard Gardner will bring with him
A gale of good sound common-sense, to blow
The fog of these delusions from his brain!

COREY (*within*)

Ho! Martha! Martha!

(*Enter* COREY)

Have you seen my saddle?

MARTHA

I saw it yesterday.

COREY

Where did you see it?

MARTHA

On a gray mare, that somebody was riding
Along the village road.

COREY

Who was it? Tell me.

MARTHA

Some one who should have stayed at home.

COREY (*restraining himself*)

I see!

Don't vex me, Martha. Tell me where it is.

MARTHA

I've hidden it away.

COREY

Go fetch it me.

MARTHA

Go find it.

COREY

No. I'll ride down to the village
Bare-back; and when the people stare and say,
"Giles Corey, where's your saddle?" I will answer,
"A Witch has stolen it." How shall you like that?

MARTHA

I shall not like it.

COREY

Then go fetch the saddle.

Exit MARTHA.

If an old man will marry a young wife,
Why then—why then—why then—he must spell Baker!*

Enter MARTHA *with the saddle, which she throws down.*

MARTHA

There! There's the saddle.

COREY

Take it up.

MARTHA

I won't.

COREY

Then let it lie there. I'll ride to the village,
And say you are a Witch!

MARTHA

No, not that, Giles.

She takes up the saddle.

COREY

Now come with me, and saddle the gray mare
With your own hands; and you shall see me ride

Along the village road as is becoming
Giles Corey of the Salem Farms, your husband!

Exeunt.

SCENE II.—*The green in front of the Meeting-house in
Salem Village. People coming and going. Enter* GILES
COREY.

COREY

A melancholy end! Who would have thought
That Bridget Bishop e'er would come to this?
Accused, convicted, and condemned to death
For Witchcraft! And so good a woman too!

A FARMER

Good morrow, neighbor Corey.

COREY (*not hearing him*)

Who is safe?
How do I know but under my own roof
I too may harbor Witches, and some Devil
Be plotting and contriving against me?

FARMER

He does not hear. Good morrow, neighbor Corey!

COREY

Good morrow.

FARMER

Have you seen John Proctor lately?

COREY

No, I have not.

FARMER

Then do not see him, Corey.

COREY

Why should I not?

FARMER

Because he's angry with you.
So keep out of his way. Avoid a quarrel.

COREY

Why does he seek to fix a quarrel on me?

FARMER

He says you burned his house.

COREY

I burn his house?
If he says that, John Proctor is a liar!
The night his house was burned I was in bed,
And I can prove it! Why, we are old friends!
He could not say that of me.

FARMER

He did say it.
I heard him say it.

COREY

Then he shall unsay it.

FARMER

He said you did it out of spite to him
For taking part against you in the quarrel
You had with your John Gloyd about his wages.

He says you murdered Goodell; that you trampled
Upon his body till he breathed no more.
And so beware of him; that's my advice!

Exit.

COREY

By Heaven! this is too much! I'll seek him out,
And make him eat his words, or strangle him.
I'll not be slandered at a time like this,
When every word is made an accusation,
When every whisper kills, and every man
Walks with a halter round his neck!
                    (*Enter* GLOYD *in haste*)
                                        What now?

GLOYD

I came to look for you. The cattle—

COREY

                                Well,
What of them? Have you found them?

GLOYD

                                They are dead.
I followed them through the woods, across the meadows;
Then they all leaped into the Ipswich River,
And swam across, but could not climb the bank,
And so were drowned.

COREY

                You are to blame for this;
For you took down the bars, and let them loose.

GLOYD

That I deny. They broke the fences down.
You know they were bewitched.

COREY

Ah, my poor cattle!
The Evil Eye was on them; that is true.
Day of disaster! Most unlucky day!
Why did I leave my ploughing and my reaping
To plough and reap this Sodom and Gomorrah?
Oh, I could drown myself for sheer vexation!

Exit.

GLOYD

He's going for his cattle. He won't find them.
By this time they have drifted out to sea.
They will not break his fences any more,
Though they may break his heart. And what care I?

Exit.

SCENE III.—COREY's *kitchen. A table with supper.* MARTHA
knitting.

MARTHA

He's come at last. I hear him in the passage.
Something has gone amiss with him today;
I know it by his step, and by the sound
The door made as he shut it. He is angry.

Enter COREY *with his riding-whip. As he speaks he takes off
his hat and gloves, and throws them down violently.*

COREY

I say if Satan ever entered man
He's in John Proctor!

MARTHA

Giles, what is the matter?
You frighten me.

273

COREY

I say if any man
Can have a Devil in him, then that man
Is Proctor,—is John Proctor, and no other!

MARTHA

Why, what has he been doing?

COREY

Everything!
What do you think I heard there in the village?

MARTHA

I'm sure I cannot guess. What did you hear?

COREY

He says I burned his house!

MARTHA

Does he say that?

COREY

He says I burned his house. I was in bed
And fast asleep that night; and I can prove it.

MARTHA

If he says that, I think the Father of Lies
Is surely in the man.

COREY

He does say that,
And that I did it to wreak vengeance on him
For taking sides against me in the quarrel
I had with that John Gloyd about his wages.

And God knows that I never bore him malice
For that, as I have told him twenty times!

MARTHA

It is John Gloyd has stirred him up to this.
I do not like that Gloyd. I think him crafty,
Not to be trusted, sullen, and untruthful.
Come, have your supper. You are tired and hungry.

COREY

I'm angry, and not hungry.

MARTHA

                  Do eat something.
You'll be the better for it.

COREY (*sitting down*)
                    I'm not hungry.

MARTHA

Let not the sun go down upon your wrath.

COREY

It has gone down upon it, and will rise
To-morrow, and go down again upon it.
They have trumped up against me the old story
Of causing Goodell's death by trampling on him.

MARTHA

Oh, that is false. I know it to be false.

COREY

He has been dead these fourteen years or more.
Why can't they let him rest? Why must they drag him
Out of his grave to give me a bad name?

I did not kill him. In his bed he died,
As most men die, because his hour had come.
I have wronged no man. Why should Proctor say
Such things about me? I will not forgive him
Till he confesses he has slandered me.
Then, I've more trouble. All my cattle gone.

MARTHA

They will come back again.

COREY

            Not in this world.
Did I not tell you they were overlooked?
They ran down through the woods, into the meadows,
And tried to swim the river, and were drowned.
It is a heavy loss.

MARTHA

         I'm sorry for it.

COREY

All my dear oxen dead. I loved them, Martha,
Next to yourself. I liked to look at them,
And watch the breath come out of their wide nostrils,
And see their patient eyes. Somehow I thought
It gave me strength only to look at them.
And how they strained their necks against the yoke
If I but spoke, or touched them with the goad!
They were my friends; and when Gloyd came and told
      me
They were all drowned, I could have drowned myself
From sheer vexation; and I said as much
To Gloyd and others.

MARTHA

           Do not trust John Gloyd
With anything you would not have repeated.

COREY

As I came through the woods this afternoon,
Impatient at my loss, and much perplexed
With all that I had heard there in the village,
The yellow leaves lit up the trees about me
Like an enchanted palace, and I wished
I knew enough of magic or of Witchcraft
To change them into gold. Then suddenly
A tree shook down some crimson leaves upon me,
Like drops of blood, and in the path before me
Stood Tituba the Indian, the old crone.

MARTHA

Were you not frightened?

COREY

        No, I do not think
I know the meaning of that word. Why frightened?
I am not one of those who think the Lord
Is waiting till He catches them some day
In the back yard alone! What should I fear?
She started from the bushes by the path,
And had a basket full of herbs and roots
For some witch-broth or other,—the old hag!

MARTHA

She has been here to-day.

COREY

        With hand outstretched
She said: "Giles Corey, will you sign the Book?"
"Avaunt!" I cried: "Get thee behind me, Satan!"
At which she laughed and left me. But a voice
Was whispering in my ear continually:
"Self-murder is no crime. The life of man
Is his, to keep it or to throw away!"

MARTHA

'T was a temptation of the Evil One!
Giles, Giles! why will you harbor these dark thoughts?

COREY (*rising*)

I am too tired to talk. I 'll go to bed.

MARTHA

First tell me something about Bridget Bishop.
How did she look? You saw her? You were there?

COREY

I'll tell you that tomorrow, not to-night.
I'll go to bed.

MARTHA

First let us pray together.

COREY

I cannot pray to-night.

MARTHA

Say the Lord's Prayer,
And that will comfort you.

COREY

I cannot say,
"As we forgive those that have sinned against us,"
When I do not forgive them.

MARTHA (*kneeling on the hearth*)

God forgive you!

COREY

I will not make believe! I say, to-night
There's something thwarts me when I wish to pray,

And thrusts into my mind, instead of prayers,
Hate and revenge, and things that are not prayers.
Something of my old self,—my old, bad life,—
And the old Adam in me, rises up,
And will not let me pray. I am afraid.
The Devil hinders me. You know I say
Just what I think, and nothing more nor less,
And, when I pray, my heart is in my prayer.
I cannot say one thing and mean another.
If I can't pray, I will not make believe!

Exit COREY. MARTHA *continues kneeling.*

ACT III

SCENE I.—GILES COREY's *kitchen. Morning.* COREY *and*
MARTHA *sitting at the breakfast-table.*

COREY (*rising*)

Well, now I 've told you all I saw and heard
Of Bridget Bishop; and I must be gone.

MARTHA

Don't go into the village, Giles, to-day.
Last night you came back tired and out of humor.

COREY

Say, angry; say, right angry. I was never
In a more devilish temper in my life.
All things went wrong with me.

MARTHA

                                        You were much vexed;
So don't go to the village.

COREY (*going*)

No, I won't.
I won't go near it. We are going to mow
The Ipswich meadows for the aftermath,
The crop of sedge and rowens.

MARTHA

Stay a moment.
I want to tell you what I dreamed last night.
Do you believe in dreams?

COREY

Why, yes and no.
When they come true, then I believe in them;
When they come false, I don't believe in them.
But let me hear. What did you dream about?

MARTHA

I dreamed that you and I were both in prison;
That we had fetters on our hands and feet;
That we were taken before the Magistrates,
And tried for Witchcraft, and condemned to death!
I wished to pray; they would not let me pray;
You tried to comfort me, and they forbade it.
But the most dreadful thing in all my dream
Was that they made you testify against me!
And then there came a kind of mist between us;
I could not see you; and I woke in terror.
I never was more thankful in my life
Than when I found you sleeping at my side!

COREY (*with tenderness*)

It was our talk last night that made you dream.
I'm sorry for it. I'll control myself
Another time, and keep my temper down!

I do not like such dreams.—Remember, Martha,
I'm going to mow the Ipswich River meadows;
If Gardner comes, you'll tell him where to find me.

Exit.

MARTHA

So this delusion grows from bad to worse.
First, a forsaken and forlorn old woman,
Ragged and wretched, and without a friend;
Then something higher. Now it's Bridget Bishop;
God only knows whose turn it will be next!
The Magistrates are blind, the people mad!
If they would only seize the Afflicted Children,
And put them in the Workhouse, where they should
        be,
There'd be an end of all this wickedness.

Exit.

Scene II.—*A street in Salem Village. Enter* MATHER *and*
HATHORNE.

MATHER

Yet one thing troubles me.

HATHORNE

                And what is that?

MATHER

May not the Devil take the outward shape
Of innocent persons? Are we not in danger,
Perhaps, of punishing some who are not guilty?

HATHORNE

As I have said, we do not trust alone
To special evidence.

MATHER

And then again,
If any shall be put to death for Witchcraft,
We do but kill the body, not the soul.
The Unclean Spirits that possessed them once
Live still, to enter into other bodies.
What have we gained? Surely, there 's nothing gained.

HATHORNE

Doth not the Scripture say, "Thou shalt not suffer
A Witch to live?"*

MATHER

The Scripture sayeth it,
But speaketh to the Jews; and we are Christians.
What say the laws of England?

HATHORNE

They make Witchcraft
Felony without the benefit of Clergy.
Witches are burned in England. You have read—
For you read all things, not a book escapes you—
The famous Demonology of King James?

MATHER

A curious volume. I remember also
The plot of the Two Hundred, with one Fian,
The Registrar of the Devil, at their head,
To drown his Majesty on his return
From Denmark; how they sailed in sieves or riddles
Unto North Berwick Kirk in Lothian,
And, landing there, danced hand in hand, and sang,
"Goodwife, go ye before! goodwife, go ye!
If ye'll not go before, goodwife, let me!"
While Geilis Duncan played the Witches' Reel
Upon a jews-harp.

HATHORNE

Then you know full well
The English law, and that in England Witches,
When lawfully convicted and attainted,
Are put to death.

MATHER

When lawfully convicted;
That is the point.

HATHORNE

You heard the evidence
Produced before us yesterday at the trial
Of Bridget Bishop.

MATHER

One of the Afflicted,
I know, bore witness to the apparition
Of ghosts unto the spectre of this Bishop,
Saying, "You murdered us!" of the truth whereof
There was in matter of fact too much suspicion.

HATHORNE

And when she cast her eyes on the Afflicted,
They were struck down; and this in such a manner
There could be no collusion in the business.
And when the accused but laid her hand upon them,
As they lay in their swoons, they straight revived,
Although they stirred not when the others touched
them.

MATHER

What most convinced me of the woman's guilt
Was finding hidden in her cellar wall
Those poppets made of rags, with headless pins

Stuck into them point outwards, and whereof
She could not give a reasonable account.

HATHORNE

When you shall read the testimony given
Before the Court in all the other cases,
I am persuaded you will find the proof
No less conclusive than it was in this.
Come, then, with me, and I will tax your patience
With reading of the documents so far
As may convince you that these sorcerers
Are lawfully convicted and attainted.
Like doubting Thomas, you shall lay your hand
Upon these wounds, and you will doubt no more.*

Exeunt.

SCENE III.—*A room in* COREY's *house.* MARTHA *and two
Deacons of the church.*

MARTHA

Be seated. I am glad to see you here.
I know what you are come for. You are come
To question me, and learn from my own lips
If I have any dealings with the Devil;
In short, if I'm a Witch.

DEACON (*sitting down*)

        Such is our purpose.
How could you know beforehand why we came?

MARTHA

'T was only a surmise.

DEACON

        We came to ask you,
You being with us in church covenant,
What part you have, if any, in these matters.

MARTHA

And I make answer, No part whatsoever.
I am a farmer's wife, a working woman;
You see my spinning-wheel, you see my loom,
You know the duties of a farmer's wife,
And are not ignorant that my life among you
Has been without reproach until this day.
Is it not true?

DEACON

So much we're bound to own;
And say it frankly, and without reserve.

MARTHA

I've heard the idle tales that are abroad;
I've heard it whispered that I am a Witch;
I cannot help it. I do not believe
In any Witchcraft. It is a delusion.

DEACON

How can you say that it is a delusion,
When all our learned and good men believe it?—
Our Ministers and worshipful Magistrates?

MARTHA

Their eyes are blinded, and see not the truth.
Perhaps one day they will be open to it.

DEACON

You answer boldly. The Afflicted Children
Say you appeared to them.

MARTHA

And did they say
What clothes I came in?

DEACON

No, they could not tell.
They said that you foresaw our visit here,
And blinded them, so that they could not see
The clothes you wore.

MARTHA

The cunning, crafty girls!
I say to you, in all sincerity,
I never have appeared to any one
In my own person. If the Devil takes
My shape to hurt these children, or afflict them,
I am not guilty of it. And I say
It's all a mere delusion of the senses.

DEACON

I greatly fear that you will find too late
It is not so.

MARTHA (rising)

They do accuse me falsely.
It is delusion, or it is deceit.
There is a story in the ancient Scriptures
Which much I wonder comes not to your minds.
Let me repeat it to you.

DEACON

We will hear it.

MARTHA

It came to pass that Naboth had a vineyard*
Hard by the palace of the King called Ahab.
And Ahab, King of Israel, spake to Naboth,
And said to him, Give unto me thy vineyard,
That I may have it for a garden of herbs,

And I will give a better vineyard for it,
Or, if it seemeth good to thee, its worth
In money. And then Naboth said to Ahab,
The Lord forbid it me that I should give
The inheritance of my fathers unto thee.
And Ahab came into his house displeased
And heavy at the words which Naboth spake,
And laid him down upon his bed, and turned
His face away; and he would eat no bread.
And Jezebel, the wife of Ahab, came
and said to him, Why is thy spirit sad?
And he said unto her, Because I spake
To Naboth, to the Jezreelite, and said,
Give me thy vineyard; and he answered, saying,
I will not give my vineyard unto thee.
And Jezebel, the wife of Ahab, said,
Dost thou not rule the realm of Israel?
Arise, eat bread, and let thy heart be merry;
I will give Naboth's vineyard unto thee.
So she wrote letters in King Ahab's name,
And sealed them with his seal, and sent the letters
Unto the elders that were in his city
Dwelling with Naboth, and unto the nobles;
And in the letters wrote, Proclaim a fast;
And set this Naboth high among the people,
And set two men, the sons of Belial,
Before him, to bear witness and to say,
Thou didst blaspheme against God and the King;
And carry him out and stone him, that he die!
And the elders and the nobles of the city
Did even as Jezebel, the wife of Ahab,
Had sent to them and written in the letters.
And then it came to pass, when Ahab heard
Naboth was dead, that Ahab rose to go
Down unto Naboth's vineyard, and to take
Possession of it. And the word of God
Came to Elijah, saying to him, Arise,

Go down to meet the King of Israel
In Naboth's vineyard, whither he hath gone
To take possession. Thou shalt speak to him,
Saying, Thus saith the Lord! What! hast thou killed
And also taken possession? In the place
Wherein the dogs have licked the blood of Naboth
Shall the dogs lick thy blood,—ay, even thine!

Both of the Deacons start from their seats.

And Ahab then, the King of Israel,
Said, Hast thou found me, O mine enemy?
Elijah the Prophet answered, I have found thee!
So will it be with those who have stirred up
The Sons of Belial here to bear false witness
And swear away the lives of innocent people;
Their enemy will find them out at last,
The Prophet's voice will thunder, I have found thee!

Exeunt.

SCENE IV.—*Meadows on Ipswich River. COREY and his men mowing; COREY in advance.*

COREY

Well done, my men. You see, I lead the field!
I'm an old man, but I can swing a scythe
Better than most of you, though you be younger.

Hangs his scythe upon a tree.

GLOYD (*aside to the others*)

How strong he is! It's supernatural.
No man so old as he is has such strength.
The Devil helps him!

COREY (*wiping his forehead*)

Now we'll rest awhile,
And take our nooning. What's the matter with you?
You are not angry with me,—are you, Gloyd?

Come, come, we will not quarrel. Let's be friends.
It's an old story, that the Raven said,
"Read the Third of Colossians and fifteenth."

GLOYD

You're handier at the scythe, but I can beat you
At wrestling.

COREY

Well, perhaps so. I don't know.
I never wrestled with you. Why, you're vexed!
Come, come, don't bear a grudge.

GLOYD

You are afraid.

COREY

What should I be afraid of? All bear witness
The challenge comes from him. Now, then, my man.
They wrestle, and GLOYD *is thrown.*

ONE OF THE MEN

That's a fair fall.

ANOTHER

'T was nothing but a foil!

OTHERS

You've hurt him!

COREY (*helping* GLOYD *rise*)
No; this meadow-land is soft.
You're not hurt,—are you, Gloyd?

GLOYD (*rising*)

No, not much hurt.

COREY

Well, then, shake hands; and there's an end of it.
How do you like that Cornish hug, my lad?
And now we'll see what's in our basket here.

GLOYD (*aside*)

The Devil and all his imps are in that man!
The clutch of his ten fingers burns like fire!

COREY (*reverentially taking off his hat*)

God bless the food He hath provided for us,
And make us thankful for it, for Christ's sake!
He lifts up a keg of cider, and drinks from it.

GLOYD

Do you see that? Don't tell me it's not Witchcraft.
Two of us could not lift that cask as he does!
COREY puts down the keg, and opens a basket.
A voice is heard calling.

VOICE

Ho! Corey, Corey!

COREY

What is that? I surely
Heard some one calling me by name!

VOICE

Giles Corey!
Enter a boy, running, and out of breath.

BOY

Is Master Corey here?

COREY

Yes, here I am.

BOY

O Master Corey!

COREY

Well?

BOY

Your wife—your wife—

COREY

What's happened to my wife?

BOY

She's sent to prison!

COREY

The dream! the dream! O God, be merciful!

BOY

She sent me here to tell you.

COREY (*putting on his jacket*)

Where's my horse?
Don't stand there staring, fellows. Where's my horse?
Exit COREY.

GLOYD

Under the trees there. Run, old man, run, run!
You've got some one to wrestle with you now
Who'll trip your heels up, with your Cornish hug.

If there's a Devil, he has got you now.
Ah, there he goes! His horse is snorting fire!

ONE OF THE MEN

John Gloyd, don't talk so! It's a shame to talk so!
He's a good master, though you quarrel with him.

GLOYD

If hard work and low wages make good masters,
Then he is one. But I think otherwise.
Come, let us have our dinner and be merry,
And talk about the old man and the Witches.
I know some stories that will make you laugh.
They sit down on the grass, and eat.
Now there are Goody Cloyse and Goody Good,
Who have not got a decent tooth between them,
And yet these children—the Afflicted Children—
Say that they bite them, and show marks of teeth
Upon their arms!

ONE OF THE MEN

That makes the wonder greater.
That's Witchcraft. Why, if they had teeth like yours,
'T would be no wonder if the girls were bitten!

GLOYD

And then those ghosts that come out of their graves
And cry, "You murdered us! you murdered us!"

ONE OF THE MEN

And all those Apparitions that stick pins
Into the flesh of the Afflicted Children!

GLOYD

Oh those Afflicted Children! They know well
Where the pins come from. I can tell you that.

And there's old Corey, he has got a horseshoe
Nailed on his doorstep to keep off the Witches,
And all the same his wife has gone to prison.

ONE OF THE MEN

Oh, she's no Witch. I'll swear that Goodwife Corey
Never did harm to any living creature.
She's a good woman, if there ever was one.

GLOYD

Well, we shall see. As for that Bridget Bishop,
She has been tried before; some years ago
A negro testified he saw her shape
Sitting upon the rafters in a barn,
And holding in its hand an egg; and while
He went to fetch his pitchfork, she had vanished.
And now be quiet, will you? I am tired,
And want to sleep here on the grass a little.
                    They stretch themselves on the grass.

ONE OF THE MEN

There may be Witches riding through the air
Over our heads on broomsticks at this moment,
Bound for some Satan's Sabbath in the woods
To be baptized.

GLOYD

            I wish they'd take you with them,
And hold you under water, head and ears,
Till you were drowned; and that would stop your
            talking,
If nothing else will. Let me sleep, I say.

GILES COREY

ACT IV

SCENE I.—*The Green in front of the village Meeting-house.*
An excited crowd gathering. Enter JOHN GLOYD.

FARMER

Who will be tried to-day?

A SECOND

     I do not know.
Here is John Gloyd. Ask him; he knows.

FARMER

            John Gloyd,
Whose turn is it to-day?

GLOYD

     It's Goodwife Corey's.

FARMER

Giles Corey's wife?

GLOYD

     The same. She is not mine.
It will go hard with her with all her praying.
The hypocrite! She's always on her knees;
But she prays to the Devil when she prays.
Let us go in.

           A trumpet blows.

FARMER

   Here come the Magistrates.

SECOND FARMER

Who's the tall man in front?

294

GLOYD

                Oh, that is Hathorne,
A Justice of the Court, and Quartermaster
In the Three County Troop. He'll sift the matter.
That's Corwin with him; and the man in black
Is Cotton Mather, Minister of Boston.

Enter HATHORNE *and other Magistrates on horseback, followed
by the Sheriff, constables, and attendants on foot. The
Magistrates dismount, and enter the Meeting-house, with
the rest.*

FARMER

The Meeting-house is full. I never saw
So great a crowd before.

GLOYD

              No matter. Come.
We shall find room enough by elbowing
Our way among them. Put your shoulder to it.

FARMER

There were not half so many at the trial
Of Goodwife Bishop.

GLOYD

          Keep close after me.
I'll find a place for you. They'll want me there.
I am a friend of Corey's, as you know,
And he can't do without me just at present.

                        Exeunt.

SCENE II.—*Interior of the Meeting-house.* MATHER *and the
Magistrates seated in front of the pulpit. Before them a
raised platform.* MARTHA *in chains.* COREY *near her,*

MARY WALCOT *in a chair. A crowd of spectators, among them* GLOYD. *Confusion and murmurs during the scene.*

HATHORNE

Call Martha Corey.

MARTHA

I am here.

HATHORNE

Come forward.
She ascends the platform.
The Jurors of our Sovereign Lord and Lady
The King and Queen, here present, do accuse you
Of having on the tenth of June last past,
And divers other times before and after,
Wickedly used and practised certain arts
Called Witchcrafts, Sorceries, and Incantations,
Against one Mary Walcot, single woman,
Of Salem Village; by which wicked arts
The aforesaid Mary Walcot was tormented,
Tortured, afflicted, pined, consumed, and wasted,
Against the peace of our Sovereign Lord and Lady
The King and Queen, as well as of the Statute
Made and provided in that case. What say you?

MARTHA

Before I answer, give me leave to pray.

HATHORNE

We have not sent for you, nor are we here,
To hear you pray, but to examine you
In whatsoever is alleged against you.
Why do you hurt this person?

MARTHA

I do not.
I am not guilty of the charge against me.

MARY

Avoid, she-devil! You torment me now!
Avoid, avoid, Witch!

MARTHA

I am innocent.
I never had to do with any Witchcraft
Since I was born. I am a gospel woman.

MARY

You are a gospel Witch!

MARTHA (*clasping her hands*)

Ah me! ah me!
Oh, give me leave to pray!

MARY (*stretching out her hands*)

She hurts me now.
See, she has pinched my hands!

HATHORNE

Who made these marks
Upon her hands?

MARTHA

I do not know. I stand
Apart from her. I did not touch her hands.

HATHORNE

Who hurt her then?

MARTHA

I know not.

HATHORNE

Do you think
She is bewitched?

MARTHA

Indeed I do not think so.
I am no Witch, and have no faith in Witches.

HATHORNE

Then answer me: When certain persons came
To see you yesterday, how did you know
Beforehand why they came?

MARTHA

I had had speech;
The children said I hurt them, and I thought
These people came to question me about it.

HATHORNE

How did you know the children had been told
To note the clothes you wore?

MARTHA

My husband told me
What others said about it.

HATHORNE

Goodman Corey,
Say, did you tell her?

COREY

I must speak the truth;
I did not tell her. It was some one else.

HATHORNE

Did you not say your husband told you so?
How dare you tell a lie in this assembly?
Who told you of the clothes? Confess the truth.
     (MARTHA *bites her lips, and is silent*)
You bite your lips, but do not answer me!

MARY

Ah, she is biting me! Avoid, avoid!

HATHORNE

You said your husband told you.

MARTHA

                    Yes, he told me
The children said I troubled them.

HATHORNE

                   Then tell me,
Why do you trouble them?

MARTHA

          I have denied it.

MARY

She threatened me; stabbed at me with her spindle;
And, when my brother thrust her with his sword,
He tore her gown, and cut a piece away.
Here are they both, the spindle and the cloth.
                    Shows them.

HATHORNE

And there are persons here who know the truth
Of what has now been said. What answer make you?

MARTHA

I make no answer. Give me leave to pray.

HATHORNE

Whom would you pray to?

MARTHA

To my God and Father.

HATHORNE

Who is your God and Father?

MARTHA

The Almighty!

HATHORNE

Doth he you pray to say that he is God?
It is the Prince of Darkness, and not God.

MARY

There is a dark shape whispering in her ear.

HATHORNE

What does it say to you?

MARTHA

I see no shape.

HATHORNE

Did you not hear it whisper?

MARTHA

> I heard nothing.

MARY

What torture! Ah, what agony I suffer!
> *Falls into a swoon.*

HATHORNE

You see this woman cannot stand before you.
If you would look for mercy, you must look
In God's way, by confession of your guilt.
Why does your spectre haunt and hurt this person?

MARTHA

I do not know. He who appeared of old
In Samuel's shape, a saint and glorified,*
May come in whatsoever shape he chooses.
I cannot help it. I am sick at heart!

COREY

O Martha, Martha! let me hold your hand.

HATHORNE

No; stand aside, old man.

MARY (*starting up*)

> Look there! Look there!
I see a little bird, a yellow bird,
Perched on her finger; and it pecks at me.
Ah, it will tear mine eyes out!

MARTHA

> I see nothing.

HATHORNE

'T is the Familiar Spirit that attends her.

MARY

Now it has flown away. It sits up there
Upon the rafters. It is gone; is vanished.

MARTHA

Giles, wipe these tears of anger from mine eyes.
Wipe the sweat from my forehead. I am faint.
                              She leans against the railing.

MARY

Oh, she is crushing me with all her weight!

HATHORNE

Did you not carry once the Devil's Book
To this young woman?

MARTHA

                      Never.

HATHORNE

                              Have you signed it,
Or touched it?

MARTHA

                  No; I never saw it.

HATHORNE

Did you not scourge her with an iron rod?

MARTHA

No, I did not. If any Evil Spirit
Has taken my shape to do these evil deeds,
I cannot help it. I am innocent.

HATHORNE

Did you not say the Magistrates were blind?
That you would open their eyes?

MARTHA (*with a scornful laugh*)

                              Yes, I said that;
If you call me a sorceress, you are blind!
If you accuse the innocent, you are blind!
Can the innocent be guilty?

HATHORNE

                      Did you not
On one occasion hide your husband's saddle
To hinder him from coming to the Sessions?

MARTHA

I thought it was a folly in a farmer
To waste his time pursuing such illusions.

HATHORNE

What was the bird that this young woman saw
Just now upon your hand?

MARTHA

                I know no bird.

HATHORNE

Have you not dealt with a Familiar Spirit?

MARTHA

No, never, never!

HATHORNE

             What then was the Book
You showed to this young woman, and besought her
To write in it?

MARTHA

Where should I have a book?
I showed her none, nor have none.

MARY

The next Sabbath
Is the Communion Day, but Martha Corey
Will not be there!

MARTHA

Ah, you are all against me.
What can I do or say?

HATHORNE

You can confess.

MARTHA

No, I cannot, for I am innocent.

HATHORNE

We have the proof of many witnesses
That you are guilty.

MARTHA

Give me leave to speak.
Will you condemn me on such evidence,—
You who have known me for so many years?
Will you condemn me in this house of God,
Where I so long have worshipped with you all?
Where I have eaten the bread and drunk the wine
So many times at our Lord's Table with you?
Bear witness, you that hear me; you all know
That I have led a blameless life among you,
That never any whisper of suspicion
Was breathed against me till this accusation.

And shall this count for nothing? Will you take
My life away from me, because this girl,
Who is distraught, and not in her right mind,
Accuses me of things I blush to name?

HATHORNE

What! is it not enough? Would you hear more?
Giles Corey!

COREY

I am here.

HATHORNE

Come forward, then.
(COREY *ascends the platform*)
Is it not true, that on a certain night
You were impeded strangely in your prayers?
That something hindered you? and that you left
This woman here, your wife, kneeling alone
Upon the hearth?

COREY

Yes; I cannot deny it.

HATHORNE

Did you not say the Devil hindered you?

COREY

I think I said some words to that effect.

HATHORNE

Is it not true, that fourteen head of cattle,
To you belonging, broke from their enclosure
And leaped into the river, and were drowned?

COREY

It is most true.

HATHORNE

And did you not then say
That they were overlooked?

COREY

So much I said.
I see; they're drawing round me closer, closer,
A net I cannot break, cannot escape from! (*Aside*)

HATHORNE

Who did these things?

COREY

I do not know who did them.

HATHORNE

Then I will tell you. It is some one near you;
You see her now; this woman, your own wife.

COREY

I call the heavens to witness, it is false!
She never harmed me, never hindered me
In anything but what I should not do.
And I bear witness in the sight of heaven,
And in God's house here, that I never knew her
As otherwise than patient, brave, and true,
Faithful, forgiving, full of charity,
A virtuous and industrious and good wife!

HATHORNE

Tut, tut, man; do not rant so in your speech;
You are a witness, not an advocate!
Here, Sheriff, take this woman back to prison.

MARTHA

O Giles, this day you've sworn away my life!

MARY

Go, go and join the Witches at the door.
Do you not hear the drum? Do you not see them?
Go quick. They're waiting for you. You are late.

Exit MARTHA; COREY *following.*

COREY

The dream! the dream! the dream!

HATHORNE

What does he say?
Giles Corey, go not hence. You are yourself
Accused of Witchcraft and of Sorcery
By many witnesses. Say, are you guilty?

COREY

I know my death is foreordained by you,—
Mine and my wife's. Therefore I will not answer.

During the rest of the scene he remains silent.

HATHORNE

Do you refuse to plead?—'T were better for you
To make confession, or to plead Not Guilty.—
Do you not hear me?—Answer, are you guilty?
Do you not know a heavier doom awaits you,
If you refuse to plead, than if found guilty?
Where is John Gloyd?

GLOYD (*coming forward*)

Here am I.

HATHORNE

Tell the Court;

Have you not seen the supernatural power
Of this old man? Have you not seen him do
Strange feats of strength?

GLOYD

I've seen him lead the field,
On a hot day, in mowing, and against
Us younger men; and I have wrestled with him.
He threw me like a feather. I have seen him
Lift up a barrel with his single hands,
Which two strong men could hardly lift together,
And, holding it above his head, drink from it.

HATHORNE

That is enough; we need not question further.
What answer do you make to this, Giles Corey?

MARY

See there! See there!

HATHORNE

What is it? I see nothing.

MARY

Look! Look! It is the ghost of Robert Goodell,
Whom fifteen years ago this man did murder
By stamping on his body! In his shroud
He comes here to bear witness to the crime!
The crowd shrinks back from COREY *in horror.*

HATHORNE

Ghosts of the dead and voices of the living
Bear witness to your guilt, and you must die!
It might have been an easier death. Your doom
Will be on your head, and not on ours.

Twice more will you be questioned of these things;
Twice more have room to plead or to confess.
If you are contumacious to the Court,
And if, when questioned, you refuse to answer,
Then by the Statute you will be condemned
To the *peine forte et dure!* To have your body
Pressed by great weights until you shall be dead!
And may the Lord have mercy on your soul!

ACT V

SCENE I.—COREY's *farm as in Act II., Scene I. Enter*
RICHARD GARDNER, *looking round him.*

GARDNER

Here stands the house as I remember it,
The four tall poplar-trees before the door;
The house, the barn, the orchard, and the well,
With its moss-covered bucket and its trough;
The garden, with its hedge of currant-bushes;
The woods, the harvest-fields; and, far beyond,
The pleasant landscape stretching to the sea.
But everything is silent and deserted!
No bleat of flocks, no bellowing of herds,
No sound of flails, that should be beating now;
Nor man nor beast astir. What can this mean?

Knocks at the door.

Who ho! Giles Corey! Hillo-ho! Giles Corey!—
No answer but the echo from the barn,
And the ill-omened cawing of the crow,
That yonder wings his flight across the fields,
As if he scented carrion in the air.

(Enter TITUBA *with a basket)*

What woman's this, that, like an apparition,
Haunts this deserted homestead in broad day?
Woman, who are you?

TITUBA

I am Tituba.
I am John Indian's wife. I am a Witch.

GARDNER

What are you doing here?

TITUBA

I'm gathering herbs,—
Cinquefoil, and saxifrage, and pennyroyal.

GARDNER (*looking at the herbs*)

This is not cinquefoil, it is deadly night-shade!
This is not saxifrage, but hellebore!
This is not pennyroyal, it is henbane!
Do you come here to poison these good people?

TITUBA

I get these for the Doctor in the Village.
Beware of Tituba. I pinch the children;
Make little poppets and stick pins in them,
And then the children cry out they are pricked.
The Black Dog came to me, and said, "Serve me!"
I was afraid. He made me hurt the children.

GARDNER

Poor soul! She's crazed, with all these Devil's doings.

TITUBA

Will you, sir, sign the Book?

GARDNER

No, I'll not sign it.
Where is Giles Corey? Do you know Giles Corey?

TITUBA

He's safe enough. He's down there in the prison.

GARDNER

Corey in prison? What is he accused of?

TITUBA

Giles Corey and Martha Corey are in prison
Down there in Salem Village. Both are Witches.
She came to me and whispered, "Kill the children!"
Both signed the Book!

GARDNER

                    Begone, you imp of darkness!
You Devil's dam!

TITUBA

Beware of Tituba!

Exit.

GARDNER

How often out at sea on stormy nights,
When the waves thundered round me, and the wind
Bellowed, and beat the canvas, and my ship
Clove through the solid darkness, like a wedge,
I've thought of him, upon his pleasant farm,
Living in quiet with his thrifty housewife,
And envied him, and wished his fate were mine!
And now I find him shipwrecked utterly,
Drifting upon this sea of sorceries,
And lost, perhaps, beyond all aid of man!

Exit.

SCENE II.—*The prison.* GILES COREY *at a table on which are some papers.*

COREY

Now I have done with earth and all its cares;
I give my worldly goods to my dear children;
My body I bequeath to my tormentors,
And my immortal soul to Him who made it.
O God! who in thy wisdom dost afflict me
With an affliction greater than most men
Have ever yet endured or shall endure,
Suffer me not in this last bitter hour
For any pains of death to fall from thee!

MARTHA *is heard singing*

Arise, O righteous Lord!
  And disappoint my foes;
They are but thine avenging sword,
  Whose wounds are swift to close.

COREY

Hark, hark! it is her voice! She is not dead!
She lives! I am not utterly forsaken!

MARTHA (*singing*)

By thine abounding grace,
  And mercies multiplied,
I shall awake, and see thy face;
  I shall be satisfied.

*COREY hides his face in his hands. Enter the JAILER,
followed by RICHARD GARDNER.*

JAILER

Here's a seafaring man, one Richard Gardner,
A friend of yours, who asks to speak with you.
                    COREY rises. They embrace.

COREY

I'm glad to see you, ay, right glad to see you.

GARDNER

And I most sorely grieved to see you thus.

COREY

Of all the friends I had in happier days,
You are the first, ay, and the only one,
That comes to seek me out in my disgrace!
And you but come in time to say farewell.
They've dug my grave already in the field.
I thank you. There is something in your presence,
I know not what it is, that gives me strength.
Perhaps it is the bearing of a man
Familiar with all dangers of the deep,
Familiar with the cries of drowning men,
With fire, and wreck, and foundering ships at sea!

GARDNER

Ah, I have never known a wreck like yours!
Would I could save you!

COREY

                    Do not speak of that.
It is too late. I am resolved to die.

GARDNER

Why would you die who have so much to live for?—
Your daughters, and—

COREY

          You cannot say the word.
My daughters have gone from me. They are married;
They have their homes, their thoughts, apart from me;
I will not say their hearts,—that were too cruel.
What would you have me do?

GARDNER

                    Confess and live.

COREY

That's what they said who came here yesterday
To lay a heavy weight upon my conscience
By telling me that I was driven forth
As an unworthy member of their church.

GARDNER

It is an awful death.

COREY

          'T is but to drown,
And have the weight of all the seas upon you.

GARDNER

Say something; say enough to fend off death
Till this tornado of fanaticism
Blows itself out. Let me come in between you
And your severer self, with my plain sense;
Do not be obstinate.

COREY

I will not plead.
If I deny, I am condemned already,
In courts where ghosts appear as witnesses,
And swear men's lives away. If I confess,
Then I confess a lie, to buy a life
Which is not life, but only death in life.
I will not bear false witness against any,
Not even against myself, whom I count least.

GARDNER (*aside*)

Ah, what a noble character is this!

COREY

I pray you, do not urge me to do that
You would not do yourself. I have already
The bitter taste of death upon my lips;
I feel the pressure of the heavy weight
That will crush out my life within this hour;
But if a word could save me, and that word
Were not the Truth; nay, if it did but swerve
A hair's-breadth from the Truth, I would not say it!

GARDNER (*aside*)

How mean I seem beside a man like this!

COREY

As for my wife, my Martha and my Martyr,—
Whose virtues, like the stars, unseen by day,
Though numberless, do but await the dark
To manifest themselves unto all eyes,—
She who first won me from my evil ways,
And taught me how to live by her example,
By her example teaches me to die,
And leads me onward to the better life!

SHERIFF (*without*)

Giles Corey! Come! The hour has struck!

COREY

I come!

Here is my body; ye may torture it,
But the immortal soul ye cannot crush!

Exeunt.

SCENE III.—*A street in the Village. Enter* GLOYD *and others.*

GLOYD

Quick, or we shall be late!

A MAN

That's not the way.
Come here; come up this lane.

GLOYD

I wonder now
If the old man will die, and will not speak?
He's obstinate enough and tough enough
For anything on earth.   *A bell tolls.*
          Hark! What is that?

A MAN

The passing bell. He's dead!

GLOYD

We are too late.
                    Exeunt in haste.

GILES COREY

SCENE IV.—*A field near the graveyard.* GILES COREY *lying dead, with a great stone on his breast. The Sheriff at his head,* RICHARD GARDNER *at his feet. A crowd behind. The bell tolling. Enter* HATHORNE *and* MATHER.

HATHORNE

This is the Potter's Field. Behold the fate
Of those who deal in Witchcrafts, and, when questioned,
Refuse to plead their guilt or innocence,
And stubbornly drag death upon themselves.

MATHER

O sight most horrible! In a land like this,
Spangled with Churches Evangelical,
Inwrapped in our salvations, must we seek
In mouldering statute-books of English Courts
Some old forgotten Law, to do such deeds?
Those who lie buried in the Potter's Field
Will rise again, as surely as ourselves
That sleep in honored graves with epitaphs;
And this poor man, whom we have made a victim,
Hereafter will be counted as a martyr!

FINALE*

SAINT JOHN

Saint John *wandering over the face of the Earth.*

SAINT JOHN

The Ages come and go,
The Centuries pass as Years;
My hair is white as the snow,
My feet are weary and slow,
The earth is wet with my tears!
The kingdoms crumble, and fall
Apart, like a ruined wall,
Or a bank that is undermined
By a river's ceaseless flow,
And leave no trace behind!
     The world itself is old;
The portals of Time unfold
On hinges of iron, that grate
And groan with the rust and the weight,
Like the hinges of a gate
That hath fallen to decay;
But the evil doth not cease;
There is war instead of peace,
Instead of Love there is hate;
And still I must wander and wait,
Still I must watch and pray,
Not forgetting in whose sight,
A thousand years in their flight
Are as a single day.

The life of man is a gleam
Of light, that comes and goes
Like the course of the Holy Stream

The cityless river, that flows
From fountains no one knows,
Through the Lake of Galilee,
Through forests and level lands,
Over rocks, and shallows, and sands
Of a wilderness wild and vast,
Till it findeth its rest at last
In the desolate Dead Sea!
But alas! alas for me
Not yet this rest shall be!

What, then! doth Charity fail?
Is Faith of no avail?
Is Hope blown out like a light
By a gust of wind in the night?
The clashing of creeds, and the strife
Of the many beliefs, that in vain
Perplex man's heart and brain,
Are naught but the rustle of leaves,
When the breath of God upheaves
The boughs of the Tree of Life,
And they subside again!
And I remember still
The words, and from whom they came,
Not he that repeateth the name,
But he that doeth the will!
And Him evermore I behold
Walking in Galilee,
Through the cornfield's waving gold,
In hamlet, in wood, and in wold,
By the shores of the Beautiful Sea.
He toucheth the sightless eyes;
Before him the demons flee;
To the dead He sayeth: Arise!
To the living: Follow me!
And that voice still soundeth on

FINALE

From the centuries that are gone,
To the centuries that shall be!

From all vain pomps and shows,
From the pride that overflows,
And the false conceits of men;
From all the narrow rules
And subtleties of Schools,
And the craft of tongue and pen;
Bewildered in its search,
Bewildered with the cry:
Lo, here! lo, there, the Church!
Poor, sad Humanity
Through all the dust and heat
Turns back with bleeding feet,
By the weary road it came,
Unto the simple thought
By the great Master taught,
And that remaineth still:
Not he that repeateth the name,
But he that doeth the will!

MORITURI SALUTAMUS*

"O CAESAR, we who are about to die
Salute you!" was the gladiators' cry
In the arena, standing face to face
With death and with the Roman populace.

O ye familiar scenes,—ye groves of pine,
That once were mine and are no longer mine,—
Thou river, widening through the meadows green
To the vast sea, so near and yet unseen,—
Ye halls, in whose seclusion and repose
Phantoms of fame, like exhalations, rose
And vanished,—we who are about to die,
Salute you; earth and air and sea and sky,
And the Imperial Sun that scatters down
His sovereign splendors upon grove and town.

Ye do not answer us! ye do not hear!
We are forgotten; and in your austere
And calm indifference, ye little care
Whether we come or go, or whence or where.
What passing generations fill these halls,
What passing voices echo from these walls,
Ye heed not; we are only as the blast,
A moment heard, and then forever past.

Not so the teachers who in earlier days
Led our bewildered feet through learning's maze;
They answer us—alas! what have I said?
What greetings come there from the voiceless dead?
What salutation, welcome, or reply?

What pressure from the hands that lifeless lie?
They are no longer here; they all are gone
Into the land of shadows,—all save one.
Honor and reverence, and the good repute
That follows faithful service as its fruit,
Be unto him, whom living we salute.

The great Italian poet, when he made
His dreadful journey to the realms of shade,
Met there the old instructor of his youth,
And cried in tones of pity and of ruth:
"Oh, never from the memory of my heart
Your dear, paternal image shall depart,
Who while on earth, ere yet by death surprised,
Taught me how mortals are immortalized;
How grateful am I for that patient care
All my life long my language shall declare."*

To-day we make the poet's words our own,
And utter them in plaintive undertone;
Nor to the living only be they said,
But to the other living called the dead,
Whose dear, paternal images appear
Not wrapped in gloom, but robed in sunshine here
Whose simple lives, complete and without flaw,
Were part and parcel of great Nature's law;
Who said not to their Lord, as if afraid,
"Here is thy talent in a napkin laid,"*
But labored in their sphere, as men who live
In the delight that work alone can give.
Peace be to them; eternal peace and rest,
And the fulfilment of the great behest:
"Ye have been faithful over a few things,
Over ten cities shall ye reign as kings."

And ye who fill the places we once filled,
And follow in the furrows that we tilled,

MORITURI SALUTAMUS

Young men, whose generous hearts are beating high,
We who are old, and are about to die,
Salute you; hail you; take your hands in ours,
And crown you with our welcome as with flowers!

How beautiful is youth! how bright it gleams
With its illusions, aspirations, dreams!
Book of Beginnings, Story without End,
Each maid a heroine, and each man a friend!
Aladdin's Lamp, and Fortunatus' Purse,
That holds the treasures of the universe!
All possibilities are in its hands,
No danger daunts it, and no foe withstands;
In its sublime audacity of faith,
"Be thou removed!" it to the mountain saith,
And with ambitious feet, secure and proud,
Ascends the ladder leaning on the cloud!

As ancient Priam at the Scæan gate
Sat on the walls of Troy in regal state
With the old men, too old and weak to fight,
Chirping like grasshoppers in their delight
To see the embattled hosts, with spear and shield,
Of Trojans and Achaians in the field;*
So from the snowy summits of our years
We see you in the plain, as each appears,
And question of you; asking, "Who is he
That towers above the others? Which may be
Atreides, Menelaus, Odysseus,
Ajax the great, or bold Idomeneus?"

Let him not boast who puts his armor on
As he who puts it off, the battle done.
Study yourselves; and most of all note well
Wherein kind Nature meant you to excel.
Not every blossom ripens into fruit;
Minerva, the inventress of the flute,

Flung it aside, when she her face surveyed
Distorted in a fountain as she played;
The unlucky Marsyas found it, and his fate
Was one to make the bravest hesitate.*

Write on your doors the saying wise and old,*
"Be bold! be bold!" and everywhere, "Be bold;
Be not too bold!" Yet better the excess
Than the defect; better the more than less;
Better like Hector in the field to die,
Than like a perfumed Paris turn and fly.*

And now, my classmates; ye remaining few
That number not the half of those we knew,
Ye, against whose familiar names not yet
The fatal asterisk of death is set,
Ye I salute! The horologe of Time
Strikes the half-century with a solemn chime,
And summons us together once again,
The joy of meeting not unmixed with pain.
Where are the others? Voices from the deep
Caverns of darkness answer me: "They sleep!"
I name no names; instinctively I feel
Each at some well-remembered grave will kneel,
And from the inscription wipe the weeds and moss,
For every heart best knoweth its own loss.
I see their scattered gravestones gleaming white
Through the pale dusk of the impending night;
O'er all alike the impartial sunset throws
Its golden lilies mingled with the rose;
We give to each a tender thought, and pass
Out of the graveyards with their tangled grass,
Unto these scenes frequented by our feet
When we were young, and life was fresh and sweet.

What shall I say to you? What can I say
Better than silence is? When I survey

MORITURI SALUTAMUS

This throng of faces turned to meet my own,
Friendly and fair, and yet to me unknown,
Transformed the very landscape seems to be;
It is the same, yet not the same to me.
So many memories crowd upon my brain,
So many ghosts are in the wooded plain,
I fain would steal away, with noiseless tread,
As from a house where some one lieth dead.
I cannot go;—I pause;—I hesitate;
My feet reluctant linger at the gate;
As one who struggles in a troubled dream
To speak and cannot, to myself I seem.

Vanish the dream! Vanish the idle fears!
Vanish the rolling mists of fifty years!
Whatever time or space may intervene,
I will not be a stranger in this scene.
Here every doubt, all indecision, ends;
Hail, my companions, comrades, classmates, friends!

Ah me! the fifty years since last we met
Seem to me fifty folios bound and set
By Time, the great transcriber, on his shelves,
Wherein are written the histories of ourselves.
What tragedies, what comedies, are there;
What joy and grief, what rapture and despair!
What chronicles of triumph and defeat,
Of struggle, and temptation, and retreat!
What records of regrets, and doubts, and fears!
What pages blotted, blistered by our tears!
What lovely landscapes on the margin shine,
What sweet, angelic faces, what divine
And holy images of love and trust,
Undimmed by age, unsoiled by damp or dust!

Whose hand shall dare to open and explore
These volumes, closed and clasped for evermore?

Not mine. With reverential feet I pass;
I hear a voice that cries, "Alas! alas!
Whatever hath been written shall remain,
Nor be erased nor written o'er again;
The unwritten only still belongs to thee:
Take heed, and ponder well what that shall be."

As children frightened by a thunder-cloud
Are reassured if some one reads aloud
A tale of wonder, with enchantment fraught,
Or wild adventure, that diverts their thought,
Let me endeavor with a tale to chase
The gathering shadows of the time and place,
And banish what we all too deeply feel
Wholly to say, or wholly to conceal.

In mediæval Rome, I know not where,*
There stood an image with its arm in air,
And on its lifted finger, shining clear,
A golden ring with the device, "Strike here!"
Greatly the people wondered, though none guessed
The meaning that these words but half expressed,
Until a learned clerk, who at noonday
With downcast eyes was passing on his way,
Paused, and observed the spot, and marked it well,
Whereon the shadow of the finger fell;
And, coming back at midnight, delved, and found
A secret stairway leading underground.
Down this he passed into a spacious hall,
Lit by a flaming jewel on the wall;
And opposite, in threatening attitude,
With bow and shaft a brazen statue stood.
Upon its forehead, like a coronet,
Were these mysterious words of menace set:
"That which I am, I am; my fatal aim
None can escape, not even yon luminous flame!"

Midway the hall was a fair table placed,
With cloth of gold, and golden cups enchased
With rubies, and the plates and knives were gold,
And gold the bread and viands manifold.
Around it, silent, motionless, and sad,
Were seated gallant knights in armor clad,
And ladies beautiful with plume and zone,
But they were stone, their hearts within were stone;
And the vast hall was filled in every part
With silent crowds, stony in face and heart.

Long at the scene, bewildered and amazed,
The trembling clerk in speechless wonder gazed;
Then from the table, by his greed made bold,
He seized a goblet and a knife of gold,
And suddenly from their seats the guests upsprang,
The vaulted ceiling with loud clamors rang,
The archer sped his arrow, at their call,
Shattering the lambent jewel on the wall,
And all was dark around and overhead;—
Stark on the floor the luckless clerk lay dead!

The writer of this legend then records
Its ghostly application in these words:
The image is the Adversary old,
Whose beckoning finger points to realms of gold,
Our lusts and passions are the downward stair
That leads the soul from a diviner air;
The archer, Death; the flaming jewel, Life;
Terrestrial goods, the goblet and the knife;
The knights and ladies, all whose flesh and bone
By avarice have been hardened into stone;
The clerk, the scholar whom the love of pelf
Tempts from his books and from his nobler self.

The scholar and the world! The endless strife,
The discord in the harmonies of life!

The love of learning, the sequestered nooks,
And all the sweet serenity of books;
The market-place, the eager love of gain,
Whose aim is vanity, and whose end is pain!

But why, you ask me, should this tale be told
To men grown old, or who are growing old?
It is too late! Ah, nothing is too late
Till the tired heart shall cease to palpitate.
Cato learned Greek at eighty; Sophocles
Wrote his grand Œdipus, and Simonides
Bore off the prize of verse from his compeers,
When each had numbered more than fourscore years,
And Theophrastus, at fourscore and ten,
Had but begun his Characters of Men.
Chaucer, at Woodstock with the nightingales,
At sixty wrote The Canterbury Tales;
Goethe at Weimar, toiling to the last,
Completed Faust when eighty years were past.
These are indeed exceptions; but they show
How far the gulf-stream of our youth may flow
Into the arctic regions of our lives,
Where little else than life itself survives.

As the barometer foretells the storm
While still the skies are clear, the weather warm,
So something in us, as old age draws near,
Betrays the pressure of the atmosphere.
The nimble mercury, ere we are aware,
Descends the elastic ladder of the air;
The telltale blood in artery and vein
Sinks from its higher levels in the brain;
Whatever poet, orator, or sage
May say of it, old age is still old age.
It is the waning, not the crescent moon;
The dusk of evening, not the blaze of noon;
It is not strength, but weakness; not desire,

But its surcease; not the fierce heat of fire,
The burning and consuming element,
But that of ashes and of embers spent,
In which some living sparks we still discern,
Enough to warm, but not enough to burn.

What then? Shall we sit idly down and say
The night hath come; it is no longer day?
The night hath not yet come; we are not quite
Cut off from labor by the failing light;
Something remains for us to do or dare;
Even the oldest tree some fruit may bear;
Not Œdipus Coloneus, or Greek Ode,
Or tales of pilgrims that one morning rode
Out of the gateway of the Tabard Inn,*
But other something, would we but begin;
For age is opportunity no less
Than youth itself, though in another dress,
And as the evening twilight fades away
The sky is filled with stars, invisible by day.

SHORTER LYRIC AND
NARRATIVE POEMS

A PSALM OF LIFE*

WHAT THE HEART OF THE YOUNG MAN SAID TO THE PSALMIST

TELL me not, in mournful numbers,
  Life is but an empty dream!—
For the soul is dead that slumbers,
  And things are not what they seem.

Life is real! Life is earnest!
  And the grave is not its goal;
Dust thou art, to dust returnest,
  Was not spoken of the soul.

Not enjoyment, and not sorrow,
  Is our destined end or way;
But to act, that each to-morrow
  Find us farther than to-day.

Art is long, and Time is fleeting,
  And our hearts, though stout and brave,
Still, like muffled drums, are beating
  Funeral marches to the grave.

In the world's broad field of battle,
  In the bivouac of Life,
Be not like dumb, driven cattle!
  Be a hero in the strife!

A PSALM OF LIFE

Trust no Future, howe'er pleasant!
  Let the dead Past bury its dead!
Act,—act in the living Present!
  Heart within, and God o'erhead!

Lives of great men all remind us
  We can make our lives sublime,
And, departing, leave behind us
  Footprints on the sands of time;

Footprints, that perhaps another,
  Sailing o'er life's solemn main,
A forlorn and shipwrecked brother,
  Seeing, shall take heart again.

Let us, then, be up and doing,
  With a heart for any fate;
Still achieving, still pursuing,
  Learn to labor and to wait.

THE SKELETON IN ARMOR

"Speak! speak! thou fearful guest!
Who, with thy hollow breast
Still in rude armor drest,
  Comest to daunt me!
Wrapt not in Eastern balms,
      But with thy fleshless palms
Stretched, as if asking alms,
  Why dost thou haunt me?"

Then, from those cavernous eyes
Pale flashes seemed to rise,
As when the Northern skies
  Gleam in December;
And, like the water's flow
Under December's snow,
Came a dull voice of woe
  From the heart's chamber.

"I was a Viking old!
My deeds, though manifold,
No Skald in song has told,*
  No Saga taught thee!
Take heed, that in thy verse
Thou dost the tale rehearse,
Else dread a dead man's curse;
  For this I sought thee.

"Far in the Northern Land,
By the wild Baltic's strand,

I, with my childish hand,
  Tamed the gerfalcon;
And, with my skates fast-bound,
Skimmed the half-frozen Sound,
That the poor whimpering hound
  Trembled to walk on.

"Oft to his frozen lair
Tracked I the grisly bear,
While from my path the hare
  Fled like a shadow;
Oft through the forest dark
Followed the were-wolf's bark,
Until the soaring lark
  Sang from the meadow.

"But when I older grew,
Joining a corsair's crew,
O'er the dark sea I flew
  With the marauders.
Wild was the life we led;
Many the souls that sped,
Many the hearts that bled,
  By our stern orders.

"Many a wassail-bout
Wore the long Winter out;
Often our midnight shout
  Set the cocks crowing,
As we the Berserk's tale
Measured in cups of ale,
Draining the oaken pail,
  Filled to o'erflowing.

"Once as I told in glee
Tales of the stormy sea,

THE SKELETON IN ARMOR

Soft eyes did gaze on me,
  Burning yet tender;
And as the white stars shine
On the dark Norway pine,
On that dark heart of mine
  Fell their soft splendor.

"I wooed the blue-eyed maid,
Yielding, yet half afraid,
And in the forest's shade
  Our vows were plighted.
Under its loosened vest
Fluttered her little breast,
Like birds within their nest
  By the hawk frighted.

"Bright in her father's hall
Shields gleamed upon the wall,
Loud sang the minstrels all,
  Chanting his glory;
When of old Hildebrand
I asked his daughter's hand
Mute did the minstrels stand
  To hear my story.

"While the brown ale he quaffed,
Loud then the champion laughed,
And as the wind-gusts waft
  The sea-foam brightly,
So the loud laugh of scorn,
Out of those lips unshorn,
From the deep drinking-horn
  Blew the foam lightly.

"She was a Prince's child,
I but a Viking wild,

And though she blushed and smiled,
  I was discarded!
Should not the dove so white
Follow the sea-mew's flight,
Why did they leave that night
  Her nest unguarded?

"Scarce had I put to sea,
Bearing the maid with me,
Fairest of all was she
  Among the Norsemen!
When on the white sea-strand,
Waving his armed hand,
Saw we old Hildebrand,
  With twenty horsemen.

"Then launched they to the blast,
Bent like a reed each mast,
Yet we were gaining fast,
  When the wind failed us;
And with a sudden flaw
Came round the gusty Skaw,
So that our foe we saw
  Laugh as he hailed us.

"And as to catch the gale
Round veered the flapping sail,
'Death!' was the helmsman's hail,
  'Death without quarter!'
Mid-ships with iron keel
Struck we her ribs of steel;
Down her black hulk did reel
  Through the black water!

"As with his wings aslant,
Sails the fierce cormorant,

Seeking some rocky haunt,
  With his prey laden,—
So toward the open main,
Beating to sea again,
Through the wild hurricane,
  Bore I the maiden.

"Three weeks we westward bore,
And when the storm was o'er,
Cloud-like we saw the shore
  Stretching to leeward;
There for my lady's bower
Built I the lofty tower,
Which, to this very hour,
  Stands looking seaward.

"There lived we many years;
Time dried the maiden's tears;
She had forgot her fears,
  She was a mother;
Death closed her mild blue eyes,
Under that tower she lies;
Ne'er shall the sun arise
  On such another!

"Still grew my bosom then,
Still as a stagnant fen!
Hateful to me were men,
  The sunlight hateful!
In the vast forest here,
Clad in my warlike gear,
Fell I upon my spear,
  Oh, death was grateful!

"Thus, seamed with many scars,
Bursting these prison bars,

339

Up to its native stars
  My soul ascended!
There from the flowing bowl
Deep drinks the warrior's soul,
Skoal! to the Northland! *skoal!*"*
  Thus the tale ended.

THE WRECK OF THE HESPERUS*

It was the schooner Hesperus,
    That sailed the wintry sea;
And the skipper had taken his little daughter,
    To bear him company.

        Blue were her eyes as the fairy-flax,
    Her cheeks like the dawn of day,
And her bosom white as the hawthorn buds,
    That ope in the month of May.

The skipper he stood beside the helm,
    His pipe was in his mouth,
And he watched how the veering flaw did blow
    The smoke now West, now South.

Then up and spake an old Sailor,
    Had sailed to the Spanish Main,
"I pray thee, put into yonder port,
    For I fear a hurricane.

"Last night, the moon had a golden ring,
    And to-night no moon we see!"
The skipper, he blew a whiff from his pipe,
    And a scornful laugh laughed he.

Colder and louder blew the wind,
    A gale from the Northeast,
The snow fell hissing in the brine,
    And the billows frothed like yeast.

THE WRECK OF THE HESPERUS

Down came the storm, and smote amain
  The vessel in its strength;
She shuddered and paused, like a frighted steed,
  Then leaped her cable's length.

"Come hither! come hither! my little daughter,
  And do not tremble so;
For I can weather the roughest gale
  That ever wind did blow."

He wrapped her warm in his seaman's coat
  Against the stinging blast;
He cut a rope from a broken spar,
  And bound her to the mast.

"O father! I hear the church-bells ring,
  Oh say, what may it be?"
" 'T is a fog-bell on a rock-bound coast!"—
  And he steered for the open sea.

"O father! I hear the sound of guns,
  Oh say, what may it be?"
"Some ship in distress, that cannot live
  In such an angry sea!"

"O father! I see a gleaming light,
  Oh say, what may it be?"
But the father answered never a word,
  A frozen corpse was he.

Lashed to the helm, all stiff and stark,
  With his face turned to the skies,
The lantern gleamed through the gleaming snow
  On his fixed and glassy eyes.

Then the maiden clasped her hands and prayed
  That savèd she might be;

THE WRECK OF THE HESPERUS

And she thought of Christ, who stilled the wave,
  On the Lake of Galilee.

And fast through the midnight dark and drear,
  Through the whistling sleet and snow,
Like a sheeted ghost, the vessel swept
  Tow'rds the reef of Norman's Woe.

And ever the fitful gusts between
  A sound came from the land;
It was the sound of the trampling surf
  On the rocks and the hard sea-sand.

The breakers were right beneath her bows,
  She drifted a dreary wreck,
And a whooping billow swept the crew
  Like icicles from her deck.

She struck where the white and fleecy waves
  Looked soft as carded wool,
But the cruel rocks, they gored her side
  Like the horns of an angry bull.

Her rattling shrouds, all sheathed in ice,
  With the masts went by the board;
Like a vessel of glass, she stove and sank,
  Ho! ho! the breakers roared!

At daybreak, on the bleak sea-beach,
  A fisherman stood aghast,
To see the form of a maiden fair,
  Lashed close to a drifting mast.

The salt sea was frozen on her breast,
  The salt tears in her eyes;
And he saw her hair, like the brown sea-weed,
  On the billows fall and rise.

THE WRECK OF THE HESPERUS

Such was the wreck of the Hesperus,
  In the midnight and the snow!
Christ save us all from a death like this,
  On the reef of Norman's Woe!

THE VILLAGE BLACKSMITH

UNDER a spreading chestnut-tree
  The village smithy stands;
The smith, a mighty man is he,
  With large and sinewy hands;
And the muscles of his brawny arms
  Are strong as iron bands.

His hair is crisp, and black, and long,
  His face is like the tan;
His brow is wet with honest sweat,
  He earns whate'er he can,
And looks the whole world in the face,
  For he owes not any man.

Week in, week out, from morn till night,
  You can hear his bellows blow;
You can hear him swing his heavy sledge,
  With measured beat and slow,
Like a sexton ringing the village bell,
  When the evening sun is low.

And children coming home from school
  Look in at the open door;
They love to see the flaming forge,
  And hear the bellows roar,
And catch the burning sparks that fly
  Like chaff from a threshing-floor.

He goes on Sunday to the church,
  And sits among his boys;

He hears the parson pray and preach,
  He hears his daughter's voice,
Singing in the village choir,
  And it makes his heart rejoice.

It sounds to him like her mother's voice,
  Singing in Paradise!
He needs must think of her once more,
  How in the grave she lies;
And with his hard, rough hand he wipes
  A tear out of his eyes.

Toiling,—rejoicing,—sorrowing,
  Onward through life he goes;
Each morning sees some task begin,
  Each evening sees it close;
Something attempted, something done,
  Has earned a night's repose.

Thanks, thanks to thee, my worthy friend,
  For the lesson thou hast taught!
Thus at the flaming forge of life
  Our fortunes must be wrought;
Thus on its sounding anvil shaped
  Each burning deed and thought.

THE SLAVE SINGING AT MIDNIGHT*

LOUD he sang the psalm of David!
He, a Negro and enslaved,
Sang of Israel's victory,
Sang of Zion, bright and free.

In that hour, when night is calmest,
Sang he from the Hebrew Psalmist,
In a voice so sweet and clear
That I could not choose but hear,

Songs of triumph, and ascriptions,
Such as reached the swart Egyptians,
When upon the Red Sea coast
Perished Pharaoh and his host.

And the voice of his devotion
Filled my soul with strange emotion;
For its tones by turns were glad,
Sweetly solemn, wildly sad.

Paul and Silas, in their prison,
Sang of Christ, the Lord arisen,
And an earthquake's arm of might
Broke their dungeon-gates at night.

But, alas! what holy angel
Brings the Slave this glad evangel?
And what earthquake's arm of might
Breaks his dungeon-gates at night?

THE WARNING*

[Written before the voyage to Europe, but not printed
until included in "Poems on Slavery."]

BEWARE! The Israelite of old, who tore
    The lion in his path,—when, poor and blind,
He saw the blessed light of heaven no more,
    Shorn of his noble strength and forced to grind
In prison, and at last led forth to be
A pander to Philistine revelry,—

Upon the pillars of the temple laid
    His desperate hands, and in its overthrow
Destroyed himself, and with him those who made
    A cruel mockery of his sightless woe;
The poor, blind Slave, the scoff and jest of all,
Expired, and thousands perished in the fall!

There is a poor, blind Samson in this land,
    Shorn of his strength and bound in bonds of steel,
Who may, in some grim revel, raise his hand,
    And shake the pillars of this Commonweal,
Till the vast Temple of our liberties
A shapeless mass of wreck and rubbish lies.

THE ARSENAL AT SPRINGFIELD*

THIS is the Arsenal. From floor to ceiling,
  Like a huge organ, rise the burnished arms;
But from their silent pipes no anthem pealing
  Startles the villages with strange alarms.

Ah! what a sound will rise, how wild and dreary,
  When the death-angel touches those swift keys!
What loud lament and dismal Miserere*
  Will mingle with their awful symphonies!

I hear even now the infinite fierce chorus,
  The cries of agony, the endless groan,
Which, through the ages that have gone before us,
  In long reverberations reach our own.

On helm and harness rings the Saxon hammer,
  Through Cimbric forest roars the Norseman's song,
And loud, amid the universal clamor,
  O'er distant deserts sounds the Tartar gong.

I hear the Florentine, who from his palace
  Wheels out his battle-bell with dreadful din,
And Aztec priests upon their teocallis
  Beat the wild war-drums made of serpent's skin;

The tumult of each sacked and burning village;
  The shout that every prayer for mercy drowns;
The soldiers' revels in the midst of pillage;
  The wail of famine in beleaguered towns;

THE ARSENAL AT SPRINGFIELD

The bursting shell, the gateway wrenched asunder,
  The rattling musketry, the clashing blade;
And ever and anon, in tones of thunder
  The diapason of the cannonade.

Is it, O man, with such discordant noises,
  With such accursed instruments as these,
Thou drownest Nature's sweet and kindly voices,
  And jarrest the celestial harmonies?

Were half the power, that fills the world with terror,
  Were half the wealth bestowed on camps and courts,
Given to redeem the human mind from error,
  There were no need of arsenals or forts:

The warrior's name would be a name abhorred!
  And every nation, that should lift again
Its hand against a brother, on its forehead
  Would wear for evermore the curse of Cain!*

Down the dark future, through long generations,
  The echoing sounds grow fainter and then cease;
And like a bell, with solemn, sweet vibrations,
  I hear once more the voice of Christ say, "Peace!"

Peace! and no longer from its brazen portals
  The blast of War's great organ shakes the skies!
But beautiful as songs of the immortals,
  The holy melodies of love arise.

THE OCCULTATION OF ORION*

I SAW, as in a dream sublime,
The balance in the hand of Time.
O'er East and West its beam impended;
And Day, with all its hours of light,
Was slowly sinking out of sight,
While, opposite, the scale of Night
Silently with the stars ascended.

Like the astrologers of eld,
In that bright vision I beheld
Greater and deeper mysteries.
I saw, with its celestial keys,
Its chords of air, its frets of fire,
The Samian's great Æolian lyre,
Rising through all its sevenfold bars,
From earth unto the fixed stars.
And through the dewy atmosphere,
Not only could I see, but hear,
Its wondrous and harmonious strings,
In sweet vibration, sphere by sphere,
From Dian's circle light and near,
Onward to vaster and wider rings,
Where, chanting through his beard of snows,
Majestic, mournful, Saturn goes,
And down the sunless realms of space
Reverberates the thunder of his bass.

Beneath the sky's triumphal arch
This music sounded like a march,
And with its chorus seemed to be

351

Preluding some great tragedy.
Sirius was rising in the East;
And, slow ascending one by one,
The kindling constellations shone.
Begirt with many a blazing star,
Stood the great giant Algebar,
Orion, hunter of the beast!
His sword hung gleaming by his side,
And, on his arm, the lion's hide
Scattered across the midnight air
The golden radiance of its hair.

The moon was pallid, but not faint;
And beautiful as some fair saint,
Serenely moving on her way
In hours of trial and dismay.
As if she heard the voice of God,
Unharmed with naked feet she trod
Upon the hot and burning stars,
As on the glowing coals and bars,
That were to prove her strength and try
Her holiness and her purity.

Thus moving on, with silent pace,
And triumph in her sweet, pale face,
She reached the station of Orion.
Aghast he stood in strange alarm!
And suddenly from his outstretched arm
Down fell the red skin of the lion
Into the river at his feet.
His mighty club no longer beat
The forehead of the bull; but he
Reeled as of yore beside the sea,
When, blinded by Œnopion,
He sought the blacksmith at his forge,
And, climbing up the mountain gorge,
Fixed his blank eyes upon the sun.

Then, through the silence overhead,
An angel with a trumpet said,
"For evermore, for evermore,
The reign of violence is o'er!"
And, like an instrument that flings
Its music on another's strings,
The trumpet of the angel cast
Upon the heavenly lyre its blast,
And on from sphere to sphere the words
Reëchoed down the burning chords,—
"For evermore, for evermore,
The reign of violence is o'er!"

THE DAY IS DONE

The day is done, and the darkness
  Falls from the wings of Night,
As a feather is wafted downward
  From an eagle in his flight.

I see the lights of the village
  Gleam through the rain and the mist,
And a feeling of sadness comes o'er me
  That my soul cannot resist:

A feeling of sadness and longing,
  That is not akin to pain,
And resembles sorrow only
  As the mist resembles the rain.

Come, read to me some poem,
  Some simple and heartfelt lay,
That shall soothe this restless feeling,
  And banish the thoughts of day.

Not from the grand old masters,
  Not from the bards sublime,
Whose distant footsteps echo
  Through the corridors of Time.

For, like strains of martial music,
  Their mighty thoughts suggest
Life's endless toil and endeavor;
  And to-night I long for rest.

THE DAY IS DONE

Read from some humbler poet,
  Whose songs gushed from his heart,
As showers from the clouds of summer,
  Or tears from the eyelids start;

Who, through long days of labor,
  And nights devoid of ease,
Still heard in his soul the music
  Of wonderful melodies.

Such songs have power to quiet
  The restless pulse of care,
And come like the benediction
  That follows after prayer.

Then read from the treasured volume
  The poem of thy choice,
And lend to the rhyme of the poet
  The beauty of thy voice.

And the night shall be filled with music,
  And the cares, that infest the day,
Shall fold their tents, like the Arabs,
  And as silently steal away.

MEZZO CAMMIN*

HALF of my life is gone, and I have let
  The years slip from me and have not fulfilled
  The aspiration of my youth, to build
  Some tower of song with lofty parapet.
Not indolence, nor pleasure, nor the fret
  Of restless passions that would not be stilled,
  But sorrow, and a care that almost killed,
  Kept me from what I may accomplish yet;
Though, halfway up the hill, I see the Past
  Lying beneath me with its sounds and sights,—
  A city in the twilight dim and vast,
With smoking roofs, soft bells, and gleaming lights,—
  And hear above me on the autumnal blast
  The cataract of Death far thundering from the heights.

SEAWEED

WHEN descends on the Atlantic
  The gigantic
Storm-wind of the equinox,
Landward in his wrath he scourges
  The toiling surges,
Laden with seaweed from the rocks:

From Bermuda's reefs; from edges
  Of sunken ledges,
In some far-off, bright Azore;
From Bahama, and the dashing,
  Silver-flashing
Surges of San Salvador;

From the tumbling surf, that buries
  The Orkneyan skerries,
Answering the hoarse Hebrides;
And from wrecks of ships, and drifting
  Spars, uplifting
On the desolate, rainy seas;—

Ever drifting, drifting, drifting,
  On the shifting
Currents of the restless main;
Till in sheltered coves, and reaches
  Of sandy beaches,
All have found repose again.

So when storms of wild emotion
  Strike the ocean

SEAWEED

Of the poet's soul, ere long
From each cave and rocky fastness,
  In its vastness,
Floats some fragment of a song:

From the far-off isles enchanted,
  Heaven has planted
With the golden fruit of Truth;
From the flashing surf, whose vision
  Gleams Elysian
In the tropic clime of Youth;

From the strong Will, and the Endeavor
  That forever
Wrestle with the tides of Fate;
From the wreck of Hopes far-scattered,
  Tempest-shattered,
Floating waste and desolate;—

Ever drifting, drifting, drifting
  On the shifting
Currents of the restless heart;
Till at length in books recorded,
  They, like hoarded
Household words, no more depart.

THE FIRE OF DRIFT-WOOD

DEVEREUX FARM, NEAR MARBLEHEAD

WE sat within the farm-house old,
  Whose windows, looking o'er the bay,
Gave to the sea-breeze damp and cold,
  An easy entrance, night and day.

Not far away we saw the port,
  The strange, old-fashioned, silent town,
The lighthouse, the dismantled fort,
  The wooden houses, quaint and brown.

We sat and talked until the night,
  Descending, filled the little room;
Our faces faded from the sight,
  Our voices only broke the gloom.

We spake of many a vanished scene,
  Of what we once had thought and said,
Of what had been, and might have been,
  And who was changed, and who was dead;

And all that fills the hearts of friends,
  When first they feel, with secret pain,
Their lives thenceforth have separate ends,
  And never can be one again;

The first slight swerving of the heart,
  That words are powerless to express,
And leave it still unsaid in part,
  Or say it in too great excess.

THE FIRE OF DRIFT-WOOD

The very tones in which we spake
  Had something strange, I could but mark;
The leaves of memory seemed to make
  A mournful rustling in the dark.

Oft died the words upon our lips,
  As suddenly, from out the fire
Built of the wreck of stranded ships,
  The flames would leap and then expire.

And, as their splendor flashed and failed,
  We thought of wrecks upon the main,
Of ships dismasted, that were hailed
  And sent no answer back again.

The windows, rattling in their frames,
  The ocean, roaring up the beach,
The gusty blast, the bickering flames,
  All mingled vaguely in our speech;

Until they made themselves a part
  Of fancies floating through the brain,
The long-lost ventures of the heart,
  That send no answers back again.

O flames that glowed! O hearts that yearned!
  They were indeed too much akin,
The drift-wood fire without that burned,
  The thoughts that burned and glowed within.

THE JEWISH CEMETERY AT NEWPORT

How strange it seems! These Hebrews in their graves,
  Close by the street of this fair seaport town,
Silent beside the never-silent waves,
  At rest in all this moving up and down!

The trees are white with dust, that o'er their sleep
  Wave their broad curtains in the south wind's breath,
While underneath these leafy tents they keep
  The long, mysterious Exodus of Death.

And these sepulchral stones, so old and brown,
  That pave with level flags their burial-place,
Seem like the tablets of the Law, thrown down
  And broken by Moses at the mountain's base.*

The very names recorded here are strange,
  Of foreign accent, and of different climes;
Alvares and Rivera interchange
  With Abraham and Jacob of old times.

"Blessed be God! for he created Death!"
  The mourners said, "and Death is rest and peace;"
Then added, in the certainty of faith,
  "And giveth Life that nevermore shall cease."

Closed are the portals of their Synagogue,
  No Psalms of David now the silence break,
No Rabbi reads the ancient Decalogue
  In the grand dialect the Prophets spake.

THE JEWISH CEMETERY AT NEWPORT

Gone are the living, but the dead remain,
  And not neglected; for a hand unseen,
Scattering its bounty, like a summer rain,
  Still keeps their graves and their remembrance green.

How came they here? What burst of Christian hate,
  What persecution, merciless and blind,
Drove o'er the sea—that desert desolate—
  These Ishmaels and Hagars of mankind?

They lived in narrow streets and lanes obscure,
  Ghetto and Judenstrass, in mirk and mire;
Taught in the school of patience to endure
  The life of anguish and the death of fire.

All their lives long, with the unleavened bread
  And bitter herbs of exile and its fears,
The wasting famine of the heart they fed,
  And slaked its thirst with marah of their tears.

Anathema maranatha! was the cry
  That rang from town to town, from street to street;
At every gate the accursed Mordecai*
  Was mocked and jeered, and spurned by Christian
      feet.

Pride and humiliation hand in hand
  Walked with them through the world where'er they
      went;
Trampled and beaten were they as the sand,
  And yet unshaken as the continent.

For in the background figures vague and vast
  Of patriarchs and of prophets rose sublime,
And all the great traditions of the Past
  They saw reflected in the coming time.

And thus forever with reverted look
  The mystic volume of the world they read,
Spelling it backward, like a Hebrew book,
  Till life became a Legend of the Dead.

But ah! what once has been shall be no more!
  The groaning earth in travail and in pain
Brings forth its races, but does not restore,
  And the dead nations never rise again.

MY LOST YOUTH

Often I think of the beautiful town
  That is seated by the sea;
Often in thought go up and down
The pleasant streets of that dear old town,
  And my youth comes back to me.
          And a verse of a Lapland song
    Is haunting my memory still:
  "A boy's will is the wind's will,
And the thoughts of youth are long, long thoughts."

I can see the shadowy lines of its trees,
  And catch, in sudden gleams,
The sheen of the far-surrounding seas,
And islands that were the Hesperides*
  Of all my boyish dreams.
    And the burden of that old song,
    It murmurs and whispers still:
  "A boy's will is the wind's will,
And the thoughts of youth are long, long thoughts."

I remember the black wharves and the slips,
  And the sea-tides tossing free
And Spanish sailors with bearded lips,
And the beauty and mystery of the ships,
  And the magic of the sea.
    And the voice of that wayward song
    Is singing and saying still:
  A boy's will is the wind's will,
And the thoughts of youth are long, long thoughts."

I remember the bulwarks by the shore,
  And the fort upon the hill;
The sunrise gun, with its hollow roar,
The drum-beat repeated o'er and o'er,
  And the bugle wild and shrill.
    And the music of that old song
    Throbs in my memory still:
  "A boy's will is the wind's will,
And the thoughts of youth are long, long thoughts."

I remember the sea-fight far away,*
  How it thundered o'er the tide!
And the dead captains, as they lay
In their graves, o'erlooking the tranquil bay,
  Where they in battle died.
    And the sound of that mournful song
    Goes through me with a thrill:
  "A boy's will is the wind's will,
And the thoughts of youth are long, long thoughts."

I can see the breezy dome of groves,
  The shadows of Deering's Woods;*
And the friendships old and the early loves
Come back with a Sabbath sound, as of doves
  In quiet neighborhoods.
    And the verse of that sweet old song,
    It flutters and murmurs still:
  "A boy's will is the wind's will,
And the thoughts of youth are long, long thoughts."

I remember the gleams and glooms that dart
  Across the school-boy's brain;
The song and the silence in the heart,
That in part are prophecies, and in part
  Are longings wild and vain.
    And the voice of that fitful song
    Sings on, and is never still:

"A boy's will is the wind's will,
And the thoughts of youth are long, long thoughts."

There are things of which I may not speak;
  There are dreams that cannot die;
There are thoughts that make the strong heart weak,
And bring pallor into the cheek,
  And a mist before the eye.
    And the words of that fatal song
    Come over me like a chill:
"A boy's will is the wind's will,
And the thoughts of youth are long, long thoughts."

Strange to me now are the forms I meet
  When I visit the dear old town;
But the native air is pure and sweet,
And the trees that o'ershadow each well-known street,
  As they balance up and down,
    Are singing the beautiful song,
    Are sighing and whispering still:
"A boy's will is the wind's will,
And the thoughts of youth are long, long thoughts."

And Deering's Woods are fresh and fair,
  And with joy that is almost pain
My heart goes back to wander there,
And among the dreams of the days that were,
  I find my lost youth again.
    And the strange and beautiful song,
    The groves are repeating it still:
"A boy's will is the wind's will,
And the thoughts of youth are long, long thoughts."

THE ROPEWALK

In that building, long and low,
With its windows all a-row,
  Like the port-holes of a hulk,
Human spiders spin and spin,
Backward down their threads so thin
  Droppping, each a hempen bulk.

At the end, an open door;
Squares of sunshine on the floor
  Light the long and dusky lane;
And the whirring of a wheel,
Dull and drowsy, makes me feel
  All its spokes are in my brain.

As the spinners to the end
Downward go and reascend,
  Gleam the long threads in the sun;
While within this brain of mine
Cobwebs brighter and more fine
  By the busy wheel are spun.

Two fair maidens in a swing,
Like white doves upon the wing,
  First before my vision pass;
Laughing, as their gentle hands
Closely clasp the twisted strands,
  At their shadow on the grass.

Then a booth of mountebanks,
With its smell of tan and planks,

    And a girl poised high in air
On a cord, in spangled dress,
With a faded loveliness,
    And a weary look of care.

Then a homestead among farms,
And a woman with bare arms
    Drawing water from a well;
As the bucket mounts apace,
With it mounts her own fair face,
    As at some magician's spell.

Then an old man in a tower,
Ringing loud the noontide hour,
    While the rope coils round and round
Like a serpent at his feet,
And again, in swift retreat,
    Nearly lifts him from the ground.

Then within a prison-yard,
Faces fixed, and stern, and hard,
    Laughter and indecent mirth;
Ah! it is the gallows-tree!
Breath of Christian charity,
Blow, and sweep it from the earth!

Then a school-boy, with his kite
Gleaming in a sky of light,
    And an eager, upward look;
Steeds pursued through land and field;
Fowlers with their snares concealed;
    And an angler by a brook.

Ships rejoicing in the breeze,
Wrecks that float o'er unknown seas,
    Anchors dragged through faithless sand;
Sea-fog drifting overhead,

And, with lessening line and lead,
  Sailors feeling for the land.

All these scenes do I behold,
These, and many left untold,
  In that building long and low;
While the wheel goes round and round,
With a drowsy, dreamy sound,
  And the spinners backward go.

THE CHILDREN'S HOUR

BETWEEN the dark and the daylight,
  When the night is beginning to lower,
Comes a pause in the day's occupations,
  That is known as the Children's Hour.

I hear in the chamber above me
  The patter of little feet,
The sound of a door that is opened,
  And voices soft and sweet.

From my study I see in the lamplight,
  Descending the broad hall stair,
Grave Alice, and laughing Allegra,
  And Edith with golden hair.

A whisper, and then a silence:
  Yet I know by their merry eyes
They are plotting and planning together
  To take me by surprise.

A sudden rush from the stairway,
  A sudden raid from the hall!
By three doors left unguarded
  They enter my castle wall!

They climb up into my turret
  O'er the arms and back of my chair;
If I try to escape, they surround me;
  They seem to be everywhere.

They almost devour me with kisses,
  Their arms about me entwine,
Till I think of the Bishop of Bingen
  In his Mouse-Tower on the Rhine!

Do you think, O blue-eyed banditti,
  Because you have scaled the wall,
Such an old mustache as I am
  Is not a match for you all!

I have you fast in my fortress,
  And will not let you depart,
But put you down into the dungeon
  In the round-tower of my heart.

And there will I keep you forever,
  Yes, forever and a day,
Till the walls shall crumble to ruin,
  And moulder in dust away!

SNOW-FLAKES

Out of the bosom of the Air,
  Out of the cloud-folds of her garments shaken,
Over the woodlands brown and bare,
  Over the harvest-fields forsaken,
    Silent, and soft, and slow
    Descends the snow.

Even as our cloudy fancies take
  Suddenly shape in some divine expression,
Even as the troubled heart doth make
  In the white countenance confession,
    The troubled sky reveals
    The grief it feels.

This is the poem of the air,
  Slowly in silent syllables recorded;
This is the secret of despair,
  Long in its cloudy bosom hoarded,
    Now whispered and revealed
    To wood and field.

HAWTHORNE*

MAY 23, 1864

How beautiful it was, that one bright day
  In the long week of rain!
Though all its splendor could not chase away
  The omnipresent pain.

The lovely town was white with apple-blooms,
  And the great elms o'erhead
Dark shadows wove on their aërial looms
  Shot through with golden thread.

Across the meadows, by the gray old manse,
  The historic river flowed:
I was as one who wanders in a trance,
  Unconscious of his road.

The faces of familiar friends seemed strange;
  Their voices I could hear,
And yet the words they uttered seemed to change
  Their meaning to my ear.

For the one face I looked for was not there,
  The one low voice was mute;
Only an unseen presence filled the air,
  And baffled my pursuit.

Now I look back, and meadow, manse, and stream
  Dimly my thought defines;

I only see—a dream within a dream—
　The hilltop hearsed with pines.

I only hear above his place of rest
　Their tender undertone,
The infinite longings of a troubled breast,
　The voice so like his own.

There in seclusion and remote from men
　The wizard hand lies cold,
Which at its topmost speed let fall the pen,
　And left the tale half told.

Ah! who shall lift that wand of magic power,
　And the lost clue regain?
The unfinished window in Aladdin's tower
　Unfinished must remain!

AFTERMATH

WHEN the summer fields are mown,
When the birds are fledged and flown,
  And the dry leaves strew the path;
With the falling of the snow,
With the cawing of the crow,
Once again the fields we mow
  And gather in the aftermath.

Not the sweet, new grass with flowers
Is this harvesting of ours;
  Not the upland clover bloom;
But the rowen mixed with weeds,
Tangled tufts from marsh and meads,
Where the poppy drops its seeds
  In the silence and the gloom.

NATURE

As fond mother, when the day is o'er,
  Leads by the hand her little child to bed,
  Half willing, half reluctant to be led,
  And leave his broken playthings on the floor,
Still gazing at them through the open door,
  Nor wholly reassured and comforted
  By promises of others in their stead,
  Which, though more splendid, may not please him
      more;

So Nature deals with us, and takes away
  Our playthings one by one, and by the hand
  Leads us to rest so gently, that we go
Scarce knowing if we wish to go or stay,
  Being too full of sleep to understand
  How far the unknown transcends the what we know.

THE CROSS OF SNOW*

In the long, sleepless watches of the night,
  A gentle face—the face of one long dead—
  Looks at me from the wall, where round its head
  The night-lamp casts a halo of pale light.
Here in this room she died; and soul more white
  Never through martyrdom of fire was led
  To its repose; nor can in books be read
  The legend of a life more benedight.

There is a mountain in the distant West
  That, sun-defying, in its deep ravines
  Displays a cross of snow upon its side.
Such is the cross I wear upon my breast
  These eighteen years, through all the changing scenes
And seasons, changeless since the day she died.

NOTES

3 *Evangeline*. This poem was written over a period of eighteen months, 1845–47, after listening to the tale of the "historical" Evangeline and Gabriel told by a friend of Hawthorne's. To this folkloric kernel, Longfellow added desultory research and imaginative heightening to this story of French settlers forcibly displaced from Nova Scotia after the British victory in the French and Indian War (1763). Immediately successful, *Evangeline* began to make Longfellow a household word.

8 *penitent Peter* After Jesus' arrest, his disciple Peter, as Jesus had predicted, three times publicly denied being Jesus' follower, then wept for shame as the crowing cock reminded him that he had broken faith.

11 *Wrestled . . . as Jacob* See Genesis 32: 24–32.

18 *Loup-garou* Werewolf.

23 *As out of Abraham's tent* In Genesis 21: 9–21, the patriarch Abraham reluctantly, at the prompting of God and his wife Sarah, expels his servant-concubine Hagar and Ishmael, the son he had by her.

34 *shipwrecked Paul* See Acts 28: 1–10.

35 *Benedicite!* Bless you.

41 *to be left to braid St. Catherine's tresses* A Norman saying, applied to a woman who does not marry.

46 *the ladder of Jacob* In Genesis 28: 12, the patriarch Jacob dreamed of a ladder from earth to heaven on which he saw angels ascending and descending.

57 *Carthusian* A monastic order, or (in this case) a member thereof.

58 *Upharsin* The last word of the mysterious biblical handwriting on the wall, interpreted as a divine inscription to King Belshazzar (Daniel 5: 24–28): you have been weighed in the balance and found wanting.

77 *The Song of Hiawatha* This poem derives its meter and some of its legendary flavor from the Finnish epic, *Kalevala*, and its anthropological content from contemporary students of American Indian culture then considered authoritative, notably J. G. E. Heckenwelder and H. R. Schoolcraft. Hiawatha is portrayed as a beloved hero who ushers in for his tribe an age of prosperity which must, however, give way before hard times and the advent of white civilization, prophesied by Hiawatha at the end. The two episodes printed here tell, respectively, of Hiawatha's conception and birth, and of the triumph that he achieves over Mondamin, the corn spirit, thereby bringing fertility to the land.

92 *The Courtship of Miles Standish* This poem elaborates, with the help of historical sources, a story that was already traditional, although the popularity of the poem has been more responsible than any other factor for its enduring fame. Longfellow's original title was "Priscilla," a better key to the poem's center of values than *Miles Standish*.

103 *Astaroth . . . and Baal* Gods worshiped by the neighbors of the ancient Israelites, and sometimes by the Israelites themselves.

111 *David's transgression* King David of Israel seduced the wife of one of his military officers, then ensured that he would be killed in battle (2 Samuel 11).

114 *Wat Tyler* D. 1381, led the first great popular rebellion in English history.

118 *Hobomok* Famous in nineteenth-century New England lore and literature as an Indian friendly to the early settlers.

Midianites and Philistines Perennial enemies of the ancient Israelites.

132 *Goliath* . . . Two enemies of gigantic stature who fought (unsuccessfully) against the Israelites (Deut. 3: 1–11; 1 Samuel 17: 4–51).

139 *Bertha the Beautiful Spinner* A quiet joke on Longfellow's part. In Norse legend, Bertha is patron of spinners and a variant name of Frigga; this figure merges with Bertha, the mother of Charlemagne, in the thirteenth-century French romance, *la Reine Pedauque*, probably the work to which Alden refers. Longfellow wrote amusedly about this work in an 1833 essay on "Ancient French Romances" (reprinted as the first item in *Drift-Wood*, volume 7 of the 1904 edition of his *Works*) because of the poem's emphasis on Bertha's splay foot, supposedly got from continually plying her treadle. "Queen Goose-Foot" is how Longfellow translates the epithet. In short, Alden's compliment is rather gauche.

142 See Ruth 4: 11–22. Matthew 1: 1–17 pictures Jesus Christ as descended from this union.

147 *valley of Eschol* Discovered by the advance guard of Israelites exploring the territory of the promised land of Canaan at Moses' request (Numbers 13: 23–24).

recalling Rebecca and Isaac The marriage of Rebecca to Isaac, Abraham's son, described at length in Genesis 24, ensured the continuity of his tribe in its new land.

148 *Tales of a Wayside Inn* The selections printed here comprise three of the seven tales told in what proved to be the first (1863) of a three-part poem (1872, 1873), set on three successive evenings in the Red Horse Inn, Sudbury, Massachusetts. The seven characters are loosely based on historical originals, including the landlord of the inn, Harvard Physics professor Daniel Treadwell (the theologian), and dentist-poet T.W. Parsons (the poet), best known as a translator of Dante. The tales are framed by interludes and by a prelude and postlude, none of which are printed here.

Paul Revere's Ride Longfellow concocted this tale from several historical sources, including, most likely, an account by Revere himself; but the poem itself is primarily responsible for the popular misimpression that Revere, who never made it to Concord, singlehandedly warned the colonists of the British attack.

152 *Torquemada* Longfellow wrote in his diary that this tale was based on a turn-of-the-seventeenth-century work: De Castro's *Protestantes Espanolas*. Torquemada (1420–98), first Grand Inquisitor of Spain, became a byword for fanaticism and bigotry. "How ingenious men are in the ways of destruction," Longfellow mused a week after the poem's completion, on a day in which he had gone to see one of the Union navy's new all-metal warships. That night he read "Torquemada" aloud to his publisher and friend, James T. Fields.

158 *The Birds of Killingworth* Though this tale is loosely based on attempts by the Connecticut town of Killingworth to

cope with an excess of birds during the eighteenth century, more than any other tale in the series, this one was Longfellow's invention.

Saxon Caedmon See the Anglo-Saxon poem *Genesis B* (Junius manuscript), l. 192b. In Longfellow's era this manuscript was wrongly attributed to the seventh-century monkpoet Caedmon.

159 *Cassandra* The Trojan prophetess who warned her compatriots against the Trojan horse; by extension, a doomcrier.

160 *Edwards on the Will* *A Careful and Strict Enquiry into the Modern Prevailing Notions of . . . Freedom of Will* (1754), the most famous work by New England's most famous Calvinist theologian, Jonathan Edwards (1703–58), much admired in eighteenth-century evangelical circles.

161 *as David did for Saul* See 1 Samuel 16: 23.

164 *Saint Bartholomew of Birds* Refers to the state-ordered 1572 massacre of French Huguenots in Paris, beginning on St. Bartholomew's Eve (August 23–24), that spiralled out of control and eventually claimed some 30,000 lives over a six-week period.

See Matthew 2: 16–18 and Acts 12: 23. Longfellow must have been aware of conflating two different Herods in this passage.

167 *The New England Tragedies* Separately published in 1868 and incorporated as Part III of *Christus* in 1872, these two verse dramas were at least nominally intended to portray the religious life of "the modern age" in the trilogy's three-part scheme, and to comment on the cardinal virtue of "charity." They constitute one of Longfellow's bleakest although most

powerful achievements. "John Endicott" was begun first, initially drafted in 1857 as "Wenlock Christison"; "Giles Corey" was done much later.

John Endicott This drama is set at the time of the Restoration of Charles II to the English throne (1660), as a result of which the New England Puritan prosecution of the Quakers was brought to an abrupt halt, although not under quite so dramatic circumstances as Longfellow envisages here. Longfellow adds unhistorical notes of pathos in creating a John Endicott, Jr., love-struck by the Quaker maiden Edith, and by having the father die partly from grief at the alienation of his son. The device of using intergenerational conflict as a means of portraying the Puritan oligarchy in an ironic light was, however, standard in nineteenth-century literature.

168 *Hope, Faith and Charity* 1 Corinthians 13: 13.

169–70 *I heard a great voice . . .* Norton, like many a fire-and-brimstone preacher, begins his discourse of quoting Revelation 16: 1–2.

172 *a quaking fell/On Daniel . . .* For the two biblical incidents alluded to here, see Daniel 10: 2ff and Isaiah 20: 2–3.

173 *as the Roman Bishop/Once received Attila* Pope Leo I "welcomed" Attila the Hun to Rome in 452.

the hand that cut/ The Red Cross In a famous act of extreme Puritan iconoclasm, Endicott had cut the red cross from the Puritan ensign in protest against the idolatrousness of Episcopacy. See also Hawthorne's tale "Endicott and the Red Cross."

175 *Saint Botolph* The patron saint of Boston in Lincolnshire, for which the Puritan metropolis was named; a seventh-century English monk.

181 *"Why dost thou persecute me"* Jesus' question during the visionary experience on the road to Damascus that converts Saul to Paul, persecutor to apostle (Acts 9: 4–6).

189 *The blood of Abel* See Genesis 4: 10.

190 *Tithing-man* A town official charged with the prevention of disorderly conduct; stereotypically an officious bigot.

205 *"Swear not at all"* Jesus' injunction in Matthew 5: 34–35.

207 *The holy man, our Founder* George Fox (1624–91), founder of Quakerism. The Vale of Beavor lies southwest of Nottingham, England.

   "Upon my handmaidens" See Joel 2: 28–29, echoed in Acts 2: 17–18.

209 *Eleazer* Moses' nephew, Aaron's son, the upright second chief priest of ancient Israel.

216 *where thou goest, I will go* Echoes Ruth's often-quoted profession of loyalty to her mother-in-law (Ruth 1: 16); of special interest here since it is the young man who pledges to follow the woman of the other "tribe."

218 *Paul of Damascus* A reference to Paul's conversion; see note on p. 116 above.

224 *Sweet as the water . . .* See John 4: 7ff.

225 *Iscariot* Judas, the disciple who betrayed Jesus.

227 *Antiochus . . .* Antiochus IV ruled the Syria-centered Seleucid kingdom at the time of the second-century B.C. Jewish revolt led by the family of the Maccabees.

228 *O Absalom* King David's lament (2 Samuel 18: 33) at the death of his rebellious but favorite son.

234 *The words/ Of the Apostle Paul* See 2 Corinthians 11: 26–27.

247 *Giles Corey* Whereas *John Endicott* deals with the first of the two most notorious cases of Puritan persecution of deviance by emphasizing primarily its consequences for the gentry, this play deals with the second and even more famous episode—Salem witchcraft—emphasizing the plight of common people, particularly that of the one accused person who refused to plead either guilty or not guilty and who was therefore condemned to be pressed to death. Another conspicuous feature of this work is Longfellow's markedly compassionate treatment of the Puritan minister Cotton Mather, who was usually scapegoated by nineteenth-century fictionalizers of witchcraft delusions.

254 *Nebuchadnezzar's furnace* See Daniel 3.

258 *Obi men* Voodoo artists.

266 *Mary Magdalene* . . . For the two biblical allusions, see Luke 8: 2, 26–33.

269 *He must spell Baker* Popular expression for doing anything difficult. In old spelling books, baker was the first word of two syllables.

282 *Doth not the Scripture say* Exodus 22: 18.

284 *Doubting Thomas* See John 20: 24–29.

286 *It came to pass that Naboth* . . . Martha here retells the story of 1 Kings 21.

301 *In Samuel's shape* Cf. 1 Samuel 28: 3–20, where Saul has the Witch of Endor summon up the ghost of Samuel, which Martha interprets as an impersonation of Samuel's shape by the devil.

318 *Finale* Jesus' disciple John is pictured as a ceaseless wanderer in accord with the tradition based on John 21: 22 that he would not see death until Jesus came again.

321 *Morituri Salutamus.* Delivered at the Bowdoin College commencement of 1875, Longfellow's fiftieth reunion.

322 *"Oh, never . . ."* In *Inferno*, xv, 80–87, Dante speaks these lines to the shade of Brunetto Latini (ca. 1220–ca. 1294), who, however, was probably not in fact Dante's master.

"Here is thy talent" See Jesus' parable in Matthew 24: 14–30.

322 *As ancient Priam . . .* Homer, *Iliad* III: 146–198.

323–24 *Minerva, the inventress . . .* In Greek mythology, the satyr Marsyas rashly challenged Apollo to a music contest after finding the flute discarded by Athena (Minerva); having won, Apollo flayed Marsyas alive, taking advantage of their agreement that the winner could do as he liked with the loser.

324 *the saying . . . "Be bold!"* See Spenser, *Faerie Queene*, III.cvii.

Hector . . . Paris In the *Iliad*, Hector is slain by Achilles in combat, while Paris runs from combat with Menelaus. Longfellow ignores the fact that Hector's courage is shown as giving way as well.

326 *In medieval Rome* Longfellow got this story from the *Gesta Romanorum*, a medieval homiletic/anecdotal compilation. The original tale is called "Of remembering death and forgetting things temporal."

329 *Tabard Inn* The inn from which Chaucer's Canterbury pilgrims depart.

333 *A Psalm of Life* Perhaps Longfellow's most anthologized poem (for better and for worse); significantly, he referred to it variously as both a psalm of life and a psalm of death. Before its publication, Longfellow read it aloud to one of his Harvard classes.

335 *skald* Ancient Scandinavian poet.

340 *skoal* Scandinavian salutation when drinking a health.

341 *The Wreck of the Hesperus* A New World rendition of the medieval ballad of "Sir Patrick Spens."

347 *The Slave Singing at Midnight* Longfellow interweaves two biblical scenes of deliverance from captivity here: the exodus of the children of Israel from Egypt across the Red Sea; and the miraculous deliverance of Paul and Silas from prison in Acts 16: 25–34. These images reflect not only Longfellow's own religious culture but that of the slaves themselves.

348 *The Warning* This poem reworks the story of Samson from Judges 13–16.

349 *The Arsenal at Springfield* Inspired by a visit to the Springfield, Massachusetts, arsenal during Longfellow's wedding

journey of 1843. Note the initial sentence, identical in form to that of *Evangeline:* Longfellow liked such abrupt openers.

Miserere Have mercy

350 *the curse of Cain* See Genesis 4: 14–16.

351 *The Occultation of Orion* Several stories about the mythical Greek hunter Orion, also a constellation, are interwoven here: that for loving the daughter of Oenopion he was blinded; that he was killed by Artemis (Diana, goddess of the moon) for insulting her; and that he was killed because he boasted that he would kill all animals. Longfellow characteristically turns the legends into a celestial drama of the triumph of light and purity, associated with the female principle, over masculine violence and strength.

356 *Mezzo Cammin* Written at the age of thirty-five—half the life span allotted to humankind in the Bible—while on the verge of leaving Europe for home. The title is taken from the opening line of Dante's *Inferno:* "Midway in the journey of our life."

361 *the tablets . . . broken by Moses* In Exodus 32: 19–20, Moses throws the stone tablets containing the Ten Commandments on the ground, in disgust at idolatry into which the Israelites had lapsed during his sojourn on Mount Sinai, communing with God.

362 *Mordecai* A general (and on gentile lips, disparaging) name for Jews.

364 *the Hesperides* In Greek mythology, islands where the golden apples grew.

365 *the sea-fight* the engagement between the American *Enterprise* and the British *Boxer* off Portland harbor in 1813.

Deering's Woods a grove of trees on the outskirts of Longfellow's home town of Portland, Maine.

373 *Hawthorne* On this date Longfellow attended the funeral of his friend and college classmate Hawthorne at Concord, Massachusetts.

377 *The Cross of Snow* This 1879 sonnet was apparently precipitated by seeing an illustration of a much-photographed natural snow-cross in a ravine of the Rockies.

CLICK ON A CLASSIC
www.penguinclassics.com

The world's greatest literature at your fingertips

Constantly updated information on more than a thousand titles, from Icelandic sagas to ancient Indian epics, Russian drama to Italian romance, American greats to African masterpieces

•

The latest news on recent additions to the list, updated editions, and specially commissioned translations

•

Original essays by leading writers

•

A wealth of background material, including biographies of every classic author from Aristotle to Zamyatin, plot synopses, readers' and teachers' guides, useful Web links

•

Online desk and examination copy assistance for academics

•

Trivia quizzes, competitions, giveaways, news on forthcoming screen adaptations

The Last of the Mohicans
James Fenimore Cooper
Introduction by Richard Slotkin
Tragic, fast-paced, and stocked with the elements of a classic Western adventure, this novel takes Natty Bumppo and his Indian friend Chingachgook through hostile Indian territory during the French and Indian War. *ISBN 0-14-039024-3*

Two Years Before the Mast: A Personal Narrative of Life at Sea
Richard Henry Dana, Jr.
Edited with an Introduction and Notes by Thomas Philbrick
Dana's account of his passage as a common seaman from Boston around Cape Horn to California, and back, is a remarkable portrait of the sea-going life. Bringing to the public's attention for the first time the plights of the most exploited segment of the American working class, he forever changed readers' romanticized perceptions of life at sea.

ISBN 0-14-039008-1

Nature and Selected Essays
Ralph Waldo Emerson
Edited with an Introduction by Larzer Ziff
This sampling includes fifteen essays that highlight the formative and significant ideas of this central American thinker: "Nature," "The American Scholar," "An Address Delivered Before the Senior Class in Divinity College, Cambridge," "Man the Reformer," "History," "Self-Reliance," "The Over-Soul," "Circles," "The Transcendentalist," "The Poet," "Experience," "Montaigne: Or, the Skeptic," "Napoleon: Or, the Man of the World," "Fate," and "Thoreau." *ISBN 0-14-243762-X*

The Scarlet Letter
Nathaniel Hawthorne
Introduction by Nina Baym with Notes by Thomas E. Connolly
Hawthorne's novel of guilt and redemption in pre-Revolutionary Massachusetts provides vivid insight into the social and religious forces that shaped early America. *ISBN 0-14-243726-3*

The Legend of Sleepy Hollow and Other Stories
Washington Irving
Introduction and Notes by William L. Hedges
Irving's delightful 1819 miscellany of essays and sketches includes the two classic tales "The Legend of Sleepy Hollow" and "Rip Van Winkle."
ISBN 0-14-043769-X

The Portable Abraham Lincoln
Abraham Lincoln
Edited by Andrew Delbanco
The essential Lincoln, including all of the great public speeches, along with less familiar letters and memoranda that chart Lincoln's political career. With an indispensable introduction, headnotes, and a chronology of Lincoln's life.   *ISBN 0-14-017031-6*

Moby-Dick
Or, The Whale
Herman Melville
Edited with an Introduction by Andrew Delbanco
Explanatory Commentary by Tom Quirk
The story of an eerily compelling madman pursuing an unholy war against a creature as vast and dangerous and unknowable as the sea itself, Melville's masterpiece is also a profound inquiry into character, faith, and the nature of perception.   *ISBN 0-14-243724-7*

The Fall of the House of Usher and Other Writings
Edgar Allan Poe
Edited with an Introduction and Notes by David Galloway
This selection includes seventeen poems, among them "The Raven," "Annabel Lee," and "The Bells"; nineteen tales, including "The Fall of the House of Usher," "The Murders in the Rue Morgue," "The Tell-Tale Heart," "The Masque of the Red Death," and "The Pit and the Pendulum"; and sixteen essays and reviews.   *ISBN 0-14-143981-5*

Uncle Tom's Cabin
Or, Life Among the Lowly
Harriet Beecher Stowe
Edited with an Introduction by Ann Douglas
Perhaps the most powerful document in the history of American abolitionism, this controversial novel goaded thousands of readers to take a stand on the issue of slavery and played a major political and social role in the Civil War period.   *ISBN 0-14-039003-0*

Walden and Civil Disobedience
Henry David Thoreau
Introduction by Michael Meyer
Two classic examinations of individuality in relation to nature, society, and government. *Walden* conveys at once a naturalist's wonder at the commonplace and a Transcendentalist's yearning for spiritual truth and self-reliance. "Civil Disobedience" is perhaps the most famous essay in American literature—and the inspiration for social activists around the world, from Gandhi to Martin Luther King, Jr.   ISBN 0-14-039044-8

Nineteenth-Century American Poetry
Edited with an Introduction and Notes by
William C. Spengemann with Jessica F. Roberts
Whitman, Dickinson, and Melville occupy the center of this anthology of nearly three hundred poems, spanning the course of the century, from Joel Barlow to Edwin Arlington Robinson, by way of Bryant, Emerson, Longfellow, Whittier, Poe, Holmes, Jones Very, Thoreau, Lowell, and Lanier.   ISBN 0-14-043587-5

Selected Poems
Henry Wadsworth Longfellow
Edited with an Introduction and Notes by Lawrence Buell
Longfellow was the most popular poet of his day. This selection includes generous samplings from his longer works—*Evangeline*, *The Courtship of Miles Standish*, and *Hiawatha*—as well as his shorter lyrics and less familiar narrative poems.   ISBN 0-14-039064-2

Leaves of Grass
Walt Whitman
Edited with an Introduction by Malcolm Cowley
This is the original and complete 1855 edition of one of the greatest masterpieces of American literature, including Whitman's own introduction to the work.   ISBN 0-14-042199-8

The Education of Henry Adams
Henry Adams
Edited with an Introduction and Notes by Jean Gooder
In this memoir Adams examines his own life as it reflects the progress of the United States from the Civil War period to the nation's ascendancy as a world power. A remarkable synthesis of history, art, politics, and philosophy, *The Education of Henry Adams* remains a provocative and stimulating interpretation of the birth of the twentieth century.
     ISBN 0-14-044557-9

Little Women
Louisa May Alcott
Edited with an Introduction by Elaine Showalter
Notes by Siobhan Kilfeather and Vinca Showalter
Alcott's beloved story of the March girls—Meg, Jo, Beth, and Amy—is a classic American feminist novel, reflecting the tension between cultural obligation and artistic and personal freedom.   ISBN 0-14-039069-3

Looking Backward
2000–1887
Edward Bellamy
Edited with an Introduction by Cecelia Tichi
When first published in 1888, *Looking Backward* initiated a national political- and social-reform movement. This profoundly utopian tale addresses the anguish and hope of its age, as well as having lasting value as an American cultural landmark.   ISBN 0-14-039018-9

Tales of Soldiers and Civilians and Other Stories
Ambrose Bierce
Edited with an Introduction and Notes by Tom Quirk
This collection gathers three dozen of Bierce's finest tales of war and the supernatural, including "An Occurrence at Owl Creek Bridge" and "The Damned Thing."   ISBN 0-14-043756-8

The Awakening and Selected Stories
Kate Chopin
Edited with an Introduction by Sandra M. Gilbert
First published in 1899, *The Awakening* shows the transformation of Edna Pontellier, who claims for herself moral and erotic freedom. Other selections include "Emancipation," "At the 'Cadian Ball," and "Désirée's Baby."   ISBN 0-14-243709-3

The Red Badge of Courage and Other Stories
Stephen Crane
Edited with an Introduction by Pascal Covici, Jr.
Here is one of the greatest novels ever written about war and its psychological effects on the individual soldier. This edition also includes the short stories "The Open Boat," "The Bride Comes to Yellow Sky," "The Blue Hotel," "A Poker Game," and "The Veteran."   ISBN 0-14-039081-2

Personal Memoirs
Ulysses S. Grant
Introduction and Notes by James M. McPherson
Grant's memoirs demonstrate the intelligence, intense determination, and laconic modesty that made him the Union's foremost commander.
ISBN 0-14-043701-0

The Luck of Roaring Camp and Other Writings
Bret Harte
Edited with an Introduction by Gary Scharnhorst
More than any other writer, Harte was at the forefront of western American literature. This volume brings together all of his best-known pieces, as well as a selection of his poetry, lesser-known essays, and three of his hilarious condensed novels—parodies of James Fenimore Cooper, Charles Dickens, and Sir Arthur Conan Doyle.   *ISBN 0-14-043917-X*

A Hazard of New Fortunes
William Dean Howells
Introduction by Phillip Lopate
Set against a vividly depicted background of fin de siècle New York, *A Hazard of New Fortunes* is both a memorable portrait of an era and profoundly moving study of human relationships.   *ISBN 0-14-043923-4*

The Portrait of a Lady
Henry James
Edited with an Introduction by Geoffrey Moore
and Notes by Patricia Crick
Regarded by many critics as James's masterpiece, this is the story of Isabel Archer, an independent American heiress captivated by the languid charms of an Englishman.   *ISBN 0-14-143963-7*

The Country of the Pointed Firs and Other Stories
Sarah Orne Jewett
Edited with an Introduction by Alison Easton
Modeled in part on Flaubert's sketches of life in provincial France, *The Country of the Pointed Firs* is a richly detailed portrait of a seaport on the Maine coast as seen through the eyes of a summer visitor. Jewett celebrates the friendships shared by the town's women, interweaving conversations and stories about poor fishermen and retired sea captains, thus capturing the spirit of community that sustains the declining town.
      ISBN 0-14-043476-3

The Adventures of Huckleberry Finn
Mark Twain
Introduction by John Seelye and Notes by Guy Cardwell
A novel of immeasurable richness, filled with adventures, ironies, and wonderfully drawn characters, all conveyed with Twain's mastery of humor and language, *The Adventures of Huckleberry Finn* is often regarded as the masterpiece of American literature.
      ISBN 0-14-243717-4